Hope Springs

OTHER PROPER ROMANCES

LONGING FOR HOME
by Sarah M. Eden

EDENBROOKE
by Julianne Donaldson

BLACKMOORE
by Julianne Donaldson

Hope Springs

SARAH M. EDEN

SHADOW MOUNTAIN

Visit us at ShadowMountain.com

Library of Congress Cataloging-in-Publication Data
Eden, Sarah M., author.
Hope Springs / Sarah M. Eden.
pages cm—(Longing for home ; book 2)
Summary: Irish-born Kate Macauley is caught in the feud that is raging between the American farmers and the Irish immigrants in the small Wyoming town of Hope Springs. She is also torn between loving two very different men.
ISBN 978-1-60907-810-2 (paperbound)
1. Irish American women—Fiction. 2. Nativism—Fiction. 3. Wyoming, setting. 4. Nineteenth century, setting. I. Title. II. Series: Eden, Sarah M. Longing for home ; bk. 2.
PS3605.D45365H67 2014
813'.6—dc23 2013033356

Printed in the United States of America
Publisher's Printing, Salt Lake City, UT

10 9 8 7 6 5 4 3 2 1

To Lois, Sarah Elva, Dora, Zelda, Barbara, and Ginny
Women of faith and determination,
who have shown me what it means
to be good and to be strong

Chapter One

However fine the day, night must eventually fall. Katie Macauley knew that truth well. For every bit of joy she'd known, life had served her an ever-increasing portion of pain and grief. Her Irish heart was just stubborn enough to keep going despite it all and just foolish enough to believe someday the balance would tip in her favor.

Finding a home amongst her displaced countrymen in a tiny town far from nowhere in the dry and unforgiving vastness of the American West seemed a fine argument in favor of optimism. Logic told her the odds of that happening were far too slim to be anything but a gift of fate. And yet the town of Hope Springs wasn't without its problems—it had a great many problems, in fact.

"Michael, bring the butter crock, lad. We're eating without your father if he's not here in another five minutes." Biddy, Katie's dearest friend in all the world, gave her a look of utter exasperation.

Katie set out the last of the dinner plates. She'd been invited to have her evening meal with Biddy and her family, an offer she appreciated more than any of them realized. Though she worked for a family who treated her with kindness and had the heart of a wonderful man—Biddy's brother-in-law, in fact—she often felt alone.

"Put the spoon in the colcannon, Mary," Biddy told her little girl. "Then fetch the soda bread, if you will."

Colcannon and soda bread. 'Twas a bit of the Emerald Isle thousands of miles from Ireland.

Biddy crossed to the narrow front window.

Katie joined her there, looking out at the dimming light of dusk.

"Never fear, Biddy. Tavish'll round Ian up and bring him home to make his apologies."

"And not a moment too soon, it seems." Biddy looked back toward the rough-hewn table, where little Mary was carefully setting down the plate of soda bread. "Thank you, love. Now you and Michael go wash your hands."

"With soap?" Mary clearly hoped the answer was no.

"Aye. Soap, and plenty of it." Biddy eyed both her children. "On with the two of you, then." She shook her head at their retreating backs. "I swear to you, Katie, they'd eat out in the muddy fields if I'd let them."

"And return to the house so filthy you could toss them against a wall and they'd stick," Katie added.

Biddy smiled, as Katie had hoped she would. But just as quickly as the lightness appeared, it faded. She set one hand on her hip and rubbed her forehead with the other. Her gaze lingered at the window.

"I am certain all's well." Katie spoke with all the conviction she could muster, but Biddy's worries were beginning to settle heavy on her as well. Tavish had left over an hour earlier and could easily have gone to town and back in that time.

As if making a finely timed entrance, the turning of wagon wheels and the pounding of hooves sounded from the yard.

"At last," Biddy breathed and made her way to the door. She pulled it open. "The two of you had best—" Biddy's eyes opened in shock, her words ending abruptly.

Katie moved swiftly to the doorway. Tavish was climbing over the back of the wagon bench to the bed. She was certain it was the look on his face that had silenced Biddy. His mouth was drawn in a tense line, his eyes snapping with something very much like anger, and also a great deal of fear.

"What's happened?" Katie called out.

"Come help me," he answered. "Quick, Katie."

Biddy stepped out with her.

"Just Katie." Tavish's voice was insistent, sharp almost. Katie had seldom heard Tavish sound anything but jovial.

"Something's happened, Katie," Biddy whispered. "Something bad."

Katie gave her hand a quick, and she hoped reassuring, squeeze. She too sensed the tension in Tavish. "I am sure all will be fine." She didn't fully believe it, but could think of nothing else to say.

Alone she moved quickly over the short distance to the waiting wagon. Tavish had made his way to the back and offered a hand to help her up.

"What's happened?" she asked again, her voice low.

Ian was nowhere to be seen. The wagon was empty except for a few crates and a messy pile of blankets.

"Why've you returned without Ian?"

"I haven't." He spoke too solemnly for Katie's peace of mind.

Tavish took hold of the nearest corner of the blanket and tossed it back.

Heavens above. 'Twas Ian beneath the blanket. Ian, bloodied and bruised and unmoving. Katie's very breath rushed from her. *Saints preserve us.*

"Keep calm, Sweet Katie. Biddy'll need you to be strong."

Katie struggled to find air enough to speak. "Is he dead?" she whispered.

"He was still breathing when I found him. But he's in a bad way."

He was, indeed. The man's face was swollen, discolored. She'd never seen anyone lie so utterly still. "Had he an accident with the wagon, or was he thrown from a horse or something?"

Tavish shook his head. The man generally wore smiles with mirthful twinkles in his deep blue eyes. Katie was not at all accustomed to seeing him somber.

"I'd wager my entire farm he was set upon by a mob."

Katie's heart fell clear to her feet. "A mob? Good heavens. Who'd do such a thing?"

And yet, she knew the answer. Hope Springs was ten years deep in a feud. Half the town was Irish. The other half hated the Irish with a passion. So, the Irish had opted to return the sentiment and hate their neighbors with equal fervor.

She set her hand lightly at Ian's heart. His chest rose and fell faintly, as though his breath was hardly there. "I'm worried for him, Tavish."

"And it's right you should be. He needs doctoring."

Katie glanced quickly at the doorway. Little Mary and Michael had joined their mother. The three of them looked on with fearful expressions.

Merciful heavens. Someone had beaten the father of these children to within an inch of his life. Beyond, perhaps.

"How bad is this feud likely to become?"

He set his hand lightly on her arm, his eyes heavy with worry. "Oh, Sweet Katie, this is only the beginning."

She pushed out a tense breath. Her eyes settled on Ian once more. "What do you need me to do, Tavish?"

"I can carry Ian in. But I'm worried for Biddy. Stick close to her side, Katie. Keep her going. And the children will need you as well."

Katie nodded. She slid to the back of the wagon and climbed down. *Keep calm, Katie. Your friends need you.*

She walked to where Biddy stood, watching with wide eyes.

"Michael," Katie said, "take your sister inside."

The lad must have sensed the urgency of the situation because he obeyed without hesitation.

"Katie?" Biddy whispered.

Katie took her hands. "Ian's been terribly injured. He's in a bad way."

Biddy's eyes darted to the wagon. Katie looked back as well. Tavish slowly walked toward them, struggling under the weight of Ian in his arms.

"Merciful heavens." Biddy's voice cracked with panicked emotion. "My Ian!"

She rushed down the porch step and toward her husband's limp frame.

"Ian. Talk to me, please, dearest. Please, Ian." Her voice shook as she pleaded with him. "Ian, darling. Ian?"

"Biddy, I have to lay him down," Tavish pleaded, attempting to continue toward the house despite Biddy blocking his path.

Katie put an arm around her friend's shoulders and pulled her out of the way. Biddy continued calling her husband's name, the word growing more indistinguishable as sobs racked her body. She fought to be freed of Katie's hold. But Tavish needed an unobstructed path into the house.

Katie walked with Biddy, swiftly, behind Tavish. But one step inside, Biddy's knees gave way. She crumbled, burying her face in her hands.

Katie knelt and wrapped her arms around Biddy.

"We'll do all we can for him," she promised.

"I can't lose him, Katie. I couldn't bear it. I can't live without him."

Katie held her even closer, her heart breaking. How quickly everything had changed.

Chapter Two

Katie had a long-standing acquaintance with death. She recognized its icy breath slithering down the back of her neck as she tended to Ian. The air hung heavy with the very real possibility that he would never awaken.

Biddy had refused to leave Ian's side, not allowing herself even a moment's rest since the evening before. But the long hours had taken a toll. She'd dropped off into a fitful sleep in the same chair she'd occupied for the last twenty-four hours, her hand still holding Ian's.

Katie laid a cool, damp cloth over his badly swollen right eye. They'd no ice left, only cold water from the river. She hummed a quiet and gentle tune. Music soothed her; it always had. If she hadn't had some tune to help her through her ministrations, she'd have been weeping out of frustration and exhaustion. The past twenty-four hours had felt like twenty-four days.

"How is Ian this evening?"

She looked up at the sound of Joseph Archer's voice. How the man managed to sneak up on her unnoticed time and again, she'd never know.

"Much the same," she answered. "His breathing is steady and deep. His pulse continues on as it should. He moves about now and then, but he doesn't talk or seem aware of any of us. He hasn't opened his eyes."

Joseph stopped beside her, looking down at Ian. "I would be surprised if he was able to open his eyes, considering how swollen his face is."

Katie had told herself as much again and again as she'd tended to Ian. 'Twas as if he hovered just on the other side of awareness, unable to cross that divide.

"Ian's a peaceable man. Why would the Red Road do this to *him?* There are so many others who jump into every fray, who antagonize the Reds at every opportunity." She immediately realized how that might be taken. "Not that I would wish this on any person." 'Twas exactly the kind of phrase her mother would have crossed herself while saying.

Joseph shoved his hands into his trouser pockets, his eyes never leaving Ian. "Hate is never logical."

She slumped in her chair, too tired to even sit up straight. She pushed out a deep and weary breath. Pain pulsed in her temples.

Joseph sat gingerly on the edge of the bed, facing her. "When did you last eat?"

She rubbed at her gritty eyes a moment, thinking. "We got a bit of broth down Ian an hour ago."

"I didn't ask how long ago *Ian* ate. I asked about you."

"Mrs. O'Connor saw to it we all had something to eat before she had to go."

"How are you holding up?" He leaned his bent arms on his legs. There were moments, like now, when his eyes seemed to look into her soul, searching out answers for themselves.

"I am so very tired, Joseph. And worry is gnawing at me. I'm so turned about I can't say whether it's on my head or on my heels I'm standing."

He reached out a hand, gently brushing his fingers over hers before seeming to recollect himself and pulling back once more. He often did just that, as though a comforting touch were the most natural thing in the world—until he remembered who she was.

She'd sat in that room alone, fretting for hours on end. The O'Connor family, in their distress, had turned to one another for comfort. Though the need felt selfish, she'd longed for someone to reach out to *her,* to touch her, even for a moment. That he'd pulled back so quickly, so entirely, only deepened her loneliness.

"I'll sit with Ian," Joseph said. "You need to rest."

A surge of guilt rushed over her at the thought of walking away from her duties in the sickroom. "Mrs. O'Connor means to come take my place in a bit, as it is. I can wait until then."

"Mrs. O'Connor will not begrudge you a moment's respite, Katie."

While that was, no doubt, true, Katie couldn't help feeling as though she would be breaking a promise by stepping away.

Joseph sat, watching her, as though he had nowhere else in the entire world to be and nothing else to do with his time. Clearly he meant to sit there until she gave over.

"I suppose a moment away wouldn't be going back on my word entirely." She rose from her chair. "And you'll be here to tend to Ian, so it's not as if I'm abandoning him altogether."

"Oh, were you expecting me to stay here?" Joseph sounded surprised, though the slightest hint of a smile tipped his mouth, enough to add something resembling laughter to his expression.

She shook her head, feeling a touch of amusement creeping over her own face. Joseph Archer could frustrate her like no one else, but he did, on occasion, make her smile in spite of herself.

"You'll not be too put out with me, will you, for having your dinner on the table late again tonight?" She'd not been so remiss in her housekeeping duties at the Archer home in all the months she'd been with them as she had since Ian's injury. "I know it's hard on the girls to be hungry longer than they're accustomed."

He shrugged as he moved to the chair she'd just left. "If they complain too loudly, I can always fire you again."

They'd worn that teasing comment near to threads. That he'd fired her twice on her first day in Hope Springs had become a source of amusement to them both. She knew he valued her and the work she did too much to let her go so carelessly. She would be moving out in another month's time as it was; his new housekeeper was set to arrive then.

"And wouldn't I just love to see you try to get on without me." She pointed a finger at him. "You'd be pained with hunger and your clothes too filthy for company. Let that teach you to appreciate me."

Though Joseph faced the bed, Katie could see enough of his face to tell he smiled.

'Twas good to be needed. She'd been in service from the time she was eight, but until coming to Hope Springs, she'd never been anything important to anyone.

She pushed aside the colorful quilt hanging in the doorway of Biddy and Ian's bedroom and stepped out. The first time she'd visited Biddy's home, it had been filled with smiles and laughter and joy. Now, it sat quiet and empty, a testament to the somber state of things. For a moment she'd forgotten how bad things truly were. A young father lay in the next room, beaten nearly to death. Half a town lived in constant worry over who would be next.

The front door opened, something that had happened again and again during the past day and a half. The O'Connor clan was plentiful and close-knit. All of Ian's siblings had come by many times, and his parents had only left his house to return to their own in order to sleep and tend to the most necessary chores on their farm.

'Twas Tavish who stepped inside. He spotted her on the instant and gave her one of his heart-melting smiles. That exact look on his face had claimed a rather permanent place in her heart.

"Good day to you, Sweet Katie." He tossed his wide-brimmed hat onto a nearby bench and shook the dust from his night-black hair with a quick swish of his hand.

"You're filthy, Tavish O'Connor. I've seen potatoes come out of the ground with less dirt clinging to them than you have just now." Katie delivered the scold with too theatrical a tone to be at all taken seriously.

"You come dragging in the whole of the earth with you and likely expect someone else to sweep up after."

His blue eyes twinkled with amusement. "You want me to go back out and take my dirt with me, leaving you here all by your lonesome?"

She shrugged as if his coming or going mattered not at all to her and received a laugh for her efforts. She loved this playful side of him. Even in her darkest hours, he could lighten her heart and take away the weight of the world sitting on her shoulders.

"You're a troublesome woman, Katie Macauley." Tavish crossed to where she stood. "What am I to do with you?"

She folded her arms across her chest. "I'm hoping you'll throw yourself in the river and wash up a bit in hopes of impressing me."

He brushed a hand along her cheek. Katie felt a blush follow his touch.

"The river's too cold for that, Sweet Katie."

She leaned her head against his shoulder, though her arms remained folded. She'd long since learned the simple joy of resting her weight against him, letting him prop her up a moment while she regained her strength.

He wrapped his arms protectively around her. "How's my brother this evening?"

"The same." She closed her eyes, shutting out the world.

"Then we'll simply have to be grateful he's no worse."

She felt him press a kiss to the top of her head, a loving gesture he'd first adopted some weeks earlier. She'd not grown entirely comfortable with shows of affection, having not known many during her life. But his attentions were so kind and gentle, she had come to love them. He put her a bit away from him, though his hands lingered on her upper arms.

"You'd best go see to cleaning your own self up a bit." He gave her an overdone look of disapproval. "You're fair covered with dust and earth and who knows what else."

She glanced down at the front of her dress and found it just as he'd declared. She was dusted with the dirt he'd brought in from the fields.

Katie shook her head, even as she smiled at him.

"That is just what I hoped to see," he said, tapping her under the chin with his finger. "Trouble hates nothing so much as a smile."

"But a smile won't cure this." She nodded in the direction of Ian's bedroom.

"Perhaps not," he said. "But neither will tears. I can do little to make my brother well again, but I mean to do all I can to see that smile of yours keeping company with your face. The two shouldn't be parted for anything in the world."

"So you plan to carry all my burdens for me, is that it?"

He nodded slowly. "I'd have followed you back to Ireland, you know that."

"I do." He'd fully intended to do just that, and she was still stunned by the enormity of that sacrifice.

"But since you've decided to stay, I'm making it my life's mission to see that you're happy here." He pressed a lingering kiss to her forehead. "Now, I'm going to see if Ian's dragged his lazy bum out of bed yet."

When she'd first met Tavish, Katie had taken his teasing remarks as a sure sign he wasn't serious enough about the realities of life. She'd since learned to know him better. Laughing was his way of dealing with the difficulties.

"You get yourself in there, you unfeeling brother." She even laughed a bit herself. "Perhaps his first act upon coming back to his senses will be to belt you hard in the gob."

Something of his humor faded for a moment. "I'd welcome it, I would. Seeing him fit enough to deliver me a fast fist to the face would do my worrying soul a great deal of good."

He slipped into the bedroom, letting the quilt fall behind him.

Katie stood a moment in the silent room, her heart heavy. She wrapped one arm around her middle and rubbed at her weary face with the other.

She had no medical training, but had spent the day caring for a man too broken to do more than wince or moan deep in his throat. No words. No eye contact. Biddy had turned to her with such trust, such complete confidence. Katie didn't at all feel equal to that responsibility.

"Losing Ian would destroy Biddy," she whispered, knowing it to be true.

Ian and Biddy were halves of a whole, two people who seemed at their happiest when with each other. If Ian did not survive, Biddy would carry a burden every bit as heavy and soul-crushing as the one Katie had carried since her sister's death. Heavier, even. Katie's heart ached at the thought of her friend hurting so deeply and permanently.

She pushed back the blanket in the bedroom doorway, peeking silently into the room. Biddy still slept in the chair near the bed. Tavish stood at the foot of the bed, watching his brother.

"If he doesn't pull through this," Tavish said to Joseph, "Biddy will need extra time to make her payment on the land."

Katie hadn't even thought of the money troubles the O'Connors would have. Would the difficulties never end?

"Ian is my best friend, Tavish. I'm not so heartless I would evict his family in the face of so much tragedy." Joseph slumped in his chair.

"What'll that do to your neutrality? The Red Road will be up in arms if you show us any mercy."

Joseph shook his head. "I have helped plenty of them through difficult times. Doing the same for Ian and Biddy won't be any different."

Tavish pushed out a breath heavy with tension and sat on the trunk at the foot of the bed. "They won't see it that way. You know they won't."

Joseph didn't answer, didn't argue.

Tavish rubbed at the back of his neck. "This will get far worse before it gets better. I'm worried about Katie living off the Irish Road. The Reds have never been happy about that."

He hadn't talked to *her* about that worry. Indeed, he'd been optimistic and more lighthearted than Katie had managed to be. His concern didn't exactly surprise her. His brother lay at death's door. He had every reason to be afraid, worried, uncertain, yet his concern still extended to include her. She was touched by that kindness.

"I know you don't have a replacement housekeeper yet," Tavish continued, "but if Katie's not safe—"

"Katie would fiercely object to being sent away before she feels she has fulfilled her obligations."

"And *I* would fiercely object to her being the next one of us beaten within an inch of her life."

She let the blanket fall back into place, her insides coiling with those words. Would the Reds truly attack her?

"It won't come to that, Tavish." Joseph's firm voice reached her from the other side of the quilt.

"This feud has driven people away." Tavish sounded wearier than he'd allowed himself to appear since discovering Ian unconscious in town. "But no one's yet died. I worry that's about to change. If not here in this room, then somewhere and someone else."

Katie closed her eyes. The simple path of life she'd thought stretched out before her had, in a few short days, turned winding and twisting and filled with fear.

Chapter Three

Joseph sat on the bench of his buggy, trying to keep his mind off the tender good-bye taking place on Biddy and Ian's front step. Tavish had staked his claim on Katie's heart weeks earlier, and she clearly returned the sentiment. Joseph could respect that. He could keep to his quiet corner of Katie's life. He could even manage some semblance of a smile for her when she mentioned Tavish's name. He could do all those things. But he didn't have to like it.

Katie reached the wagon a moment later, and he offered her a hand up.

"Thank you, Joseph." Even after three months, she still seemed surprised when he showed her that civility.

She settled on the bench and tucked her feet behind her skirts as she always did, keeping her battered shoes out of sight. He knew that the state of her footwear bothered her but that the broken and scarred state of her feet bothered her even more. He wished he could do something for her, anything to ease even one of her burdens.

"If only Hope Springs had a real doctor." Katie sighed, long and heavy. "Mrs. Claire is a fine midwife and knows every folk remedy ever thought of, and she's been so very helpful with Ian, but it would ease my mind considerably to have an actual man of medicine to consult. I worried all day that I'd make a mistake, and he'd be the worse for it."

He tightened his grip on the reins, resisting the urge to take her hand in his and offer some words of comfort. *You are her employer. And she has given her heart to someone else.*

"There is nothing for it but to wait and see what the next few days hold for him." Joseph took some pride in his businesslike tone. If he could feign indifference, perhaps he would eventually learn to feel it.

Katie nodded. "We've a saying in Ireland much like that. 'For what cannot be cured, patience is best.'"

He flicked the reins, urging the horse along. Patience was all well and good, but it wasn't the most satisfying companion. Distraction was more often the best approach where his feelings for Katie were concerned. He certainly had enough to worry about.

His first thought upon hearing of Ian's condition was fear for his friend. But immediately afterward came concern for Katie. Was she still safe in his home? Would the Red Road take out their anger on her? He hated that he did not know the answer to those questions.

The wagon rolled over the bridge that led off the Irish Road. His house sat first after the bridge, the no-man's-land in the town's decade-long feud. He was caught in the middle in every sense of the word.

"Seems the girls arrived home before we did." Katie motioned toward the barn, easily visible from the bridge.

Finbarr O'Connor sat in the back of his father's wagon, playing some kind of game with Joseph's daughters. Though only sixteen, Finbarr had the patience of a saint and the uncanny ability to keep the girls occupied. Ivy saw him as a fun friend and playmate; Emma was half in love with him. If Emma hadn't been only nine years old and if Finbarr hadn't been the most trustworthy young man of Joseph's acquaintance, he might have worried about that.

Joseph raised his hand in greeting to Mr. O'Connor and received the same gesture in return. He pulled up to the side of the O'Connor wagon.

"How's my son?" Mr. O'Connor asked, his expression tight and worried.

"There's been no change." Katie's tone twisted with guilt. She blamed herself for far too many things that weren't her fault.

The discouragement in all of their faces pricked at Joseph. These were good people, yet terrible things continually happened to them.

"At least he isn't growing worse," Joseph put in, hoping to give them at least a little hope to cling to.

Their nods of acknowledgment were noticeably low on enthusiasm.

Joseph lifted his daughters down from the O'Connor wagon, keeping little Ivy in his arms. "Send word if you need anything."

Mr. O'Connor nodded in understanding and with a quick twitch of the reins, had his wagon turned about and on its way back toward the Irish side of the valley.

"Pompah." Ivy turned his head with her tiny hands, bringing his gaze to her face. "Is Mary's papa still ill?"

"Yes, dearest. He is still very ill." Joseph had decided the moment he heard about the nature and extent of Ian's injuries to spare his daughters those details. They'd seen too much hatred in their short lives without knowing just how deep it ran in Hope Springs.

Ivy laid her head on his shoulder. Joseph felt Emma's hand slip in his. He glanced down. Her nine-year-old eyes were often too old and knowing for his peace of mind. She, it seemed, suspected there was more to the difficulties than he'd let on. He tried to smile reassuringly, but he could see she still worried.

"What say you to a steaming pot of potato-and-leek soup?" Katie jumped in.

Joseph could see in the strain of her smile that she made every effort to appear cheerful. Did she sense the girls' uneasiness as well? Though she'd thoroughly protested her inadequacy as a caregiver for the children initially, she'd proven her worth again and again.

"Can we have bread too?" Ivy asked hopefully.

Katie put her hands on her hips and eyed Ivy with a teasing scold. "Now what kind of baker woman would I be if I didn't serve bread with the soup? You just tell me that, now."

"No kind of baker woman at all." Ivy shook her finger in rhythm to her words, even managing the tiniest bit of an Irish inflection.

Joseph smiled to hear it. He very much liked the idea of Katie being an influence in his daughters' lives. They would do well to learn from her strength and determination.

"Could it be soda bread?" Ivy pleaded.

Katie nodded. "I think it'd best be; we haven't time enough for making anything else."

Ivy's grin was wide as a Wyoming horizon.

"Come on then, sweet thing." Katie reached out for her. "We'll get you and your sister washed up just quick as can be and have your supper on the table as well."

Ivy willingly made the switch from Joseph's arms to Katie's. Though he loved the feel of his little girl in his embrace, giving her over to Katie felt as natural as anything in the world.

Katie loved both his girls. She simply didn't love *him.*

Emma moved to Katie's side as well. Joseph nodded her on toward the house; he needed to tend to the horse. And he needed a few minutes of quiet to settle his thoughts.

He'd only just turned in the direction of the barn when Katie's voice, steady but uncertain, called out to him. "You seem to have yourself a visitor, Joseph Archer."

A visitor? He looked back over his shoulder. A silhouette stepped out of the shadows of the back porch. Joseph knew him after a moment. Bob Archibald.

Bob Archibald despised the Irish more than anyone else in town did, and he'd never attempted to hide his animosity. He'd been behind most of the escalations in the Hope Springs feud over the years. Though he had no proof, Joseph firmly suspected Bob Archibald had a hand in Ian's current state.

Katie had frozen in the yard, the girls standing close at her side. Joseph crossed the yard in a few quick strides. He'd not have Bob infecting the girls with his vitriol. And he absolutely would not allow the man to insult or threaten Katie.

"Bob." He nodded his acknowledgment.

"I came to see how that Paddy is doing." Bob's smile was that of a man enjoying another's suffering.

Katie's posture stiffened. The Reds called every Irish person in Hope Springs "Paddy" and in the same sneering tone Bob Archibald had used.

Joseph joined Katie and the girls. "Go on inside," he told them in as quiet and calm a voice as he could manage. To his unwelcome visitor he said, "I don't know anyone named Paddy."

"You know the one," Bob answered. "Rumor has it he fell and hurt himself."

Emma's worried eyes turned up to Joseph. He motioned her once more toward the door. Katie took her hand and pulled her along. That she knew what to do without him specifically asking was a blessing.

As soon as Katie and the girls were inside, Joseph took up the discussion with Bob once more. "I think you know perfectly well that Ian O'Connor didn't fall."

Bob managed an almost believable look of uncertainty and rubbed his chin as if in thought. "Is that so? I am certain I heard he tripped."

As much as he hated playing the snake's game, Joseph could see no other way of getting the information he sought, short of storming down the Red Road himself and demanding the guilty parties identify themselves.

"One has to wonder why a man as peaceable as Ian O'Connor, one who never causes trouble nor stirs things up, would 'trip' that way," Joseph said. "One would expect such a thing to happen to someone with a reputation for fanning the flames."

"Yes, one does have to wonder about that." The oily smile disappeared, replaced by a look so pointedly serious Joseph couldn't help but feel a wave of apprehension. "It seems to me it would be best if *everyone* got it into their heads where they belong." His eyes darted quickly, almost imperceptibly, toward Joseph's house.

Joseph forced himself to take a calming breath. As angry as the feud made him, he alone stood in a position to reason with both sides. Pummeling Bob Archibald would not help in the long run.

"I have to disagree with you there," Joseph said. "What would actually be best is for both sides of this ridiculous argument to forget about beating each other down and mind their own business for once in their lives."

One side of Bob's mouth tipped. He plopped his hat on his head. "You had best keep a weather eye out, Archer. Things can get a little stormy this time of year."

Joseph watched him go, a weight settling in his stomach. Bob hadn't come simply to gloat over Ian's injuries; Joseph felt certain of that.

The Red Road had never been happy about Katie living off the Irish Road. They had made an issue of it almost from the beginning.

Panic flared on the instant. Ian's injuries remained fresh in his mind. If that happened to Katie . . .

Having her nearby was the greatest thing that had happened to him since his wife died. The girls loved her. *He* loved her. But if she wasn't safe in his home, on his land, he could not—*would* not—keep her there.

His new housekeeper would not arrive until the end of harvest, some weeks down the road. Practicality demanded he keep Katie there until he had a replacement. His own loneliness called out for the same. More than mere loneliness—she was such a crucial part of his life that he couldn't imagine his days without her. But how could he ask her to stay if there was even the tiniest possibility any harm would come to her?

He couldn't. He wouldn't allow Katie to remain in danger.

He sat through dinner, debating how to go about insisting she leave without either wounding her feelings or alarming her. She'd been mistreated by far too many people in her life. He didn't want his name added to that list.

He stepped into the kitchen after the girls had finished their meal.

She looked up at him. "I've been meaning to ask you a question, Joseph." She continued working as she spoke. "I saw a stack of letters on your writing desk. Does there happen to be one for me in there?"

Katie had written to her ailing father in Ireland and was clearly hoping for a response.

"There hasn't been enough time yet for a letter to reach here from Belfast," he told her, hoping to ease her disappointment.

"Are you trying to tell me that patience is a virtue?" Her light tone and smile did his heart good.

He loved her smile. Though she had arrived somber and painfully unsure of herself, Katie had eased into life in Hope Springs and in his home. She fit there like a piece in a puzzle.

Joseph leaned against the countertop near the sink where she worked. "Bob Archibald's visit has me thinking."

Katie's smile dimmed visibly. "Is it terrible that I'm convinced within myself that he was behind Ian's beating? I know I've not a bit of proof, and maybe it's only my own dislike of the man talking, but I blame him for it. I blame him entirely." She gave a tiny shake of her head, shrugging as she did. "'Tis likely terribly unfair of me, I know."

"I doubt there is a single person in all of Hope Springs who *doesn't* think Bob Archibald is responsible for Ian's condition."

Her hands stilled in the dishwater. She pressed her lips together, mouth downturned. "I've heard whispers," she said hesitantly, "that many suspect Ian was set upon by an entire group of people."

Joseph was certain of that. Even caught off guard, Ian could have defended himself against a single attacker. Still, Katie was worried enough; she didn't need to know the feud had truly descended into mob attacks. He could only hope more violence would not follow.

"You think that as well, do you?" Katie returned to her washing, scrubbing with more determination than she had before. He'd learned that about her—she cleaned with vigor when she was upset. "That is a terrible, terrible thing to do to a man. Did Bob Archibald say anything to you about it?" She spoke uncertainly, watching him closely. "Did he say what might happen next? If . . . if there's more danger?"

Leave it to Katie to strike directly at the heart of the matter. He'd never known her to shy away from a problem, little or great. "Archibald didn't make any specific threats, but I didn't care for his tone."

She dried her hands on a dishrag, her brows drawn as she spoke to him. "Did he make *vague* threats, then?"

Nothing got past Katie. He was grateful in that moment to have someone to talk with. "His main point of complaint was 'people not staying where they belong.'"

She turned the tiniest bit pale. "He was speaking of me, was he?"

Joseph brushed his fingers against her arm, wanting to reassure her. He never allowed himself anything but the friendliest connection, a momentary touch on the arm, an encouraging word or two. He never crossed beyond that no matter how desperately his heart cried out for her companionship. Touching her was torturous.

His touch brought a half-smile to her face. His own burden lightened seeing even a tiny bit of her worries lifted. He wished he was in a position to do more than that.

"I don't want to bring trouble to you here, Joseph." Katie took up position next to him, leaning against the countertop. "But what am I to do if the Reds mean to make problems?"

He kept himself still, resisting the urge to put an arm around her shoulders and draw her closer. "I think, Katie, it would be best if you go live on the Irish Road."

"I intend to, just as soon as your new housekeeper arrives."

He knew in his bones that waiting even another few days would be a mistake. "Bob's demeanor worried me, and you know I am not easily shaken. I can't be certain the Reds' patience will hold out long enough for my new housekeeper to get here. I think you need to make the move tomorrow."

Her eyes widened and her voice rose. "*Tomorrow?*"

He nodded.

"That is so soon. Who'll look after the house and the meals?"

He had no idea. More likely than not, everything would fall apart. He and the girls would have to go back to his questionable cooking skills. But if Katie thought her departure would cause them difficulty, she would insist on staying. "We'll manage."

"Joseph." Doubt and scolding filled her tone. Clearly he hadn't convinced her. "I saw the state of things when I arrived. You need me here, and you need me badly."

She had no concept of how true that was. "I need you on the Irish Road, Katie."

Her eyes narrowed. "Are you firing me?"

He couldn't tell if her posture was more angry or hurt. "No. I simply think it would be best if you left as soon as possible."

Hurt. Definitely hurt.

He held up his hands in a show of innocence. "I am not complaining about your work, nor am I saying we don't want you here with us. We do. We want and need and love having you here. I am only thinking of your safety and the girls'."

"The girls' safety?" Her gaze bored into his. "Surely no one would do anything to either of them."

He didn't think so. He hoped not, anyway. But hatred made people unpredictable. "I would rather not find out the hard way that I was overly confident about their safety."

Worry knit her brows. She pressed her fingertips to her downturned lips. "I would never forgive myself if anything happened to them."

The very thought settled as a weight on his chest. "Things will not be easy here without you, but sending you away is the only option I can accept right now."

"I could come back each day, cook meals and such, straighten up a bit."

So long as she lived on the Irish Road, would the Reds object to her continuing to work for him? Finbarr had been working for him for years. He wanted to believe they would have no objection to Katie still working in his home if she didn't live there.

But what if I am wrong?

"It is tempting, I assure you, but the Reds need to see that—"

"That I've been put where I belong." Though she spoke the words with dignity, Joseph knew her well enough to see the bruised feelings hiding under the declaration. She turned away. "It seems the Irish really do lose every battle in this town."

Again his well-intentioned actions were being construed as taking sides.

"*Et tu,* Katie?" he muttered.

The reference clearly confused her. He didn't explain. If she were in the mood to accuse him of turning on her, nothing he said would likely convince her otherwise

He paced away. He'd passed a hard twenty-four hours, watching his closest friend hover near death, being plagued by questions of what came next and how bad things would become, wondering what he could possibly do. Behind all of it was the very real truth that he would once again endure barbed comments and thinly veiled accusations from both sides of the feud.

Even Katie was questioning his loyalties. She had always seemed like the only one who truly understood his desire to stay out of it all. She too had worked to distance herself from the feuding, though, in the end, her nationality had pulled her into the fray.

Weariness dragged at him. How many times had he pulled the town back from the brink of self-destruction? He'd saved them from themselves by keeping himself apart from them all. What was his reward for that? What did he get for his sacrifice?

Loneliness. Deep, unending loneliness.

"I'll drop you off at Mrs. Claire's in the morning when I take the girls to the Scotts' house for the day. Have your things packed. We'll leave after breakfast."

He didn't look back at her or wait for a response. She'd either be hurt by his dismissal or thunderous. In that moment, he couldn't bear to see either one.

Chapter Four

Tavish dropped an armful of firewood into the basket near the fireplace. 'Twas ten in the morning already, and he hadn't yet been out to Ian's fields. Between the chores at his own place and those he'd taken on at his brother's, he'd worked without a moment's pause since well before sunrise.

He pulled his hat from his head and wiped at the sweat trickling along his hairline. His gaze wandered toward Ian's room. Biddy said there'd been no change overnight, that Ian stirred now and then, even made the occasional sound, but never truly woke. Tavish had managed an encouraging word for her, but his own hopes were flagging.

He crossed to the bedroom doorway and pulled back the quilt. Biddy looked up from her position beside the bed.

"How is he?" Tavish asked.

Her gaze returned to her husband. The worry in her face answered his question. "If only he'd open his eyes and look at me, or squeeze my hand. Anything. He feels so far away."

"Ignoring you, is he? Seems to me you've a right lazy bum of a husband." Striking a laughing tone was painfully difficult. He wanted to rage at the injustice of it all. He wanted to weep at seeing his brother so beaten. But Biddy needed someone to buoy her spirits, and there was no one but him to do it.

That role had always been his. Even as a child on the boat from Ireland, with his heart breaking for his lost home and the beloved grandparents they'd left behind, he had been charged with bringing smiles and laughter to his family. No one else could manage it, and they were in desperate need of cheering. Though smiling through troubles didn't always come easily, he'd found strength in it.

"You know, Biddy, when Ian was just a boy, Da would bribe him with butter candy. Perhaps you ought to give that a go."

She gave him a small smile. "I've already tried offering him sweet rolls and barm brack."

"He didn't awaken for barm brack? Now that *is* a stubborn man, that is."

Biddy adjusted Ian's blankets. "I even offered to milk the cow every day from now on if only he'd wake up."

Tavish leaned against the doorframe, arms folded loosely over his chest. "Not having to milk the cow—any man would jump at that opportunity. Perhaps if you also promise to muck out the stalls, he'll quit being so headstrong and just get up."

Biddy took Ian's limp hand in hers. "I love you, dearest." She kissed his hand and pressed it to her cheek. "But I'm not mucking out your stalls."

Tavish smiled in relief. Hearing even a tiny bit of humor from Biddy put his heart at ease.

"How long until you need to feed him again?" he asked her. Biddy couldn't hold Ian up and dribble broth down his throat without help.

"About an hour."

He could see to a few more chores before then. "I'll come back."

He looked once more at Ian, hoping to see something encouraging. The swelling had, perhaps, gone down a bit. He lay peacefully; no look of pain marred his features. Tavish supposed that was something. But

Ian hadn't spoken or even shown the slightest sign of awareness in nearly forty-eight hours. That made optimism a bit hard to come by.

"If you need anything, I'll be out in the barn mucking out the stalls."

Biddy nodded as she smoothed Ian's blanket.

Tavish slipped from the room, crossing to the front door. Something had to change for the better with Ian, or they'd all lose hope.

The front door squeaked as he opened it. The hinges didn't look rusted, but a bit of grease would do them good. Tavish added that to the list in his mind. He'd have his brother's house in as fine shape as he could get it. If he awoke—Tavish hated that he thought of Ian's recovery in terms of "if"—he'd need his strength for recovering from his injuries, not tending to his home.

He stepped out beneath the front overhang and saw his Sweet Katie sitting on the step. Her back was to him, knees pulled up close, her arms wrapped around her legs.

"This is a fine surprise," he said, pushing all thoughts of hinges and repairs out of his mind. "Did Joseph give you the day off again to come help Biddy?"

She shook her head without speaking a word.

"You've slipped off, then? It's not like you to skip out on your work."

In a tiny voice, she answered, "I've been fired."

For a moment the words made no sense. "Joseph fired you?" He stepped closer to her.

"He let me go, which amounts to the same thing, really. I've been sent off from a job, something that's never happened to me once in all my life." Katie leaned her chin on her knees. She looked so terribly small and vulnerable sitting there.

Tavish sat on the step beside her. "Did Joseph say why he let you go?"

"So the Red Road won't be angry about me living there. And because if I stayed I might not be safe." She turned her head enough to look over at him. No tears hung in her eyes, but plenty of hurt hovered there. "I understand the whys of it, but that doesn't make it any less frustrating."

Poor Katie. Troubles did seem to stack on top of one another. He'd have to do what he could to lift her spirits. It would be a pleasure, really.

"Granny Claire let you in the door, I'm assuming."

Katie smiled at him. His entire world lit up whenever she smiled, however small and quivery the attempt.

"Aye. She let me in. So I've a place to live and bread to sell and, all things considered, am in a fine situation." She sat up a bit, but her shoulders slumped. "I'm only discouraged is all, and so very tired."

Tavish wrapped his arm around her, pulling her closer. She leaned her head on his shoulder, though her arms remained crossed over her knees. They'd grown close over the past weeks. She'd shared a great deal of her thoughts and worries with him, yet she still felt distant at times, as though she still held something back.

He wished he could promise her that all would be well, that Ian would recover, that the feud would resolve itself peacefully, that she'd have the money she needed. He couldn't, but neither would he speak of heavy things when she was already weighed down. He pressed a kiss to her hair. "You smell like flowers, love. And you feel like heaven."

The tiniest of laughs answered. "You always do manage to think of honeyed words, don't you?"

"And what if I further said that, if we have a *céilí* this Saturday, I'd like for you to be my particular companion for the evening?"

She pulled away enough to look up at him fully. "*If* we have a céilí? There is always a céilí."

He motioned with his head back toward the house. "With all that's happened, I can't say anyone will feel much like holding a party."

"So the Red Road'll take that from us as well?" She pushed out an audible breath. "I hate that the Irish are always the ones who lose in this feud."

He took her hand in his. Hers were hardworking hands, roughened with years of labor, but tiny and gentle all the same. "I, for one, am feeling more optimistic all the time."

He turned her hand over and pressed a kiss to her palm.

She blushed red as a strawberry.

"Keep doing that, Tavish O'Connor, and I'll begin to suspect you fancy me."

He loved when she teased him back. The first few weeks he'd known her, she had been far too serious. "What do I need to do to get you from 'suspecting' to 'believing'?"

"You could lend me a hammer and nails."

He laughed right out loud at the unexpected request. Her smile grew to a grin, sending his heart into a racing rhythm. He'd made progress in his courtship, quite a bit, in fact, but Katie was not one to be quickly won over. Slow and steady was the only approach that would work.

"And what do you need the hammer and nails for, Sweet Katie?"

"There're a few things in my new room at Granny Claire's that need mending."

"Tavish!"

He jumped at Biddy's sudden voice. She peeked out the door, her face frantic.

"I need your help. Please."

He sprang to his feet. "Ian," he whispered, his heart dropping to his toes.

With Katie at his side, he rushed into the house, fearing the worst.

Chapter Five

Katie followed close on Tavish's heels, hoping desperately that they'd find Ian on the mend rather than worse off.

"He's thrashing about." Biddy walked and spoke swiftly, a frantic edge to her voice. "He's too big. I can't hold him still, but I don't want him hurting himself."

Did more movement mean Ian was improving? Or was this even more reason to worry?

Ian was, indeed, moving about, enough to warrant concern. He might injure himself further. Tavish took up position at the side of the bed, holding his brother down by both arms. Katie, taking her cue from him, set her hands on Ian's ankles, hidden beneath the blanket. She didn't hold them so tightly he couldn't move, but with enough force to keep him from kicking anyone.

"Ian." Tavish spoke sharply. "Settle yourself down, man."

"He's in pain." Biddy's heartbreak sounded in each word. "I don't know how to help him."

Ian's expression remained anguished, though he seemed to settle a bit.

"Have you any powders?" Tavish asked.

Ian's head jerked from side to side again, eyes pulled tight, mouth drawn.

Biddy shook her head. "Your da went into town this morning and meant to bring some back, but he's not come by yet."

Ian quieted a little, just as he had a moment earlier. Indeed, he settled a bit every time Biddy spoke.

"Talk to him, Biddy," Katie said. "I think it calms him."

A heart-wrenching mixture of hope and doubt filled Biddy's face. She sat on the edge of the bed. "Ian, love?"

He moaned deep in his throat, a sound of sheer pain.

"Ian?" Biddy tried again. She set her hand on his cheek. "Come on, then. Look at me, darling."

He didn't open his eyes. His grimace remained firmly in place. Still, he quieted.

"We're getting you something for the pain, love." Biddy spoke soothingly. "'Twill help you rest, it will. You only need endure a bit longer."

Ian seemed calmer. Katie looked to Tavish, wanting his opinion. Their eyes met across the bed. He gave her a tiny nod.

"Keep talking," he said to Biddy. "I'll see if I can't find Da."

He came around the foot of the bed and paused long enough to press a light kiss to Katie's temple. Her heart both jumped and warmed at the brief contact.

"Stay with Biddy," he whispered. "She'll need you." He left the room in a hurry.

"Of course." Katie crossed to the side of the bed where Tavish had stood. She pressed her hand to Ian's forehead.

"He's a touch feverish," she said quietly.

Biddy held Ian's hand in one of hers. She nodded, brow creased. "If only his da would hurry with the powders. I'm not sure what to do otherwise."

Katie didn't either, but clearly Biddy needed someone to at least appear confident. "We'll do what we've done all along. Wet cloths to cool him off. Water so he doesn't grow thirsty." That had seen him through the past two days. "Perhaps he'll be able to eat more now that he's a bit more awake."

Biddy nodded, a glimmer of optimism behind her pallor.

Ian's eyes scrunched tighter, and he whimpered.

"I wish I could do more for him." Biddy touched his face, absolute heartbreak in her eyes. "Are you thirsty, dearest? Hungry?"

He didn't answer but simply lay there with the same look of misery on his face. They'd worried so much when he wasn't waking up. But was this any better? Ian was more awake but in too much pain to rest. And if he couldn't rest, how could he possibly heal?

"Do you sing, Biddy? Or hum or anything?"

"A little." The question clearly confused her.

"Music soothes the soul," Katie explained. "We've nothing else to give him for the pain. We can at least give him that."

Biddy nodded but still looked terribly uncertain. After a moment she began to hum quietly, the notes broken a bit. Katie didn't immediately recognize the tune, but Ian stilled—that was all that truly mattered.

Pain still etched his features, but bits of his agony melted into something like contemplation. Was he aware enough to be pondering on things?

Katie dipped the rag that had been on his forehead in the bowl of cool water. She wrung it out and, taking advantage of Ian's calm, laid it over his brow. Her eyes met Biddy's, an unspoken recognition passing between them. The quiet tune was weaving its magic. Katie knew she should recognize the melody, though she couldn't quite pull it from her memory.

Biddy held her husband's hand in her own, pressing them both to her cheek as she hummed. Katie had heard many talented musicians in her lifetime. Biddy's unpolished, heartfelt tune topped every one of them, not for ability, but for sheer depth of feeling.

Ian moved a bit. 'Twasn't the jerking, desperate flailing of earlier. He simply turned slightly toward Biddy, as if listening more closely.

In the next instant Katie realized what the tune was Biddy hummed:

"I Am Asleep and Don't Awaken Me." She smiled at Biddy's choice. They'd tried all of the past two days to awaken Ian from his pained slumber and there Biddy was humming a tune about *not* waking a person.

Biddy stroked Ian's hair above the cooling cloth. The weight in her expression had eased.

Ian's mouth opened, though no words emerged. Was he trying to speak?

Again he moved his lips. Biddy grew instantly silent, her gaze riveted to her husband.

Words shaking and broken, Ian whispered, "Don't stop."

Biddy took an audible, gasping breath. "Dearest?"

He winced. His breaths seemed labored. "I liked . . . the song."

"Recognized it, did you?" The hope written on her face was heartbreaking.

Ian nodded a tiny bit.

Please open your eyes. She needs to see you there.

"And do you know *me,* love?" Tears hovered in Biddy's eyes.

Ian took a shaking breath. "Biddy," he whispered.

Relief surged through Katie. Ian was speaking. He had recognized a song almost before Katie did. He knew the sound of his wife's voice. Surely these were good signs that he would recover in time.

Biddy turned her head enough to press a kiss to Ian's palm before returning his hand to her cheek.

"Keep singing, woman." Ian's hoarse voice had grown ever quieter in the tiny moment since he'd last spoken. "Distract me . . . from . . . the pain."

"Your da's gone for powders," Biddy said.

He nodded weakly. "'Irish Lamentation,' Biddy."

"But that tune's so sad."

Ian took a shallow breath, wincing as he did. "Please."

Biddy took up the melody, clinging to his hand. The desperate hope in her expression tugged at Katie's heart. The past days had been so very hard on Biddy.

"I'll see if I can't find Mr. O'Connor," Katie said. She was as anxious to get Ian the powders as she was to give Biddy and her husband a moment of privacy. There was something intimately tender in the moment they were sharing. Katie didn't belong there with them.

She stepped beyond the hanging quilt. Alone in the open space beyond, she wrapped her arms around herself. The sound of Biddy's voice humming "Irish Lamentation" filled the silence.

Katie closed her eyes. *Music soothes the soul.* She'd said it herself, but she wasn't feeling very soothed. Weight pressed against her heart. The tunes of home took her thoughts back across the ocean. Did Father have music to calm him in his final illness? Was Mother humming to him?

Katie had his fiddle there in Wyoming with her. He hadn't even that instrument to offer solace. She'd meant to take it back to him, but her plans had changed. Her father was dying in Belfast, while she remained where she was.

She needed her music, needed the feel of the fiddle in her hand and under her chin, the sound of the old tunes echoing inside. She needed quiet and peace. She needed—

The door opened. Katie looked up.

Tavish.

He stepped inside with his father at his side. They both wore nearly identical looks of deep, worried contemplation as they spoke in low voices to one another. Tavish would likely have too many difficulties of his own to see her through her moment of weariness.

His eyes met hers. She tried to smile. The gesture must have failed miserably. Concern immediately filled his expression.

"Ian—?"

Katie cut across him. "He is still awake. He's even speaking a bit."

Such a mingle of emotions flitted across the men's faces. Amazement. Hope. Wariness.

Mr. O'Connor crossed quickly to the blanket-hung doorway. Katie fully expected Tavish to do the same. He surprised her by crossing directly to *her* instead.

"Seems to me, Sweet Katie, you're feeling a bit crushed by the weight of all this."

"We've passed a difficult few days," she said.

He pulled her into an embrace. 'Twas his answer for everything, really—a solution she'd come to value. She leaned against his chest, breathing in deep the masculine scent of him. His hand rubbed slow circles over her back, the repetition calming her.

"Seems I've done nothing but fall apart lately." Katie had been something of a mess in the short weeks since word of her father's illness arrived.

"Nonsense." Tavish's voice rumbled in his chest. "You've held up better than anyone could have expected, considering all that's happened. And besides, what's the use of having a man about if he can't help piece you back together now and then?"

She could smile at that. "No use at all, I say."

She felt him laugh. That sound had lifted her spirits so many times. Her grief ebbed, allowing clear thought to return.

"Ian'll be feeling better now that he has something to take for the pain," she said.

"Da wasn't able to get the powders."

She pulled back and looked up at him. "Didn't get any? Was the mercantile out?" That seemed unlikely.

Tavish shook his head. "The Irish price for medicine's gone up. Johnson's asking five dollars a bottle."

She took a shocked step backward. "*Five dollars?* That's a fortune."

"Until today, a bottle of powders was only two bits." He shook his head. "But, then, not until today did someone on this road need the powders for something the other road did to him. We're to be doubly punished, it seems."

"*Five dollars?*" That was three months' salary at Joseph's, the highest-paying job she'd ever had.

Tavish reached out, cupping her jaw with his hand. "Now, don't you go fretting yourself over this. You've plenty on your mind as it is. We'll see to Ian."

How could she help but worry? Biddy would never rest so long as Ian was suffering, and Ian would suffer so long as he had nothing to ease his pain.

"How can Johnson set so high a price on medicine he knows is so badly needed? It's inhumane, is what it is."

"Son?"

They both turned at the sound of Mr. O'Connor's voice.

"Run up the road, Tavish, and let your ma know her boy's awake."

"Aye, Da." Tavish turned to Katie. "Care to walk with me a piece?"

The offer was tempting, but Katie's mind was churning too much on the latest difficulty to go for a stroll, even with him. "Actually, I'd best get back to Granny Claire's."

He walked with her as far as the road, then pressed a lingering kiss to the back of her hand. "A fine good day to you, Sweet Katie."

"And to you."

Tavish walked farther up the road, while Katie made her way down toward her new home.

Five dollars. The price echoed as painful beats in her heart. Harvest was yet a few weeks off. Farming families wouldn't have a great deal of cash on hand until after they sold their crop.

Aye. But you have some. Hidden in an old, dented biscuit tin in her new room was the money she'd saved over the past eighteen years, her sole means of returning home. In the few short days since she'd decided to remain in Wyoming she'd begun imagining what she might do with her precious savings. Land of her own had been the excited answer. She could have a place of her own, a home she could never be thrown off of. If her connection to Tavish progressed, that money would help support them both, perhaps pay off the note on his land, free him of that burden.

Five dollars would set you back quite a spell.

She needed her savings in the short-term as well. 'Twas the only money she had to live on now that she hadn't a job. And what little she brought in from selling her bread went to buy supplies for making more bread; there was no true profit in it yet.

She stepped inside Mrs. Claire's house. 'Twould take her some time to grow used to calling her "Granny" as the kind woman had requested.

Mrs. Claire—*Granny*—sat in her rocker beneath the front window, as always. She pierced Katie with a concerned look. "Has Ian improved at all?"

"He's awake and talking a very little, but he's hurting something terrible."

Mrs. Claire gave one of her wizened nods. "Poor man'll likely be pained for days to come. Weeks, maybe. My younger brother fell from a wall when he was a lad. His head pained him for months afterwards."

Months. Would Ian suffer that long? How would he recover without anything to give him relief? How would he even begin to do the work that needed doing on a farm in the midst of harvest? Could he manage any of it in so much pain?

"You look worn to a thread, Katie," Granny said.

"I am pulled a touch thin." Indeed, Katie felt run clear off her feet. "I need to rest my own four bones a spell."

Granny smiled her wrinkly grin. "Your 'own four bones.'" She shook her head in amusement. "You'll have me thinking I'm back in Ireland again, talking that way."

Katie nodded. "That was part of our bargain, if I remember correctly."

"Indeed." Granny gave her a sharp look. "You just set your mind to rummaging up a few more words and phrases from the Old Country, and try not to worry."

A moment later, Katie stood in the room Granny Claire had given her. Despite Granny's words, Katie's mind returned to the question of Ian's medicine. *Five dollars.* It would take her at least a year to earn that much money baking and selling her bread.

But Ian's voice sounded in her memory: "Distract me from the pain." And with it came her tiny sister's voice from nearly two decades earlier: "I'm cold, Katie."

She'd not been able to do a thing for little Eimear. Not a single thing. She'd simply lay beside her in the bitter cold as the girl slowly froze to death that terrible night.

Was five dollars really so enormous a price to pay to help Ian and Biddy?

Katie pulled her old, trusted biscuit tin from under the bedtick. She pried the tight-fitting lid off and dumped the contents on the faded quilt spread over her new bed. She could spare five dollars. She could. Ian needed the powders desperately, and Biddy would fall clear to pieces if Ian didn't recover. Biddy was like family to her.

Though she couldn't read, Katie had been taught upon arriving in America how to recognize the different paper moneys by the faces on each. Most of her bills were American, and nearly all worth only one dollar. She had a great many coins, but America had in recent years become enamored of paper dollars, and she'd been paid that way of late.

She counted out five of the bills worth one dollar each. Spending the money she'd painstakingly saved caused her a touch of panic. Growing up in poverty had left her that way, always a little afraid of deprivations yet to come.

Katie slipped the bills into the pocket of her dress. She snapped the lid back on her tin and stuffed it in its cozy hiding spot once more.

She would have the powders for Ian. She would not fail him the way she had her sister.

Chapter Six

Katie had done her best to avoid Johnson's Mercantile since her first week in Hope Springs. Mr. Johnson had spent that visit belittling and insulting her. She'd been told to keep to the shadows and keep quiet. From all Katie had learned of the shopkeeper since, she expected more of the same.

She stood beneath the overhang in front of the mercantile, taking a moment to build up the fortitude she knew she'd need. She was about to hand over some of her precious savings to a man who would treat her terribly from the moment she entered his establishment. But she needed medicinal powders, and he was the only one who had them.

Filthy Irishwoman. Mr. Johnson's words echoed anew in her memory. The venom in his voice had shocked her then. Little about the hatred in Hope Springs surprised her anymore. It still hurt. It hurt deeply, but it was no longer unexpected.

She took a deep breath, then another. She opened the door, a bell sounding overhead. She held her chin at a confident angle, determined to prevent Mr. Johnson from seeing that he intimidated her. Some of that confidence slipped, though, upon seeing he was not alone. Nearly any other customer, except perhaps Mr. Archibald, would have been more welcome than Reverend Ford. Her one and only encounter with him had not ended well either.

"Good day." She managed a smile, though she knew it didn't precisely ring with enthusiasm.

The reverend seemed surprised to see her. Mr. Johnson simply looked annoyed.

"I am a busy man," the shopkeeper said as he stood behind his counter doing, as near as Katie could tell, absolutely nothing.

She nodded. "I've come to make a purchase, whenever you've time to see to it."

Mr. Johnson's attention shifted back to the preacher. Katie hung back a step or two. She'd give them room to conduct any business they had, but she'd not allow herself to be completely forgotten.

"How long before your wife is likely to deliver?" the reverend asked.

Katie hadn't heard Mrs. Johnson was in a family way, but she didn't interact with anyone on the Red Road, nor did she attend Sunday services.

"Another two months or more," Mr. Johnson said. "But she's already finding her chores here too cumbersome." He shrugged, though the gesture seemed more resigned than dismissive. "No one here is looking for work. I haven't had a single inquiry since putting the sign up, and it's been months."

Katie muscled down a smile at the irony of his words. She'd been trying to find a permanent job since her second day in town. She'd been told the sign he hung in his window specifically said he wasn't hiring Irish, otherwise he might have filled the position long ago.

"Have you hired a teacher yet?" Mr. Johnson asked.

The reverend shook his head.

Katie let her thoughts and eyes wander.

The mercantile was not quite so tidy as she remembered it from when she'd last stepped inside months earlier. Perhaps she was only looking about with a more critical eye now that she knew just how much she didn't care for the man. Or, more likely still, Mrs. Johnson's now-cumbersome chores involved straightening and sweeping and dusting the shop, and those things simply weren't getting done as often.

"What is it you want?"

She realized with a jolt that Mr. Johnson was addressing her. "I've come to purchase medicinal powders." She spoke with a steady, confident voice.

Something like a laugh entered his eyes. "A popular inquiry for y'all today."

Katie gave a small nod.

"You've heard the price is five dollars?" Mr. Johnson clearly doubted she had the money.

"I have." She glanced at the preacher, still standing near the counter. "And have you heard, Reverend, that Ian O'Connor, who I feel the need to remind you is among the faithful members of your congregation, is lying up the road, bruised and broken, and, more than once these past days, hovering on the very cliff of death?"

He held himself stiffly. "I have."

Katie tipped her head as if in thought. "Odd, that. If you knew a member of your flock was ailing so bad—tiptoeing at the edge of his very life—why is it the family's not seen you once in the days since he was laid so low? I thought that was a duty held sacred by a man of the cloth."

The reverend blustered a moment.

"And neither did I hear a squeak of protest when Mr. Johnson, here, declared that, now that the powders are needed by one in a most terrible hour of suffering, he's raised the price from two bits yesterday to five dollars today. Do you not find that inhumane?"

"Now, just one moment—" Mr. Johnson protested loudly.

Katie spoke over him. "Let us hope, Reverend Ford, you do not find yourself laid low some awful day and our local merchant decides to use your misfortune to line his pockets."

Mr. Johnson leaned closer to her. "I do believe the price for those powders has just increased to *seven* dollars. Keep talking, and I'll go higher."

She didn't let a hint of her concern show. "You've not seen fit to visit the O'Connors in their time of need, Reverend. Will you not at least help see that Ian has something to relieve his suffering? Will you allow him to fall victim to such a lack of basic kindness from this man?"

The preacher's face pinked with unbecoming blotches. Katie fully expected him to rail at her, to protest his innocence, to insult her presumptuousness. He surprised her.

"You told the woman five dollars, Jeremiah," he said in a quiet, calm voice. "The Christian thing would be to keep your word."

"Reverend—"

"The Red Road pays two bits," the preacher said. "I am certain you are making a tidy profit charging her five dollars. You cannot claim financial hardship."

Mr. Johnson's mouth pulled in a tight line. His eyes narrowed. Katie held her breath. She didn't have seven dollars in her pocket. She had not even a ha'penny more than five. Five dollars was a painful enough sacrifice; seven would likely bring her to tears.

The preacher, to his credit, did not abandon the issue and cleared his throat meaningfully.

Mr. Johnson reached behind him, pulling down a bottle of powders and setting it on the counter in front of Katie.

"Five dollars." The words came out as a growl.

Katie ignored his tone. As unfair as it was, five dollars was better than seven.

She set the small pile of money from her pocket on the counter. Though the man pictured on the bills was not the same on all five, she'd been told they were worth the same amount, that the face had changed only the year before. Both Mr. Johnson and the reverend seemed satisfied. The merchant took her money, and she took the medicine.

Clutching the bottle, she turned to face the preacher, feeling a bit ashamed of her harsh words earlier. Perhaps he'd deserved them, but he *had* done her a great service, one she'd not foreseen. Katie wouldn't let that moment of kindness pass unacknowledged.

"I thank you for this, Reverend."

Was he as surprised as she was to find them allies even for a fleeting moment?

He gave a brief nod but didn't look her fully in the eye. Apparently he found the situation more uncomfortable than unexpected. Perhaps the best expression of gratitude would be to leave and let him explain away in his own mind the short time they'd spent in agreement with each other.

She hurried up the road, offering a quick wave to Seamus Kelly, standing outside his blacksmith shop, as she passed. Worry and hope pushed her on. Ian would find some relief once he had the powders. He'd sleep, and heal. And Biddy's mind and heart would find some peace as well.

Katie stopped briefly at Granny Claire's home to pick up her fiddle before continuing to Biddy and Ian's. The house was full when she arrived, chaotic almost. Ian's sisters and brothers wove about in a tapestry of busyness. They stood and sat and moved about, some eating, some talking, a couple even dusting and straightening up. Katie stood at the door, watching them, unnoticed.

She'd learned to love this family. Watching them help one another and care for one another filled an almost lifelong void in her heart. She'd once been part of a loving family. She'd once had parents and siblings who watched over her. But she'd lost everything while still a small child. She'd been alone since she was eight years old. Nearly two decades of loneliness had taken quite a toll. How she wanted to be part of what the O'Connors had.

She pulled the door closed behind her. Ciara, Tavish's youngest sister, smiled at Katie as she stepped inside, but returned quickly to tending to her niece and nephew. Katie nodded a greeting to a few of the others in the room, slowly making her way among them all. They knew each other so well. No one fumbled about like she did, searching for their place and their role.

Is this to be my lot in life, then? She walked on her own toward Ian's bedroom, holding the bottle of powders tightly in her hand. *Among them, but not really a part of them?*

Tavish stepped out of his brother's bedroom in the very next instant. His smile blossomed on the spot. "Why, hello there, Sweet Katie."

Katie took a deep and purifying breath. Relief took hold inside. So long as she had Tavish, she wouldn't be alone.

"Hello, then," she said. "Did you miss me?"

He leaned against the doorframe. "Did I miss you? When did you start asking daft questions?" He brushed a hand along her cheek. "I always miss you when you're gone."

Heat spread up her neck. His touch did that to her every time, no matter how brief the contact. Bless Tavish O'Connor. He didn't forget her. He didn't overlook her. She was part of his world without needing to ask.

"I have something for—*Ian.*" Katie smiled at Tavish's look of highly exaggerated shock. "Thought I brought *you* something special, did you?"

"If my brother weren't looking all beaten and pathetic, I might be horribly jealous of him just now."

She held up her fiddle case. "I thought I'd give Biddy a rest from her humming."

"Ah, music from our Katie." Tavish smiled fondly. "That'll be a treat, to be sure."

She held out the bottle of powders. "And I've brought Ian this."

Tavish's smile vanished. "Begorra, Katie. Johnson was demanding five dollars for a bottle."

"I had some savings," she said. Uncertainty touched her shrinking feeling of accomplishment.

"But five dollars, Katie. That's too dear."

She shook her head. "Ian cannot heal if he cannot rest, and he cannot rest if he is in pain."

He looked almost upset, somewhere just shy of angry. "That was your going-home money, Katie."

It *was* her going-home money, but it was more than that. It was her funds for giving Father back his land, money for her sister's headstone. But none of that was on her horizon any longer. Having chosen to stay in Hope Springs, it was now her money for starting over again. It was her future.

Keep your head above water on this, Katie. You need to be strong.

"I meant to get the powders my own self, Katie, once I'd finished my day's work. I'll pay you back the five dollars."

"No, Tavish. I can do this for them."

"You *can,* certainly, but you don't have to. We're his family; we'll see to it he has the medicines he needs. You needn't worry."

We're his family. Meaning, of course, she wasn't. She wasn't anyone's family.

"Is Biddy about?" A change of topic would save her from an embarrassing breakdown. "I'd like to give her the powders."

"She's in the sickroom, where else?"

Biddy near about cried when Katie gave her the medicine. The flow of gratitude flustered Katie a little. Clearly her contribution had been unexpected. *We're his family.* It would take time, she told herself. A person didn't simply toss themselves into someone else's family.

"And I've brought my fiddle," she said. "If you think anyone would enjoy a tune or two. Of course, if I'd only be in the way—"

"Oh, dear Katie." Biddy squeezed her free hand. "Your music would be a gift from heaven itself. Soothing to the soul, just as you said."

The music did, in fact, bring a change to those gathered there. More smiles were evident, fewer furrowed brows. Ian remained in bed, but Biddy said she knew he could hear the tunes and appreciated them.

Katie left the house feeling better than she had on her arrival. Tavish insisted again he'd repay her for the powders. She hoped he wouldn't. Making the sacrifice helped her feel part of them all. So many of the worries plaguing her were either out of her control or things she'd already failed at. This was something she could do to help.

Her mind spun wildly about as she lay in bed that night. Her thoughts battered her raw emotions. Too much had happened too quickly. She had changed plans she'd had her entire life. It was too much. Far, far too much.

She hoped that one day her heart and mind would wrap around the changes she'd made in her life. She would find joy to outweigh the pain. There in Wyoming she'd find a family to be part of, people to belong to.

In time, she hoped, the emptiness she felt would ease.

Chapter Seven

Joseph pulled his buggy to a halt in front of Mrs. Claire's house. The girls were spending the day with the Kesters down the Red Road. He really ought to have been out in his fields. Yet, there he was, out paying a visit. He'd tried to focus on his work, but his mind constantly returned to Katie. There was nothing for it but to go see her and clear his thoughts.

He had a barrel of flour for her. She likely wouldn't need it for another week or more. But flour was the perfect excuse to come see her, if only for a moment.

Finbarr helped him heft the barrel out of the buggy. Joseph could roll it inside and leave it wherever Katie wanted it.

"Let me know if Ian or Biddy need anything," Joseph said.

The boy nodded and made his way up the path toward the road.

Joseph knocked and waited. Would Katie think him a fool for bringing her supplies before she'd told him she needed them? Perhaps he really was a fool. She'd only been gone thirty-six hours and he was already spending precious time concocting reasons to visit a woman who had pledged her heart to another. He *was* a fool, a complete and utter fool.

He could be friendly, but really nothing beyond.

The door opened and there she was. Not even a second could have passed before a smile appeared on Katie's face.

"Why, Joseph Archer! And what is it brings you around here?"

Friendly. Nothing beyond. "I was in town this morning and thought I'd pick up your next barrel of flour while I was there."

"That was very kind of you."

She sounded happy, so why, then, did strain show behind her eyes? He studied her for some clue, but found none. Katie was frustratingly good at keeping her thoughts hidden.

"Where would you like me to put the barrel?" he asked.

She pondered a moment. "There is not a great deal of room in the kitchen area. I'd best keep my supplies in my own room."

Katie pulled the door open all the way, making space for him to pass through. He rolled the barrel through the doorway. Mrs. Claire sat inside, comfortably settled in her rocking chair.

"A fine good afternoon to you, Joseph Archer."

"And the rest of the day to you, Mrs. Claire."

Her wrinkled face turned up in an amused grin. "Well, then, Katie. I see you taught him a thing or two while you lived at his house. That there was a right proper answer to an Irish greeting."

Joseph's breath caught for a brief instant at the bright-eyed smile Katie gave the older woman. That was the smile he'd come to see, the one he'd closed his eyes to remember as he'd stood in his empty kitchen that morning.

"I tried," Katie told Mrs. Claire. "I was determined to make an Irishman out of him, but, alas, I ran out of time."

That seemed to be the theme of his and Katie's connection: wanting something but not having sufficient time to accomplish it. He'd once hoped to court her after she left his employ, but Tavish was there before he had the opportunity.

"You can roll that right in through here," Katie said, motioning him toward the far end of the fireplace where a short hallway jutted off.

The house was small; he reached his destination in only a few steps. Katie threw Mrs. Claire another friendly smile over her shoulder. But,

Joseph noticed, that smile slid quickly away as she stepped into the dim bedroom she called her own. The strain he'd seen in her face at the door returned.

What was weighing so heavily on her?

"If you'd place that in the corner, I'd be grateful."

He took a quick look around the room as he followed the instructions. The space could use another lantern, a candle at the very least. Even in the afternoon, the small window didn't let in enough light to make the room as cheerful as it ought to be.

He had no argument with the simplicity of the furnishings, only their obvious need for repairs.

He wanted more for her, at least a few of life's comforts. If only there was a way to give her the relative luxuries she'd had only two days before. She'd had a bedframe and a comfortable mattress at his house; now she had only a straw tick on a pallet for a bed. But she'd never accept anything from him. She was too proud, too stubborn. He understood, admired her for it even, but it could be very frustrating. She likely wouldn't even let him bring the curtains from her old room to add some femininity to this new space. Women liked curtains. She would probably enjoy having them there. But she'd never take them from him.

"Is it still three dollars for the barrel?"

Her question pulled his thoughts together. He nodded.

Katie crossed to the opposite corner and knelt in front of her battered carpetbag. She opened it and pulled out a small drawstring bag.

Joseph could see she hadn't unpacked her things.

"Is something wrong with the chest of drawers?" he asked, nodding toward the bureau.

She moved to the pallet bed and sat. "The drawer frames are pulling apart." She turned out the contents of her small coin purse on the bedtick and began counting coins.

"Do you have a hammer and nails?" Joseph asked. He couldn't give her fine furniture or luxurious comforts, but he could at least fix the drawers.

"Aye, just there on the floor. I borrowed them from Tavish yesterday but haven't had time to see to the mending."

Joseph hung his hat on the doorknob and slid out of his heavy jacket. "I have some time right now. I'll fix the drawers."

She looked up at him, surprise and uncertainty in her gaze. "You don't have to do that, Joseph. I know you're busy."

"I'm never too busy to help." He left unspoken that helping *her,* most specifically, was very near the top of his list of priorities. Only his girls and the most pressing work on his farm came anywhere near Katie's well-being in his mind. Even if the repairs took all day, it would be well worth his time.

He knelt in front of the short chest and pulled out each drawer. Just as Katie had described, the framing was loose and no longer square. A few nails in the right places would help.

"If you're staying for a piece, would you mind if I bent your ear a bit?"

He looked over his shoulder at her. "I know I've heard you use that phrase before, but I don't remember what it means."

She laughed lightly, a sound that did his heart as much good as hearing her music did. So many times he'd stood at the kitchen door or at his own bedroom window listening to the strains of her violin from across the fields. He knew the music had calmed her, but did she have any idea how much he had needed it as well?

"I'm only asking if I can bother you with a great deal of talking and asking advice," Katie said.

"Of course."

The earnestness in her deep brown eyes was enough to nearly undermine his determination to keep his feelings hidden. He focused on his task, turning over the first drawer he meant to mend. If he didn't actually look at her, she might not see his heart hanging there in his eyes.

"I've been wondering on something these past weeks," she said. "Mr. Johnson threatened to charge you the Irish price for the flour you buy me, but your cost hasn't gone up. How is it you convinced him not to cheat you? Did you threaten him?"

"No." He lined up a nail. "I needed the flour price to remain the same, so I discovered something Johnson needed just as much. We came to a mutual agreement."

"What was it he was needing?"

"A loan." He pounded in the first nail, followed quickly by a second. Already the drawer was sturdier. "The trail to the train station isn't passable for much of the winter. Johnson has to bring in all his inventory before the snow comes. He didn't have the funds on hand to cover that expense this time around."

He didn't hear her footsteps over the sound of the next two nails driving into place. He simply looked up to find her sitting on the floor near him. The familiarity of her look of pondering, of her simple, tidy work dress, of those wisps of hair that always came loose by the end of the day, settled over him. For just a moment he knelt there, hammer still in his hand, a nail held between his teeth, just looking at her.

I could sit with her like this all day.

He shook himself back to some presence of mind. There was no point losing his head.

"What else does he need, I wonder?" Katie muttered the words, as if talking entirely to herself.

"What else does *who* need?" He lined up his next nail, grateful for the double distraction of conversation and repairs.

"Mr. Johnson. He's raised the Irish price on wool and shoes and even medicine. The winter will be hard without wool cloth to make coats. The Irish can't afford to replace the shoes their children have outgrown."

Joseph drove in another nail. "Next Seamus Kelly will raise his prices for blacksmithing and shoeing," he said. "Then both sides will decide that is reason enough to be at one another's throats. That is the cycle of life in Hope Springs."

"But if someone among us responded to the mercantile by swapping needs with Mr. Johnson, like you've done, rather than punishing the Red Road, maybe that cycle would stop."

He tested the sturdiness of the newly repaired drawer and found it much improved. "The key isn't finding just any need, but one that holds equal weight as his reason for raising prices."

"His *reason* is he hates the lot of us. What could possibly be traded to outweigh that?"

Joseph realized she wasn't speaking in hypotheticals. He slid the mended drawer back into the chest and looked at her, reminding himself to remain simply friendly, helpful, emotionally neutral.

"Are you hoping to get the Irish prices down to what the Red Road pays?" That was, he knew all too well, a fool's errand. "He'll never do it."

She gave him a worried, pleading look. It was too much. He set his eyes on the next drawer. Work was as good a distraction as any.

"Things weren't supposed to turn out this way, Joseph."

You have no idea. "Turn out what way, exactly?"

He heard her sigh. "I gave up home for this. I stayed here because I love it, because I thought it would be a happy place to live."

He thought she'd decided to stay because of Tavish. That had worried him. His late wife had given up the only hometown she'd ever known to come with him to Wyoming, and she had regretted it every year she'd spent there. She'd been miserable. He didn't want that for Katie.

Joseph focused on the next drawer. He didn't look up at her. Seeing her upset would eat away at him. "Are you unhappy?" he asked quietly.

"Not *un*happy. I'm more frustrated, I suppose. Between Ian's troubles and Biddy's worries and the Irish not knowing if they can afford to survive the winter, I'm weighed down. And . . . I—"

She stopped. Joseph looked up and immediately wished he hadn't. Her chin quivered and a tear coursed down her face. He had to grip his hammer tight to keep from reaching out for her.

Katie pressed her eyes closed, turning her face toward the ceiling. "I never used to be a crier, Joseph. Hope Springs has ruined me for it, I'm afraid."

She was smiling a little, even through her tears. Joseph had never known anyone quite like Katie Macauley. "What has brought the tears on this time?"

She shrugged with one shoulder, but Joseph didn't believe the dismissive gesture for a moment. Katie wasn't one to grow upset over something small.

"I was only thinking of my father." Her voice broke on the last word. She pushed out a breath and composed herself on the spot. "He's dying, and I'm so far away."

"Do you regret staying?" He hoped she didn't.

She shook her head. "I only feel helpless. I can't do anything for him, and nothing I do here seems to help anyone either." She picked up a few of the spare nails, fiddling with them in an absentminded way. "I used some of my savings to get Ian medicine—Mr. Johnson was asking five dollars instead of two bits, and the O'Connors couldn't afford it."

"Five dollars?"

"Aye. That's the new Irish price."

Joseph bit back a curse. Johnson had no conscience. "I wish you had told me, Katie. I could have bought the medicine for two bits."

"I didn't even think of that." She pushed out a puff of air, her expression falling. "Now I feel foolish *and* helpless."

He hadn't meant to add to her burdens. What Katie needed was encouragement.

"You did a good thing, Katie. You helped Ian and Biddy when they needed it."

She didn't look reassured. "It doesn't solve the bigger problem, though. You can't purchase everything that every Irish family is overcharged for. And I haven't the means of buying wool for all their coats or paying for dozens of shoes. If others grow ill, I'll run out of money before I can get medicine for all of them. I can't even pay you the three dollars I owe you for flour without dipping further into my savings."

"Don't worry yourself about—"

"I *will* pay you," she cut across him. "I just haven't made my bread deliveries this week, so I don't have enough money from *that* to pay you with, and I need my savings to live on now that I don't have a regular job."

He knew she wasn't trying to make him feel guilty, but he felt so just the same. "I am sorry you couldn't stay at our house. We've missed you there already."

She smiled at him. "I've missed you as well—all of you. The mornings are far too quiet here."

"I missed our morning chat at breakfast this morning as well." He had to look away or he knew he'd reach out for her. *She chose someone else.*

Katie handed him a nail, and he set back to work. He was nearly done with the last drawer when a knock sounded from the front. The house was small enough that they easily heard Mrs. Claire invite the visitor in.

A moment later, Katie's face lit with a brilliant smile as her eyes settled just past Joseph.

"Tavish."

Joseph drove in the final nail with a force that surprised him. He thought he'd come to terms with Katie's choice. Apparently not.

"Hello there, Sweet Katie." Joseph thought he heard a question in Tavish's tone.

"I wasn't expecting you, Tavish, but I'm pleased you've come." Katie's tone had lightened. How was it Tavish managed to do that for her when he had only managed to talk about heavy things, topics that made her cry? Maybe it was for the best that she'd chosen Tavish. "Joseph brought me my bread flour and was kind enough to stay and mend the chest of drawers I'd not gotten around to."

"I would have done that for you," Tavish said. "You needed only ask me."

"I didn't actually ask Joseph. He simply took on the task," Katie said. "He can be very bossy, you know."

He glanced up at her. Her teasing smile pulled an answering one from him. The connection was a brief one, over almost the moment it began. Katie rose and walked past him, no doubt straight to Tavish.

Joseph slid the newly repaired drawer into place. He didn't look behind him. Katie would be holding Tavish's hand or leaning into his embrace. He had no desire to see that.

"I came by to offer to drive you about while you made your bread deliveries," Tavish said, "but I don't smell any loaves fresh out of the oven."

Joseph scooped up the nails and dropped them on top of the bureau. He set the hammer beside them.

"I didn't have time for baking today," Katie said. "If you're free tomorrow, I'll take you up on your offer."

"I'll make certain I am. As for today, Finbarr is tending Ian's animals, so I am at your disposal for the afternoon. What else needs mending?"

"I've been meaning to put a couple nails in the wall to hang my dresses on," Katie said. "And there's a shelf in the kitchen that's not terribly sturdy."

"I'll get started, then. You keep adding to that list. I've an entire afternoon."

Joseph knew an invitation to leave when he heard one. Tavish had arrived, and Joseph was no longer needed or welcome. He picked his coat up off the floor and stepped past Katie and Tavish to where his hat hung on the doorknob.

"Thank you for bringing the flour," Katie said. Joseph fancied that he heard a small thread of regret in her words. Perhaps she'd enjoyed his company, though likely not as much as he'd needed hers. "I'll pay you for it just as soon as I can."

"Don't fret over it. Take your time." He set his hat on his head and turned to Tavish. He could at least try to show the man that he held no true malice toward him. Jealousy, certainly. Envy, yes. But even with all that, Joseph couldn't actually hate him. Tavish was a good man, and lucky. "How's Ian?"

"Better."

Tavish's eyes locked with his own. He made a miniscule nod in Katie's direction and took her hand.

"Show me where you want your dresses hung." Tavish smiled at Katie.

Joseph could easily read the warning there. The time had come for him to beat a hasty retreat.

He slipped from the room and down the short hallway to where Mrs. Claire sat rocking by the window.

"Is there anything I can do for you before I go?" he asked.

"Quitting the field so soon, then?"

"Quitting the field?"

She clicked her tongue. "It wasn't yesterday I was born, Joseph Archer. You've been sweet on our Katie almost since she first came. Seems to me you've given up terrible quick, you have."

"She made her choice. I am determined to respect that."

The look on the older woman's face clearly showed her lack of faith in his intelligence. "I thought you a man of greater determination than that."

"What I am is a man who doesn't believe in trespassing."

Mrs. Claire's gaze narrowed as though she were studying his very soul. Joseph didn't particularly want his most guarded feelings laid bare.

"Katie has made her choice," Joseph said firmly, reminding himself as much as Mrs. Claire.

"Has she now?"

That was a tone of doubt if ever he'd heard one.

"I worry for her." Sadness touched Mrs. Claire's expression. "She's known so much suffering in her life. I only want her to find the happiness she deserves."

"So do I," Joseph said. "And she seems happy with Tavish." As much as he hated acknowledging that, it was true.

"I've seen the way she looks at you, Joseph. I've heard the way she speaks of you and *with* you. What if you're right for her after all?" Mrs. Claire asked, resuming her rocking. "Doesn't she deserve to know she has a choice?"

"It seems a little underhanded."

Mrs. Claire actually rolled her eyes. "Saints above, Joseph Archer, I'm not suggesting you kidnap the lass."

He shook his head a little at the picture Mrs. Claire painted. "Kidnap her? My house is in shambles already, and the girls are so angry at me for 'letting Katie leave,' I'll soon have a mutiny on my hands. Kidnapping her may be my best option."

"And now I've lost all faith in you, lad." Still, she was grinning, her eyes dancing with laughter. "What sort of a ham-fisted suitor are you anyway, stealing the girl off to do *housework?*"

"And that, Mrs. Claire, is the reason I leave the courting to men like Tavish, who know how to do the thing properly."

"Think on what I said." She gave him what his childhood nanny had called "the look"—a combination of pointed reprimand and fond condescension. "At least give the lass a chance to know you—the man and not the employer—better."

"Good day to you, Mrs. Claire." He tipped his hat and stepped out.

He shut the door behind him and stood silent and tense under the front overhang. For just a moment Mrs. Claire's words tempted him. He hovered on the thought of Katie being in his life again, of holding her hand the way Tavish did, of courting her as he'd planned to.

I've seen the way she looks at you. What had Mrs. Claire meant by that? Was there reason to hope after all?

Then he remembered the smile that lit Katie's face when Tavish had arrived. Tavish made her happy in a way he never had. He couldn't take that away from her, not when she was so burdened by life. He could be her friend, help her where and when he could. He'd keep himself to that. Eventually he might even learn to accept it.

Give her a chance to know you better.

Perhaps he could do that, too.

Chapter Eight

A man could do far worse than to have Katie Macauley riding up beside him in a buggy, even if that buggy was not exclusively his and they'd nothing finer to see than the very familiar Irish Road. Tavish had driven her about the past few afternoons, but that Sunday evening was different. They weren't making deliveries, weren't rushed for time. This wasn't business. 'Twas courting, true and proper, something there'd not been time for before.

"I still say 'tis a full shame there was no céilí yesterday." Katie had sorrowed over that a few times during their drive. "I look forward to the music all week."

"A fine fiddler such as yourself can have music whenever she pleases." He kept the horse at a sedate pace. Driving a fair lady about ought to take time, after all.

Katie tossed him a smile. "Granny and I had plenty of music last evening. Between my fiddle and her talent for tapping spoons, we had tunes all night. Our own little céilí, it was."

"And you didn't invite me?" He scoffed dramatically. "I'm fully offended, Katie Macauley. Fully offended."

She rolled her eyes, and he couldn't help a grin.

"What would you have contributed to our little party?" Katie asked. "No one was allowed admittance unless he added to the music."

"I'd have sung for you, Sweet Katie." He could see the comment intrigued her.

"Have you a talent for it, Tavish? Or are you of the sort to frighten off small children?"

"Perhaps if you're very nice, dear, you'll find out one day."

He loved that her smile grew when he teased her. In the first weeks of their acquaintance his joking had seemed to only confuse or upset her. She understood him better now.

"Why is it you don't toss your voice in at the céilís? Are you more terrible than you're letting on? Can't keep a tune in a brand-new bucket, is that it?"

"Are you trying to trick me into serenading you, you troublesome woman?" He laughed as he clicked the reins, setting the horse going a bit. "I'll tell you here and now, Sweet Katie, I don't sing for just anyone, nor for just any occasion."

"But you would have graced our tiny little céilí last evening?"

He shrugged. "Perhaps. But, you should know, my own family can likely count on just one hand how many times I've joined in a tune with any of them these past few years."

"What's made you stop?"

The answer came in a single word: *Bridget.* He'd sung often with his poor sweetheart before she died. While he wasn't full mourning her passing any longer, there were some things that still pricked at his heart too much, even after a half-decade.

"You tell me you have a fine voice, and then you refuse to prove it." Katie shook her head, a twinkle in her eyes. "You're terrible, Tavish. Terrible. Terrible."

"And you shouldn't be forced to ride about with a terrible man." He gave her his most dramatic look of empathy. "I'll just slow the wagon down enough so you can jump out and walk the rest of the way home."

Her face lit with silent laughter. She slipped her arm through his, scooting closer to him. He could grow quite used to having Katie sitting beside him, hugging his arm with hers. Even the ache of thinking back on Bridget tucked itself firmly away when Katie was with him. She leaned her head against him. He wished the Irish Road were longer. Their drive would be over in but a few more minutes.

"Is there anything else needing attention at your new home?" Between Katie's bread deliveries and repairs at Granny's house, Tavish had managed to spend some time with her the last few days, but not near as much as he would have liked. He was strung thin, trying to see to his own farm and Ian's.

"Everything is holding up," Katie answered. "We're quite snug there." She slid her hand into his, still managing to keep her arm wrapped around his arm. "Did you know I never had a room all to myself before coming here? Servants share quarters. And my sister and I shared the loft in our home growing up. The boys slept there too before they all left—only a blanket hung up to divide the tiny space in half."

A small house with little but a family space and a loft. Tavish's current home could be described in exactly the same way. He'd put all his profits into paying down his debt on the land itself. Only in the last year had he begun putting aside what he needed to begin adding on to the house. 'Twas that money, and what he could have gotten from Joseph Archer for selling off his land, that he'd meant to live on in order to follow Katie to Ireland. He hadn't, in the short time since those plans had changed, given any real thought to what he'd do with the funds from his berries.

"So you enjoy having your own room, do you?"

"It makes me feel very fancy." Her smile was a touch whimsical. "A person feels less—I don't know, less dispensable when she has a space all her own. She feels more important, I suppose. A person has to be truly needed for her to be worth more than a tiny corner of an attic or a blanket on the kitchen floor."

Tavish knew in that instant exactly how he meant to spend the bit of savings he'd set aside. He meant to court Katie and, in time, he'd ask her to marry him. But when he brought her to his home—to *her* new home—she'd find a room waiting there just for her. If a room was what she needed to feel essential in his life, that was exactly what he would give her.

He turned the buggy in at Ian and Biddy's. He and Ian shared ownership of the buggy. Ian had acquired it in a shrewd deal two years back whilst they were down at the train depot selling off grain. It was something of an extravagance—not useful really, but a fine thing to have for riding about or making a quick trip into town.

Tavish brought the buggy to a stop just outside the barn. Katie made to climb down, as she always did.

"At least give me a chance to be a gentleman," he lightly scolded.

They'd had this very conversation a few times. She stopped at the edge of the bench and waited for him to make his way around. He reached up and lifted her down.

"I don't know why it is you insist on doing this," she said as her feet reached the ground. "I can get down on my own."

"Oh, I know you *can.*" He kept his hands at her waist and leaned in toward her. "But it gives me a rare opportunity to stand particularly close to you."

Color stained her cheeks when she looked up at him. She made no attempt to slip away. A good sign, he felt certain. She could sometimes be jumpy, quick to put up walls between them. A past filled with too much pain and heartache had left her wary, but she was well worth the time and patience he'd need to win her over, if only life would grant him more time to court her properly.

He lightly brushed his lips along her hairline, not kissing her, just barely touching. Her hands slid from his shoulders to his neck. Tavish closed his eyes and tried very hard to think clearly. He was never entirely sure what to do around Katie. If he pulled her tight to him and kissed her soundly, would she melt or would she run? Each possibility was equally likely.

He took a deep breath in through his nose, hoping to calm his thoughts and his pulse. "Did you know you smell like flowers?" He had no idea which variety, but he'd noticed that about her almost from the beginning.

"Scented water." She whispered the reply. Clearly she was not entirely indifferent to his touch.

He slipped one hand from her waist to behind her back, pulling her ever so slightly closer to him. She made no protest. Tavish lowered his head, giving her ample time to push away or pull back if she wanted to.

Katie tipped her head in his direction, and their lips came within a breath of each other.

"Looks to me as though I ought to be taking my wife out for a Sunday afternoon drive so I can get myself a nice squeeze afterwards," Da's deep, gravelly voice said from nearby.

"Quit interrupting *my* squeeze, will ya, Da?" He didn't release Katie by so much as an inch.

"Can't do that, son. The lass hasn't a father here to see to it suitors treat her as they ought. I've taken that task to my own self, I have."

Da *would* set himself to such a task. What was more, he'd undertake it in earnest.

Katie pulled back from him, not entirely, but enough to look over at the door of the house where Da stood.

"He's been a perfect gentleman, I assure you."

Tavish grinned. "I've been *perfect,* have I?"

Katie pressed her lips together. He'd wager she was holding back a smile of her own.

"Aye." Da's tone hadn't lightened. "And he'll continue to be a gentleman, else I'll take a switch to him like I done when he was little and making mischief."

Tavish took her hand in his and pressed it to his lips. "Off with ya, then, before my father decides to flog me."

"That's quite enough, lad. Let the sweet *ógbhean* go on inside."

Tavish smiled at her. "When he starts speaking Gaelic, I know I'm in trouble." He kissed her fingers one more time before letting her go.

She stepped around him. Tavish watched her go. Da met her just at the edge of Ian's porch.

"He really was behaving himself," he heard Katie say.

"Oh, I know it," Da said. "And Tavish knows I know it. And he further knows it would be a *scalladh-croidhe* to his poor mother should she hear of him acting elsewise."

Tavish could hear him well and clear, just as he imagined Da wanted him to. He leaned against the buggy with his arms folded across his chest, watching the two of them. Da had a way with ladies, young and old. He wove a kind of spell about them all, putting them at ease and making them trust him. He'd been able to soothe the often-prickly Katie from the earliest days of their acquaintance.

"What has brought on the sad face, Katie?" Da asked.

"Hearing you speak Gaelic puts me in mind of my father. He spoke Irish more often than English."

"I'm told your father is ailing," Da said.

Tavish stood up straight, intending to jump into the conversation if need be. Katie was not bearing up entirely under the weight of her father's impending death. Da would make her cry with such a topic.

"He is," Katie answered simply.

Da stuffed his hands in the pockets of his trousers, nodding slowly. "Do you think your da would allow me to look out for you while you're here?"

Tavish fully expected her to avoid the topic as she'd done many times before. She surprised him.

A bit of a smile touched her lips. "I think he would thank you for it. And I'd thank you for it too. I've not had a father to care about me in many, many years."

Da's very Irish, very blue eyes twinkled back at her. Tavish relaxed, torn between gratitude that Da had worked his magic once more and wishing he himself could so easily earn her faith.

"In that case," Da said, "if any of the other lads hereabout come around courting you, I fully expect you to tell me so. I mean to make it a particular duty of mine to be certain they're good men and treating you as they ought."

"I will, though I don't imagine there's likely to be a great many men knocking on my door."

"We'll see." Da nodded quickly and firmly. "Now, I'd be much obliged if you'd step inside and say hello to Biddy before you make your way home. She's missed you this past day or more."

Katie looked back at Tavish, a smile playing about her lips, though not fully blossoming. He winked at her, and she slipped inside the house. Da remained behind on the porch.

"A sweet lass," Da said.

"Aye. That she is."

Da had given Katie a look of tender concern; the gaze he turned on Tavish was edged with warning. "You're treating her as you ought?"

"Aye."

"Don't let me hear otherwise."

Tavish nodded his understanding. He moved to unhitch the horse.

"And, son?"

He looked back to the porch.

"Our Katie's quite a catch. Don't let her slip through your fingers."

"I don't intend to."

"That's a good lad." Da crossed to where Tavish stood. Together they unhitched the horse. Da rubbed its nose, something he'd done with every horse they'd ever had. "We've trouble ahead of us, Tavish." Da's hands slid over the horse's head.

Tavish patted the animal on the back, following as Da led it into the barn.

"More of the same?"

Da nodded. "Johnson told your ma after services today that he means to raise prices on a few more things."

That sounded decidedly bad. "What things?"

"He didn't give particulars. Only mentioned it with that smile of his that makes you feel as though you've been drinking sour milk."

Tavish rubbed at the back of his neck. "He means to starve us out, then? Keep us from buying food this winter?"

"Food. Clothing. Supplies. We're to freeze and starve and, should any grow ill, suffer all the more for want of medicines."

Tavish took the bridle off the horse and hung it on its peg. "How many will he drive away this year, do you think?"

Da only shook his head.

"Katie gave up Ireland for this, Da. She stayed to make a future here."

"I know, son."

"I can't let it fall apart. Not when it means so much to her."

Da took to rubbing down the horse while Tavish leaned against the stall wall.

"You know, I was having me a fine bit of courting until you pushed your nosey self out the door."

Da kept at his work. "I'd wager our Katie doesn't have a lot of experience with proper courting. I worry about her. About both of you. She's likely to have her head turned by sweet words and lingering kisses, not really knowing how to discover what it is that she wants and needs most."

He looked at his da. "Isn't that what courting is supposed to do? Turn a person's head?"

"Unless that courting turns her *heart,* it won't be enough."

Tavish shifted a bit. "I have to convince her to fall in love with me, is that it?"

"To fall *the rest of the way* in love with you," Da corrected. "She likes you well enough, cares for you truly and deeply, but you've some work yet to do."

"I don't know how to make someone love me, especially her." Though he'd thought it many times, he'd never admitted his misgivings out loud. "Katie isn't like anyone I've known before. 'Tis fully impossible to know exactly what she's thinking or feeling. Sometimes I am certain she loves me. Other times—" What could he do but shrug?

"Well, then." Da took a step away from the horse. "Best of luck to you with that."

That brought a smile back to Tavish's face. "You are no help at all."

They laughed as they returned to Ian's house. But underneath the smile, Tavish's mind spun.

Unless that courting turns her heart, *it won't be enough.*

How could any person truly win a heart as closely guarded as Katie's?

Chapter Nine

"Well now, Tavish, you seem to be having a party and I wasn't invited." Katie stood in the doorway of Tavish's house. He and the women of his family were up to their elbows in glass jars and berries.

He tossed her a lopsided grin. "This here is one of our famous preserving parties."

Tavish had told her once about his female relations gathering to help him put up jellies and such from his berries. 'Twas how he made his living, going about the territory selling what they preserved. Why, then, hadn't she been asked to join in?

"Is there room for one more?" She tried to keep disappointment out of her voice.

"There is always room for you, Katie," he said as he set back to his work. 'Twasn't the most flattering invitation, but it was a welcome one at least.

Always room for her. That, she knew all too well, was not true. There'd not been room for her in her family's home by the end of things. She was supposed to go to Manchester because they couldn't keep her, because there'd not been a place for her in her own home. That reality haunted her even now.

It would have been different going back. If she'd returned, her parents would have wanted her there. They needed her. She might have helped during the few remaining months that lay ahead of Father. She might have been a balm to her mother's loneliness. She would have been welcomed. They would have made a place for her. Surely they would have.

"Katie?"

Tavish's voice broke through some of the fog of memory, but it was his gentle touch on her hand that brought her fully back to the moment.

She tried for an unaffected smile. He clearly didn't believe it.

Still, she pressed ahead. "I am quite handy with a canning jar or a paring knife. Give me a task, Tavish. I'm looking for a spot of work."

He squeezed the hand he held. "You've had a difficult couple weeks, Katie. What you need is rest, not more work."

Katie plopped her hands on her hips. "And where do you get off, Tavish O'Connor, dictating to me what *I* need?" Work had been her escape for a very long time. Music soothed her, but work gave her purpose.

The scolding widened his eyes. Perhaps she'd snapped a bit more than necessary, but she never had liked being told what to do. He likely hadn't meant the words to feel that way, but they had just the same.

"Biddy's had a harder go of it than I have, and she's here."

Tavish's gaze slid to his sister-in-law. "She needed the distraction."

"At the moment, Tavish, I need one as well."

His free hand slipped around her waist and he pulled her close. "There are far better distractions than putting up preserves," he whispered to her.

Her entire face heated even as a tiny smile echoed from her heart. "Do you never stop flirting, Tavish O'Connor?"

"Of course. But I needed to see that smile of yours, Sweet Katie." He spoke quietly, his breath tickling the hair near her temple. "Everything's right in my world when you smile."

"If the two of you are done loving on each other, you might give us a hand." Tavish's older sister, Mary, gave him a look of pure scolding, but she winked at Katie.

"Have I mentioned that being under my sister's iron thumb for these few days every year is my absolute favorite part of being a berry farmer?" The sarcasm in his voice made Katie smile ever brighter.

"What is it you need me to do?" She directed the question to Mary and earned a grin wide as the River Foyle.

"I see our Katie knows just who is in charge here," Mary said.

Tavish laughed. "It's only that you're so everlastingly bossy."

Mary stuck her tongue out at him just as she'd likely done when they were small children.

"Have a sit down, Sweet Katie."

"We're mashing and straining these for jellies." Mary indicated the bowls of berries on the table. "We'd be most grateful for your help."

Every woman in the room gave Tavish an "I told you so" look. Katie could almost feel sorry for the man. He was terribly outnumbered.

Katie pulled a pail of blackberries close to her and took up a mashing implement. She'd spent enough hours kneading dough that she knew she had the strength for this task. Work would do her good, just as she'd said it would. Using her muscles helped clear her mind.

The berries were small, but a beautiful color. Katie had had the chance to eat a few over the past weeks as they'd ripened, so she knew they were as delicious as they looked.

Tavish returned to his own work, with something of resignation in his demeanor. Was he upset with her for arguing with him?

He looked up briefly, just long enough to indicate his sister with a jerk of his head and roll his eyes theatrically. They shared a quick moment of amusement. Katie knew then all was forgiven.

"'Tis a very good thing you had the jars already, Tavish," Mary said as she stirred a large pot heating on an ancient stove. "I hear Johnson has raised his price."

"Aye." Tavish crushed more berries. "He's trying to put me out of business, no doubt. No one else needs jars as much as I do. But if we run out of sugar, I really am in trouble. He's tripled the price for us 'Paddies.'"

Medicine. Cloth. Jars. And now sugar prices had gone up as well? Where would Johnson stop?

"Is it true about salt?" Biddy's voice was so small it drew all their eyes to her. She was too pale. Dark circles shadowed her eyes.

"Aye. 'Tis true enough," Tavish said.

Biddy took the tiniest step back from the table. Her shoulders slumped a bit. "How are we to preserve the meat when it's time for the hog slaughter if we can't afford salt? We'll have no meat for the winter. What'll we eat? The children—."

All the others exchanged uncertain, worried looks.

"We'll manage, Biddy," Ciara, the youngest sister, said. "We always manage."

A tear gathered in Biddy's eye. Her lips shook. Biddy had been so strong through the difficulties she'd faced. To see her break down over the price of salt was heartrending.

Katie spoke up. "Do you think you can see to the mashing on your own, Tavish? I've a longing for a walk in the fresh air, if Biddy'll come along."

"I really should stay and help." Biddy's protest was halfhearted at best. "Tavish has done so much since Ian's . . . injury."

Katie threaded her arm around her friend's elbow. Biddy allowed herself to be led away. "He has two sisters helping him just now. That'll do fine."

She opened the front door and looked back once more at Tavish. He smiled and nodded encouragingly, mouthing a "thank you." She led Biddy outside. The day had turned a bit cool. Winter was coming early to Wyoming.

Biddy hesitated at the edge of the porch. "Tavish's ma usually helps with this as well, but she's looking after my Ian and the little ones. Tavish is shorthanded without her. I can't just walk out."

Katie kept Biddy at her side and walked slowly toward the road. "We'll double back after a moment," she said. "But just now I need you to talk to me. Tell me what's weighing on you."

Biddy shook her head. "You have troubles enough of your own."

Why did everyone seem to think her incapable of bearing difficulties? She'd not crumbled under the weight of the last eighteen years—she wasn't about to do so now.

"Friends are supposed to share burdens, Biddy. I am your friend, aren't I?"

"Of course you are." Biddy actually looked shocked that she would question it. But Katie had never really had a true friend before. She often felt as though she were guessing her way through their friendship.

"Then tell me what's brought on the tears. I may not be able to help, but I can at least listen."

They turned up the road, not heading anywhere in particular.

"I overheard my father-in-law and my brothers-in-law talking when everyone was over on Sunday evening. They don't think Ian will be very well recovered for the busiest parts of the harvest."

Katie had her doubts on that score as well, but had kept the thoughts to herself. Biddy had enough reasons for worry.

"They all mean to help bring our crop in, but they have their own to see to. And Tavish is already behind in preparing for his deliveries. He lost some of his berries because we didn't preserve them quickly enough. He can't afford to lose any more."

Tavish hadn't said anything to Katie about that.

"We're going to lose some of our crop." Biddy spoke quick and low, as though the thoughts were simply pouring out of her now that she'd started. "And the prices at market are expected to be low this year as it is. Now Mr. Johnson is raising the Irish prices again. I don't know how we'll get through this next year."

"You've made it through before." Katie hoped the words didn't sound hollow. She simply didn't know what else to say.

"This time is different."

"Because of Ian?"

"And—" Biddy swiped at a tear and then at another.

"And *what?*"

Biddy stopped at the side of the road. She slumped under an invisible weight. "I'm to have a baby, Katie. Toward the end of winter."

"But this is good news, is it not?" Katie couldn't at all tell just by looking at Biddy.

"We were so happy when we realized." Biddy rubbed at her own arms. Katie wished she'd brought shawls or something as a shield against the constant wind. "We lost a little one to the fever all those years ago, a sweet little girl, in age between Michael and Mary. There's been such an emptiness in the home since then. Not that this babe will ever take little Fíona's place, but we were so happy at the thought of another."

"And that's changed?"

Biddy began walking again, something like pacing but all in the same direction. "Mary's shoes are falling to bits. Michael's outgrown his coat. Ian has a very long and difficult time ahead of him. And I have a wee babe inside depending on me. There'll not be any extra money coming in this year. We'll be fortunate if we can purchase the seed we need for next year and make our payment on the land."

"Surely Joseph would give you more time to pay him." She knew for certain he would—had heard him say as much, in fact.

But Biddy was already shaking her head. "I cannot ask him to do that."

"But he *would*."

"Too much depends on his control over the farms here. Undermining that would put us all at risk."

Katie walked with Biddy a while longer, grateful when she saw some calm return to her expression. She was understandably exhausted and overwhelmed, but talking of her worries seemed to have helped. Katie only wished she could do more.

She didn't know how much Ian and Biddy's payment was on their land. Perhaps she had enough in her savings to make it for them, or part of it at least. But would they even accept her help? She knew enough of

Irish stubbornness to doubt it very much. And what would *she* live on if she spent every penny she had? She and Granny Claire would be in dire straits without money. Neither of them had paying jobs. Katie's baking hardly covered its own costs. How many others on the Irish Road were looking ahead with fear?

She didn't sleep much that night. Too many heavy questions weighed on her. She lay on her bedtick, staring into the darkness.

What am I to do, Eimear? she asked her long-dead sister. There'd never been anyone else to listen to her worries over the years. But Eimear never had answers for her, and, in that moment, she needed an answer badly.

"How do I stop a greedy and hateful man from robbing his neighbors?" She whispered the question into the night.

It was late and the night was very cold. Otherwise, Katie would have slipped outside with her fiddle, letting the music clear her thoughts. Playing inside was out of the question with Granny sleeping so nearby. She closed her eyes and quietly hummed. "The Dear Irish Boy." "Abigail in Breitamain." She had hummed twice through "Éamonn a' Chnuic" when an answer began to formulate in her mind.

It started as little more than a breeze of memory, a conversation she couldn't quite recall. She'd spoken to Joseph about Mr. Johnson and his prices. He'd managed to talk the merchant down from a price increase by loaning him money.

Katie sat up, searching her mind for the rest of it. Weariness and worry slowed her thoughts.

"I needed the flour price to remain the same," Joseph had said, "so I discovered something Johnson needed just as much."

That was the key. If she could trade on something Mr. Johnson needed—more than he needed to put the Irish in their place, to punish them for existing—she might convince him to bring the prices back to where they'd been and to not raise any others over the winter.

But what did he need? What could a man with an entire mercantile at his disposal possibly need?

The words came clear and precise.

Help wanted.

Mr. Johnson needed an employee. Based on the look of his shop, he needed someone to straighten and organize and clean. He needed a housekeeper for his shop. A housekeeper.

Katie's heart lodged firmly in her throat. She knew perfectly well how the rest of that sign read: "No Irish need apply."

But if she *could* somehow convince him to take her, then she would have income, beyond the mere pennies she brought in with her bread. Perhaps she'd have enough to support herself and Granny, and then she could use her savings to help Ian and Biddy.

But what of the rest of the Irish? She didn't have enough money for them all.

Think, Katie. The answer is there somewhere.

She stood up and walked to the small bedroom window. 'Twas a clear enough night to see the stars. She watched them sparkle above her.

He needs a housekeeper. You have more experience at that than anyone.

But you're Irish.

Jeremiah Johnson would no sooner pay an Irishwoman a salary than he would dance a bare-skinned jig in a rainstorm.

He will never pay an Irishwoman a salary.

She took a gasping breath, a thought dropping fully formed into her mind. He wouldn't pay her to work for him, but he might be willing to trade: her labor in exchange for lowering the Irish prices to where they had been.

Could she really do it? He would be a horrible person to work for. Every day would likely be miserable. And she'd be making no money. Not a single cent.

But if she didn't at least try, the Irish would be driven out one by one. She'd lose this new home she'd chosen for herself. Her plan might very well fall to pieces. But she had to try. She wasn't ready to give up yet.

Chapter Ten

Granny Claire opted to spend Friday keeping company with Mrs. O'Connor, they being good friends despite their age difference. Katie couldn't imagine anyone not being instantly charmed by the sweet old woman.

With Granny gone for the day, Katie had her first opportunity to go to town and approach Mr. Johnson with her idea. She felt certain any of her Irish neighbors would argue against her efforts if they knew what she was up to. She was unsure enough of her plan that she might just be talked out of trying.

If only she were still living at Joseph's house. She could have spoken to him about it over breakfast. He always listened, and he was smart about these kind of things. She could sort out even the most complicated of worries by talking through them with him. But she was on her own now. Her problems were hers alone.

Town was quiet, but not empty. Having witnesses about might very well ruin Katie's chances. She stepped into the mercantile, but kept to the back wall, waiting until Mr. Johnson finished with his customer. The shop appeared to be in greater disarray than it had been during her last visit just over a week earlier. Perhaps Mr. Johnson was feeling a bit frustrated. That might help her cause.

Dusting. Organizing displays. A good waxing of the floors. Katie mentally listed the various jobs needing done. *Straighten and coordinate the bolts of fabric. Sweep up the bits of spilled flour. Wash the windows.*

Only one customer stood inside, Matthew Scott from down the Irish Road. His farm sat just past Granny Claire's.

"No sugar, then, this time." His voice held an edge of forced acceptance. "Just the flour."

"Wool?" Mrs. Johnson was at the counter alongside her husband, which was unusual.

Mr. Scott shook his head. "Not this time."

The answer seemed to surprise and confuse Mrs. Johnson. "But it's nearing winter," she pointed out. "You cannot underestimate the value of a good coat when the weather turns."

Mr. Scott held his chin at a proud angle. "I know its value well enough, as does your husband, it would seem. He further knows why you're not selling much wool lately."

Mr. Johnson dropped a heavy bag of flour in front of Mr. Scott.

Mr. Scott slapped a handful of coins on the counter, the clanging echoing in the uncomfortable silence. He took the bag of flour under his arm and left without further comment.

"How high have you raised the prices, Jeremiah?" Mrs. Johnson asked under her breath. "They've always bought goods before, even at the higher cost."

"They'll buy," he said stubbornly. "Eventually they'll be cold and hungry enough to buy."

"And if they don't?"

"Then they'll leave or starve. Either way, it'll take care of the problem."

His venom struck at Katie's resolve. How could any person speak so coldly of another person's suffering, their possible demise, even? Convincing him to even appear merciful would be an uphill struggle, and no denying it.

She put firmly in her mind Joseph Archer's manner of dealing with her during that first day she'd worked for him. He'd shown nothing but resolve and businesslike logic. She'd struggled to find any way of arguing with him. That was exactly how she needed to approach the Johnsons.

Katie stepped up to the counter, her shoulders back and her posture unbending. "Good morning, Mr. Johnson, Mrs. Johnson."

"Another one," Mr. Johnson muttered. "What do you want?"

"I want a word with you, if you must know."

"I don't have time for—"

Katie spoke right over him, as if they were equals. "If you're losing sales the likes of what I just saw with Mr. Scott, I'd wager you don't have time *not* to listen. I've come with a business idea that I think will bring your profits back up."

"My profits are just fine."

"I've my suspicions that's not so true as you're letting on. You've a pile of unsold shoes so high it's gone and toppled over. There's dust on your bolts of wool. There's dust on most everything, in fact."

Mr. Johnson's eyes narrowed, and not in a ponderous way. She was pricking him where it was most tender.

"I've no formal training in such things," Katie admitted with only the slightest, momentary dip of her head, "but I do think you've put your prices out of the reach of those who would buy these things. Wanting or not wanting them isn't a consideration any longer. There's simply no money."

"I'll not have some Irish filth coming up out of the ditches to tell me how to run my business."

Katie kept her dignity ahead of her like a shield. Half the town was depending on her, whether they knew it or not.

"If you lowered the Irish prices to where they were before—which is still considerably higher than the Red Road prices, I'll point out—your sales would likely return to normal."

Mrs. Johnson actually seemed to be listening to her argument.

Perhaps if she proceeded carefully, she might convince the woman to help talk her husband around.

"If you are asking me to show mercy to a bunch of lazy heathens—"

"I know too much of you to try any such thing," Katie said. "I'm not speaking of mercy or pity. I'm talking about a trade—a business trade."

That got his attention, though he only barely let her see as much.

"What kind of trade?" Mrs. Johnson asked.

"Hush, Carol," Mr. Johnson ground out.

Katie ignored him and continued with her point. "You've a sign in your window advertising a position. That sign's been hanging there for all the months I've lived in Hope Springs. Now, if you'd be honest with yourself, you'd admit that if no one's come forward yet in three months or more, no one will."

Neither of the Johnsons responded, though both were watching her closely.

"As near as I can tell, you're needing someone to straighten and dust and clean, perhaps organize displays, wash windows, wax the floor."

Mrs. Johnson gave several small nods of her head. Mr. Johnson's complexion grew a touch splotchy, as though he fought down a hint of embarrassment at the obvious state of his place of business. Katie was careful to keep any hint of accusation or disapproval from her tone. She remembered the inarguable logic of Joseph's reasoning that first day. She could mimic that tone, to a degree at least.

"I've worked as a household servant since I was eight years old. All I've done these past eighteen years and more is straighten and dust and clean. I've organized pantries and cupboards and linen closets. I've even waxed floors and kept windows clear as a lake on a cloudless day. You'll not find a soul anywhere in Hope Springs, perhaps anywhere in all of Wyoming Territory, who can do the job you need faster or better than I can."

Mr. Johnson's splotchiness gave way to full-faced redness. "I'm not hiring Irish." He spat the final word.

Katie was unmoved. "I'm not speaking of hiring, nor salaries, nor true employment in the sense you're thinking. I'm speaking of a trade."

Mrs. Johnson spoke first. "What kind of trade?"

"Hush, woman."

Mrs. Johnson held up a hand. "No, I want to hear what she has to say. I will not be able to do my work around here until well after this child arrives. We need someone to see to it."

"But she is Irish."

Mrs. Johnson looked her husband dead in the eye. "She is also the only person in four months to ask about the job. The only one, Jeremiah."

He muttered something under his breath and paced away from the counter. Mrs. Johnson looked at Katie, and with an almost regal nod of her head, indicated Katie should continue. 'Twas very much like the superior gestures she'd so often received from the ladies of the houses where she'd worked for so many years. Oddly enough, it put Katie at ease. Here was a give-and-take she understood.

"I am offering to do your sweeping and straightening and cleaning, at least a few days a week, in exchange for returning everything to the prices they were before."

"The Irish price?" Mrs. Johnson asked.

Katie nodded. "You'll not be losing any profit over what you made before. And, in exchange for returning your prices to normal, you'd get that job filled you've been advertising for these many weeks. You'd win on both counts."

Mrs. Johnson appeared to mull that over. "It would be very nice to have the position filled, but it would mean having an Irishwoman working here. I cannot say that would be looked well on by everyone. Some would be upset, in fact."

Clearly Mr. Johnson was among that number.

"I understand." Katie let some of her defiant posture soften. "But I wouldn't be at the counter, wouldn't interact with any customers. I work quickly and quietly. I'd keep out of the way. Other than looking out over a neat and tidy shop, you'd hardly even know I was here."

"Except I'll have to listen to that ridiculous accent of yours, hearing the way you butcher the English language." Mr. Johnson still hadn't returned to the counter.

Katie wanted to argue that the heavy influence of the American South in his voice made his words sound odd to *her* ears, but she opted to keep her mouth shut and simply let him think.

A Red Road customer came inside. Katie melted back, doing her best to simply blend in. She could show the Johnsons just how invisible she could truly be. The customer, whom Katie didn't recognize, dug through the pile of shoes, toppling it in a few places. Mr. Johnson moved to help pick up the pairs that tumbled to the ground. Mrs. Johnson watched from behind the counter, a look of ponderous concern on her face.

When the customer repeatedly had to wipe dust from her fingertips after touching a tabletop or display, both Johnsons grew noticeably flustered. Katie couldn't have hoped for better timing.

Please let this work out. Please.

Mrs. Flannigan came in during the dust difficulties. She held a small change purse in her hands and asked Mrs. Johnson about the price of sugar. When, after checking with her husband, Mrs. Johnson quoted the recently raised price, Mrs. Flannigan left without making a purchase. Katie's heart broke to see it, even as a small flicker of hope grew inside.

She stood silent and still, waiting for the Johnsons to think through what she'd said and what they'd just seen.

The shop was empty for a full five minutes before Mr. Johnson, behind the counter once more, turned toward her. He pointed a menacing finger directly at her.

"Be here by six in the morning, every morning. You'll work until noon."

Katie nodded. She'd originally imagined three full days, not every single morning. But the look of disappointment on Mrs. Flannigan's face and the tears in Biddy's voice earlier that week, decided it for her.

"And," Mr. Johnson added with a flash in his eyes, "you'll keep your mouth shut while you're working here. I don't want to hear any *'twas* or *'tis* or any of your Irish words."

She almost answered with a "Yes, Mr. Johnson," but thought better of it. If he wanted silence, he'd have it.

"And—"

"Jeremiah." Katie thought Mrs. Johnson's tone was promising. She at least was making a minimal effort to put an end to Mr. Johnson's demands.

Mr. Johnson kept right on at it. "I don't want you near the customers or talking to them. You keep out of the way. Give me one lick of trouble and this trade of ours is off. Understand?"

Katie nodded firmly.

Mr. Johnson slammed his ledger book on the counter, taking up his pen. "Now get to work." His gaze dropped to his account book.

Katie was torn between grinning in triumph and sinking with the enormity of the troubles she'd just invited. Mr. Johnson would be a difficult employer. If past experience was any indication, she'd likely be insulted and belittled again and again. But it would be worth it.

Chapter Eleven

Joseph bit back a few tense words, working at being patient with his girls. They were both trying very hard to help with dinner but were only making things worse. They'd attempted to make pancakes, but after four eggs dropped to the floor, followed by nearly an entire pitcher of milk and a good amount of flour, Joseph had opted for something with fewer steps and, thus, fewer opportunities for disaster. But fried eggs had proven just as unsuccessful. If Hope Springs had even one restaurant, he'd have thrown in the towel and driven the girls into town.

Emma and Ivy were both on their hands and knees wiping up the mess with towels. He'd likely be paying Harriet Kester extra this week for laundering. If only Katie could have stayed until the new housekeeper came. Disaster after disaster had plagued the house since she left.

And I miss her. He planned to drop by the next day and talk with her. He'd been working on an excuse. Katie had taken a job at the mercantile; the idea didn't sit well with him, and he wanted to ask her about it. If he happened to find another reason to stay, perhaps something else needing repairs, so be it. He'd enjoyed the few minutes he'd spent the last week fixing her chest of drawers. Katie had sat nearby and talked with him. He'd missed that since she left.

"It's like paste, Pompah." Ivy squished her hand in the sticky mess of eggs, milk, and flour mashed together on the floor. She clapped her sticky hands together, then stretched out the viscous mixture between them.

"You're a mess, sweetheart." He motioned her toward him. "I think you can both be done now."

"But we're not finished cleaning it up," Emma protested from her own corner of the messy floor. The hem and front of her dress were filthy, covered in the same concoction as Ivy's hands and face.

"You've helped quite a lot." He felt justified in the white lie. Things would go far more quickly and smoothly if he didn't have to clean them up as well. "I'll finish what's left."

Emma's floured forehead puckered. "But we were supposed to do the low parts, and you were going to do the high parts."

Most children would have gladly been released from chores. His Emma almost seemed offended.

"What are we going to eat?" Ivy had happily handed over the cleaning assignment.

"I'm not certain yet," Joseph said. "But I can't make anything until I clean this up."

"I can help, Papa." Emma's look was so earnest, Joseph couldn't bring himself to turn her away. But letting her continue to help would only make the mess bigger.

He rubbed a hand over his mouth and chin, trying to sort out the difficulty. Until Katie had left he'd never really asked either of the girls to do chores. His late wife had absolutely recoiled at the idea of her daughters doing "servants' work." But they no longer had any servants, and there was still plenty of work to be done.

A knock echoed through the kitchen.

"Me! Me!" Ivy rushed to the door.

Joseph tried to catch her before she answered it. Ivy was hardly in any state to be greeting visitors. He reached her just as she opened the door.

Katie, of all people, stood on the back porch. Why did she have to come right at the height of this failure? She'd see how entirely they'd undone the work she'd accomplished during her time there.

Her eyes seemed to take it all in: Ivy's sticky face and hands; his own less-than-pristine state; Emma, standing behind him, with her dress caked in goo; the kitchen, filthy and chaotic.

Slowly, a smile blossomed across her face. Then she laughed. She laughed so hard and deep that she struggled for breath.

Ivy pressed her messy hands to her mouth and giggled. Joseph glanced back at Emma to find a smile on her face as well.

"We've been making dinner," Joseph explained, feeling equal parts foolish and amused.

"You ought to make it in a mixing bowl like a right regular person, Joseph Archer, instead of stirring it on the floor."

"Is that the step I missed?" Even in his humiliation, Joseph found he could laugh.

"If you've any appetite left, I've brought you a plate of sweet rolls."

Ivy immediately began jumping up and down making almost desperate sounds of longing.

"Please, Pompah. Please can we have them? Please?"

Joseph patted the top of her head, about the only part of her that wasn't dirty. "I think that would make a fine dinner."

Such relief crossed Emma's face that Katie started laughing all over again. She stepped gingerly inside, somehow managing to avoid both the mess on the floor and Ivy's gluey fingers. She set her plate, with a dishtowel over it, on the countertop near the pile of dishes Joseph hadn't yet gotten around to washing.

She crooked a finger at Emma and Ivy, drawing them closer. She held Ivy's hands over the sink and pumped water. As she washed the mess from Ivy's hands, she spoke to the girls. "I want the both of you to go up to your bedroom, being ever so careful not to touch a single thing, and slip out of your dresses. Put on your nightgowns and come back down. Bring these dresses back with you. Can you do that, now?"

The girls nodded solemnly.

"Off with you, then."

They rushed out, an eagerness in their movements, no doubt inspired by empty stomachs and the promise of Katie's famous sweet rolls.

"Do I dare ask just what this concoction is down here?" Katie looked warily at the mess on the floor.

"Broken eggs, spattered milk, and spilled flour."

She seemed to ponder that a moment. "Eggs, milk, and flour. Was it to be *pancóga* for dinner tonight?"

"*Pancóga?*"

She winced dramatically, no doubt at his horrible attempt to pronounce her Gaelic word. "*Pancóga* is . . . drop scones." She shook her head. "No. That's the Scottish word. I can't remember what you call them here."

"Pancakes?" Joseph suggested.

"Yes. That's it."

"We *were* trying to make pancakes, but the girls were a little too eager to help."

Her eyes returned to him. He couldn't say if he saw more laughter or empathy in her face. "Bless your heart, Joseph Archer, but you do have your hands full."

"Two more weeks, Katie. In two weeks I'll take my grain to the station to sell and come back with a new housekeeper."

"This new housekeeper, she seems like a good fit for you, does she?"

Joseph nodded. He'd been much more thorough in finding Katie's replacement than he'd been when hiring *her.* Mrs. Smith was neither young nor Irish. And he'd received references that assured him she had experience with children. "I think she will be a good fit."

"Would you like a bit of help cleaning this up?"

"If you're offering, I'm accepting."

Katie pushed back the sleeves of her dress and grabbed a dishrag from the drawer where she'd kept them. He'd spent enough time lingering in the kitchen after meals to know exactly where to find the rags after she'd gone.

"If you'll fetch the slop bucket," she said, "we can get this cleared away quick as rain."

He slipped outside to do just that, and by the time he returned, she had a heaping dustpan of the doughy mess all ready for him. She scooped and dumped a few more dustpans' worth of the concoction, while Joseph scrubbed the floor with the damp dishtowel.

"Thank you for your help," he said, rinsing and wringing the rag in the sink.

She smiled up at him. "You're quite welcome, Joseph."

"And for the rolls," he added. "I hate to even admit it, but they are likely to be the girls' entire dinner tonight. We've had a few too many disasters today."

"I'm a regular heavenly messenger, it seems. Bringing you miracle upon miracle, I am."

"We've needed a few miracles around here lately."

Katie pulled another rag from the drawer and stood beside him at the sink, rinsing it. "When does Emma start school?"

"Next week." It didn't at all surprise him that Katie remembered what was happening in Emma's life, nor that she would ask after her. Katie and Emma had a special bond, one Joseph didn't fully understand but for which he was daily grateful. Emma was a quiet and lonely girl. Katie had lit a candle inside the child, and she absolutely glowed when Katie was nearby.

"The younger children start school first," he continued. "Those old enough to help with the reaping won't start back to school until after all the crops are brought in."

Talking with her again, Joseph could almost imagine things were the way they'd been before. She was doing her daily work, and he was there talking with her, helping where he could, simply enjoying having her nearby. Odd that *this* had become his idea of "normal," when Katie had only been with them for three months. How quickly his view of the world and the things he wanted out of life had changed.

"I'd wager Emma's a fine student." Katie wiped down the front of the stove, which hadn't escaped the pancake-batter explosion. "She's such a clever girl. She must do very well in school."

"She does." Emma was exceptionally bright. She often amazed him, in fact.

"Have you a clean pot? A small one?"

He searched about in the cupboards until he found one. She had the pitcher of milk in hand by the time he handed her the pot. Katie poured a generous amount in and placed it on the stovetop, stirring with a spoon she'd retrieved at some point.

"I would have liked to have gone to school." She spoke wistfully, without bitterness.

He leaned against the nearby countertop and watched her stir. What a moonling he'd become, so happy to stand about staring at a woman who was out of his reach. "What would you have studied if you'd gone to school?"

"Everything. Numbers and ciphering and the world. Just everything." Her eyes unfocused, growing thoughtful and distant. "I might have learned how to write my name. Wouldn't that be a wonderful thing, to take up a pen and write my very own name?"

The longing in her tone pierced him. "I could teach you that. If you want to learn to write your name, I could show you."

"Perhaps you might find a moment between working your land and keeping up your house and tending to your children," she answered with a touch of amused dryness. "I know perfectly well you have far too much to do to be wasting your time on something so . . . silly."

"I am in earnest, Katie." Nothing that would make her happy would ever be "silly" to him.

She tucked a wisp of hair behind her ear. "You once told me you are always in earnest."

"At the time I said that I believe I was firing you."

"Something you have done far too many times." She pointed a teasing finger at him.

One side of his mouth tugged upward. "What are you making?"

"Warm milk. To go with the sweet rolls. 'Twill—it will be a fine treat for you and the girls."

Joseph had never heard Katie trade out her Irish expressions for American ones. Why had she started now? He found himself studying her more closely.

She looked tired. More than tired, *exhausted.*

He set a hand on her arm. "Are you unwell?"

She shook her head. "I am quite well."

"You don't look it."

Hurt and embarrassment immediately filled her expression. "That's a fine thing to say to a woman who, out of the goodness of her heart, has made you something edible for dinner."

"I didn't mean it like that."

Her coloring was a touch off. And, no matter her protests, she did look very tired. His late wife had been pale and worn-looking in the day or two before the fever took hold. Was Katie truly "quite well" or was she more ill than she let on?

"Katie?"

She tapped her spoon on the side of the pot, something she did every time she cooked. That sound would forever make him think of her.

"Don't start fussing like an old nursemaid," she said. "I've had a couple long days is all. I'm behind on my bread deliveries, so I've been up all day and late into the night baking."

"Now I'm feeling guilty that you made us rolls." He struck a lighter tone.

"The rolls are a bribe."

"A bribe?" That was unexpected.

She set the pot off the heat and turned to face him. Something in the very straight set of her shoulders spoke volumes of her nervousness. Was she afraid to talk to him?

"I don't have all the money I owe you for the flour yet," she said, a feigned firmness in her voice that contrasted with the worry in her eyes. "I fell behind with my bread and haven't sold as many loaves as I expected to. If I can sell all that I usually do, I can give you the rest of what I owe you by the end of the month."

"Katie—"

"I thought I'd have more time for baking and deliveries since my duties here no longer fill my days, but it simply hasn't worked out that way." Her shoulders slumped a little. "There has been so very much to do at Mrs. Claire's house, with repairs and cleaning and cooking. And she was so low on everything essential. I honestly don't know what she's lived on. Stocking her cupboards took a good bit of money."

Joseph led her to the table and pulled a chair out for her. She sat. He took the chair diagonal from hers.

"There's just been so much to do." She sighed deeply. Her beautiful brown eyes met his, pleading and worry heavy in their depths. "I will get you the money, I promise."

"I am not at all worried about that, Katie. I know you well enough to not doubt you for a moment."

Her brow only creased more as she shook her head in what looked like disappointment. In herself. "But I gave you my word."

He set his hand on top of hers, which were clasped together on the tabletop. "Your word is good enough for me. Please don't worry about the money when you clearly have other things on your mind."

She sat in silence, shoulders drooping, head lowered. Joseph didn't pull his hand back. Tavish wouldn't approve, but Tavish wasn't there. Katie needed *someone* to reach out to her.

"Why must people be so horrible?" she whispered. A catch in her voice added a tone of misery.

"What happened?"

She gave the tiniest shake of her head. "I've only been thinking of Ian and the terrible way the Red Road treats the Irish. And of what a poisonous snake Mr. Johnson can be at times."

There was the very topic he'd meant to discuss with her the next time he saw her. He'd clearly been justified in his uneasiness with her new position. "I'd heard you were working for him. Is he mistreating you?"

She pulled one of her hands from his, upturning it and propping her head there. Her other hand, though, remained with his.

"If he is making you miserable—"

"Not miserable, really. At least not so much that I can't endure it." She looked so weary. Joseph's heart ached at the sight. "Besides, my work is making a difference. He brought the Irish prices back down. I don't know if you heard that."

He had, but hadn't realized she was connected to the change. "You talked him down?" He was impressed.

"Not exactly. I work for him six hours every morning, and he agrees not to starve the Irish out of town. That is our arrangement."

She wasn't being paid? That was little better than slavery. "It sounds to me like a very one-sided arrangement."

She closed her eyes, her head still resting against her palm. "I've seen the fear leave my neighbors' eyes. I've seen the wee ones with shoes on their feet and their mothers making coats for the coming winter. I'm well paid in that, I promise you."

"Then why do you sound so defeated, Katie?"

"Do not you lecture me on this too, Joseph." She stood rather abruptly, pacing away from him. "Tavish already told me I was every sort of a fool. He insisted I should let everyone else worry about the Irish prices as I've enough troubles of my own."

"He does have something of a point." Joseph stood, tempted to move closer, but choosing, instead, to keep his distance.

"Sometimes I think he thinks I'm helpless, that I'm weak or incapable or something. He turns the subject whenever our conversations touch on hard things. Every time I attempt something difficult, he insists that I shouldn't."

Katie weak or incapable? That was so inaccurate it was almost laughable. "My guess is he worries about you. That he cares so much he'd do anything to save you from pain and heartache and worry, but he doesn't know how." He took a step in her direction. "He probably is astounded at how strong and capable you are, but wishes you didn't have to carry so much weight on your shoulders."

She looked at him, her gaze riveted to his face. Did she realize he was actually speaking of himself?

"If he only knew how to help, Katie, if he could believe he was allowed to walk with you when you are passing through troubles, I think he would jump at the opportunity. I think he would do anything in the world for you."

She took a shaky breath. Katie seldom looked emotional, but she did in that moment. Joseph hated that he didn't know what it meant or what she was feeling.

"What can I do, Katie? I'll do anything you need me to, anything at all."

She held her hands up in a gesture of frustrated helplessness. "I'm only tired. So very, very tired."

Her voice broke, and her expression crumbled on the final words. She pressed her hands to her face.

He didn't even have to think. His arms were around her the moment he reached her side. She sobbed against his chest. He refused to diminish her burden with empty words of dismissal or reassurance. If she was exhausted enough to be weeping in his kitchen, he wouldn't tell her to hush or that it wasn't as bad as she thought. If life had brought her to this state, it was bad enough to warrant tears.

"I'm not sleeping much," she said. "I have to be to town by six o'clock every morning but Sunday. And I try to have breakfast waiting for Granny when she wakes up. Once I finish at the mercantile, I have to make my deliveries. Just as soon as those are done, I drop in on Biddy to do what I can for her. Then I return home and make the bread for the next day.

That takes me late into the night. And it all just starts up again the next morning."

It was little wonder she was exhausted to the point of tears. "I wish I could help. I'd offer to put a day in at the mercantile, but I can't clean worth anything."

"I know," she muttered.

He smiled a bit. "And I am absolutely certain no one would buy a loaf of bread I made."

"Especially if they knew you mixed it on the floor."

"A very good point, Katie." He laughed through the words and felt her chuckle against him.

He kept her close, hoping doing so didn't make him selfish. She needed comfort and had turned to him. She was being courted by someone else. Yet, she'd turned to him.

He was very confused. But, Katie was there, with him. He'd made her laugh. That was something.

She leaned back enough to wipe her wet cheeks. A wobbly smile tugged at her lips. "I have a confession. I didn't bring the rolls only as a bribe."

"What, then?"

She shrugged a single shoulder. A bit of color touched her pale cheeks. He was glad to see it. "I couldn't think of a good excuse to come talk to you, and I wanted to."

"Did you?" He could tell he was smiling like an idiot. He couldn't help it.

"I knew you wouldn't scold me or tell me I couldn't hold up under my burdens. I needed to talk to someone who would just listen."

The girls clambered back into the kitchen. Katie slipped out of his embrace. He felt empty the moment she stepped away.

Katie had a smile for the girls, quite as if she hadn't been struggling under the weight of the world only a moment earlier.

In a flurry of excitement and almost maternal fussing, she had the girls seated at the table with a sweet roll and a glass of warm milk set before each of them. If he hadn't stopped her, she likely would have brought him his food as well, as if she still worked for them instead of being a guest for the evening. He saw to his own roll and milk while she rinsed out the girls' dirty dresses in the sink.

The girls were beside themselves with praise for Katie's rolls. They'd endured *his* cooking for too long. Katie smiled in her quiet way and hung their damp dresses over the back of a chair pulled up near the warm stove.

"I do need to be getting back to Mrs. Claire's house," she said.

The girls protested. She gave them each a kiss on the top of their heads. She spared a moment for Emma, telling her how she hoped to hear all about school and the wonderful things she would be learning. The look of threatening tears in Emma's eyes flitted away, replaced by a contented smile.

Joseph walked Katie to the edge of the back porch.

"Thank you for letting me talk," she said. "I'm certain my grumbling wasn't what you hoped to endure tonight. But . . . but I needed it so badly."

In that moment she looked lonely. She, who had the entire Irish Road cheering over her decision to stay in Hope Springs, who had sacrificed her sleep and peace of mind to save her neighbors from starvation, seemed nearly desolate.

"Come talk any time, Katie. Any time at all. No sweet rolls necessary."

"Thank you, Joseph Archer." She stretched up on her toes and, without even the tiniest hint of warning, kissed his cheek.

Kissed his cheek.

Then she was gone, leaving him staring after her. Katie had come to him with her troubles. She had cried on his shoulder, had laughed with him. He thought she left less burdened than she'd arrived. His home had felt whole and warm again with her there.

What if you are best for her, after all?

Chapter Twelve

Tavish tucked Katie's fiddle under his arm. He gave Granny Claire a quick kiss on the cheek before sending her off in his little sister's care.

Granny said Katie had gone to Joseph's house on a matter of business. Tavish meant to bring her home for a much-needed bit of merrymaking. She needed it. And he needed her.

He turned back, fully intending to fetch her from the Archer place, only to find her not many paces off, walking toward him.

She waved as she drew closer. "A fine good evening to you, Tavish."

Heavens, it was nice to see her smiling again. She had been fatigued and burdened the last time he'd seen her. He'd tried convincing her to end her employment at the mercantile. She needed the sleep and some time to herself. She most certainly *didn't* need Johnson's insulting and belittling treatment.

"What's that you're carrying?" she asked.

"This?" He held up her fiddle case. "It's a fiddle, Sweet Katie. An odd contraption with strings that makes music."

She gave him a look of scolding that held a heavy hint of amusement. "I know perfectly well what a fiddle is. And *that* fiddle looks like mine."

"Probably because it is."

"But why are you carrying my—" Absolute panic entered her

expression. "Has something happened to it? Please tell me it's not broken. I can't lose it. I need the music."

He set his free hand on her arm. "Your fiddle is perfectly sound. I've simply come to take it—and you—to the céilí."

The explanation didn't appear to settle in for the length of a breath. Relief followed. Close on its heels came a whisper of eagerness.

"There's to be a céilí tonight?"

Tavish nodded. "The Irish have reason to celebrate. Ian is out of bed and looks likely to eventually recover. The harvest promises to be plentiful. And, perhaps the greatest miracle of all, there's been no more feud violence."

Katie's shoulders rose and fell with a deep breath. "I've worried about that. And about Ian, and the harvest."

He slipped his arm about her waist, pulling her close to him as they walked on.

"I suppose I worry too much," she said with a sigh.

Tavish pressed a kiss to the top of her head.

"Is that a 'yes, you do,' then?" Katie asked.

"That is an 'I can't possibly answer without getting myself into trouble.'"

He thought he felt her laugh a tiny bit. That did him a world of good. Katie ought to laugh and smile more.

He leaned in close and spoke softly. "Tonight you are to do nothing but smile and laugh, play your music if you wish, and enjoy your friends' company."

"And *your* company?"

He grinned back at her. "Thought of me first thing, did you?"

She threw him a saucy look. "Second or third thing, at least."

"You're in better spirits than you have been of late," he said, grateful to see it.

"I feel better—less weighed down," she said. "And to have a céilí is a fine thing."

They turned in at Ma and Da's place where the céilís were always held. Such a look of peace entered Katie's expression.

"'Twas these parties that first made Hope Springs feel like home to me. These parties and these people." She smiled fondly as she looked over the crowd that had already gathered. "I would have died a bit to leave it all behind."

"And there is yet another reason I'm happy you've chosen to stay."

She looked up at him. No one but Katie had ever worn such a look of mingled determination and weariness. "I fully intend to be happy here, Tavish. No matter what it takes."

Tavish pressed a kiss to her forehead. He couldn't say when he'd begun doing that, but he'd found he liked it very much. Something in the simple tenderness of the gesture felt very right.

"Enough of that, lad," Da said.

Tavish pushed out an amused and exasperated breath. "Why is it you always seem to be sneaking up on me just when I'm having a tender moment with this sweet colleen?"

Da kept his expression stern, though an unmistakable twinkle shone in his eyes. "Is it not a father's duty to look out for his girl?"

"Aren't you meant to look after your son as well?" Tavish matched his da's teasing tone.

Da shrugged. "I like our Katie better than I like you. So you can just look out for your own self."

Katie slipped from Tavish's side. She gave Da a hug, something Tavish would never have expected her to do only a few short weeks earlier.

Da returned her embrace, smiling at her fondly. "Biddy's been asking after you, hoping you meant to come to the céilí."

"Biddy is here?"

Da nodded. "My wife's sitting with Ian so Biddy could have some time away."

"Let's find her, then," Katie said. She turned back and held her hand out to Tavish, an invitation he readily accepted.

They walked amongst their neighbors. Every single soul they passed had a word of greeting for Katie. How quickly she'd become an indispensable part of their lives.

They spotted Biddy not far from the tables of food. Katie was off in a rush. She and Biddy embraced each other, falling into easy conversation.

"She has been a good friend to Biddy," Da observed. "And such a comfort to her since Ian was laid low. Visits her every day, she does. I don't know how Biddy could have endured all she has without Katie at her side."

Tavish remembered how standoffish Katie had been the day she met Biddy and smiled.

"How is your courtship going, lad?" Da asked.

"It would be going vastly better if a certain nosy Irishman didn't keep interrupting me."

Da chuckled. He slapped a friendly hand on Tavish's shoulder. "See if you can't get the lass to play her fiddle tonight. She does the lot of us a world of good with her music."

Tavish kept to Katie's side the remainder of the evening. For a woman who had arrived so utterly alone, she had made the entire Irish Road her friends. She played her fiddle for them all, filling the cool night air with the tunes of home played to perfection.

Seamus took up the usual storytelling, and Katie took up her place at Tavish's side, leaning against his arm as the evening drew out. The air turned more and more chill as night fell. He wrapped his arm about her, pulling her close. As the tales gave way to the quiet tunes that always ended their céilís, Katie's head grew heavy against him.

Though Tavish would have followed her to Ireland, he was grateful she'd chosen to stay. As she'd said, Hope Springs was home.

Chapter Thirteen

Katie stretched up on her toes, trying to reach the very highest shelf in the mercantile's storeroom. She'd spent every minute of the past seven mornings, excepting Sunday, among the shelves and boxes.

She'd nearly finished organizing the storeroom. A week of carrying boxes and cans and heavy bags across the room, pulling them off shelves only to lift them onto others, had left her sore and tired. She'd taken the chaos she'd found in the storage room and created structure. Mr. Johnson would know in a glance what was there, how much, where to find it. 'Twas an enormous improvement.

She slid a box off the highest shelf. It was lighter than she expected, but awkward coming from as high up as it was. The stepladder teetered once as she climbed back down. She set the box on the ground and pulled it open.

Handkerchiefs. The pile out front was down to three.

Katie tucked the box under her arm and stepped out of the storage room. The mercantile was empty, just as it had been most of the week she'd worked there. Harvest kept the residents of Hope Springs busy and away from town.

"What are you doing out here?" Mr. Johnson skewered her with an accusatory look. "Get in the back where you belong."

"I'm only—"

His livid expression stopped her on the spot. Mr. Johnson only permitted her to speak in whispers. Her accent, she'd been told many times over the last week, made "his ears bleed."

"I'm putting out the handkerchiefs." She kept the words barely audible. "There are but three remaining in the display."

"But *tree* remaining?" He mimicked her pronunciation with an obvious desire to offend.

Katie kept still and quiet.

"Fine. But be quick about it." He returned to his ledgers.

She crossed to the long table where the Johnsons displayed gloves and scarves and handkerchiefs. She laid her box on the table and pulled out one square of linen at a time, setting each out very precisely. Not a single handkerchief was so much as a hair's breadth farther to one side or the other than the one before it.

Mr. Johnson was very particular about everything she did. She'd spent a full hour arranging a display of shiny leather boots the morning before, only to have him topple them over because one of the rows wasn't as straight as he wanted it to be. Just that morning he'd kicked over her bucket of mop water for missing a bit of dirt.

The door chime sounded. Katie looked up from her work and straight to Mr. Johnson. She wasn't supposed to be out when customers came around. But there was no way of returning to the storage room without passing by the new arrival.

Mr. Johnson jabbed his finger in her direction. "Not a word. Keep to the corner."

Katie nodded. The last thing she wanted was trouble. She returned to laying out the handkerchiefs. Surely the table sat far enough in the corner to satisfy Mr. Johnson's edict.

"Have you come by for a treat?" Mr. Johnson said to his customer.

Katie kept her head down and her hands moving. She'd had an employer very much like Mr. Johnson before. Her first job in Derry had been filled with beatings and angry, insulting words. She'd learned then to work hard and keep out of the way. She flexed her fingers as she stood in the corner of the mercantile. Her first mistress had beaten her hands so many times for the smallest things that she still bore the scars.

At least Mr. Johnson hasn't resorted to that. She was belittled and yelled at but hadn't yet been beaten.

"Katie?"

She knew that voice in an instant. *Emma.*

The sweet child stood at the display of candies, smiling across at her. Was she the customer who'd come inside? A happy surprise, that.

Katie pressed her lips together to keep from calling out a greeting. She did, however, give the tiniest wave of her fingers and a smile she hoped communicated her very real pleasure at seeing Emma again.

Emma's face lit up. She came to the corner where Katie was working.

"Hello, Katie."

"Hello, sweetheart." She kept her voice quiet. "What brings you to the mercantile? Are you here on your own?"

She couldn't imagine Joseph would leave Emma to fend for herself.

"Papa came to get me from school and gave me a penny for a sweet." She held her hand open, palm up, with a single bronze coin lying there. "He said I could pick whatever candy I wanted."

Katie smiled. "A butterscotch, I'd wager."

"You remembered." Emma actually seemed surprised by that.

"Butterscotch sweets. Chocolate cake. Potato-and-leek soup." Katie counted off the items on her fingers. "I think I remember most of your favorites."

"When will you come see us again? We never found the tune I liked."

Emma had overheard her playing her fiddle one night and became particularly attached to a tune she'd played. Though Katie had spent many evenings playing through the tunes she knew, they hadn't yet found the one Emma wished to hear again.

"Perhaps your papa will let you come visit me at my new house and we can have a wee little céilí of our own."

"I told you I won't have you using any of your asinine Irish words in this shop."

Katie hadn't even heard Mr. Johnson approach. She looked quickly at Emma. The girl was sensitive. Had Mr. Johnson's angry tone upset her? But Emma looked more confused than upset.

"I'm sorry, Mr. Johnson. I'll—"

He stopped her short with the same look of warning she received every time she spoke. He stood there glaring at her, a small box under his arm.

Katie bent lower, so she could speak to Emma while keeping her voice low. "Go pick out your sweet."

Emma nodded, her eyes darting between Katie and Mr. Johnson. She moved slowly back toward the candy display, glancing repeatedly over her shoulder as she went.

"I told you not to talk to the customers. If you can't follow simple instructions—"

"She came and spoke to me. I kept to the corner just like you told me to."

Though Katie thought her reasoning was sound, Mr. Johnson didn't seem satisfied. His lips all but disappeared as his mouth narrowed.

He slammed his small box on the table. "What is this?"

She glanced inside. "Ribbons, Mr. Johnson."

"And who put the ribbons in this box?"

"I did, sir."

"Why would you put ribbons in a box that is clearly labeled 'laces'? Are you trying to sabotage my business? Make me look like a fool?"

Heat flamed across Katie's face even as her stomach dropped to her shoes. She'd seen the lettering on the front of the box and, looking inside to find a single spool of ribbon, had assumed the word was "ribbon."

"I'm not meaning to make you look foolish at all, I assure you. I'd not meant to place the ribbons in the wrong container."

His eyes were hard and disbelieving. "You 'didn't mean' to put ribbons in the lace box? Are you a simpleton, then? You can't understand that lace goes in the lace box and ribbons in the ribbon box?"

"I am not stupid." She spoke quietly but firmly.

"You're either stupid or playing me for a fool." He snatched up the box and tipped it upside down, dumping the rolls of ribbon on the floor. "Put the ribbon in the ribbon box and the lace in this one. Are those instructions simple enough, or do I need to use smaller words?"

Katie lowered her eyes, a position beaten into a servant until it became an instinct as deeply rooted as breathing itself. "I don't know where the ribbon box is, sir." She had thought the box now sitting upturned on the table *was* the ribbon box.

"It is on the display shelves where this one was. Everything is labeled. This should be simple."

Katie clasped her hands in front of her. She kept her head down. "I can't read the labels, sir. I've been looking inside the boxes to see what goes where."

"Are you commenting on my wife's handwriting?" Was the man determined to be offended by everything she said? "She has fine penmanship."

"Aye. I'm certain she does."

"Do not say 'aye.' If you can't speak proper English, you'll be out on the street quick as lightning."

"Yes, sir."

"Now get back to work." He pushed a spool of ribbon toward her with the toe of his shoe. "And do it right this time."

"Yes, sir."

He grumbled as he walked off. Katie stood in frustrated silence. After all she'd accomplished in the storeroom—she hadn't taken anything out of their boxes, so she knew she hadn't misunderstood any labeling there—and the fine displays she'd created out in the shop, she was rebuked over a box of ribbons. *Are you a simpleton?* She could endure his complaints about her work, but she hated being treated as though she were stupid.

Emma was not at the candy display. Apparently she'd made her purchase and slipped out quietly. Katie hadn't even heard the door chime.

She bent down to gather up the ribbons. 'Twas an unfortunate thing Mr. Johnson had taken the "lace" box back with him. Keeping all the spools in her arms without any spilling over would be a juggling act.

Katie piled them one by one into her arms, the stack nearly reaching her chin. She stood awkwardly, trying to keep the ribbons balanced. Mr. Johnson had disturbed her nearly perfect arrangement of handkerchiefs. She'd have to return to fix that, but he seemed more concerned with the ribbons at the moment.

She managed to carry her unstable load all the way to the tall shelves where sat boxes and baskets of smaller goods. Buttons, ribbons, thread, needles, and other sewing notions. Every container was labeled in letters she could not read. It seemed the boxes were in as desperate a state of disarray as the rest of the mercantile. She ought not to have assumed the contents and the labels matched.

A few spools slid from her grasp.

"Your job is to clean, not make a mess." Mr. Johnson spoke without even looking up at her.

"Yes, sir."

"And keep quiet. I don't want to hear your voice the rest of the day."

She set the spools in a small pile at the base of the shelves.

Silence for the rest of the day? That shouldn't be hard. She hadn't been much of a talker before coming to Hope Springs. Keeping quiet had simply been part of being a servant. Joseph had spoiled her for that. He talked to her and encouraged her to keep up the conversation. She was treated with kindness. She'd almost forgotten that was not normal.

She looked over the boxes and baskets and realized she had something of a puzzle staring at her. She was to put the ribbons in their correct box, but she couldn't read a single word. She didn't know which box she was looking for. And she was not supposed to talk.

How do I get around this difficulty, Eimear?

She couldn't simply look inside all the boxes. That method had put her in this difficulty in the first place. She would simply have to ask.

"Mr. Johnson, I—"

"I said no more talking."

"I don't know where to put the ribbon."

His head jerked up, eyes snapping with annoyance. "In the ribbon box." He spoke slowly.

Katie held herself perfectly still, enduring the barb without so much as a wince. This was old, familiar territory. "Which is the—?"

"Read the labels, you half-wit."

The word struck her like a slap. *Half-wit.* Confessing she couldn't read would convince him of that even more. Perhaps he was right. But she couldn't do her work properly if he didn't read the labels for her.

Pride was a fickle companion. It seldom improved a situation.

"I cannot read, sir. Not a word."

His first look was one of surprise. "Can't read? Why, even that child who just left can read. My own little Marianne can read."

She might have defended herself with arguments over opportunities and education, but the words died unspoken. She stood in silence, as she'd been ordered to.

"No wonder your people are such a plague." Mr. Johnson turned back to his papers.

"If you'll but tell me where to put the ribbons, Mr. Johnson."

He slowly turned his head toward the shelves. "Third shelf from the top, second basket from the right. Or can't you count either?"

She let the insult pass and set back to her work. She need only endure a little while longer, then she could return to the peace and quiet of Granny's house. That would become her daily routine, she imagined.

The door chimed once again. Another customer.

Katie spoke without looking back. "Do you want me to step into the storage room?"

"I want you to shut up."

She closed her eyes and her heart to his words. If she let him wound her, she would eventually die inside.

"I told you, Papa. There she is."

Hearing Emma's voice pulled Katie around. Sure enough, there the child stood with her father at her side, both looking at Katie.

"What can I do for you, Joseph?" Mr. Johnson spoke respectfully, with deference and consideration.

She stood at the shelves, too embarrassed to flee and too afraid she'd lose her position if she even attempted to explain.

Joseph's gaze traveled between her and Mr. Johnson. His expression had often been unreadable in the first weeks she'd known him. In the months that had followed, she thought she'd come to understand him better. But she couldn't say at all what he was thinking.

"Emma came for a butterscotch." Though Joseph spoke without the slightest hint of a question, Katie sensed something hovering beneath the surface of his words.

"Of course." Mr. Johnson moved quickly around the counter to join Joseph and Emma at the candy jars. "I hoped you would come back and pick out your sweet."

Katie faced the shelves. She pulled down the third-down-second-over box. Kneeling on the floor, she set the ribbon spools neatly inside, organizing them by color. Mr. Johnson could not with any degree of honesty complain about how hard she worked. He likely *would* complain, but the complaints wouldn't be warranted.

She slid the box, now nearly full, back into its place on the shelf. As she turned to slip into the back room, she found Joseph standing directly beside her.

She opened her mouth to say hello but closed it again immediately. She didn't want to endure another scolding. All she needed to do was finish out her morning. If she could manage that without being yelled at again, she might not spend her walk home fighting tears of exhaustion and humiliation.

"Emma said Mr. Johnson called you a simpleton."

She glanced at Mr. Johnson. Though he stood near Emma as she looked at the sweets display, his eyes were on Katie and Joseph. She wasn't supposed to talk. She looked back at Joseph, silently pleading with him not to press her for an answer.

He proved very uncooperative. "She also told me he was yelling at you and threw a box of ribbons at your head."

She just shook her head no, keeping her lips tightly closed.

Tavish, of all people, spoke next. "I'd wager Miss Emma had the right of it."

Katie spun about. Tavish stood at the counter, looking over the lot of them with a confused lift of one ebony eyebrow. Katie hadn't even heard the door chime.

"Have you sunk so low as to throw things at women's heads?" Tavish spoke to Mr. Johnson, though his eyes darted back to her more than once.

"No. At *Irish* heads, and only the insufferably incompetent ones."

Katie made to move to the storage room, away from his complaints and out of sight of Joseph and Tavish, but Joseph took hold of her hand. His gaze hadn't left her face. His earlier question still lingered in his expression. *What is going on?*

Mr. Johnson caught her eye. "Not one word, Paddy," he muttered. He stood with his arms folded across his chest. At least he wasn't flashing that feigned smile he so often wore for the Irish. That smile always made her feel uneasy.

She couldn't bring herself to even look at the two men. She hoped Emma wasn't too upset by the confrontation.

Mr. Johnson yanked the door to the storage room open and nodded for her to step inside. "You can work in here for the rest of the day."

She gave a quick nod of her head, pulled her hand away from Joseph's, and stepped inside.

"Don't ever forget," Mr. Johnson spat at her as she passed, "I could have driven every last one of you out of here. Without clothes or food, this Irish scourge would have been gone for good, and y'all would have run straight back to where you came from."

He snapped the door shut. Whatever conversation or confrontation took place in the shop, she was not privy to it. She stood in the storage room for several long moments without moving, simply attempting to reassure herself that all would be well in time. But the peace she looked for, the sense of calm contentment, didn't come. She didn't believe in second sight or premonitions, but she couldn't shake the feeling that the path ahead of her was anything but smooth.

Chapter Fourteen

Having an Irish Road meeting called a mere two days before the entire town was scheduled to take their harvests to the depot did not bode well. Something had to have upset a good number of people or else the gathering would have been postponed. Tavish stepped inside his parents' home in a less-than-optimistic frame of mind.

He acknowledged his brothers-in-law with a quick nod and exchanged a questioning glance with Da. His father looked out over the gathering of men.

"Seamus," Da said, "you had a concern to bring before everyone."

Seamus stood. His blacksmith's build was intimidating, even to those who knew him well. But it was the fearsome look on his face that made Tavish nervous. Seamus was fun and lively, until he was riled. The man, Tavish had heard tell, had been part of the Young Irelanders Rebellion in '48. Seamus had, if the story was true, spent time in prison for his role in that uprising and had either been released or had escaped. There were moments when Tavish saw in Seamus's expression just enough fury to make him believe every rumor he'd heard about Seamus's past.

"How many of you are missing chickens?"

It would have been an odd question if Tavish himself hadn't noticed both he and Ian were short a few laying hens. Every hand around the room was raised.

Not a good sign at all.

"That's what we were afraid of." Seamus frowned. "Though I'd not like to make an accusation without some proof"—Seamus had done that more than once—"this seems too big a problem to be a coincidence."

A few noises of agreement answered that declaration. Tavish glanced at Da. He looked as uncomfortable as Tavish felt.

"I'd wager," Seamus continued, "we're not experiencing an early winter migration amongst our domestic fowl."

The smiles at that were heavily tinged with uncertainty, worry even.

"It seems to me," Seamus said, "someone's making off with our birds."

"The Red Road, no doubt." Eoin O'Donaghue spoke what the rest were thinking, even Tavish.

Seamus eyed them all in turn. "It's not been many weeks since Tavish's horse had its tail clipped and its body bruised in the incident."

Tavish was still angry at that, though he'd done his best to stay calm.

"Ian O'Connor couldn't even be here with us tonight, as he's not yet recovered enough from the Reds' cowardly attack." Seamus had entirely lost his light and cheery storyteller's voice. This was as near to a call-to-arms as Tavish had heard in a few years. "Now they're on our road at night, sneaking onto our land, making off with our animals. They've brought this fight to us, no matter that we've tried to keep the peace."

Matthew Scott spoke up. "Just what would you have us do, Seamus? We can't prove they've done anything, and even if we could, would not provoking them leave us open to far worse things than missing chickens?"

Seamus was not always the most patient of men, but he took no offense at the question. "Times are perilous. We, none of us, can deny that."

"Certainly not," a voice in the crowd answered cautiously.

"But how long do you imagine we have before the mercantile decides to raise prices despite Katie's admirable efforts?" Seamus asked. "How long before the Red Road goes fully on the attack and we, as always, suffer for it?"

Worry etched into every face. Tavish knew what they were feeling. He'd felt it himself for weeks. Trouble was brewing again, and they all knew far too well what came next.

"Do you think they'll make more mischief before the harvest exodus?" Matthew asked.

Seamus gave a firm nod.

Tavish offered a slightly different opinion. "Bear in mind, the lot of them are getting ready to sell their grain just like we are. The workload this next week will be too great for much troublemaking."

Eyes slid in Da's direction. He'd often been looked to as a voice of wisdom. Too bad Seamus so often undermined that with his relentless determination to rush into a fight with shillelaghs flying.

"This won't come to a head before the harvest run," Da said. "But neither do I think we'll have uninterrupted peace and quiet until then. I'd advise watchfulness and great care. Keep an eye out for one another, but keep peaceable and calm. This feud will still be here when we all return."

"And what of the womenfolk?" Seamus shot back. "They'll be here without their husbands and fathers."

"Admit it, Seamus," Tavish called out, "the women aren't the problem in this town. If we leave them here long enough on their own, they're likely to solve our difficulties all neat and tidy."

The group chuckled at that. Nothing about the feud was actually so simple, but the women were by far the most peaceable group in Hope Springs, excepting perhaps the children.

The meeting dispersed with no more conclusion than that. Apparently they were all going to watch and see what happened. 'Twasn't exactly a vote of confidence, simply resignation. The feud would flare; they all knew that much. There was simply no knowing when, nor just how hot the flames would burn.

Tavish hung back as everyone else filed out. He needed to talk to Da.

"I've not seen Ian today," Tavish said when the room was empty again. "How is he?"

"Better a bit at a time. Biddy's sinking under the weight of it all, but your ma means to rally a few of the Irishwomen to her cause."

Tavish had no doubt Ma would have things firmly in hand in no time.

"I've a feeling," Da said, "it's not your brother you truly wish to inquire after."

Nothing got past him. "I'm worried about Katie."

"Aye, poor lass." Da shook his head. "As if we'd not put enough weight on her shoulders, now she bears the burden of our very survival, but with no actual power to see it through."

Poor Katie, indeed. "Johnson was vicious to her today. I was only there for a few minutes, but he had me spitting mad. Called her terrible names and spoke down to her. We cannot expect her to endure that."

Da sat near the fire, lighting his pipe. "What else is she to do? If she quits, the prices will go up again, perhaps higher than they were."

"If she continues as she is, they might still go up. And she'll have suffered needlessly." Tavish paced toward the fireplace. "I've tried convincing her to walk away, before things have gone too far. At this point there'd still be time to come up with a new solution."

Da gave him a look generally reserved for Tavish's least intelligent moments. "Dictating to a woman of her determination will get you nowhere, lad."

"I cannot just leave her in that situation. I was there this morning, Da, and saw how he treated her. I only wish she'd told me of her idea beforehand. I might have talked some sense into her."

"So is it concern for Katie that's gnawing at you, son, or is it your wounded pride?"

He hadn't thought of it that way. 'Twas likely a bit of both. He knew Katie had turned to Joseph when she first pondered the idea of selling her bread. She'd trusted Joseph with her plans and her difficulties, so why was he left out in the dark?

"Katie is an independent sort," Da said. "Comes from being on her own for so long. And you are the rescuing sort, always looking for ways to fix people's troubles. I'd say most times, though, a woman doesn't need saving; she needs someone to walk at her side while she works out her own rescue."

Tavish rubbed at the tension in the back of his neck. "Now you sound like Joseph. He quite smugly told me this afternoon that I'd best leave Katie to her decisions if I knew what was best for myself and my courtship." What right did Joseph have to comment on his and Katie's relationship?

"I hate to say it, Tavish, but I think Joseph may have the right of it."

That was not at all what he needed to hear. Tavish sat on a chair near his da's. He forced himself to say out loud what he'd only permitted himself to think. "I believe Joseph may be courting her."

"There's no 'may be' about it, son. There has long been a fondness in Joseph's eyes when he speaks of her."

"I've noticed that myself." But that hint of fondness had grown into something more of late. "I can't like the idea of being set up to compete with Joseph Archer. He has every advantage."

"Is that so?" Da scratched his chin and gave him a look of deepest pondering. "Here I was thinking *you* had the advantage of being the first to court her, of sharing a heritage with her. And I could have sworn *you* had always had an easy way with women, a handsome enough face to turn heads wherever you go, and a personality one can't help but grow fond of. And, fool that I am, I believed *you* were the one to whom she'd first opened her past and her heart."

"Then why is it, Da, I can't shake off the worry that I might be losing her?"

Da's expression turned empathetic. "Likely because you lost Bridget and you know how it feels when someone you love slips away. That's a fear that, once learned, never entirely leaves us."

An ache gnawed in his heart at the reminder of the tender woman

Bridget Claire had been and how deeply he'd loved her. He didn't allow himself to think of her often. Poor Bridget. She'd been so young. They both had been.

"A sweet, sweet lass," Da said.

Tavish pushed out a deep sigh of regret. "Aye, that she was."

"I was speaking of Katie, actually. But, yes, Bridget was a dear." Da's expression softened. "I will say this for you, my boy. You do know how to choose well for yourself."

Tavish rubbed at the pulsing pain between his eyes. "How do I make certain Katie chooses *me* for herself?"

"There are no guarantees in love, Tavish. You be who you are, and you love her the best you can. If you're what she needs most, she'll choose you."

There *were* no guarantees in love or in life. Tavish knew that well. But he'd learned long ago that giving up never solved anything.

Mornings came far too early during harvest. For weeks, they'd all been in the fields day after day, cutting and bundling grain, hauling it around by the wagonful, praying for the dry weather to continue. Long days of backbreaking labor, followed by minimal amounts of sleep, took its toll quickly.

Tavish hadn't slept well that night in particular. Katie still weighed on his mind too much for rest. Though Da had insisted he need only be himself to make his case, he felt a greater urgency than that. He wanted her to see what she meant to him. He intended to purchase the lumber he needed to build a proper bedroom onto his one-room house. Katie had told him she'd always longed for a room of her own, and he meant to give her one. While he built it, he'd put more effort into turning Katie's heart fully in his direction. Once he had that, he'd ask her to marry him.

Tavish pulled on his overcoat and stepped out into the crisp morning.

He pushed open the door of his barn. He'd become quite adept over the years at hitching up his horse in the dimness of an early-morning barn. Even with questions heavy on his mind, he went through the motions with hardly a thought. He pulled the bridle off its hook and opened the stall door.

His horse was not inside. How had he not noticed that? Apparently worrying about Katie was turning him just a touch daft.

Perhaps more than a touch. Looking about, he could see his cow was gone as well. He'd not even noticed how very silent the barn was. But where had the animals gone? They weren't wandering about. The barn door had been closed. In his experience, livestock didn't close the door behind themselves.

He stepped outside once more, looking out over the brightening horizon. Where were his animals?

"Ériu." His horse could generally be counted on to nicker in response to her name, provided she was near enough to hear it. There was nothing but silence.

He wandered out to the road, hoping to see some sign of his animals. Nothing. Perhaps they'd gone in search of water. He would look down at the river first, then try the lake at the back of his property. If he didn't find them there, he had no idea where to search next. The animals had never gotten loose before, except a few weeks earlier when the Red Road cut Ériu's tail and set her to run wild in her panic.

Tavish stopped in the middle of the road, an uneasy thought settling in his mind. His horse had never slipped out before except as part of the Red Road's mischief, and the animal was out now. It was not at all unreasonable to wonder if the Reds were behind this as well.

As he walked down the road in the direction of the bridge, he kept an eye out in both directions. He didn't spot his animals, but saw several of his neighbors out and about. Harvest had the entire area up early. The morning air nipped at him, even through his jacket. Soon enough he'd need his heavier coat.

He whistled "When a Man's in Love" as he walked along. 'Twas the song most often in his head of late.

"You've a fine whistle, Tavish O'Connor."

The sound of Katie's voice floating on the brisk dawn air tugged him in all different directions. She was up early, likely on her way to the mercantile. She began her hours there before the shop even opened. Perhaps he could walk with her.

She kept to her spot as he approached, watching him with that half-smile of hers that always made him ponder just what it would take to bring it fully into blossom.

"You look cold, Sweet Katie," he said as he came closer.

"The mornings here in this town of yours are right frigid, I'm discovering."

"Oh, darling." He shook his head, trying not to laugh. "We've not even reached autumn."

Dread filled her expression. "I don't like to be cold." She shuddered as if an arctic wind were beating against her.

Tavish simply pulled her into his warming embrace. Saints, she was cold to the touch.

"How long have you been standing out here, love?" He rubbed her arms and back, hoping to drive away some of the chill.

"Mr. O'Donaghue's trying to find his horses and cow. I've been looking about Granny's place for them."

He set her away from him enough to look her in the face, while still rubbing her cold arms. "O'Donaghue's animals have gone missing too?"

"*Too?* Are you missing animals? I mean other than all the chickens that disappeared a few days back."

Tavish nodded. "And I suspect O'Donaghue and I aren't the only ones."

"This is Red Road mischief, then?"

"As always. I think I'd best check at Ciara and Keefe's." He motioned his head in the direction of his sister's home. "D'you want to walk up with me?"

She didn't hesitate. "Certainly."

He wrapped an arm about her waist. Heavens, she felt good right there beside him. The distance he'd worried was growing between them felt far narrower just then.

"Biddy tells me you'll be gone for a full month making your deliveries." She leaned a bit against him as they walked.

"Aye." He'd never before dreaded making his deliveries. In the past he'd found the endeavor rewarding, the fulfillment of all his work and planning. But, one day out from his annual trip, the miles ahead of him felt long and lonely. "Of course, if the entire Irish Road spends the day trying to find our animals instead of finishing the last of our preparations for the journey, we may not be leaving in the morning after all."

"I hadn't thought of that."

He'd be willing to wager every cent he'd make on that year's crop that the Red Road had most certainly "thought of that."

"My guess is whoever took it upon themselves to sneak about our barns and let the animals out did so late into the night. The animals could have been wandering for hours. It's possible some of them won't ever be found."

"What a terrible thing to do."

The Reds had done it before. Ian had lost a fine milk cow a few winters back. 'Twas a hard thing for a family with wee ones to be without milk all winter, but there hadn't been time to replace the animal before the snows had come.

"Every man, woman, and child down the Irish Road'll be wearing their shoes thin today rounding up animals." Tavish shook his head in frustration. "An entire day's work lost, most likely. And the Reds'll be preparing for their journey completely at their leisure."

They'd reached Ciara's house. Keefe stood at the barn doors, hat in his hands, a look of boiling anger on his face.

"Yours as well?" Keefe asked.

Tavish gave a quick nod.

Keefe slapped his hat against his thigh, muttering a few words in Gaelic that would have earned Tavish a lashing from Da when he was younger.

"How well do you remember your Gaelic, Katie?" Tavish asked.

In perfect, almost poetic Irish, Katie told him she remembered quite well.

To hear the old tongue in her dear voice brought such a flood of memory. He missed home in that moment. "When I get back from the harvest run, I think we should have an Irish Day."

He loved that she looked curious. "What is an Irish Day?"

"I am so pleased you asked. We'll spend a day being as Irish as the two of us can manage. Irish food. Irish tunes. And speaking only the proud and beautiful Irish language."

She smiled. "I left Ireland only two years ago, Tavish, and I served on a very Irish staff there. I spoke Gaelic every day until I came to America. I'm not sure *your* Irish is up to the challenge."

Even if he made a fool of himself, he'd enjoy that day. "I look forward to finding out."

"Perhaps for now we should look about for some missing animals," Katie reminded him.

Yes. The matter at hand. To his brother-in-law, he said, "We're likely looking for Ian's animals as well as our own."

Keefe stuffed his hat on his head. "I'll follow the river north. The two of you can follow it south."

A good plan. Tavish turned about, intending to make his way to the bridge to begin the search. Katie kept up with his quick pace without speaking a word.

They reached the bridge. Tavish turned south. Katie caught his arm.

"I can't stay and help," she said. "I've got to get to work. I'm nearly late as it is."

"I hate that you work for Johnson, Katie."

She gave him such a look. "Do not scold me, Tavish."

"I wasn't scolding." He squeezed her hand. "I only worry, is all."

"No one will starve this winter, Tavish. That is the most important thing. No one will be hungry."

He cupped his hand under her chin. "You are a good woman, Katie Macauley."

She blushed a little, smiled a little. "Thank you."

Thank you. Leave it to Katie to thank him for simply telling her the truth.

"I do need to go." She at least looked reluctant. "No use giving Mr. Johnson a real reason to fire me." Her eyes darted between Tavish and the bridge and the Irish Road stretching out long and far. "I wish I could stay here instead."

"I wish you could as well." For quite a few reasons. Staying meant she would avoid Mr. Johnson's poisonous barbs. Staying meant they'd have time together. He summoned a smile, not wanting her to leave thinking he was put out with her. "Go quickly so you're not late."

Katie slipped away before he could say anything else. He stood on the spot where she'd left him, watching her go. Katie paused halfway over the bridge, turning back to wave at him.

He gave her a wave and smile in return. She wrapped her shawl more closely around her shoulders.

I should have given her my jacket to wear. Next time.

Just the thought of "next time" brought a smile to his face. The few moments they'd spent together that morning had returned the smile to her face and restored a connection between them that he had feared was slipping away.

Chapter Fifteen

Joseph could sense the tension as he drove his buggy down the Irish Road. No one in Hope Springs was unaware of the chaos reigning on both sides of town. The morning before, all the Irish had woken to find their animals missing. That morning, every single horse on the Red Road had mysteriously lost their shoes overnight. The Red Road, instead of leaving to take their grain to the depot, had spent hours lined up at the blacksmith shop, having their horses shod.

Seamus Kelly, to his credit, hadn't raised his prices—he'd done that in the past during crises—but he'd certainly made a pretty penny off the suspicious circumstances.

The Irish had spent the day catching up on the work they'd missed doing the day before while chasing down their livestock. The two groups would be leaving the same day after all. Years ago they'd decided to take different routes to different depots in order to avoid open warfare on the trail. He hoped everyone would keep to that agreement.

The renewed hostilities had left him with a dilemma. He'd intended to leave the girls with Mrs. O'Connor while he was gone, but doing so would likely be seen as taking sides with the Irish. Leaving the girls with the Kesters would look like siding with the Reds. He absolutely could not leave them on their own, and he couldn't take them with him.

His only hope was Katie. She lived among the Irish, but worked, once more, off the Irish Road. She was as close to a neutral choice as he was likely to find. And he trusted her without reservation.

Why, then, he wondered, standing at Mrs. Claire's front door, shifting his hat nervously around in his hands, was he so afraid she would say no? He'd brought the girls with him as an added bit of convincing. They had Katie wrapped around their adorable little fingers, whether or not she realized it.

Mrs. Claire peeked through her window. She had a smile for Joseph and a wave of invitation to come inside.

"Now, mind your manners," he reminded the girls.

He turned the knob and opened the door. The smell of fresh bread hovered in the air. He had missed that smell. Was there anything that he didn't now associate with Katie? The smell of bread and coffee. Music. The quiet stillness just before dawn when she used to talk to him in the kitchen.

"Is Katie here?" he asked Mrs. Claire, trying to keep himself focused.

"Standing right over there, or aren't your eyes working today?" Mrs. Claire seemed to be laughing at him.

Katie spotted them in the next instant. "Why, girls, have you come to see me at last?"

Emma and Ivy rushed across the small room and threw themselves at Katie, wrapping their arms about her legs. She stroked the top of their heads, smiling down at them.

"What brings you by?"

"Pompah bringed us."

Katie looked up at Joseph.

He pressed ahead. "I've come to talk to you about something."

All the lightness left her eyes. She looked instantly wary. "Have you, now?" Katie turned to address the girls. "I've a plate of fresh rolls on the table just over there. You can each have one if your father agrees."

Joseph gave a quick nod. The girls scampered off.

"What is it you've come to talk to me about? Have I done something wrong?"

He shook his head. "No, nothing like that."

"Truly?" She was clearly unconvinced.

"Do I generally come by to criticize you?"

"Our Katie's had a great many visitors today," Mrs. Claire said from her chair by the window.

Obviously their conversation wasn't as private as Joseph might have liked. "A lot of visitors?" He pieced that together in the next moment. "And *they* have come with criticisms."

Katie pushed out a puff of breath. "'Katie Macauley, you have to march in to town with banners flying or you're no countrywoman of ours.' Or 'Katie Macauley, if you don't act as a spy at the mercantile, you've betrayed us all.' And the Reds come into the mercantile all the day long and help Mr. Johnson point out everything they could possibly say I've done wrong, and he threatens to toss me out. I must apologize at least twenty times every single morning."

Joseph didn't want to add to her burdens. Would she agree to watch the girls out of a sense of obligation? Perhaps if he talked to her more privately, gave her the opportunity to say no if she really needed to without an audience.

"Would you take a little walk with me?" He hadn't been this nervous the first time he'd asked his late wife to ride out with him. Perhaps because he'd known *she* would agree. Nothing was ever that certain with Katie.

She nodded, but without enthusiasm.

"Off with the both of you." Mrs. Claire shooed them away with a wave of her hand. "The girls and I will get on famous without you."

He held the door for Katie. She passed through without a word. Silence was the theme of their walk as the minutes dragged on.

Katie was hurting. He couldn't ask another favor of her.

After a time, she sighed. "Things have grown difficult, Joseph."

"Tell me."

She picked a long blade of wild grass, using it to swipe at the grass growing around her. "I couldn't help the Irish gather up their missing animals because I had to work. The Irish were disappointed in me for that. And Mr. Johnson is mean as a cat that's had its tail stepped on."

He could easily believe that.

"I am growing terribly weary of being called a half-wit simply because I don't know all the fancy words he uses. I am convinced within myself he does that in order to confuse me. He likes having reason to make me feel stupid."

"You know that you aren't, don't you?"

She rubbed her arms through her shawl and gave a half shrug. "He makes me feel . . . small."

He pulled off his jacket and set it around her shoulders. She pulled it tight around her. They walked on for a while. Joseph didn't know quite what to say. He wouldn't tell her she had no reason to feel the way she did; Johnson was trying to make her feel stupid and unimportant. That was one of Katie's particularly tender topics, so arguing that she was one of the sharper people he knew would likely seem to her like empty flattery.

"I should start dropping in Gaelic words once in a while when I talk to him. Then *he* would be the one who didn't know the words being said to him."

There was the resilient Katie he knew.

"You make a very good point, Katie. He can say all he wants about your intelligence, but he can't argue with the fact that you speak two languages while he knows only the one."

"Hmm." Her steps slowed a bit. After a moment she looked at him again. Her lips turned up a little until she fully smiled. "Now, isn't that a fine discovery. I know something he doesn't."

"Not just *something.* An entire language."

She laughed. "Maybe that is why he doesn't want me to use any Irish words, because it makes *him* feel stupid."

Katie slipped her arms into the jacket sleeves. She looked adorable, so undersized for his coat. And she was smiling again. He'd longed to see that smile every day since she'd left.

She set her fingers in his, though they only just poked out of the jacket sleeve. She had reached for his hand. He adjusted their hands enough to hold hers properly. She didn't pull back, didn't object.

He'd been wondering for some time if he ought to try to win her affection. He had debated with himself, arguing that she had chosen Tavish, counterarguing that letting his feelings be known wouldn't be a bad thing. But that moment, walking alone with her, hand in hand, he knew he couldn't simply walk away.

"I wish you would come visit more often, Joseph Archer."

He intended to. But right then, he had particular business to attend to.

"I've come for more than a visit," he confessed. "I've come to ask a favor."

"What is it?"

"I need someone to look after the girls while I'm taking my crop to market. The girls love you and have missed you a great deal since you left. I know they would jump at the opportunity to spend a few days with you again."

"I'm not qualified to look after children, Joseph. You know what happened to my sister, and you know it was my fault."

"Katie." He gave her a stern look. "What I know is that it wasn't your fault, only that you blame yourself for it. And I further know that you can be trusted despite your misgivings. And I do trust you, enough to have no qualms about leaving the two most precious things in my life to your care—if you are willing to look after them. I have full faith in you, Katie."

He watched her take a deep breath. She gave a quick nod. "Well, I do speak two languages, you know."

Joseph squeezed her fingers, smiling at her humor. Her history haunted her, and it pained him to see her still hurting. That she was trying to keep her optimism through it all was commendable. "You plan to end every sentence with that from now on, don't you? 'Why, yes, I do make very good sweet rolls, and I speak two languages as well.'"

Katie laughed, swinging their arms between them. "I'll need to ask Granny Claire if she can keep an eye on the girls while I'm working at the mercantile."

That difficulty had occurred to him, but true to form, Katie had tackled the problem head-on.

"Emma will be in school many of those days," Joseph pointed out. "That should relieve some of the burden."

"Oh, the girls are never burdensome. The children in the first house I worked in were positively demons compared to Ivy and Emma. Demons, Joseph."

He smiled at her forceful tone. "I am relieved my angels have proven themselves better than their predecessors."

"Vastly better."

They turned back in the direction of Mrs. Claire's house.

"Now are you certain," she asked, "the Red Road won't take exception to your girls staying down this road while you're gone?"

"They will a bit," he admitted. "But oddly enough, the fact that you work at the mercantile seems to make the Reds find you less threatening."

Katie looked equal parts annoyed and frustrated. "Probably because they have seen for themselves how firmly I am under Mr. Johnson's thumb while I'm there. A caged enemy is hardly a dangerous one."

"I don't know about that, Katie. Cage any creature long enough and it will fight back."

Katie shook her head. "Either fight back or curl up and die."

"Don't you dare curl up and die."

His vehemence clearly surprised her. Indeed, it surprised *him.* He tried to cover his outburst with a shrug and a half smile. But there was no explaining away the thread of panic woven into his words at the thought of Katie and all her fire and determination dying under the weight of Hope Springs' hatred.

"I don't intend to give up, Joseph Archer. Complain a great deal, certainly—especially when you're so willing to listen—but I'll not give my troubles the satisfaction of beating me."

That's my Katie.

By the growing look of surprise on Katie's face, he'd said the words out loud. Her surprise turned to a blush. That was encouraging.

The visit was a quick one. Katie returned Joseph's jacket, kissed the girls good-bye, and with a smile acknowledged she would see them all in the morning. He would have Katie's company twice in only a few hours. Joseph could easily grow accustomed to that.

Ivy was still half asleep, but Joseph needed to be on his way and couldn't wait for a later hour. So he'd arrived at Katie's door before sunrise, with Ivy heavy in his arms and Emma only slightly more awake beside him.

Katie let them in with her usual command of any task, despite the early hour.

"I'll just lay this sweet one down on my bed." She took Ivy out of his arms.

"Thank you." Though he wanted to bid his tiny girl farewell before he left, he knew Ivy would be impossible the rest of the day if she didn't get the sleep she needed.

Emma clung to his hand, looking about uncertainly. "Why can't we sleep in our own house, Papa?"

"Because that would inconvenience Katie. She needs to keep close to Mrs. Claire. And all her baking things are here."

Emma nodded in understanding, though her brows still turned down with worry.

"You'll enjoy being with Katie again," he reminded her. "I would guess she'll play her violin for you—I know how much you've missed that." They all had.

"Why can't I go with you, Papa?" Emma looked up at him, a threat of tears in her eyes. "I could help. I am a very hard worker."

Joseph pulled her up against his side. "You *are* a very hard worker, dear. But you need to be in school." That argument would likely sting less than a reminder that she was far too small for a trip to the grain markets. "And Katie will need your help with Ivy."

"I don't want to be left behind." That had been Emma's constant worry for too many years. She wanted to go everywhere he did, needed reassurance that when they were apart, he would return.

"I'll come back in a little more than a week," he reminded her. "Sooner, if things go really well. And I'll bring you back something as I always do. Plus I'll have our new housekeeper with me, so you won't be eating burnt toast and runny eggs in a messy kitchen every single day any longer."

That earned him the tiniest, most fleeting of smiles. "Will she be nice, Papa?"

"The new housekeeper?"

Emma nodded.

"I am sure she will be." *She had better be.*

Katie emerged from the hallway, her arms now empty. The house was quiet with both Ivy and Mrs. Claire sleeping and night not yet entirely fled outside.

Emma's grip on his hand tightened. "You promise you will come back?"

"I give you my solemn word." He tried to convey with a look just how sincere he was, but she still looked worried.

Joseph tried very hard not to think ill of his late wife, but at this time each year he found himself cursing her in frustration. She had planted these fears in Emma. She had cruelly taught Emma to expect abandonment.

"I always come back, Emma." *He* always had.

"But you always leave too. You always leave me here."

Katie came and stood beside him, standing so close he could smell the flowery scent that had once filled his home while she lived there. He'd missed that about her as well. He'd missed everything.

She motioned him over to the side. Emma stayed where she was, a look of forlorn grief on her face. What was he going to do? He couldn't break the girl's heart again.

"Why is she so upset?" Katie asked. "Other than missing you, of course. It seems more than that."

"She doesn't want to be left behind."

"Because she'll miss you? Or she'll worry about you?"

He shook his head. "Because her mother left her behind."

Katie laid her hand gently on his arm. "When she died?"

If only it were that. "No." He dropped his voice to the smallest of whispers. "Not long after Ivy was born, Vivian decided she'd had enough of Hope Springs and Wyoming and farming, and she ran off with a cowhand from one of the ranches here in the valley."

"Merciful heavens."

"It wasn't a 'romantic' connection. She simply wanted to return to Baltimore, and she offered him a small fortune if he would help her get there." He hadn't confessed this to anyone but Ian. How was Katie pulling this from him with nothing more than an empathetic look? "She took all her clothes and prized belongings and Ivy, and she left."

"Wait. She took Ivy?"

Joseph sighed. "Yes. Ivy—and not Emma. Poor Emma didn't understand the reasons her mother left; she only remembers that she was left behind."

Katie said something in Gaelic. From the tone and inflection, it was not a flattering reflection on Vivian's actions.

"My thoughts exactly," he muttered.

"How could any woman do that to her child?"

"I tracked Vivian down and brought her back, but she died of the fever not long after. There was no time for Emma to feel secure again."

Katie glanced briefly in Emma's direction. She pulled Joseph a single step down the hallway.

"I have a suggestion."

"For Emma?"

"For the both of you."

"What do you have in mind?" He'd listen to any suggestion Katie had.

They took another step away from Emma—not far enough to cause the girl alarm.

"The poor dear is worried out of all reason that you're not coming back for her. That is a fear I know all too well." A flash of pain crossed Katie's face. "I know what it is to watch my father leave me behind. But he never looked back; he never returned."

He took her hand. The stories she'd told him of her past returned with force to his mind. She'd known too much heartache in her life.

"The thing that pulled me through those days was having my father's fiddle," she said. "'Twas a part of him I had with me to touch and to hold. So long as I had something of his, he didn't feel completely lost to me."

Her suggestion became instantly clear. He needed to give Emma something of his to cling to while he was away. "That is a brilliant idea."

He stepped around her and knelt in front of Emma. He pulled from his jacket his pocket watch. "I need you to look after something for me, Emma. Do you think you could?"

She nodded, some curiosity sneaking into her worried expression. He set the watch in her hand and wrapped her fingers around it.

"I need you to keep this for me, hold on to it until I return." He gave her a most serious look. "I know you'll take very good care of it."

"Oh, I will, Papa." Her grip on the watch tightened. "I won't lose it or anything. I'll still have it when you get back."

He leaned in very close and whispered, "I will always come back, Emma. Always."

Emma pressed the watch to her heart. He ran a hand along her still-messy hair.

"Pompah, this isn't our house." Ivy tottered in from the hall, one eye closed, the other heavy with sleep. She rubbed a fist against the eye she hadn't opened. "This is Mrs. Claire's house."

Joseph looked up at Katie from his position kneeling in front of Emma. "She will be difficult today if she's tired."

"She will be fine." Katie spoke with a confidence that contrasted sharply with her full-bodied uncertainty the first day she met the girls. "Let her have a good-bye."

He had to drop his gaze away from her beautiful brown eyes. She distracted and tortured him, and she had no idea.

Katie knelt beside Ivy, wrapping a protective arm around her. Ivy leaned her head on Katie's shoulder. Emma wandered to Katie's side, her gaze continually dropping to his watch.

There they were, side by side, the three people in all the world he would miss more than anyone else over the next week. A quick good-bye seemed best. Ivy would be too sleepy for protests. Emma had found some solace in keeping his watch with her—the tears that hovered in her eyes seemed to have dried. And Katie was there beside them both. She would offer them the comfort they needed.

"Good-bye, sweet girls." Reminding himself to be quick and on his way, he pressed kisses to their cheeks. "And thank you, Katie."

She nodded. He flattered himself that she looked sad to see him go.

He stood and stepped out. Emma and Ivy gathered in the doorway, with Katie right beside them. Joseph made his way up the walk.

Still within sight, he turned back one more time, wanting a last look at his girls before he left. They waved. He waved as well, and set himself firmly back on the path.

He'd only gone a step or two when the sound of swishing fabric and quick footsteps stopped him. He turned back. Katie reached him and, without warning, threw her arms around his neck.

His heart lodged in his throat, pounding painfully. His mind couldn't settle on a single thought, couldn't focus on anything except Katie, in his arms, embracing him.

He stood a moment, too shocked to move an inch. But she didn't pull away. He slowly wrapped his arms around her, fully expecting her to object. She didn't. He wasn't complaining; he was only very, very confused.

He somehow managed to find his voice. "What has brought this on, Katie?" Whatever it was, he'd make certain to do it again and again.

She pulled away enough to look into his face. He kept his arms close about her.

"You looked back." Her voice quivered a bit. "The girls were standing there, missing you already, and you looked back."

She'd tossed herself into his arms because he'd glanced back over his shoulder? But the answer came in the next moment. *Her* father had left her, never intending to return. And he hadn't so much as looked back at her one last time.

Joseph rubbed her back, remembering with clarity the heartache in her eyes when she'd first told him of being left behind. How long had she been waiting for someone to regret leaving her? The painful longing lingered in her eyes.

He let his mind memorize the moment. Loving her was sometimes a physically painful thing—it too often felt pointless.

"Thank you, again," he said, "for watching the girls while I'm gone."

She smiled at him, and his heart cracked that much more.

"Have a safe journey, Joseph Archer," she said. "Come back to us whole."

He lightly touched her face. He couldn't help himself. Color touched her cheeks, but she didn't flinch.

"I'll see you in about a week," he said.

She gave a small nod. Her eyes never left his face. He thought he saw a question there, but he couldn't be sure.

He stepped back. She dropped her gaze. An odd tension pulled between them, an awkwardness that was not usually there.

A week. In another week he could begin making his case in earnest. Maybe, just maybe, he would be permitted to hold Katie Macauley in his arms again.

Chapter Sixteen

Katie was a mess.

She'd bid Tavish farewell, his good humor turning what would have otherwise been a painful departure into a morning of smiles and laughter. Even the girls, still longing for their father, had giggled a great deal. Tavish brought joy everywhere he went. She missed that about him when he was away, and he was often away.

Why, then, in the two days since the men had left to take their crop to market, had her thoughts turned as often to Joseph as to Tavish? What kind of woman had a heart so fickle it felt pulled by two men at the same time? Tavish had been willing to give up so much for her. He had touched her heart, and that heart, she'd firmly believed, had chosen him. So why was there suddenly room in her thoughts and longings for Joseph?

There had been a time not long before when she'd admitted to growing feelings for both men, but she thought she'd put that confusion behind her.

What was she to do?

"Quit daydreaming and get back to work," Mr. Johnson snapped.

Katie jumped at the interruption.

"Lazy foreigners," Mr. Johnson muttered.

She quickly set back to sweeping the floor. Wind had driven dust in under the door the day before. Katie had been at work two hours and had done nothing but dust off tables, counters, baskets. She'd only just turned her attention to the floors. Two hours of working dirt out of the narrowest grooves of the furniture and still she was labeled lazy.

But I can speak two languages. That had been her silent response to all Mr. Johnson's complaints lately. It never failed to calm her mind and set her at peace again. She found she could even smile.

Katie passed the tidy display of ankle boots. She'd taken to brushing her fingers along the leather upper-soles, letting herself dream for the most fleeting of moments that she could afford to buy herself a fine pair of new shoes.

"Don't even think about stealing them."

She looked back at her employer. "Stealing them? The shoes?"

"Did I say you could talk?"

Katie managed not to roll her eyes as she turned back to her work. He'd been very particular the last few days about her not speaking. The man was even more grumpy than usual of late.

"I'm making you shake out your shawl before you go," Mr. Johnson said. "I can only guess how many things you're planning to sneak off with."

Katie didn't comment. Didn't defend herself despite the unfairness of the accusation. Ignoring Mr. Johnson and focusing on her work had seen her through many difficult mornings at the mercantile. It'd do again.

Marykate Kelly stopped to talk to her on her way home from the mercantile that day, thanking her for all she had done for the Irish. Katie had not had many conversations with Seamus's wife, finding her a touch too embittered by the feud and their difficulties.

"'Tis more than merely keeping prices down," Mrs. Kelly said. "Mr. Johnson is . . . well, not exactly friendly, but he seems easier to deal with."

"I don't know that I can take credit for that." She'd not really noticed such a change, but hoped it was there just the same.

"Well, I cannot deny you've done something." For the first time since Katie had known the woman, Mrs. Kelly's expression lightened, as if the tiniest glimmer of hope was beginning to break through years of darkness. "Mr. Johnson's changed a bit. More than that, even, the Irish are doing better."

"Because of the prices?" They walked side by side down the Irish Road.

Mrs. Kelly half shook her head, half nodded. "You've given them reason to keep fighting. For the first time in memory, we're not losing this battle."

Those words stayed with her through the frustrations of working at the mercantile. Keeping in mind the difference she was making helped her survive. She put on a brave face every day before returning home. The girls didn't need to know of her troubles. They were doing well, considering they still missed their father. Katie had warm biscuits ready for Emma when she reached the house after school each day; she walked to and from with Michael O'Connor and a few of the other Irish children.

The fifth morning after the men in town had left, Katie stood on the mercantile's porch, sweeping. She paused in her work, watching Emma in front of the school. The children were playing. Some were skipping rope or chasing each other around the yard. Emma was walking about with little Marianne Johnson, Mr. and Mrs. Johnson's eight-year-old daughter.

Marianne had shown herself a sweet-hearted girl. She offered a "hello" whenever their paths crossed, though she immediately clamped her mouth shut and sent a nervous look in her father's direction. Clearly the little one had been warned against being friendly to the unwanted Irishwoman.

Katie had liked Marianne from the first time the child had smiled at her. There was something in the friendly greeting that was purely natural, untainted by the hatred around her. But to see that Marianne was a friend of Emma's solidified her good opinion. Being blessed with a friend to walk about the schoolyard with and a sister who played with her at home and a father as loving and kind as Joseph, Emma would never be as alone in the world as Katie had always been.

She smiled, watching the girls chatter as they made a wide circuit of the schoolyard. If Marianne's parents weren't so set against the Irish, Katie would have eagerly extended an invitation for Marianne to come home with Emma so the girls could spend the afternoon together. But the Johnsons would never allow their daughter to set a single foot on the Irish Road.

"Standing around again?" Mr. Johnson stood in the doorway, leaning against the frame. He pointed a finger, jabbing it in her general direction with each word. "Lazy, every last one of y'all."

Katie knew the rest of the complaint and said the words silently in her head, perfectly timed with his declaration.

"Lazy, no-good foreigners."

He took a step out onto the porch. His gait swayed oddly. Was he unwell?

"I won't take pity on your sniveling friends in exchange for you standing around all day doing nothing." The words, slow and oddly toned, melted together a bit. "Is that clear, Paddy?"

Looking at his watery, red eyes and swaying posture, and noticing the unfortunate smell of him, something became even clearer than his threats. The man was drunk.

Katie had never seen him drink so much as a drop of spirits while working. He'd always been perfectly in control, entirely sober.

"'Tis quite clear, sir." She watched him closely, confused by the change in him.

"Don't say *'tis*." His words pulled and lisped awkwardly.

She kept quiet and nodded.

He stumbled back inside.

Blazing drunk, he is.

Though she had no high opinion of the man, seeing him walloped had her worried for him. A man of business wouldn't risk being full drunk while open to customers. He was too responsible for such a thing.

Katie took up her broom once more, but her thoughts continually drifted inside. Was she working for a drunkard after all? She'd known a few people over the years who loved their liquor too much. Some became violent, others overly sad. What kind of drunk would he be? What if he made drinking a habit and proved himself a dangerous person to be around?

Placing herself in harm's way day after day would be a steep price to pay for her neighbors' well-being. Yet she couldn't turn her back on their needs.

You're getting quite far ahead of yourself there, Katie. No use greeting the devil 'til he's knocking on your door.

Down the road, the school bell rang. Reverend Ford stood on the step outside the school building where church was held on Sundays. All the children made their way inside, some very slowly and reluctantly.

Katie watched Emma, smiling to herself as she did. Emma moved with more enthusiasm than most of the other children. She enjoyed school. She'd told Katie as much every day.

The preacher brought the children in from their lunchtime play at precisely the hour Katie's time at the mercantile ended. She carried her broom inside, ready to make her way back to Granny's house.

The shop was very quiet. Usually Mr. Johnson was moving about. Often he had a few choice words for her within moments of her arrival into his line of sight.

Nothing. He wasn't even agonizing over his ledgers as he so often did. Perhaps she could just slip out without enduring his usual end-of-day lecture about all the ways in which she fell short of his expectations. 'Twould be a fine change from the usual.

Katie stepped lightly toward the storage room. If she didn't make much noise, Mr. Johnson might not realize she was leaving. She set the broom in the storage room, then turned to tiptoe out of the mercantile.

But she caught sight of Mr. Johnson sitting on the floor behind the counter.

"Have you misplaced something, sir?"

He didn't seem to be looking for anything, only sitting, his back to the cupboards, his head dropped into his hands.

"Leave me be, you filthy Paddy."

A fine "thank you for your concern" that was. He sounded even more drunk than he did ungrateful. Perhaps it was the hard drink that had him sitting on the floor like a beggarman.

And he accuses the Irish of being drunken layabouts.

Katie shook her head at the ridiculousness of it all. She'd leave Mr. Johnson to his pitiful state.

She looked one last time at him, committing his position to memory so she'd have something to think back on when he was insulting and belittling her. Remembering this moment would do wonders for her pride.

There was something dark on his hand cupping his head. She looked a little closer.

Good heavens. It looks like blood.

Katie knelt near enough to him to get a better look. It was blood indeed.

"Sir? Have you hurt yourself?"

"Get away from me," he growled, swatting gracelessly in her general direction with his clean hand.

"You have blood running out your fingers, Mr. Johnson." It wasn't exactly a flood of bleeding but enough to be worrisome. "Have you cut your hand?"

"You—" He pointed a finger in her direction, though it wove around quite a bit. "You left something out. You left it out, and I tripped on it. It's your fault."

Absolutely nothing was lying about on the floor other than him. He more likely than not had tripped over his own drunken feet. Wasn't that just like a Red in Hope Springs—aye, like so many in America who were determined to blame their every problem on the immigrants from Ireland?

"I'll just leave you to your bleeding and drinking, then," she said and stood up. "A fine combination, that."

Katie set her chin at a proud angle and pulled back her shoulders. For once she was not the one at a disadvantage. The man was likely too soaked to remember the moment come morning, but she'd enjoy it while it lasted.

"Miserable foreigners, all of you." He pulled his blood-covered hand from his face for the first time, shaking his fist at her.

Katie felt her eyes widen in shock. A wide, gaping cut marred his forehead, blood trickling from it. The man was truly hurt, and it appeared to be no small thing. She snatched a rag from the basket where she kept the clean ones.

"Sir." She retook her position, kneeling on the floor in front of him. "Press this to your wound, sir."

Either he was in a great deal of pain or he'd rattled his brain, because he obeyed her instructions without comment. Katie took a good look at his state. She wasn't at all easy with what she saw. He'd clearly been bleeding a lot, the front of his shirt splattered by it, his hand and arm covered in trickles. His coloring was pale to the point of worry. He had most likely hit his head on the countertop, an unforgiving and thick bit of solid wood. It would have dealt him a severe blow indeed. Perhaps it was not only the alcohol slurring his words and wreaking havoc on his movements.

Blood hadn't yet seeped through the rag, a good sign he wasn't about to bleed to death there on the floor. Still, she'd seen the cut and knew it was nothing to be ignored.

"I'll be back directly, sir."

He muttered words she couldn't make out.

She moved swiftly to the door that connected the shop to the Johnsons' home behind the mercantile. Mr. Johnson needed care, but Katie couldn't be certain her assistance would be welcomed. She couldn't simply leave him there.

"Mrs. Johnson, ma'am?" she called out. "Mrs. Johnson?"

She looked back at her employer. He still sat with his back against the cupboards, rag pressed to his bleeding head.

"Mrs. Johnson?" she tried again, louder.

The woman, moving slow with the weight of her wee one growing inside, stepped into the sitting room from the room beyond. "What is it?" Hers was not a patient expression.

"Your husband's fallen, ma'am. His head's bleeding a great deal, and I'm worried for him."

She'd not finished her explanation before Mrs. Johnson rushed toward the shop. Katie followed close on her heels.

Mrs. Johnson gasped, her hand pressed to her heart. "Dear heavens. All that blood."

It was an alarming sight now that Katie truly looked. Why was it wounds on the head always bled so very much?

"Jeremiah." Mrs. Johnson sat next to him. "Let me see your head."

She pulled back her husband's hand. The underside of the rag had turned a bright red. Mr. Johnson's wound looked worse than it had before.

Mrs. Johnson's eyes fluttered shut a moment. She made the tiniest of whimpering moans.

"Ma'am, are you unwell?"

She shook her head. "Blood tends to make my head spin a bit, is all."

"Do you need smelling salts? I know where they are."

"No. I'll be fine."

Katie looked closely at Mr. Johnson's cut. He glared at her, but she ignored it. His wife wasn't holding up and he needed attention. She was all he had.

The cut was quite wide. "This may need stitching up."

Mrs. Johnson's whimper was her only answer.

Katie fetched a new rag and traded it for the bloodstained one, instructing Mr. Johnson to press it against his cut again. She scooted across the floor until she was positioned next to Mrs. Johnson. The woman hadn't always been kind to her, but Katie couldn't bear the look of worried pain on her face.

"Mrs. Johnson?"

She looked at her, a reluctant pleading in her eyes. She seemed to know how much she and her husband needed Katie, though she disliked the needing very much indeed.

"I can see to the stitching, if it'd help. But I don't think the floor of the mercantile is the best place for sewing up wounds."

Mrs. Johnson's face cleared. She adopted a look of purpose and rose to her feet. "Let me lock up the shop so we won't have any interruptions."

A moment later, she'd returned.

"Between the two of us," Katie said, "I think we could get him to the house. We'd best set him on a sofa or a bed or wherever would be easiest for you to look after him the rest of the day."

Mrs. Johnson's brows pulled in, her eyes looking off in the distance. "I think the sofa in the sitting room would be best, then I needn't climb the stairs more often than need be."

"That'll do, ma'am."

Mr. Johnson's eyes were scrunched tight. He hadn't lodged a single complaint about Katie talking too much nor insulted her heritage since before his wife arrived. She knew from experience Mrs. Johnson's presence didn't generally make him more civil. She'd wager pain was the silencer this time around.

Together Katie and Mrs. Johnson managed to help him to the sitting room sofa. He was aware and strong enough to keep the rag pressed to his wound as his wife slipped a pillow beneath his head and eased him back.

"Have you a sewing kit?" Katie asked.

Mrs. Johnson fluttered about a bit before pulling herself to her purpose. She retrieved a sewing kit from beside a chair near the front window.

"And a bit of good strong soap?"

Mrs. Johnson nodded and set the sewing kit in Katie's hands. She made her way as quickly as her swollen middle would allow. Katie pulled a tasseled ottoman over next to the sofa and sat.

"Are you planning to poke me with pins?" Mr. Johnson grumbled. "Torture me while I'm already suffering?"

"That, sir, is not the Irish way of doing things." She pulled out a spool of thick black thread and the sharpest needle she could find. "If you'll forgive me for saying so, drinking yourself into a stupor doesn't strike me as *your* way of doing things."

He looked annoyed. "It's been a difficult day," he muttered.

Katie snipped the thread into just the right length for sewing a few knots in the man's forehead. 'Twas an odd task to be preparing for.

"Was the day difficult before you burst your head wide open, or mostly afterwards?" She threaded the needle and set it on the highly polished end table, laying out the other lengths of thread next to it.

Mr. Johnson examined his bloody rag. With a deep and shaky sigh, he pressed it back to his head. Katie could almost feel sorry for the man.

"Today is my brother's birthday." His words were still slurring badly.

And that was reason to get drunk as a wheelbarrow? Perhaps it was a tradition in the South where he came from.

Mrs. Johnson returned with a cake of soap and a fine blue-and-white porcelain washbowl. "I have a teakettle heating on the stove," she said. "I'll fill the bowl just as soon as the water is hot."

Mrs. Johnson glanced uneasily at her husband. Her eyes lingered on his wounded forehead. She took a deep breath in through her nose. "I am sorry. I am not usually this overwhelmed by . . ." She pressed her fingertips to her mouth, even as she laid her other hand on her belly.

Poor woman. She had quite enough to be dealing with just then. "Clean cloths would be quite helpful also," Katie hinted.

Mrs. Johnson gave her a grateful look and quickly left the room.

Into the uncomfortable silence, Katie attempted to undertake a bit of light chatter. "Your brother with the birthday—is he older or younger than you?"

"Gabriel is dead."

'Twas a quick end to a very short conversation, but it did explain a great deal. Tavish had previously told her that Mr. Johnson's brother had died fighting an Irish regiment at Gettysburg; likely the brother he was mourning that day. The pain of his loss was driving him to drink.

Katie had never indulged in liquor. She'd seen too many footmen and stable hands and masters of the house change in terrible ways under the influence of hard drink. But she'd also been told that alcohol numbed the heart and mind. Perhaps Mr. Johnson was grieving too hard to endure it without something to take the sting out.

"I am sorry for that, sir. 'Tis a hard thing to lose a family member."

"And what do you know of it?" he snapped.

"What do *I* know of losing a loved one?" 'Twas such a ridiculous thing she couldn't help staring at him a moment. "You know, Mr. Johnson, if you'd step away from your determination to hate everyone you think's different from you, you just might discover we've a few things in common."

He didn't answer, but lay there, petulant and frowning.

"I had three brothers and a sister myself," Katie said.

He eyed her sidelong. *"Had?"*

"Aye. We'd a famine in Ireland, a Great Hunger. The food we needed ran out and the people starved. My brothers left, one by one, their bellies and their pockets empty. They left in search of work, because, though so many here in America prefer to think otherwise, the Irish are willing, eager even, to work for what we're given, be it food or money or a roof over our heads."

He didn't look at her, but she could tell he was listening. She'd likely never have another opportunity to tell the man how wrong he was about so many of his neighbors.

"I never saw any of my brothers again. Not a single one. They were gone from us forever." The loss still hurt, but she pushed on. "And my wee little sister, so tiny and frail, she starved to death in front of our very eyes. She starved full to death, Mr. Johnson. And still there was not food enough for my parents and me. They found me work and left me, so I lost them as well."

Something that almost looked like sympathy shone a moment in his eyes, though she refused to believe it entirely.

"You ask what I could possibly know about losing someone I love. I assure you, sir, I know that pain well. I know it far too well. I lost every single person I loved. Every one."

Mrs. Johnson returned with a stack of fresh cloths and set them on the table beside the washbowl. "I think the water is probably hot enough," she said and slipped out again.

Katie sat quite still, focusing on her coming task. She'd never sewn together a wound before, though she'd seen it done a few times. Servants didn't warrant the cost of a man of medicine. When they were ill or injured, they physicked each other. 'Twas precisely how her feet had become so terribly deformed. No surgeon had been sent for when frostbite and infection turned her toes black. The blacksmith had undertaken the removal, and he'd done an unsightly job of it.

Now she was preparing herself to act as doctor for a man of means who deeply hated her. She could make her efforts quite painful for him, pulling and tugging more than necessary. She could also make large, inexpert stitches that would do little to pull the wound together. He'd be left with a thick, unsightly scar that would likely not heal quickly. She could do all those things. But she wouldn't. She wouldn't because, no matter how horrible he was to her, no matter how unfairly he treated the Irish in Hope Springs, purposely hurting the man would be wrong.

"Hot water." Mrs. Johnson came in. She poured steaming water into the washbowl, before rushing the kettle back to the kitchen.

Katie set to washing the dried blood from Mr. Johnson's head. She could see he was as uncomfortable with the arrangement as she was. Sworn enemies make awkward sickroom companions.

She took a new cloth, dipped it in the hot water, and rubbed the cake of soap along it. "I'll make my apologies now, sir, for I know quite well this is going to hurt."

He winced as she cleaned the cut itself with her soapy rag. To his credit, he didn't curse at her or swat her hand away. Perhaps he'd make it through the stitching without tears.

Mrs. Johnson returned, hovering about the sofa with a look of complete uncertainty.

"Perhaps," Katie suggested gently, "you might sit here and hold his hand. You needn't look at the wound."

"Would you like that, Jeremiah?" Mrs. Johnson asked hopefully.

"I would, sugar."

Sugar? Katie had never heard the Johnsons use pet names for each other. Knowing they did made them seem . . . sweet.

Mrs. Johnson sat on the edge of the sofa with her husband's hand in hers. 'Twas a loving sight.

Katie finished cleaning the cut as best she could, then set to washing the needle and threads. "Again, sir, I'm sorry for the pain of this."

He gave a quick, silent nod and closed his eyes.

As the needle jabbed his skin, he sucked in a loud breath. Katie pulled it up through the other side of the wound, then tied the thread in as strong a knot as she knew how to make. She washed the needle again and set to rethreading it.

"I'm sorry about your family," Mr. Johnson said.

His words hovered between them a moment. Her mind refused at first to accept them whole. But he'd said them. He'd said them without provocation, without reluctance.

"And I'm sorry about your brother." She made another stitch.

"He was a soldier." Mr. Johnson spoke quietly, his words not entirely steady.

"In the war between your states?" Though she knew the answer, she sensed in him a need to tell the history himself.

He made a noise of agreement. "He fought for the Confederacy, and he died at Gettysburg."

"The O'Connors lost two sons at that same battle." She tied off the stitch, grateful he had some topic to distract him.

Mrs. Johnson sat silent, her eyes firmly fixed on her husband's hand held between her own.

Katie made a third stitch. His wound would likely need two more.

"Gettysburg was a bloody affair," Mr. Johnson said.

"Everything I've heard of that battle purely horrifies me."

Just as she was preparing to begin a fourth stitch, a tiny cry sounded. Was there a child at home? Katie knew the Johnsons had an older son—Joshua, who was seventeen or eighteen years old—and she knew of Marianne and the wee babe not born yet.

Mrs. Johnson's eyes raised to the ceiling before shifting to Katie. "That'll be Thomas waking from his nap. I probably should go get him."

Katie nodded her understanding.

Mrs. Johnson kissed her husband's hand and promised to return quickly.

Katie had only ever thought of them as horrible, hateful people. But they were so sweet and loving just then. 'Twould likely make them harder to dislike.

"Gabriel was a good man," Mr. Johnson said into the silence. "And brave. A better man than I am."

Katie didn't know if the drink or the pain had brought this unusual humility to the surface.

"I know that feeling well. My sister was an angel." She tied off the thread. "Far better than I."

He opened his eyes and met her gaze. Something uncomfortably close to understanding passed between them.

Katie finished her work and cleaned up as best she could, considering she didn't know where to put everything, and suddenly found herself increasingly anxious to be on her way. She was perfectly willing to help Mr. Johnson, but she wasn't at all prepared to feel a kinship with the man.

Mrs. Johnson came in the sitting room after a while with a small boy clutching her skirts. The sleepy-eyed little one could not have been much older than three years old. He looked a great deal like his dark-haired father.

"I'm sorry to leave you a bit of a mess," Katie said, "but I don't know where to put everything."

Mrs. Johnson shook her head. "I can take care of it. Let me walk you to the door."

They'd reached the door to the mercantile when little Thomas spoke. "Why is one of *them* here, Mother?"

One of *them.* Katie knew precisely what the child meant. What was an Irishwoman doing in their home?

"Father hurt himself. Miss Katie was helping him."

He looked confused. "Do they help people?"

Mrs. Johnson looked uncomfortable. She glanced at Katie, face blotchy with embarrassed color. "Yes, Thomas," she finally said. "They do, indeed."

Chapter Seventeen

When two people are predisposed to hate each other, feeling anything resembling a kinship with one another is not at all a comfortable experience. Katie felt absolutely certain that was the reason for the awkwardness between her and Mr. Johnson as the week wore on. He, with light bandaging wrapped around the sewn-up wound on his head, didn't seem quite able to make eye contact with her. He still complained a great deal, but in a muttered voice instead of the ringing tone of confidence he'd been using.

For her part, Katie found doing her very best work about the shop less grating than before. The look of pain on his face as he'd told her of his brother echoed the ache she felt when thinking of her sister.

Circumstances forbade them from actually liking each other. But that brief moment in his sitting room would not allow them to fully hate each other any longer either.

Katie wished Joseph were in town. He had more experience than anyone in dealing with that kind of oddity. He hated the way the town fought, and it often got in the way of friendships he might have had. Yet, he liked the people too much to dislike them entirely. He would understand her dilemma. He would likely even have some advice for her.

She walked down the Irish Road, her large basket hung over one arm. Between working at the mercantile and making daily bread deliveries and seeing to the girls in the evening, she was exhausted. And with Tavish gone and Biddy busy caring for Ian during his recovery, she was also feeling lonely. Mrs. Claire was sweet and kept her company. The girls were a treat as well. But she still longed for something more, for someone else.

A month earlier she'd have known just exactly who that "someone else" was. Now she wasn't entirely sure. She longed for Tavish's laughter and smile. She missed Joseph's friendship, his willingness to hear her troubles and help her solve her problems.

She turned up the walk toward Ian and Biddy's, having saved their loaf for last that day. She needed a good gab with her friend.

Little Mary answered the door.

"Good day to you, Mary. Is your ma about?"

Mary nodded with a gap-toothed grin. She opened the door fully and ushered Katie inside. Ian sat on a chair near the empty fireplace. If the chill in the air were any indication, there'd be a fire burning there soon enough.

"Well, now, Ian," Katie said. "You're looking hale and hearty."

His expression was clearly disbelieving. "I'm pale and sickly yet, and don't I know it. I feel like an utter fool with all the men in town off working and me sitting here on my bum all the day long."

The man needed a bit of cheering. Tavish would have seen to that were he there. Katie thought she'd learned a thing or two from him about how to do the job properly.

"A fool, is it? You ought to be feeling like a rooster, strutting about the town, knowing you're near about the only male in a valley full of hens." Katie made the tiniest show of strutting right there on the spot.

Ian shook his head even as he smiled at her antics. "You've been spending far too much time with Tavish."

"I've done a fine job of mimicking him, have I?" Katie set her nearly empty basket on the floor near the door and crossed to the bench next to Ian's chair. Heavens, the man looked tired.

He leaned back. "Tavish would have been quite proud of that bit of teasing, though he'd have done a great deal more strutting, not stopping until every person was wiping tears of laughter from their eyes."

"Tavish says he prefers tears of laughter to tears of sadness."

Ian nodded. "Aye, but sometimes I don't think he's allowed himself enough of the latter." The conversation had taken a somber tone she hadn't expected. "We saw a lot of death during The Hunger. We saw more of it on the boat over—we were unfortunate enough to find ourselves on board a coffin ship, you see." Ian's expression grew a touch distant. "Tavish was here the day my wee girl died of the fever."

Katie pushed back an unexpected rush of emotion. She could remember so clearly the physical pain in her own parents' faces when their tiny angel had died. She remembered the pain of losing her sister. How much greater that ache must have been for her mother and father.

"Tavish was with his fiancée when she passed—her and her entire family," Ian said. "Those few days were the closest I've seen him to breaking down. He was frantic with worry, but he didn't cry. I stood beside him the day she was buried and saw no tears, though I know for absolute certain his heart was breaking. Even now, five years since the fever, whenever her name is mentioned, he turns the topic away, finding something to laugh about so he doesn't have to think on her. I've known him all of his almost thirty years, and I've never once seen him cry. Not once, though he's had ample reason to."

"Perhaps he's simply not one to show what he's feeling." Katie knew she was very much that way.

Ian's gaze remained focused on the fireplace. "I think, rather, he doesn't allow himself to feel it at all."

'Twasn't the most flattering picture, but not a truly terrible one, either.

"A good evening to you, Katie." Biddy spoke as she stepped inside. "Mary came and said you'd stopped in. I'm pleased to see she was right."

Katie was so happy to see her friend. Too much time had passed between visits.

Biddy gave the small basket she carried to Mary. "Go put the eggs in the cupboard where they belong."

Mary agreed and moved away very carefully.

"Have you time for a gab?" Katie asked.

"I do, indeed." She looked past Katie to where Ian sat. "Do you think you can get along without me for a bit, love?"

"Perhaps for a very little bit." He had a half smile for his wife.

She crossed to him and pressed a loving kiss to his check. That brought his smile to full measure. The small bit of affection between them lit both their faces and brought such peace and tenderness to their eyes. 'Twas the very thing she'd seen pass between the Johnsons.

How long Katie had despaired of ever finding for herself someone who would look at her that way, who would bring that same contented happiness to her own eyes. Now there she was with two men claiming a place in her heart.

A moment later, Katie and Biddy were comfortably situated on the porch.

"How is Ian's recovery coming along?" Katie asked.

Biddy let out a small, tense breath, the tiny sound telling its own story. "Slower than any of us would like, I'm afraid. He grows tired fast. His head aches him at the slightest thing. His body is still bruised. Worst of all, though, his spirits are low."

"He's frustrated by it," Katie said.

"He's been ill before, enough to be laid low for some time. But I've not seen him like this." Biddy pressed her fingertips to her temples. "He has more of a temper—not a violent one, thank the heavens. He's simply more quick to grow upset and less likely to smile or laugh through a difficulty."

Katie reached over and took her hand. "Oh, Biddy."

"I've yet to see that twinkle back in his eye that I love so well. It's as though my sweetheart is just out of reach, as though I can see him but I can't get him to come out and say hello."

The loneliness she saw in her friend's face tore her up inside. "Perhaps 'tis nothing more than the pain and the weariness weighing him down."

Biddy nodded absentmindedly. "I only pray it's not a permanent change in him."

"Have you spoken to anyone about this?" She hated to think Biddy was enduring this heartache alone.

"His parents have noticed the change, but they've no more answers than I do."

"What about Tavish?"

Biddy shook her head. "He'd only laugh and make a joke. I know it's his way of dealing with what's hard, but I don't think I could bear it just now."

Katie squeezed Biddy's hand. "I think you underestimate him. I've told him of difficult things in my life, and he listened without a single jest or laugh."

Biddy allowed a bit of amusement in her eyes, though Katie could see it didn't come easily. "I suppose I've something of a sister's inability to think of her brother in any way but as something of a child. He's grown a lot since you came here, Katie. You've made him a better person."

"Don't set that task on my shoulders," Katie said. "He has a mind of his own, and don't I know it."

The first bits of a true smile began on Biddy's face. "So has he written to you while he's been away? I wager he's thought of you plenty enough."

Katie chuckled. "Tavish knows full well that I can't read a single word. I don't think he'd send me a letter knowing that."

"Aye, and it would be an embarrassing thing to have someone reading his loving words out loud."

"Precisely."

Biddy rocked on her chair, pulling her coat more tightly around herself. "And has Joseph sent word?"

"Joseph?" Katie nearly choked on the name. What sent Biddy's thoughts in that direction?

Biddy actually laughed. Though the sound did Katie good, it also brought a swift rush of heat to her face. "I didn't mean a love letter, though when I think on it, such a thing isn't entirely out of the question."

"Biddy O'Connor, what are you pressing at?"

Biddy only smiled at her. "I asked the question at first only because I know the Archer girls are staying with you and Mrs. Claire. But now that I've set my thoughts in that direction, I begin to wonder if the poor man's thoughts aren't as often on you as they are on his daughters while he's been away."

She realized her mouth hung open and managed to close it.

"Now look there," Biddy said with a great deal too much enjoyment, "I've hit upon something, I have. You've been thinking on Joseph, I'd wager."

"Only because of the girls, like you said. My heart's with Tavish, you know that."

"I know you fancy my handsome brother-in-law, and I approve, I assure you. He's a fine man. But I do recall a certain newly arrived Irishwoman lamenting not two or three months ago that her foolish heart was pulling itself in two different directions."

Katie gave herself a moment to formulate a response. She wanted to sound less confused than she felt. "There was a time—"

"Oh, piddle," Biddy interrupted. "*Was* a time, she says. I know a look of heart-deep confusion when I see it, my dear friend."

"But that would be wrong." Katie let her thoughts spill. She needed someone to share her worries with. "I can't love two men at once, Biddy. What kind of woman would that make me?"

"A very normal one, I'd say." Biddy didn't look like she disapproved of the idea. "They're both fine men, with much to recommend them. They're alike in the ways that matter—men of integrity and kindness, with a very real fondness for you. And they're unalike in ways that make them very different choices for your heart as well. You've every reason to be unsure. And you'd be wise to sort this out *before* you decide on either one of them."

Katie rubbed at her newly aching head. "I've pledged my heart to Tavish. He knows that. Everyone does."

"But is that what you want?"

"Of course." Still, she felt the tiniest bit of doubt. "He was willing to give up his entire life for me. No one's ever done that for me before."

"I'll not argue that he doesn't care for you, nor that he doesn't love you. I know he does."

She nodded at the words of confirmation. "And I love him too, I know I do. And if I do, then I can't love someone else."

"And yet, Joseph's claimed a bit of your heart as well?"

She dropped her face into her upturned hands. What a mess it all was. "He comes by to visit, and my heart jumps about at the sight of him. He's even held my hand a few times. He hugged me when he left town. Actually, I hugged him, but the way he held me . . ." Her heart flipped over at the memory. "I cannot feel this way for two men, Biddy. It doesn't make sense."

"The beginnings of love can be like that, Katie. Give your heart a chance to sort itself out and you will, in time, reach a point where there's no question, no tugging and pulling inside. You'll simply know."

"But Tavish—"

"Tavish deserves to be loved entirely by someone who isn't secretly wondering in her heart if she made the right decision. So does Joseph. Give yourself time to know for sure. If the one you choose is worthy of your heart at all, he'll be there still."

Katie could see the wisdom in it, but she still felt all sorts of a fool for being so confused. "And, of course, there is the very real possibility that I'd throw myself heart and soul into pursuing one or the other of them only to discover I've overestimated the depth of his feelings. I might make an utter fool of myself and break my heart in the process."

Biddy nodded her head. "Love does make a mess of our lives, doesn't it?"

"What am I to do if I can't sort all of this out?"

"Well, then, you come over here and we'll cast lots."

Their laughter rang out around them. Katie felt better for letting that out. If they could laugh at the dilemma her heart had made for her, then perhaps the situation was not as terrible as she feared. Both men would return in the following weeks. She'd simply see how she felt, and she'd pay very close attention.

And with any luck, the answer would be clear in time.

Chapter Eighteen

Housekeepers, Joseph discovered, were not the most predictable sort. His newest one, Mrs. Smith, who had, true to her word, been waiting at the depot, was as different from Katie as seemingly possible. She was at least twice Katie's age, considerably taller and far thicker built. She was also of a somber disposition, though not necessarily unhappy. Where Katie took to quiet contemplation, Mrs. Smith spoke her mind quickly and to the point.

She would take some getting used to. But, then, so had Katie.

"Is that your town?" Mrs. Smith pointed ahead, past the bridge they were about to drive over.

"It is."

"Is that all of it?" she pressed.

Joseph nodded. "A mercantile, a blacksmith shop, and the school, which is also the church."

"It is very small."

He couldn't say if her words were a condemnation or simply an observation. Her tone was, without exception, straightforward, very businesslike. He hoped she wouldn't ruffle too many feathers.

"It *is* very small," he said. "You will get to know everyone easily that way."

He'd gone over in great detail all the things he'd written in his telegrams to her. There would be no misunderstandings this time. He'd quite specifically reiterated that she was not to get involved in the town feud. She didn't have to agree with both sides; she could even be sympathetic to one over the other. She simply could not become actively entangled in it and bring the arguing to his home.

He'd given Katie those same requirements. Though she'd tried, it had, in the end, proven impossible. Still, his first housekeeper had never involved herself so Joseph knew it could be done.

The town was relatively empty. Evening had come, and the children had long since come home from school. Joseph knew he was the first to return from taking in his crop. He had the advantage of many years' experience with business transactions and a great deal of information gathered ahead of time. His arrangements could be made with very little delay.

The other men would start arriving some time the next morning, he'd guess. In the meantime, he had his girls to pick up and Katie to face again. Their last moments together threaded through his thoughts as he pulled up to the barn.

Katie had run after him. Though he knew she'd done so more out of a reaction to him as a father to his children than out of any true attraction to him as a man, he hadn't been able to clear his mind of it. His pulse still pounded when he thought back on it. Things always seemed that way between them. She thought of him as a friend and neighbor, while he loved her with every beat of his heart.

He hadn't changed his mind about courting her, but he wasn't any more confident about his success.

He carried Mrs. Smith's trunks into the house and showed her to Katie's—*the housekeeper's*—room. He would have to grow used to the idea of someone else being in there.

"I'll give you a chance to settle in," he said. "It is late enough the girls will likely have eaten already. And I have enough left from the traveling supplies to see to my own meal. Feel free to make yourself something to eat from what you find in the kitchen."

He'd stocked his cupboards before leaving with things that wouldn't spoil. She'd be able to feed herself without difficulty.

Mrs. Smith gave a quick nod and turned to her unpacking. She would likely have the room entirely converted to her own space by the time he returned. Maybe that would help him stop thinking of the room as Katie's.

He knocked at Mrs. Claire's house and, while he waited, prepared himself to see Katie again. He could be friendly and appear unaffected by that embrace they'd shared. She certainly would be.

The door opened.

"Pompah, you're back!"

A smile spread across his face. "My sweet Ivy." He reached down and scooped his tiny daughter into his arms.

She wrapped her arms around his neck, squeezing like she meant to pop his head right off. "We didn't think you'd be here 'til tomorrow."

"I rushed back," he told her. "Did you miss me?"

"Oh, yes, Pompah. And we had ever so much fun. Mrs. Claire taught us how to cro—cro—" She shook her head. "I can't say the word, but it's pretty, and Katie said, 'Ivy, you've a fine talent for it, you do.' Just like that."

Joseph laughed out loud to hear the remarkably good Irish accent Ivy managed to produce. If she'd had the voice of a twenty-six-year-old rather than an almost six-year-old, she would have sounded very much like Katie.

"And did Emma learn to do this thing you did?" Joseph couldn't begin to guess just what Mrs. Claire had taught the girls. He simply loved hearing Ivy talk about it.

Ivy nodded emphatically. "But she mostly just did her schoolwork and read a book to Katie."

That sounded very much like Emma.

"And Katie said that Emma is a fine reader and quite the smartest child she's ever, ever known in all her days. 'Bright as the sun in June, you are,' Katie said."

Here was one of the many reasons why he hadn't worried about leaving the girls with Katie. She treated them so sweetly and seemed to know just what they needed to hear.

Emma came into the doorway. "Hello, Papa."

Joseph reached out and pulled her close to him. "I've missed you, Emma."

She smiled up at him. "Katie says to tell Ivy to let you come in instead of making you stand on the porch like a beggarman."

He laughed. Katie had likely said exactly that.

He stepped inside with his two girls by his side. Mrs. Claire sat in her customary place near the door, rocking calmly and peacefully.

"Good evening, Mrs. Claire."

"And to you. How was your trip to market?"

"Very good. I sold all my crop and picked up a housekeeper and returned quicker than expected."

Mrs. Claire nodded in rhythm with her rocking.

Emma tugged at his pant leg. "I have your watch," she said, looking up eagerly into his face. "I took very good care of it."

He smiled down at her. "I had every confidence in you, sweetheart."

"Have you eaten, Joseph Archer?" He knew the sound of Katie's voice instantly.

He braced himself to meet her eyes again. She stood over a pot at the stove, looking at him. The steam had brought color to her cheeks and a hint of curl to her hair. She looked, in a word, adorable.

"I have not," he answered.

"Well, then." She tapped her spoon on the edge of the pot. "We'll just add some water to the soup, I suppose."

Water to the soup? He refused to be a burden. "That's not necessary, Katie. I can—"

Why were Katie and the girls laughing? Clearly he'd missed something. He gave Ivy a questioning look—she could be counted on to spill any secret with very little encouragement.

"Katie always says that," Ivy said with a giggle. "We have imaginary guests every night, Pompah, and Katie says, 'We'll just add some water to the soup.' She says it even if we aren't eating soup."

He set Ivy down. She and Emma pulled him by the hand in Katie's direction. He did his best to keep his nervousness hidden.

"You have had a lot of imaginary guests?"

Emma nodded. "Last night was Queen Victoria."

Joseph looked to Katie. "Royalty?" He let the girls see how impressed he was with their dignified guest list.

Katie nodded seriously. "Only the very best guests for us." She looked down at the girls with a grin. "And what did we feed the queen?"

"Praties!" Emma and Ivy answered in unison, before dissolving into laughter.

Katie bit down on her lips as if holding back laughter of her own. Even Mrs. Claire chuckled.

"Have I missed something?" He didn't understand the joke.

"The fine queen wouldn't ever eat potatoes—peasant food, you understand." Katie wiped her hands on a dishrag. "So what did we do, girls?"

"We told her we were eating praties," Ivy said with a grin wider than Joseph had seen in some time. "And she thought it was something fancy instead of just regular old potatoes."

"We fooled her," Emma added. He loved hearing Emma laugh and act more like the carefree child she ought to always have been.

"We fooled her fine and well, we did," Katie added.

Again all the women laughed. This was the kind of happy home he'd wanted to raise his daughters in. His late wife hadn't been one for teasing or imaginary dinner companions. There had been very little laughter.

Joseph moved directly to Katie's side at the stove. "What can I do to help?"

"Oh, I've seen the disaster you make of meals, Joseph Archer. I'll not let you anywhere near this one." She looked past him. "Time to set the table, girls. You know your parts. Show your father how well you do it."

Emma and Ivy sprang into action, pulling out plates and cups and flatware with the familiarity of practice.

"You have taught them to set the table?"

Katie nodded, watching the girls fondly. "And they do a fine job of it, with hardly a complaint. Sweet girls."

"They didn't give you too much trouble?"

"Not at all. But they did miss you."

He let his gaze turn to the girls as well. They were so vibrant and alive under Katie's care. He knew already that Mrs. Smith would not be Katie's equal in that. He only hoped his newest housekeeper wouldn't prove a complete disaster.

"How have you been?" He thought it a relatively safe beginning to a conversation.

"A little worn, but I'm holding up. The girls have become quite the little helpers this past week. I've been grateful to have them here."

"How are things at the mercantile? Is Johnson still making your life miserable?"

"He slipped and hit his head the other day."

A blow to the head could be quite serious. "Was he badly hurt?"

"He cut his forehead open—it needed stitching." Katie spoke as she cut a loaf of bread into thick slices. "As there's no doctor in town, that task fell to me."

"You sewed up a man's head?" Was there nothing this woman couldn't do?

"Aye, and he's none too happy about it. Things between us have become terribly awkward. I don't think he knows just how to behave now. Knowing I did something nice for him, he can't in good conscience act hateful toward me, but neither can he bring himself to be nice to me."

Leave it to Katie to be the first Irish resident of Hope Springs to change Jeremiah Johnson's perception of her fellow countrymen even the tiniest bit. No one else had managed it in the almost ten years since Johnson's arrival.

"Oh, I meant to ask—" Katie took hold of his arm.

He felt the touch echo through him. In his mind he was immediately back on the path with Katie in his arms. That moment had only grown more detailed in his memory during the days that had passed. It had kept him up at night and driven him to distraction during the day.

"Did you get a good price for your grain?" Katie asked. "I know there has been some worry about prices this year."

"I didn't get as much for it as last year, but still not terrible." He was proud of how steady his response was. Her touch upended him, and she still hadn't pulled her hand back.

"That is a relief. I hope the others did well also."

"So do I." Tensions were high enough in town without adding the burden of money troubles. He'd thought on that during his trip back. It was good to have someone to talk with about it.

"We'd best get your daughters fed." Katie took her hand from his arm and reached for a thick kitchen towel.

He liked that she'd referred to them together. They made a good "we," he thought. But how to convince her of that?

The girls had the table set and were waiting patiently for dinner. Mrs. Claire shuffled over, taking the chair at the far end. Joseph carried the large pot of what appeared to be bean soup. Katie followed close behind with the loaf of bread. He'd missed Katie's bread.

They weren't more than a few bites into their meal before the girls were vying for control of the conversation. Even Emma, who tended to be very quiet, had a great deal to say.

"Some of the children at school are fighting," she said. "Billy Archibald hit Ryan Kelly in the stomach and said he was nothing but a filthy foreigner."

Katie's spoon stilled halfway to her mouth, her gaze riveted to Emma. "He said that at school? Did Reverend Ford say anything about it?"

"We were out playing. Reverend Ford didn't hear him."

"Did anyone tell the preacher?" Katie pressed.

Emma shrugged. "Yes, but the boys hit each other enough that Reverend Ford said they were both being bad."

Katie's eyes shifted to Mrs. Claire, then to Joseph. They all knew that adult arguments often found their way to the schoolyard.

"This must have happened in the afternoon," Katie said. "I was outside during your lunch-hour playtime and I didn't notice any scuffles."

Emma swallowed a large mouthful of soup. "They were hitting each other *after* school."

Katie's eyes met his. "You don't seem terribly surprised, Joseph," she said quietly.

"This has, unfortunately, happened before."

Her coloring fell a little. "Is Emma in danger?" She didn't speak above a whisper.

He set his hand on hers where it rested on the table. "Emma is fine. She isn't likely to spend time with Billy Archibald or Ryan Kelly or any of the other children who are prone to get into a skirmish."

Katie's mouth tipped in a half-smile. "You're telling me I worry too much, is that it?"

He smiled back and wrapped his fingers more fully around her hand.

His gaze happened to meet Mrs. Claire's. She very pointedly looked at his and Katie's hands. A grin slowly spread across the woman's happily wrinkled face. Joseph gave her a look he hoped communicated his determination to keep things just as they were. He was offering comfort to a woman who was worried, and, further, a woman who had laid her hand on his arm only a few minutes earlier, and, further still, a woman who was not objecting to his attention.

Why isn't she objecting?

He studied her, looking for some clue. Katie's eyes shifted from the girls to him. Color touched her cheeks.

"It's good to have you back, Joseph," she said quietly. She turned her hand enough in his to take hold of his fingers. She was, for all intents and purposes, truly holding his hand.

It's good to have you back. She'd missed him. She was happy to have him there. A woman whose heart was wholly set on another man wouldn't look at him that way or hold fast to his hand.

"It's good to be back, Katie."

Chapter Nineteen

Tavish found it odd being out on the road with Finbarr instead of Ian. He had made the harvest run with his older brother for ten years. Not having him there served as a constant reminder of the difficulties he'd left behind at home. Was Ian improving at all? Would the price they'd negotiated on their brother's crop be enough to see his family through until the next harvest?

Did Katie miss him? She was of such an independent nature, Tavish could never be certain if she needed him around at all.

"This is a lot of lumber." Finbarr slid a plank onto the wagon bed, not the first nor the last they'd loaded up that day. "Are you building a cathedral or something?"

"Not a cathedral. Only a very fine room." The absolute finest he could manage, in fact.

"What kind of room?"

"I told you—a very fine room."

Finbarr slid another plank in place without rising to the bait. He did, however, toss Tavish a look of curious inquiry. They'd been traveling together for over two weeks and hadn't had anything resembling a lengthy conversation. Finbarr had always been that way, contentedly reserved.

Tavish was more accustomed to Ian's voice helping him pass the long hours of travel.

"I'm building a proper bedroom onto my place," he said, answering the question Finbarr hadn't actually asked. "A room unto itself, not the nook behind the fireplace where I've been laying my head these past years. Something nice."

"Does this mean you intend to ask Miss Macauley to marry you?"

That was a surprisingly direct question, especially coming from someone as quiet as Finbarr.

"I might be." Tavish tossed the bag of nails he'd purchased into the back with the wood. "But if you think I'll make more of a confession than that to a scrawny sixteen-year-old boy, you'd best think that through again."

Finbarr helped him set the remaining crates of preserves and such on top of the tightly piled lumber. Tavish would have preferred to get his supplies last, but it didn't make sense to drive all the way back and so far out of his way. There were no better prices for wood anywhere else along his route. He tied the crates securely in the wagon to keep them from shifting.

They tied down the canvas cover over the back of the wagon bed. The topic of Katie seemed to have been dropped between them.

Tavish checked that everything was secure, then motioned his brother back up on the bench. They set off again, the usual silence between them. He'd had a profitable two weeks, if a touch disappointing. Grain hadn't sold for as much this year as in the past. And he'd not had as many bottles of preserves or cordials or wines to sell. The upheaval of the past month had taken its toll in many ways.

Still, there'd been enough to cover the cost of his building supplies, with money left over to make his payment on his land. Once he sold the rest of his jars, he ought to have enough to live on for another year. Barring any catastrophes—he quickly crossed himself, a habit he'd learned well from his mother—he'd not have any money worries.

"I like Miss Macauley," Finbarr said without warning.

There was an unspoken "but" at the end of that sentence. Tavish raised his eyebrows expectantly, eyeing his brother as long as he dared, considering he was driving his wagon out of a relatively busy town.

"I didn't know you two were on the verge of making things permanent."

How could he have thought otherwise? "I was prepared to go back to Ireland for her, Finbarr."

He didn't look convinced, but didn't offer an argument.

"Spill your budget," Tavish insisted. "I can see there's more you're wishing to say."

Finbarr only shook his head.

"'Tis a long road home, brother. You might as well start talking."

Finbarr slumped on the seat, his eyes focused ahead. There was nothing belligerent in his posture. 'Twas something far more thoughtful.

"Miss Macauley hasn't ever come for Sunday cake with the family," Finbarr said. "Keefe came nearly every week once he and Ciara were serious about one another."

"Until recently, Katie was working Sunday evenings for Joseph," Tavish pointed out. "Since then, we've not had many Sunday gatherings, what with Ian still not well."

"That's true." Finbarr still looked thoughtful.

"Is there something else weighing on you, lad?"

Finbarr looked uncomfortable, but pressed ahead. "Do you love her?"

"Of course I do."

Why would Finbarr wonder about that? Everyone in Hope Springs knew Tavish's feelings for Katie.

"Mr. Archer is mad in love with her as well," Finbarr said.

Tavish rolled the tension from his shoulders. He'd never been jealous of any man except for Joseph Archer. The feeling had actually started long before Katie had arrived. Joseph had everything. He had a fine family, a fine house. He had more money than he knew what to do with. The only thing Tavish had that Joseph didn't was Katie's affection. Curse the man for making him unsure of even that.

"He told you that, did he?"

Finbarr shook his head. "I can just tell. He always built the fire for her because being near the flames made her nervous. And Mr. Archer ordered her a pair of thick woolen stockings. He said she takes great comfort in having warm feet."

Tavish didn't know that.

"It must be an odd thing for her to have two men in love with her at the same time," Finbarr said. "And, I'd guess, a bit strange for the two of you as well."

"For a lad who rarely speaks a word, you certainly have plenty to say today."

Finbarr crossed his arms over his chest. "You asked," he muttered.

His younger brother had always had a strange knack for shifting between being wise beyond his years and being the very picture of the child he actually was. In that moment, Tavish didn't particularly appreciate either one.

Tavish flicked the reins, setting his horses at a faster clip now that they'd reached the edge of town. As the wagon rolled, Tavish's thoughts spun as fast as the wheels. He'd taken his future with Katie as a given thing. 'Twas a hard thing realizing that wasn't the case. Winning over Bridget had been easy. They'd simply fallen in love with nothing to come between them, and no one to tear them apart. Even with that promising beginning, she'd been taken from him. He couldn't bear the thought of losing Katie as well.

Finbarr sat quietly, his gaze focused straight ahead. Their conversation hadn't ended well. Tavish knew they would pass an awkward week or more if they spent it in uneasy silence.

"Is that little Emma still sweet on you?" he asked.

A smile returned to Finbarr's face. "That she is."

"But she's rather like a sister to you, I'd wager." Tavish had watched his youngest brother interact with the Archer girls enough to know how Finbarr saw them. "Someday when you're both grown and married, you'll look back on her puppy love of you and laugh."

A brotherly fondness filled Finbarr's expression. "I am going to enjoy watching both those girls grow up. They are sweet little ones."

"Aye, that they are," Tavish said.

Finbarr gave a nod and slouched comfortably on the wagon bench. Quick as that, they were on good terms again. If only he could settle the matter of Katie's feelings so easily.

Chapter Twenty

Katie took Biddy's advice to heart. Time had come and passed for sorting out her terribly confused feelings.

Joseph had come by a handful of times since returning to town. He always brought the girls, then spent the evening sitting with *her.* They talked about any number of things: his worries, her difficulties, amusing stories from their pasts. He'd talked to her about the situation with Mr. Johnson, and they had decided between them that this was a rare opportunity to help the shopkeeper see her countrymen in a different light. Joseph asked her each night to play her fiddle. She wondered if he really liked the music as much as he seemed to or if he simply knew she needed it at the end of a difficult day.

She valued his company. She looked forward to seeing him. Her heart even flipped around the few times he'd held her hand.

But she felt all those things for Tavish. Did she feel them for him still? Who did she feel them for most? She couldn't know without seeing Tavish again. Aside from all that, she *wanted* to see him again. She missed him.

What a complete and utter mess she was.

Katie watched the wagons roll back into town from her vantage point at the mercantile. Tavish and Finbarr wouldn't be back for at least another week.

"The return of the wagons," Mr. Johnson muttered. "That always means winter is coming."

He'd taken to grumbling and mumbling over the week or more since Katie had sewn his bleeding head back together. But he didn't insult her or belittle her anymore. She didn't point out the change, didn't press it. She and Joseph had talked through it and decided that, if left to his own thoughts, Mr. Johnson might very well change his own mind in light of what she'd done. Katie hoped that was true. If even one person on the Red Road could learn to let go of their hatred for the Irish, Hope Springs might begin to put the feud behind itself.

"I've heard the winters are bad hereabouts," Katie said, wondering if he'd take up the try at conversation.

"Bad? They're brutal," Mr. Johnson said. "It's so cold the snow begs to be let in out of the weather."

She couldn't help laughing at that. Mr. Johnson even smiled. But the moment his eyes met hers, his lips pulled down once more. Her chuckle died abruptly.

Mr. Johnson set back to piling shoe blacking neatly on the shelves near the counter.

Katie continued cleaning the glass jars that held the sweets. She watched Mr. Johnson as she worked. He glanced at her furtively. His frown remained firmly in place.

For a moment things had been almost friendly between them. She wasn't foolish enough to think they could truly be friends, but she thought at least they'd moved toward something better than enemies.

Mr. Johnson absentmindedly rubbed at the skin around his sewn-up wound. Thought about it, did he? She hoped so.

A few townspeople wandered in over the course of the morning, mostly the men looking to begin gathering supplies for the coming winter now that they had money from selling their crops.

"Hello, Katie."

"And a good day to you, Mr. Scott."

He looked tired, no doubt from days spent riding in a wagon on the rough trails of Wyoming. Mr. Scott had always been a kind man, slow to anger. He moved up to the counter, placing his order with the quiet and humble voice many Irish had adopted when doing business at the mercantile. Katie hated seeing good people reduced almost to begging in a place of business.

Mr. Johnson quoted him the price of the things he'd ordered. Mr. Scott looked surprised.

"The price hasn't gone up, then?"

For the briefest of moments, Mr. Johnson's eyes met hers, then quickly returned to his customer. "No, the prices have not increased."

Mr. Scott stood silent, mouth moving but no sound coming out. Clearly he'd expected to return to Hope Springs and find the Irish prices soaring to the heavens. Katie knew a moment of deep relief, pride even, at this new proof she was making a difference.

Mr. Scott spoke low and quick to her as he made his way out. "Prices have always increased after the harvest run. Always. Thank you for this, Katie. Thank you."

The next moment brought another customer.

"That's Archibald," Mr. Johnson said. "Get in the back."

She hadn't been sent into hiding in days. But she knew Mr. Archibald could be counted on to cause problems. While she wanted to think Mr. Johnson was saving her from the insults she'd have to endure, 'twas far more likely he only wanted to avoid earning the displeasure of the Reddest of Reds in Hope Springs.

Katie followed his instructions without comment. For the next twenty minutes she sat on a crate in the storage room, listening to the conversation outside. 'Twas a very one-sided discussion, with Mr. Archibald lodging complaint after complaint.

"The blacksmith's prices are still outrageous."

"The crops didn't sell for as much as we wanted."

"The Irish beat us to the depot. *Our* depot. They knew the higher bidders would be there. The filthy cheats beat us to them before we even had a chance."

Didn't the two men have anything else to talk about other than the feud? How could they possibly be friends if there was no other connection between them?

"Is that girl-Paddy still working here?" Mr. Archibald asked.

"She is," Mr. Johnson said.

"I'm warning you, Jeremiah. The Red Road put up with her being here because you were the one on the better end of the bargain. But after that trick the Irish pulled—taking the horses' shoes, rushing to market, *stealing* our profits—the Reds won't like seeing her face here every time we come to town."

"She stays in the back," Mr. Johnson said. "And she doesn't talk, so y'all won't have to hear her Irish voice, either. It will be fine."

'Twasn't exactly a compliment nor a defense of her value. She shouldn't have expected more than that, but she had hoped for it.

I sewed up the man's head, for heaven's sake. And he can't be bothered to tell his neighbor that he's glad to have me here.

"You need to fire her, Jeremiah," Mr. Archibald said. "Fire her before this gets out of hand."

Katie held her breath and listened.

"She's keeping the place clean so Carol doesn't have to. I'm getting a lot of work out of her."

He was, indeed. If Katie could say one thing for herself, it was that she knew how to work hard.

"So you've found yourself an Irish slave," Mr. Archibald summed up.

"More or less."

For Katie, sitting on the crate, tucked away in the back, those words cut painfully deep. She was his "Irish slave." For all the progress she thought she'd made, that declaration hurled her back to the moment when Mr. Johnson had declared her a "filthy Irishwoman." Despite all she'd done for him and his family, the work she tirelessly undertook, her efforts at tending to his injuries when she might as easily have left him bleeding on the floor, she was still worthless in the man's eyes. Nothing more than a bit of Irish garbage to be tossed aside and never thought of again.

She tried to clear those words from her mind, but they echoed within her, piercing her heart with each repetition. *Irish slave.* She thought her time at the mercantile was making a difference, that she was beginning to change Mr. Johnson's mind, perhaps even softening his heart a bit. Disappointment sat heavy on her shoulders.

She offered Mr. Johnson a quick and silent nod of farewell as she left, unwilling to meet his eyes and see hatred sitting there. Perhaps this feud could not be ended after all. Perhaps she was a fool for even hoping.

The children were still out in the schoolyard as she passed by. Emma waved and quickly walked over to her. The hug she received was a desperately needed balm.

"Thank you for this bit of loving, my sweet Emma," she whispered, returning the embrace.

"You look sad today, Katie." Emma studied her face.

"I am only weary."

Her forehead creased. "Does that mean 'tired'?"

"Aye, that it does."

Marianne Johnson, who'd stood nearby watching Katie and Emma with quiet curiosity, spoke up. "Why do you say 'aye'? What does it mean?"

"'Tis a very Irish way of saying 'yes,' and quite common across the way in Scotland as well."

Marianne smiled and two adorable dimples showed on her rounded cheeks. "I always thought the Irish people were saying 'eye.'" She pointed at her own eye. "It seemed silly."

Katie nodded. "That would be very silly indeed." She winked at Emma. "Emma, here, had to explain to me about 'cookies,' as I'd been calling them 'biscuits' and sounding like a regular chicken-head."

Marianne laughed. Emma joined her. Katie hoped Marianne was

always such a lightening influence on Emma. The somber little girl needed it.

Katie took Emma's hand and the three of them walked along the road where it ran along the schoolyard. "How are you adjusting to your new housekeeper?"

Emma hesitated, her mouth turned down. She knew Emma was not fond of changes in her life. The response was more than that, though.

"She is old," Emma finally said.

When Katie had first arrived, Joseph hadn't liked that she was so young. He'd obviously been quite careful not to make that mistake again.

"Though she's older than you expected, does she keep you fed and the house kept up?"

Emma nodded. Katie's worries eased. The girl was simply learning to accept change.

"Does she comb your hair in the mornings?" Katie truly doubted Joseph had managed the two tidy braids hanging down Emma's back.

Another silent nod answered her question. Katie wondered at that. Emma had always been quiet and reserved, but less so of late, at least with *her*. She couldn't entirely shake the feeling that something else was weighing on Emma.

The sound of the school bell signaled the end of their little walk.

Marianne took Emma's other hand. "The bell, Emma."

Katie smiled. "Have a lovely day at school, sweet one."

She received a tiny smile for that. Marianne waved once before the girls, in perfect unison, turned and ran back toward the school. Why was the Johnson family like that? Taken one at a time, they could be surprisingly friendly. The moment they were in company with the Red Road or even one another, though, that bit of civility flew right out the window.

She continued down the road, feeling every bit as weary as she'd told Emma she was. Life was hard sometimes. Other times it was nothing short of exhausting. Her mind hardly noted the scenery as she walked.

Before even realizing how far she'd gone, she stood at the fork in the road, looking directly at Joseph Archer's home.

She hadn't realized until leaving the place behind just how fond she'd grown of the dormer windows with their lovely shutters, the tall tree in the yard, and the porch that spanned the full length of the house. 'Twas the first home in which she'd felt valued and welcomed and cared about. Even in her childhood home, the strain of starvation and the threat of eviction had tempered any show of affection. Behind every expression of love and welcome was the sure knowledge that each mouth to feed was a burden.

"I need a moment in your home, Joseph Archer," she whispered as she stood alone. But she knew it wouldn't be the same. She no longer belonged to this home where she'd once felt loved.

Loved. The word struck her. 'Twas, indeed, loved that she'd felt. Loved like a family member. Loved like a friend. And more than that, even. There'd been more than that in Joseph. She needed to discover just how much more.

The prospect frightened her more than she had expected it to. But she'd never been such a coward. She'd given up far too much in choosing this new life. She did not mean to live it ruled by fear.

You've a mess of a heart to sort out. Now's the time to be brave, Katie girl.

She scrubbed the last few tears from her face and rolled back her shoulders. She'd courage enough for this.

Katie marched herself with purpose around the back of the house. She fully intended to step onto the porch and knock at the kitchen door. She knew better than to think herself a front-door visitor. Only the properest of people came to the front door. She wasn't anything more than a servant.

A queue of men spilled out of the barn, all of them dressed in the humble clothing of working farmers. Joseph, more likely than not, was in *there.* She turned toward the barn. As she drew closer, she recognized the gathering. Irish, every last one of them. It was like a céilí, but with no songs or dancing and quite a bit more somber expressions.

"What's this, then?" she asked Mr. MacCormack.

"Land payments."

That made sense. Joseph owned the entire valley. With their crops newly sold, the farming families would have money on hand to make a payment against their note.

Their usual chatter was noticeably subdued. They stood with uncertain looks, drawn mouths. Care sat heavy on their shoulders. These were people worried for their families. Poverty and the fear of losing his land had made her own father hard. She could see the beginnings of it in these good people as well.

Katie slipped around the queue at the door. Joseph stood at a high, roughly hewn, narrow desk, with an account ledger, much like the one Mr. Johnson used, open in front of him. He was speaking to Mr. O'Donaghue. The men exchanged nods and handshakes. Mr. O'Donaghue stepped away, slipping his hat back on his head. Joseph leaned over his ledger, writing something.

She'd clearly chosen a bad time to drop by.

Joseph looked up and saw her. He said something to the next man in the queue, Mr. Murphy, then walked over to her.

"Good afternoon, Katie."

Tavish had always been the one with the melting smile. Why was it Joseph's small one flipped her heart about?

"You are hosting quite the fancy party here, Joseph."

"Not exactly." He wasn't the roaring-laughter type, but he could, with the smallest raise of an eyebrow or quirk of his mouth, show his amusement as surely as if he were clutching his sides.

"I know rent day when I see it." Katie tried to hold back a remembered shudder. "I hated rent days. Standing in queue with Father while he clutched that meager bit of money and rehearsed his list of crops he'd grown for the landlord. I hated watching him shuffle and mutter and lower himself, begging the way he had to. I—I hated it."

"There is no begging here, Katie," he said. "There never is."

"That, Joseph, is because there are no tenants. Not in the way we were tenants."

Joseph brushed a gentle hand along her cheek. Her heart leaped about, as if desperate to get her attention. She was not indifferent to his touch. Not at all. Here was yet more evidence that he'd captured her heart as much as she suspected he had.

"You will not ever have to live that way again," Joseph said, a firmness underlying his words.

"Promises are dangerous things, Joseph Archer. When they break, they wound. Deeply."

'Twas in that moment Katie remembered the men of the Irish Road were standing about watching. They likely had noticed her studying Joseph and wondering about him. There might not have been begging at Joseph's payment collection day, but she was providing ample moments of speculation.

"I hadn't meant to interrupt," she said. "I only . . ." An awkward swallow seemed in order. "I only came by for a little chat."

"Ah." He nodded slowly. "Now that the men have returned, I'll be doing this"—he motioned to the crowd gathered around—"for a few days. Today and tomorrow I'll meet with the Irish Road. The two days or so after that, I'll meet with the Red Road."

"Is that why you rushed back?"

His gaze grew more focused on her. "That's not the reason," he said quietly, almost as though he didn't realize he'd spoken.

The air around them grew tense, her lungs struggling to breathe. She thought she knew his reasons. He'd come back quickly because he'd missed her. A warmth began deep inside her at the thought.

Somehow she found enough voice to speak. "I'll let you get back to it." She stepped away. "Thank you for taking a minute to say hello."

"Katie?" He stopped her while she was still close enough for something of a private conversation.

She looked back uncertainly.

"Would you . . . Would you join us for dinner?"

The invitation surprised her. What exactly did he mean by it? Perhaps the girls had asked after her. Maybe he thought she was hungry and could use the free food. Perhaps he meant it as a social engagement.

For just a moment, she entertained the idea, thought about sitting to table with a family of means like a fine lady. A handsome and kindhearted man would pull out her chair for her, perhaps walk with her on his arm. She'd have a housekeeper setting a meal before her, rather than setting the meal herself.

The daydream ended there. She was only Katie. Plain Katie, the servant.

"'Twould be terrible odd, don't you think, being there while Mrs. Smith is still finding her place?"

His nod was reluctant. Did he regret, then, that she'd turned down the invitation? The thought almost made her smile. He *did* miss her.

He tipped his head to her, then made his way back to his desk, with his usual confident stride.

"Mr. Murphy," Joseph said in greeting. He didn't immediately turn to his ledger, but kept his attention on Mr. Murphy. "Were you able to see the dentist while you were at the station?"

"Aye, and a good thing I did. The tooth was broken clear through and rotting inside."

"It was little wonder, then, you were in such pain." Joseph spoke with clear concern. "Dr. Philips does good work."

"That he does and charges very little," Mr. Murphy said. "I thank you for recommending him. I would likely have continued on in agony otherwise, too afraid I couldn't afford it."

"My pleasure."

They set themselves to their business and parted with a friendly handshake. The pattern held true with each person who stepped up to Joseph's desk. He asked after their families, knew of their individual difficulties and struggles.

The feud had often kept him from forming true friendships with his neighbors. He was forced to be something of an outsider in Hope Springs. How easily he might have simply become indifferent to the people around him, seeing them as little more than an opportunity for profit as did so many landlords in Ireland.

But Joseph so clearly cared about them all. She'd long known he was a good-hearted man. The truth of that struck her anew as she stood there, and she loved him all the more for it.

Chapter Twenty-One

Joseph hadn't been this nervous when he was courting his late wife. Their match had been something of a foregone conclusion, so there had been very little pressure and no real possibility of failure. With Katie he felt an overwhelming amount of both.

She'd been friendlier of late, smiling at him, blushing, seeming to enjoy the brief moments when he'd held her hand or touched her face. He'd vowed to respect her choice if she was truly set on Tavish, but her attitude toward *him* seemed to indicate that a decision was still somewhat up in the air.

Five days had passed since she'd appeared like a vision from heaven in his darkened barn as he undertook his business with the Irish. He simultaneously enjoyed and hated payment days. Business, though it was not his first love, was in his blood, and he was good at it. To see those skills help an entire valley of people was satisfying, fulfilling. But taking money from people who had so little only brought to mind all the reasons he'd disliked the cold heartlessness of finance.

The men of Hope Springs had been trickling in for nearly a week. He'd spent every evening going over accounts, helping the illiterate understand the state of their finances while trying hard not to sound condescending. He worried that, in his eagerness to help them make sense of sometimes complicated things, he'd make them feel unintelligent or small or unimportant. Equally frustrating were those who, at every payment day, felt the need to argue over every little detail. Thankfully, his father had taught him to keep meticulous records and to always put business arrangements in writing.

After nearly a week of dealing with high emotions and tempers made sharp with worry, he needed a break. The promise of Katie's company beckoned to him like a lighthouse in a thick fog. So he put the girls to bed a little early, informed Mrs. Smith he would be out for some time, and, taking with him a few special packages from town, walked up the Irish Road. Mrs. Claire's was the second house on the right and an easy distance from the bridge.

He held the packages under his arm as he knocked at the door.

Katie opened it. "Why, Joseph. Have you decided to come by at long last?"

He nodded. A joking response was likely called for, probably even expected, but he was too nervous for anything else.

I'm like a schoolboy again in the throes of first love.

"I haven't had an evening to myself since the harvest run ended," he explained. "Except for Sunday, but the girls were feeling rather desperate for some attention."

Katie held her hand out to him. He took it gladly and allowed her to lead him inside. For a woman who'd been so standoffish when she first arrived at his home, she was very affectionate of late. He wasn't complaining, only trying to keep himself realistic.

"You look tired, Joseph."

"I would say the same to you, but I learned long ago it isn't wise to tell a woman when she is looking less than her best—not if you wish to remain on good terms with her."

Katie clearly took no offense. If anything, she seemed to warm to the topic. "But a woman who wishes to be lied to doesn't seem the kind worth being on good terms with."

He had missed Katie's conversations. She could debate a topic with him, matching him point for point, but without growing petty or angry as too many did. She challenged him and impressed him at every turn. A man could spend the rest of his days in conversation with such a woman and never grow bored.

"I wasn't arguing in favor of constant untruths," Joseph said. "I was making a case for discretion and tact."

Katie's mouth twisted to one side, then the other. "So if ever I see you about town and you *don't* tell me that I'm looking fine as feathers, am I to assume that I look rather horrid and you're simply being tactful?"

"Only if you are hoping to be offended on a regular basis."

"Am I looking horrid 'on a regular basis,' then?"

Joseph set his packages on the table. "Twisting words, Katie?" He'd long ago begun scolding her in jest for that.

Her shrug was coy to say the least. The gesture pulled at him. His collar, though it wasn't buttoned all the way to his neck, felt tight, overly warm. He managed to keep himself from tugging at it.

"Where is Mrs. Claire?" He hadn't noticed until then that she wasn't in her usual spot at the front window.

"She is just down the street visiting with Ciara Fulton."

He hadn't intended to visit while Katie was alone. Such a thing would have been considered inappropriate in the extreme amongst society in Baltimore. The first time he'd been truly alone with Vivian before they were married was the five minutes they were granted in her parents' rose garden so that he could propose. For just a moment he wondered if things might not have turned out differently had he been permitted a closer acquaintance before they'd wed. There'd been a great deal about her he hadn't known. She likely would have said the same of him.

"Can I make you a cup of coffee?" Katie asked.

Though she made the best coffee he'd had in a long time, and certainly better than anything he'd had since she left his home, he didn't want to spend their time together with her working in the kitchen. "Thank you, but no."

Her eyes darted to the packages and back. "What have you brought with you?"

"Some things I picked up while I was at the train depot."

Katie leaned over the table. She held her hands behind her back as if keeping herself from touching the packages. "There is quite a bit of lettering on them. Were they mailed, then?"

They had come a long way, in fact. "One is from Baltimore. The other came from Belfast."

That brought her head around, eyes wide. "Belfast? What did you have mailed from there?"

He hadn't wanted to make a fuss about it in case she was disappointed. It seemed the fuss was unavoidable now. "It's something for you."

He hadn't thought her eyes could get wider, but they did. "For *me?* From Ireland?"

"It isn't anything so amazing or fine as I'm afraid you're imagining."

"But it is for *me.* I've so seldom been given anything. 'Tis a treat no matter what it might be."

She'd seldom been given anything? Didn't Tavish bring her little tokens of affection? What kind of courtship was the man undertaking? Joseph shook off the uncharitable thought. Tavish had probably brought her wildflowers. Or given her berries from his bushes. Tavish was not a wealthy man. It likely was all he could afford to give. Just so long as he was doing something. A woman ought to be important enough to a man for him to make an effort to show her he thought of her often.

"May I open it?" Katie asked.

He forced his thoughts back into the moment. "The top package is the one from Belfast."

Katie pulled out the chair nearest the packages and sat. Joseph braced himself against her coming disappointment. She took the package in her hand and gave it a squeeze, apparently surprised to find it wasn't rigid.

"I'm full dying of curiosity now." She tore back the brown paper. One at a time, she pulled out three pair of thick woolen stockings.

"I told you it wasn't anything particularly exciting."

She rubbed the last pair against her cheek, then held it to her nose, closing her eyes as she inhaled. "This is Irish wool, Joseph. I'd know it anywhere."

"And it's the thickest you'll find, I'm told."

"I don't understand. There must be hundreds upon hundreds of places to buy stockings that are closer than Belfast. That is such a vast deal of trouble to go to."

How could he explain himself without looking like a fool?

"Wyoming winters can be brutally cold," he said. "I haven't been able to get out of my head the thought of you being so cold that your toes were taken by frostbite." He didn't look at her as he explained. Never had he felt so unsure of himself. "I thought if your feet could at least be warm during your winters here, you would be less miserable. And I've heard Ian and Biddy both talk of how soft and warm they remember the wool in Ireland being. I wanted you to have a little bit of that with you."

He hazarded a glance in her direction. She was smelling the wool with such a look of longing. Had they really kept a scent of home during the long journey to Wyoming, or was her memory filling in the empty spaces?

"You must have sent for these weeks and weeks ago."

He pulled out the chair next to hers and lowered himself into it. "I first had the idea that night you told me about your feet. I sent the order with Johnson's oldest boy on his very next trip to the train depot. It takes a very long time to ship things from Ireland, even with the telegram speeding up the process."

He'd sent another telegram to Belfast not long after Katie had received word of her father's illness. He had hoped to find an answer waiting at the telegraph office when he was there selling his crop, but nothing had come yet. He didn't intend to tell Katie about it until he received an answer. *If* he received an answer.

"You must have felt like you'd wasted the effort when I decided to go back to Ireland. The stockings would have come, but I would have already been gone."

When Katie had told him of her intention to leave Hope Springs for good, the very last thing on his mind had been those stockings.

"Thank you," she said, rubbing them against her cheek again. "I'd worried a great deal about the coming winter, having heard so much of how cold it'll be. But if I can have warm feet, I can endure anything."

She'd accepted the gift with grace. Seeing her so happy over something so small spurred him on.

"The other package is for you as well. A token of my gratitude for all the work you did while you lived at our house and for watching the girls while I was away."

"They were a delight. You needn't offer me gifts for doing something I enjoy."

"I want to." He had sent for that particular package just before she left to live on the Irish Road, unsure how he would convince her to keep it. Her birthday wasn't until after the New Year. Christmas was still some time off. A gift for no particular occasion would have been a difficult thing to explain.

Katie lifted the package up. "It's heavy."

Joseph all but held his breath. He had no idea what she would think of his gift. If only she would love it the way he hoped she would.

She tore back the paper. "A book?" She was clearly confused.

"This is no ordinary book," he said. "A Frenchman invented a machine a few years ago called a phonautograph. It creates patterns, pictures from sound waves."

Katie gave the tiniest shake of her head. "I don't know what sound waves are."

"I would be willing to wager you do but you just haven't heard them called that."

She looked more intrigued by the moment.

"When you speak or sing, you feel a vibration in your throat or perhaps in your chest. And when you play your violin, it vibrates inside."

"Aye."

"That vibrating you feel is sound waves."

"I didn't know there was a word for it." She looked back at the still-closed book. "This man from France—how does his machine make pictures from sound waves?"

Joseph flipped the book open to a drawing of the phonautograph. "The person speaks or sings or plays an instrument into this part here." He tapped the sketch, indicating the cone-shaped piece of the phonautograph. "And the vibrating makes this part here shake exactly the same way the sound itself is shaking."

"And it makes a picture of the shaking?" She was already putting it together, though he'd not told her enough for the concept to be entirely clear.

"Around this cylinder is a long sheet of paper covered in lampblack. The moving part has something very much like a needle at the end, and that needle scratches a pattern into the blacking."

Her eyes moved about as she studied the drawing. He could almost see the thoughts as they swirled through her mind. "Those patterns, then, are—" Her forehead creased and her eyes narrowed. She tipped her head to one side, still examining the drawing. "Those patterns are what sound *looks* like? If we could see music, it would look like the patterns this machine makes?" She tapped the drawing.

"Yes, exactly."

She slowly turned her head in his direction. Awe filled her face. "They are like photographs of music. Not people playing music, but the music itself."

"Yes. Music and spoken words and general sounds. Any noise at all makes a pattern in the air."

She clasped her hands together and pressed her fingertips to her lips, leaning back in her chair. It was exactly the posture of a woman in a state of full amazement. After a moment, she said, "Can I see the . . . the pictures? I don't the know proper name for them."

"They are phonautograms. And of course you can look at them." Joseph flipped through the first few pages, past the explanation of how the machine was invented and the principles on which it worked, until he found the first phonautogram print.

"These wavy lines, here?" Katie spoke before he had a chance to. "Are these the pho—phon—"

"Phonautograms. Yes."

She stared, hardly blinking. She said simply, "They're beautiful."

He'd known she would think that. He'd known it. She who loved music so deeply couldn't help but be moved by the sight of its physical form.

She traced her finger along the up-and-down pattern of the line that stretched the length of the entire page. "Does it say what sound this is?"

Joseph read the inscription. "It says this is a man's voice singing 'Au Claire de Lune.'"

"This is music, then." She shook her head in amazement. "I have often closed my eyes while playing my fiddle and imagined the music as swirls of color and light. But I never knew it had a shape, an actual shape. If we could see it floating in the air around us, it would have a shape."

"This shape, in fact," Joseph said, a smile around the edge of his mouth.

They turned page after page, Katie watching in wonder, asking countless questions. Joseph read the inscription under each image so she would know exactly what she was seeing. How quickly she grasped a concept based in physics and mathematics having never studied either one. Here was one of many reasons he'd come to love her as he did. She had an intellect not only open to new ideas but eager for them and more than capable of learning anything she put her mind to.

"This is really for me to keep all for myself?" she asked before they had even reached the end of the book.

"Yes, it is. I wanted you to have something that you would love but not necessarily need."

"I don't understand."

He didn't entirely himself. "I just wanted to give you something that would make you happy."

"It has, Joseph. It's like holding a bit of magic." She closed the book, running her hand lovingly over its cover.

Something about that set his heart pounding again. Perhaps because she'd liked his gift so much. Perhaps it was the sparkle of excitement and joy in her eyes. Maybe the grace of even her smallest movements.

He slowly, carefully, slid his hand over hers where it rested on the book.

"Thank you, Joseph. I will treasure this."

He wrapped his fingers around her hand and pulled it to his lips. He pressed a quick kiss to her fingers. His heart nearly jumped out of his chest.

Katie sat very still, watching him. He couldn't quite decide what expression she wore. Confusion. Enjoyment. Uncertainty. Pleasure. It was a mixture of all of those things. He waited for her to pull away or speak or let him know if the gesture was welcome.

She did nothing but sit frozen on the spot, her gaze never leaving him.

"Katie, I—"

A knock interrupted the words he'd not yet decided upon. Katie hesitated a moment.

"I should answer that." Her voice was small, unsteady. Her eyes remained firmly locked with his.

Joseph nodded and released her hand.

Katie crossed to the door. Joseph hoped whoever it was would keep their conversation short so he could have more time with her.

But the moment she opened the door, he knew his time was over. A quick intake of breath preceded her happy cry of "Tavish!"

Tavish scooped her up, spinning her about. "Did you miss me, lass?"

For just a moment Joseph had forgotten that he had a rival for Katie's affections, a rival with a prior claim. He rose as Tavish came in, nodding in what he hoped appeared to be unconcerned friendliness.

"Joseph." Tavish held out his hand and Joseph shook it.

"Were your deliveries successful?" Joseph asked.

Tavish said they were. He didn't seem overly worried about finding another man spending an evening with the woman he was courting. Either Tavish didn't care as deeply as Joseph thought—something he doubted very much—or Tavish was confident in the strength of Katie's regard.

Joseph bid them both good night. He received a sincere, if awkward, thank you from Katie. He nodded his acceptance as he slipped out the door.

He'd made progress that night and had some reason for optimism. But the end was far from decided.

Though failure was a very real possibility, he didn't intend to lose without a fight.

Chapter Twenty-Two

Tavish pounded nails into the cow stall he and Ian were repairing in Ian's barn. While working alongside his brother once more was a relief, Ian wasn't entirely his old self again. He moved slower and without the stamina he once had. Tavish wanted his brother back, whole again.

"How is your new addition coming along?" Ian asked, helping Tavish lift the next plank into place.

"It is taking shape at last. The work has been slower than I expected."

"A great many things have been slower than expected lately." Ian looked unmistakably frustrated.

"How *are* you doing, then?" Tavish worried for him. "You seem a bit better at least."

Ian pounded in a nail, securing the plank. "Each day I'm a little improved, but I was no help at all during harvest. We lost a great deal of crop."

Tavish knew that well, and he was sorry for it. Even with all the men in the O'Connor family working one another's land, without Ian working alongside them, they'd not been able to bring in all the grain.

Ian set to sanding the top plank of the wall. "We weren't able to make our full payment on the land," he admitted in a quiet and frustrated voice. "Not even half the amount owed."

"You're not alone in that, brother. Hardly a soul in this valley made their payment in full. Times are hard for everyone."

They worked in silence for some time. Ian's thoughts were, no doubt, filled with his own worries. Tavish's mind was full of Katie, as always. Seeing Joseph Archer with her the very night Tavish returned to town had left him worrying once more.

Joseph could give her more than a small room tacked onto one end of a very simple and humble house. Joseph could give her the finest home in all of Hope Springs. If she wished for it, he could give her the whole world.

Tavish could offer her very little.

"How's our Katie holding up?" Ian asked without warning. "Has she heard from her father?"

"I don't believe she has." Indeed, Katie sometimes had such a look of sorrow in her eyes, the same sadness he'd seen there the day word had arrived of her father's illness.

"Da has full adopted her, you know." A quick smile crossed Ian's face. Tavish was glad to see it. "He's as protective of Katie as he ever was of Ciara and Mary. Whenever she comes 'round and Da is here, he asks how you're treating her and how Joseph's treating her and if she's happy."

Da asks after Joseph. Is there anyone who doesn't realize I've lost ground to that man?

Tavish laid his hammer on the barn floor near his bag of nails. They were nearly finished with the stall.

Ian chuckled lightly, pulling Tavish's eyes in that direction. Ian hadn't laughed much lately. Tavish hoped it meant he was mending.

"Do you remember how frustrated Ciara always was with Da when he'd quiz her about her beaux?"

Tavish smiled at the memory. "Does Katie prick at it as well?"

Ian shook his head. "She only smiles and embraces Da as if she's too grateful for words. A sweet woman she is."

"You don't have to convince me of that." Tavish gave their handiwork a close inspection. The stall was sturdy. "We've done some fine work here, Ian."

"We always were an impressive team, you and I. Well, mostly *I,* but you helped a bit here and there."

Tavish shook his head and laughed. Here was yet another glimpse of the brother he feared he had lost.

"Isn't this just like the two of you," Biddy said from a few steps away. "Laughing when you ought to be working." She smiled broadly as she came to where they stood.

Ian slipped his arms around her without a moment's hesitation and kissed her soundly. Tavish wished he had received that kind of greeting from Katie when he arrived at her doorstep a few days earlier, but at least she had embraced him.

Well, I *embraced* her, *but she didn't object. She hugged me back right there in front of Joseph. That has to count for something.*

What did he know of the workings of the female mind? Katie cared for him, he knew that much. He even believed she *loved* him. That did not, however, mean she didn't have any affection for Joseph Archer. She might not be entirely sure what she felt.

Which doesn't help my cause at all.

Biddy settled easily into Ian's embrace and her gaze fell on Tavish. "'Tis your day for fetching the wee'uns."

He had nearly forgotten.

There'd been a few scuffles between children in the schoolyard, and the preacher had asked that the children be collected at the end of each day by their parents or neighbors or family to ensure they returned home without getting themselves in fights along the way.

"I'll come by your place tomorrow and help with your new room," Ian offered.

Tavish gave him a firm nod of acknowledgment. He welcomed the help and the reassurance that Ian was recovering.

As he left, he saw Ian pull Biddy closer and press a kiss to her forehead.

That picture remained with him as he walked to town. Ian and Biddy had precisely the deep and abiding connection Tavish longed for. They completed one another, two halves of a whole. They found strength and comfort in the other. He wanted that for himself.

I think Katie feels that way toward me. But do I feel that way for her?

He nodded to his neighbors, gathered in town. The school days had been shortened. All the children left at lunchtime now; no more outside playtime, and thus no opportunities for fistfights behind the school building. The children left every day with somber faces and a look one would expect to see in the eyes of a caged animal. Tavish fully intended to let the children he'd come to collect run all the way down the Irish Road—they'd be restless after being kept inside all morning.

He stood among the other adults waiting for school to let out. Even now they were clearly divided. The Red Road parents stood by the mercantile; the Irish stood outside the smithy. Everyone's eyes darted between the school and the rival gathering, discomfort and, in many cases, downright hatred in their expressions.

How have we come to this?

"Back inside, Paddy, where we don't have to look at you."

The sneering command from the gathered Red Roaders pulled all the Irish eyes in that direction. Katie stood on the mercantile porch with her broom in hand. Tavish took a step toward her, but Mr. Johnson appeared on the porch. Tavish worried he'd only cause her more trouble if he made a scene.

Mr. Johnson said something. Katie nodded immediately and stepped back into the mercantile.

The children began emerging from the schoolhouse. Reverend Ford dismissed the Red Road children first. They rushed over to their parents. When the Irish children were dismissed, they did precisely the same thing. Even with the two groups separated by the wide dirt road, the movement of so many bodies was chaotic.

Tavish craned his neck searching for his own nieces and nephews. He had Michael at his side first. His sister's brood found him next.

"We'll just stay a moment and make certain all the children have someone to walk them home, shall we?" he asked his charges.

They all agreed, though he could see the idea of standing still for any length of time was not their favorite suggestion.

As the crowd began trickling away from town, they were careful to keep to their sides of the road. Most people lingered outside their chosen business establishment, chatting with one another and listening to their children speak of their school day.

Tavish caught sight of Katie carefully weaving her way through the Red Road crowd, receiving glares and words of disapproval for her efforts. She kept her chin up throughout the ordeal.

"Katie!" a little voice called out. At the edge of the Red Road crowd, Ivy Archer pulled away from the grip of a woman Tavish recognized from church the Sunday before.

She was the Archers' new housekeeper. The woman, as far as he'd been able to tell, didn't smile, didn't truly frown, and had very decided ideas about everything. Mrs. Smith had accepted the reverend's odd way of introducing new arrivals in town. When told she would find herself best suited to the red side of the chapel as opposed to the green, she'd thanked him for his concern, explained that she was charged with the welfare of the Archer girls and, thus, would sit with them, and took her seat on the centered back pew with the Archer family. It was far from the reprimand Katie had given the preacher but, still, it was the second refusal to comply in as many introductions. Tavish had seen the confusion in Reverend Ford's eyes and something like doubt creeping over his expression.

Katie was, at that moment, surrounded by Emma and Ivy Archer and, if Tavish was recognizing her correctly, the little Johnson girl. They stood in the middle of the road. Katie's gaze shifted between all three girls as each spoke over the other. Her smile was genuine. Tavish couldn't help a smile of his own.

"Shall we see if Miss Macauley wishes to rove home with us?" he asked his nieces and nephews.

They agreed and followed him as he moved in Katie's direction.

"Mama will have warm cookies waiting," the Johnson girl was saying. "I am sure she'd let us all have some."

Katie, it appeared, was included in the invitation. Had she actually managed to be on friendly terms with any members of that family?

"'Tis a sweet offer, Marianne, but I've a great deal of bread to be cooking this afternoon. I have to rush home, I'm afraid."

"That's quite enough loping about, girls." Mrs. Smith stood behind the Archer girls, her usual stern expression in place. "I have too much work to do to be standing here."

"Couldn't—?" Ivy bit down on her lip. "Couldn't we—?" She didn't finish the question.

Emma didn't speak either.

Katie's happy expression turned concerned. "The girls have been invited to enjoy some warm cookies with their particular friend Marianne Johnson. I believe they're wishing to ask permission to accept."

Tavish enjoyed seeing this side of her. She'd been so uncomfortable around the wee ones when she'd first arrived in Hope Springs. Her natural kindness had finally broken through the worry of uncertainty.

Mrs. Smith's face didn't transform in even the tiniest way. "I believe I already told the girls that it was time to go home," she said to Katie. "Come along, children."

"Yes, Mrs. Smith," they said in near-perfect unison and followed their housekeeper down the road home.

Katie gave Marianne an empathetic look. "I am sorry your friends couldn't stay for a bit."

Marianne didn't look devastated. "Mrs. Smith doesn't work Sunday afternoons. Emma is going to ask her papa if she can come to my house after church."

Katie nodded in approval. "A fine idea, that. I'd wager it'll work perfectly."

Marianne giggled and skipped off toward the mercantile, waving back at Katie as she went.

"You've made a fine friend, there, Sweet Katie."

"Aye. Marianne's a dear little girl." She turned around to face him. "I saw you hovering about. Wondered if you meant to say good day to me or not."

"I didn't want to interrupt."

She looked at the children hanging about him. "Have you picked up a few strays?"

"Aye. No one wanted this scraggly bunch, so I'm taking them down the Irish Road to see if anyone'll take pity on them and feed them lunch."

Katie winked at his niece Margaret. "I can think of a couple houses where I imagine they'd be welcomed."

Margaret giggled. "Ma'll let us in."

Tavish set his features in an expression of dawning understanding. "Then I suggest we take you there first."

"Excellent idea," Katie said.

"Come on, Uncle Tavish," Margaret pleaded. "Can't we go yet?"

He motioned them off. "But don't get so far ahead you can't hear or see us, understand?"

They nodded eagerly and began walking quickly up the road.

Tavish offered Katie his hand. She took it, and they followed after the children.

"So what did you do at work today, Sweet Katie?"

"Mr. Johnson had a fancy word for it, but mostly I just moved things around. What he thought would sell more during the winter was moved out onto the displays. The things he thought wouldn't sell much until next summer I moved into the storeroom."

'Twas no wonder, then, she looked so tired. "That is very demanding work."

She tossed him a saucy look. "Oh, I've muscles enough for it, I assure you."

"If only I could convince you to come move things about at my house." He spoke as though it was entirely a jest, but having Katie at his home, and not at all as an employee, had been on his mind a great deal lately.

"I'll not undertake putting your place to rights, Tavish. I've heard whispers up and down the road that you're tearing things apart over there. You've some great secret project going on, I'm told."

His neighbors were likely saying that very thing. The Irish took great delight in pulling stories the way others pulled taffy. "'Tis no great secret. I'm building onto my house is all, adding some extra space."

"I don't believe that boring explanation for a moment. You're digging a tunnel to the ocean or something, aren't you?"

He put a finger to his lips. "Shhh. You'll give away my dastardly plan, you will."

Her smile of amusement set his entire day to rights. He slipped his hand free of hers and wrapped his arm around her, pulling her closer to his side as they walked.

"Do you know where you ought to dig that tunnel to?" Katie went on.

"Where?" 'Twas a fine thing to have her at his side again.

"I've heard tell that north of Belfast there is a place where the rocks are tall towers, with sides fitted together like puzzles. Thousands and thousands of them all pressed together." Her expression was distant and longing. "I always wanted to go there, to see if it's as amazing as it sounded."

"The 'Giant's Causeway'?"

Her eyes widened. "You've heard of it?"

He nodded. "But I never got to see it either."

"You should dig your tunnel to *there,* Tavish. We could have our Irish Day at the Giant's Causeway."

"Our Irish—?" His deliveries and building project had pushed that idea clear out of his thoughts. "I'd forgotten. We do need to do that."

"I thought it might have slipped your mind—along with your promise to show me the 'finest view in all of Hope Springs.'"

He'd forgotten that as well. It'd been weeks and weeks since he'd told her about his favorite spot in the valley. He never had taken her there.

"You could come around just for a bit of gab, you know," she said. "It doesn't have to be a fancy, planned-out sort of day."

"I do need to come by more. Or"—another idea jumped into his mind—"you should stop by and see what I'm building. We could make a picnic of it."

"In this weather?" She shook her head as though it were the most nonsensical thing she'd ever heard. "We'd fair freeze to death."

"An indoor picnic, then."

"That would be nice." She threaded her arm through his. "I've not seen much of you, and I . . . I need to have some time with you, Tavish. That likely sounds very, I don't know, silly or—"

Tavish squeezed her arm with his. "Not silly at all. What kind of courtship is this if we never see each other?"

She didn't react to the word "courtship." He didn't know what to make of that.

Raised voices up ahead interrupted his pondering. In the length of a single breath, Tavish knew precisely what was happening. Damion MacCormack and Bob Archibald were standing nearly nose to nose on the road, shouting at one another.

"Tavish, the children."

Of course, that had to be the first priority. "Michael," he called out, getting the boy's attention quickly. "Take your cousins home without delay. You hear me?"

Michael took charge immediately. He was a boy much like Finbarr, mature beyond his age. He could be counted on to see through any task he was given.

Katie had already slipped from Tavish's side, guiding the other Irish around the coming scuffle, offering encouraging smiles to the children.

Tavish knew he couldn't reason with Archibald. No one could, not even the others on the Red Road. The man's temper was beyond legendary. But Damion could sometimes be talked down. He strode to where they were growling and glaring and spitting words at one another.

"This is hardly the time or place."

"Stand off, Tavish," Damion warned. "I've reason enough to settle this now."

"True though that may be, it can wait."

"Isn't that just like a Paddy," Archibald sneered. "You take his side because his blood is green like yours."

Tavish shot him a look of warning. "Keep running your mouth like that and you'll find out just what color your own blood is, Archibald."

"Is that a threat?" He ground the words out through his teeth.

Tavish took a breath to keep himself calm. "No. It's a reminder that brawling in the street isn't going to solve anything. And there are children about." He looked at both of them. "Are you willing to risk their well-being so you can feel like big men, throwing your fists to prove something?"

Archibald shoved him hard in the chest. Though Tavish was more solidly built, the attack caught him off guard. He stumbled back a single step before regaining his balance.

"You really shouldn't have done that," Tavish warned in a low, deliberate voice.

"Do you intend to fight back?" Archibald seemed amused by the thought.

Tavish shook his head. "But I'm not going to stop him"—he motioned at Damion with his head—"from having at you. Perhaps you didn't know he was a prizefighter in Galway."

For the first time, Archibald looked less certain of himself. Tavish glanced about. The children had all been herded down their respective roads. No one was near enough to be hurt except the two men who'd brought it on themselves. It might even break some of the tension hanging over the town to let a couple combatants go at each other to their hearts' content.

Katie stood near the bridge, watching him and waiting. He gave her a quick wave to assure her he'd be there in a moment.

To Damion he said, in a voice loud and clear enough for Archibald to understand, "Just don't *kill* him."

He didn't look back as he walked to where Katie stood. He knew the sounds of a scuffle when he heard them. The men hadn't wasted any time.

"You didn't stop them?" Katie asked, surprise and concern in her tone.

"When two people are that determined to lay into each other, sometimes the only thing to be done is delay them until there's no one else about to get caught in the brawl."

Her worried gaze remained on the road behind them. "Fighting can't be the answer. People only get hurt that way."

She'd not been in Hope Springs long enough to truly understand. "The tension's been thick since before the harvest run. *This* will release some of that."

"This is brutality."

He followed her gaze. The men were, indeed, beating each other good. Tavish turned her face away with the lightest pressure of his hand. "Watching it isn't going to help, sweetheart."

"But pretending it's not there doesn't make it go away." Clearly the situation upset her more than he'd expected it to.

"They'd have been fighting eventually. I've seen it often enough. It's either the two of them looking like fools on an empty road, or dozens of people slugging it out with no regard for the welfare of anyone who might be nearby." He took her hands and squeezed them. "I know it isn't pleasant, but it is what it is."

"You've given up, then?"

"Not given up. I'm only hoping to keep the town from actually killing each other while we search for some kind of real solution." He tried to coax a smile from her, but it didn't work. "Come on. I know you've bread to make today."

She nodded and went with him, but her eyes remained clouded.

"I suppose Hope Springs isn't quite the paradise you hoped it would be," he said.

In a voice quiet and heavy, she answered, "Nothing is quite what I expected it to be."

Though she walked at his side, her hand in his, Tavish could feel a distance between them. Was she pulling away from him personally, or simply reacting to the anger and hatred she'd seen on the road? He couldn't be sure either way.

Chapter Twenty-Three

Joseph was about a breath away from consigning all of Hope Springs to perdition and letting them happily take themselves there. Though the ranch owners out at the farthest reaches of both the roads were a rough and often argumentative group, he'd reached the point where he far preferred their company to any of his nearer neighbors.

Almost every day that week he'd had a new report of one side or the other causing problems. Eggs had been stolen. Animals were being let out at night, leading to creative methods of locking barns or rigging pans to the doors so they would clang about should anyone try to break in. Hay had disappeared. Equipment had as well.

Bob Archibald and Damion MacCormack had spent much of an afternoon a few days earlier fighting on the road to town. Chester Smith and Eoin O'Donaghue undertook the same task, but along the banks of the river. No one was quite certain where Gerald Jones and Seamus Kelly had held their boxing match, but they looked every bit as bad as the others.

They were stealing from each other, pounding one another into a pulp, and generally doing their utmost to make life for their neighbors as miserable as possible. Their animosity increased day by day. The likelihood of widespread violence continued to grow. At some point, Joseph realized with frustrated resignation, he would have to once again threaten them into a cease-fire.

He'd seldom felt less like going to church than he did that Sunday morning. In the past, the Sunday after the final harvest had been a favorite. His mind was clear of work for once. But that day going to church felt like another chore.

"Are you ready to go, girls?" he asked, stepping into the parlor as he straightened his lapels.

Mrs. Smith finished tying a white ribbon on one of Emma's long braids. The woman gave him a single quick nod, a gesture he'd come to recognize as her most common. It meant everything from agreement to reprimand to acknowledgment of an assignment. She didn't say much. What she did say tended to be a touch too blunt. He almost preferred her silence.

"Come along." He motioned the girls toward the dining room.

They passed through it to the kitchen and out the back door. Mrs. Smith followed along in their wake. He helped the girls onto the back bench of the buggy. Mrs. Smith preferred to sit up front. That had taken some getting used to, as the girls had grown accustomed to sitting beside him. Still, it kept the peace, which was all he wanted.

The drive to church was a quiet one. Ivy didn't chatter away, and Emma's usual silence felt quieter somehow. Had the tension in Hope Springs settled on his girls as well?

Inside the church building the townspeople sat like statues. Backs were ramrod straight. Eyes remained firmly ahead. Both sides refused to acknowledge the other. Though Joseph could see nothing but the backs of their heads from his place in the rear of the room, their postures were unmistakable. Anger and distrust and pride rippled through the entire congregation. Even his own girls looked somber and withdrawn.

Joseph slumped a little on the bench, tired to his core. If everyone would simply try to get along, life would be far easier for all of them. He was sick of the whole town at that moment.

Every one of them except Katie. He'd taken the girls to visit her again the night before. The feud had come up in conversation. Though he hadn't said anything, Katie seemed to understand he didn't want to talk about it. She quickly changed the topic—he didn't even remember what to—and they spent the rest of the night on light subjects. She played her violin. The girls danced. Ivy even sang a song Katie had taught her. He'd had to force himself to leave without begging her to come home with them.

He'd gone home alone, put the girls to bed alone.

"Stop fidgeting, children." Mrs. Smith spoke without even looking at the girls. Her eyes remained properly straight ahead where Reverend Ford was seated near the pulpit reading in his Bible.

Joseph didn't think the girls were moving all that much. A shift in weight now and then, but considering their ages, that was admirable. They stilled their small movements and sat very properly on the bench.

Reverend Ford rose to begin the service. If he noticed the undercurrents of battle in the air, he didn't let on. His words of welcome didn't differ in the slightest from the ones he usually spoke. The congregation muttered the morning hymn more than sang it.

The preacher got no further than "The topic of today's sermon is taken from—" before he was interrupted.

Bob Archibald—Joseph would recognize his acerbic tones anywhere—called out, "You should preach about not stealing another man's animals."

Reverend Ford's face froze, his eyes darting about as if searching for an explanation for the interruption.

"Only if you Reds'll listen," someone on the Irish side called back.

Are they planning to fight inside the church now?

"This is hardly the place," Reverend Ford insisted.

Bob Archibald was on his feet. "The church is just the place to tell these heathens they can't get away with wringing my rooster's neck."

One of Archibald's animals was *killed?* Joseph hadn't heard that.

"I know it was one of you." Archibald pointed a finger at the other side of the room. "I found the poor animal dead at the door of my barn this morning." He glared at the Irish. "Don't think this won't go unanswered."

Damion MacCormack jumped to his feet. "Then maybe you'd care to answer for my calf. 'Twas let out of the barn the week of the harvest run, and we've not found it yet. *That* needs answering."

Shouts became general. Accusations flew across the room like cannon shot. Men had each other by the collars, shaking and shouting. The women yelled and pointed and glared. Even their children joined in the growing anarchy.

Joseph glanced at his little ones. Ivy clasped her hands over her ears, a look of misery on her face. Emma's chin began to quiver, her eyes wide with fear. *This* was the utopia he'd left Baltimore for, the peaceful, happy place he'd wanted to raise his children, the community Katie had given up her dreams of Ireland to be part of?

Little Marianne Johnson rushed down the aisle to the centered back bench where Joseph and his family sat. The pleading in her expression was clear. She wished to escape the shouting and anger. Joseph nodded, and she climbed up on the bench next to Emma. The two girls held each other's hands, watching the battle playing out in front of them with growing worry and anguish.

Perhaps Katie was the wisest of all of them, choosing not to attend services. She'd denounced the entire thing as hypocritical her very first week in town.

These were good people when they weren't fighting. If they'd just calm down, let their tempers cool, this difficulty might pass and quit frightening their own children.

Someone—Joseph couldn't see exactly who through all the chaos—shoved someone else, and he knew the time for sitting back had passed.

He set two fingers in his mouth and blew. An ear-splitting, shrill whistle ricocheted mercilessly around the room. All eyes turned toward him. He slowly rose, looking them in the eye one by one. He walked with deliberate steps up the center aisle. The crowd of combatants parted, most dropping their gaze the moment he captured it. Perhaps they could still be convinced to step back—not reasoned with, necessarily, but momentarily appeased.

He nodded to Reverend Ford when he reached the spot just in front of the pulpit. The slightest nod of the reverend's head seemed to indicate permission to usurp command of the service for a moment.

"Sit down." Joseph addressed the group in a voice that was not so much calm as it was thick with vexation. They obeyed, though many did so reluctantly. "Is this what you've come to? Brawling in a church? Dragging your little children into your own blinding hatred?"

A few people had the decency to look shamefaced.

"I have never made myself an enemy to any of you, never taken sides." He locked eyes with anyone willing to keep their gaze off the floor. "All of you know how I feel about your determination to destroy each other. If you keep things relatively peaceful, I stay out of it. But we've seen fistfights at school, on the road. We almost had one here a moment ago. Animals are being stolen, let loose and killed. This stops now." He emphasized each word of his final sentence.

For a moment he simply stared them all down. They needed to see his disgust with the situation, his determination to end it.

"Prices were low at market, and many of you on *both* sides of this feud came to me asking for time, for consideration, for mercy in your land payments. I didn't call in those debts, though the terms of your notes allow me to." More eyes dropped. More faces fell in humility. "But if you aren't willing to give each other consideration and mercy, then neither am I."

Suddenly he had the full attention of every adult in the room. Most of these families—nearly all of them, in fact—hadn't been in a position to make a full payment on their land. If he called in their notes, they would be forced from their homes.

Please don't let it come to that.

"So long as you keep the peace between each other, nothing will change. But start this up again, start brawling and stealing from and destroying each other, and I will call in every single debt owed to me in this town."

He hated that the only way to get through to his neighbors was to make them fear him. He wanted friends, associates with whom he could laugh and spend an evening of amiable conversation. Instead, he'd forced himself into isolation by the necessity of his threats.

"I don't want to have to do this," he assured them.

Thomas Dempsey called back, "We don't want you to have to either, Joseph Archer."

He could smile the tiniest bit at that. Leave it to one of the O'Connors, even an in-law, to break some of the tension.

"So keep quiet and peaceable," Joseph said. "And let the reverend deliver his sermon without interruption."

As he walked back to his seat in silence, his eyes caught Emma's. She looked at him as if she hardly knew him, as if he frightened her.

They've turned my own child against me.

He hadn't the heart to sit beside her and feel that condemnation. Rather than take his seat, he instead slipped out the back door. He leaned against the outside wall of the church building and closed his eyes. Would Emma look at him differently now? Would Ivy?

Would Katie? If anyone would understand, she would. He found some comfort in the belief that she wouldn't condemn him outright.

Acting the part of the coldhearted man of business had cost him some associates over the years and come in the way of friendships. If it cost him Katie, he didn't think he could bear it.

Chapter Twenty-Four

Mrs. Claire gave Katie a detailed report of all that had happened at church and how Joseph had threatened to evict the entire valley. She'd heard before that he'd had to use that leverage to keep the peace. She understood it, but she couldn't like it. All she could think of was the time as a child when her landlord had decided to clear his land and had evicted families in the cruelest, most heartless way. How could Joseph even think of doing something like that? It did not at all sound like him.

She stewed over it all day. Joseph was a good man, she knew that for a fact. Surely if evictions proved necessary, he would show compassion.

Compassion or not, those families will still be out in the cold.

Biddy arrived in the midst of Katie's swirling thoughts. Her waistline had expanded since last they'd seen each other; a close observer would be able to tell she was expecting. The strain in Biddy's eyes had grown as well.

"Good evening to you, Katie. I've come for a gab."

"That is just grand, as I've been longing for one, myself." Katie happily showed her inside. "Would you care for a cup of coffee or tea?"

"Tea would be lovely. 'Tis such a terribly cold night out."

They chatted as Katie prepared the kettle. Before coming to Hope

Springs, Katie had never really had a friend. Biddy had filled that void to perfection. Hardly a day went by when they didn't see each other.

"I've a feeling you heard of the difficulties at church today. Tavish likely mentioned it."

Katie pulled the tin of tea from its shelf. "He might very well have mentioned it if he'd come by."

"Not been by?" Biddy stared a fraction of a moment before shaking off her surprise. "Sunday courting is a time-honored tradition."

"Tell that to my lazy bum of a grandson, will you?" Mrs. Claire called from her rocking chair. "He's not been by in a month of Sundays. Stops in now and then and flashes a melting smile or offers a mouthful of sweet words, then he disappears for days on end."

"You know as well as I do, Granny, that Tavish is a busy man," Katie said. "Further, my own schedule is just as packed full as it can be. He'd more likely than not stop by and not find me here."

She received a look of exasperation in response. "Aye, it's busy we all are, including Joseph Archer, but we can't seem to get rid of *that* man."

'Twas a truth sure enough. Katie's heart warmed at the reminder of his attentiveness and the joy of his company. She had liked him whilst working in his home, but having come to know him outside of that had taught her to love him in a way she hadn't anticipated.

"Joseph comes by now and then, does he?" Biddy looked between Katie and Granny, eyes wide with anticipation.

Granny answered before Katie could. "More accurate to say he '*leaves* now and then.'"

To her credit, Biddy didn't laugh right out loud, though she grinned wide enough to make her amusement clear. She lowered her voice so Granny wouldn't hear her next words.

"Have Joseph's visits helped you decide which direction your heart's leaning?"

Katie busied herself with the tea. "I've grown more fond of him, certainly."

"More *fond?*" Biddy did allow a small chuckle at that. "I've a feeling Joseph's hoping for more than fondness. But if that's all you're feeling, that may be the answer you're looking for."

Katie shook her head. With a sigh, she confessed, "It's more than fondness. It's a vast deal more than fondness."

"Then why do you sound so sad about that?"

"A woman's affections don't change so easily. They *shouldn't,* anyway."

"Katie." Biddy spoke right over her. "If you'd declared suddenly one day that you had absolutely no feelings for Tavish and had, for no real reason whatsoever, decided Joseph was the very man for you, then I'd agree your affections had changed easily. But, my dear friend, there's been nothing easy about the debate you've been waging with yourself. It's been weeks and weeks you've argued with yourself over this."

"Because I don't know what to do." Uncertainty coiled inside her at the reminder of how turned about she felt in the matter of Joseph and Tavish. "I've never had *one* man vying for my heart, let alone two. And I've been on my own for nearly all my life with no mother or sisters or anyone to help me know how to make this kind of decision. I feel so lost."

"And it isn't as though you're choosing between a wonderful man and a horrible one," Biddy added.

"Aye. That'd be an easy decision for anyone." Katie rubbed at the tension in her neck and let out a deep breath. "I'm certain there are plenty of people who would declare me inexcusably stupid for not knowing the answer to this. It likely would be obvious to someone with more experience in these matters."

Biddy took Katie's hands in hers and looked directly into her eyes. "'Tis the easiest thing in all the world for someone looking on from the outside to declare that the choice is obvious, that you ought to have magically known from the very first moment, that you ought to know both their hearts and minds."

Katie smiled a bit at the idea. "It would simplify things if I could know what both of them were feeling. As it is, I have to guess."

"You are trying to make a decision that will change your entire life," Biddy said. "If you made such an important choice without giving it enough thought to be truly sure—even if you belabored it more than others might think necessary—*that* would be 'inexcusably stupid.' So don't you give a moment's thought to whether or not someone might insist this is an easy decision. If it mattered less, it might be simpler."

"Bring the tea over, you two," Granny instructed. "I'd like a bit of gossip myself."

A moment later they were all settled, sipping at their steaming cups. Apparently by "gossip" Granny meant "talk about Katie's love difficulties." The topic didn't wander at all from that one.

Granny rocked as she sipped. "Tell me this, Katie: how do you feel when the two of them are about?"

She hardly had to think to explain her feelings in Tavish's company. "Tavish makes me smile. I only need to see him across the way and my heart lightens. He makes me happy."

Biddy nodded, the gesture one of complete understanding. "Tavish has a way of bringing joy wherever he goes."

"And when he's nearby, I know I don't have to worry about the hard and heavy things," Katie added. "Tavish offers a respite, and that's something I've not had in my life."

"Is that what you want?" Granny asked. "Someone to take away your burdens?"

To take away my burdens? Sometimes.

"What of Joseph?" Granny pressed. "How do you feel with him?"

That was a more difficult question. "I don't rightly know how to explain it. I'm always glad to see him, for sure, but I don't get that immediate urge to grin like I do with Tavish."

Granny didn't seem to think that a discouraging thing. "Joseph is of a more somber bent; that makes perfect sense."

"But I *am* happy to see him," Katie quickly clarified. "Indeed, I find myself watching for him even when he isn't expected. And when he does show up on the doorstep, I feel as though I've been holding my breath all the day long and can finally let it out. It's almost like . . . like relief. When he's with me, the difficulties and struggles of life are less overwhelming. He doesn't take my burdens away; he just helps me face them."

Both women watched her closely, neither offering insights.

Katie continued sorting the dilemma out loud. "Both are good reactions, aren't they? It isn't as though I don't wish to see them or they make me miserable or any such thing. A person wants to smile and be happy. And a person also wants someone in her life who lifts the weight of the day simply by being there with her."

"Aye." Granny sipped and rocked and nodded. "But which is it you need most, Katie? Which man brings you that sense of completeness you can't quite seem to find without him? For which of them do *you* conjure up that same feeling of being complete?"

What could she do but hold her hands up in a show of utter bafflement?

Granny gave her a look that quite perfectly spoke of knowing the answer her own self, but choosing to leave the words unspoken. "You'll sort it out. Give it a bit of time, and you'll realize the truth that's staring you in the face."

"You make it sound very simple," Katie said.

"I hadn't meant to, dear. It's anything but."

Biddy took a quick sip of tea. "I passed Tavish's house on my way here, and he is making progress on his building project."

"I hadn't heard exactly what it is he's building," Katie said, happy to have the topic turned from her very confused heart. "A room of some kind."

"Aye." Biddy nodded. "A proper bedroom. He's slept all these years in a wee nook behind the fireplace. It will be nice for him to have something finer than that. He deserves it."

"That he does," Granny agreed.

"And, though he had a lean year like the rest of us, he's managed to purchase materials and make a full payment on his land. Very few in Hope Springs were able to pay all they owed." A heaviness settled on Biddy's face, a sure sign she and Ian were among the number who came up short.

"Is Joseph truly threatening to evict the whole valley?" Katie asked.

"Aye," Granny answered. "We've not given him much choice with all this fighting and stealing going on. That threat is likely the only thing that will get through to everyone."

"Will he have to do it in the end, do you think?" Katie's heart sank at the thought.

"I certainly hope not," Biddy said. "For our sake as well as his."

As well as his. Joseph cared deeply about his neighbors. Being forced to toss them out would tear him apart. 'Twas nothing short of an impossible situation.

Granny was feeling poorly on Monday, so Katie left the mercantile a little earlier than usual. She thought it a sign of progress that Mr. Johnson was willing to grant her the time. Perhaps others in the valley would follow Mr. Johnson's lead and set aside some of their animosity. 'Twould save everyone a great deal of heartache.

Her mind was heavy as she walked along the road leading away from town. She feared for her neighbors and the future of Hope Springs. She worried about Joseph and the role he'd been forced to take on.

The sound of footsteps pulled her from her musings. She glanced over her shoulder. Bob Archibald walked not many paces behind her. Katie slowed her steps and moved to the edge of the road, giving him ample room to pass her. But he didn't. Mr. Archibald kept directly behind her, matching her pace. She sped up once more, and he did the same.

Was he following her? Why?

School wouldn't be out for a while yet. She was a good distance from town, too far to simply turn back. No one else was on the road. Katie's heart pounded with the realization that she was alone and being closely followed by a man who hated her, a man with a violent temper.

Trying to keep her growing panic from showing, Katie kept a smooth but quick pace. The Irish Road would be every bit as empty. Did she dare try to get all the way to Granny's house with Bob Archibald on her trail? If he didn't catch her before she got home, what was to stop him from forcing his way inside? Granny certainly couldn't defend either of them.

She didn't know for certain that Mr. Archibald intended to hurt her, but she didn't dare take that chance. There was only one real choice.

Joseph's home.

She cut across the front lawn and directly to the door. She knocked, then glanced back over her shoulder to see if Mr. Archibald was still there. He stood at the fork, arms folded across his chest, watching her. The man was unnerving. At least he hadn't come closer.

She knocked again.

Mrs. Smith answered. "The family is not at home to visitors." She made to close the door, but Katie slipped her foot inside enough to stop the door.

"Please tell Mr. Archer I am here."

"I will not," Mrs. Smith said. "He is a busy man and not to be disturbed."

"Did Mr. Archer tell you specifically that if I came to the door, you were to turn me away?" Katie only asked because she knew it wasn't true. "Your job is to answer for visitors; your employer decides who stays and who goes. I will not be turned away by you."

Katie didn't at all like the snapping displeasure in the older woman's eyes. Still, she held her ground. Between Mrs. Smith and Mr. Archibald, she'd rather face down Mrs. Smith.

"Mr. Archer is not currently in the house. I am a busy woman and will not go hunting him down."

Katie glanced back over her shoulder. Mr. Archibald was still on the road, but he'd begun moving slowly toward the bridge to the Irish side. He meant to cut her off.

"Please, Mrs. Smith—"

"This is no longer your place of residence or employment. I suggest you get that fact firmly lodged in your mind." Mrs. Smith shut the door with a snap. Katie heard the door lock.

What do I do now? She couldn't go back to town. Though Seamus Kelly would help her—and she felt certain if she returned to the mercantile, Mr. Johnson wouldn't allow her to be harmed either—she didn't think she could walk all that way fast enough to elude Mr. Archibald. The Red Road was absolutely out of the question.

Oh, Joseph, where are you? She turned slowly away from the house, surveying the area and the situation. What was she to do? She couldn't be entirely certain Bob Archibald wouldn't do her a physical harm. Staying on the porch wouldn't help—he'd already seen that she couldn't expect assistance from those inside the house—but neither could she get past him to the bridge.

He moved too slowly for his pace to be anything but deliberate. The man knew how to make her afraid.

Katie moved down to the first step, watching Mr. Archibald's back. There was no reason he'd be headed toward the Irish Road, no *good* reason at least. He was waiting for her.

You got yourself from Derry to Belfast all on your own at only thirteen years of age, Katie Macauley. You're no autumn leaf falling down at the first stiff breeze.

She stepped off the porch and onto the path. The wind pushed and pressed at her, as if trying to convince her to return to the shelter of the porch. But she couldn't hide forever. The safety it offered was a ruse. So long as she was outside the house, there was no real protection there.

A show of confidence couldn't hurt, though she wasn't convinced it would help. She held tight to her woolen shawl. It had been woefully inadequate against the cold of the past week, but it was all she had.

One step at a time she moved closer to the bridge and to Mr. Archibald.

Where are you, Joseph? I need you.

Mr. Archibald stopped—he'd reached the bridge—and leaned against a post, watching her approach.

Her feet stopped. 'Twould be foolish to simply walk directly into the trap he was clearly setting for her. But where could she go?

She was closer to the barn than Mr. Archibald was. She might be able to beat him there. Her first night in Hope Springs, she'd hidden in Biddy and Ian's barn. Tavish had found her there. Perhaps if she ducked inside Joseph's barn, someone would come to her aid. Or she'd simply trap herself inside with no way out.

Aye, but you might find a pitchfork or something.

It wasn't the best plan, but it was all she could think of. She set herself to a faster pace, heading directly toward the barn. Mr. Archibald seemed to realize her destination after a moment and moved that way himself.

She walked faster. So did he.

So she ran.

He was likely only steps behind her. She ducked inside the barn. The dimness inside forced her to slow down.

"Joseph?" she called out, hoping against hope to find him there. Only silence answered.

She stumbled about as her eyes tried to adjust to the low light. She'd not spent a lot of time in Joseph's barn. Where did he keep his tools? She couldn't remember.

"What have we here?" Mr. Archibald stood in the doorway. "A little Irish mouse that's wandered too far from home."

She took a frantic step backward and lost her footing. Her shoulder slammed into the wooden wall of an animal stall. Her face scraped up against it before she could entirely right herself. She could likely see better in the dimness than he could yet. That was her only advantage.

She slipped farther back into the barn, looking about for anything she might use to defend herself.

"There is only one way out of here." Mr. Archibald hadn't left the doorway.

Find a pitchfork. A shovel. Anything.

"What is it you want, Mr. Archibald?" She searched around her as she spoke, her eyes settling on a gardening hoe. That would have to do.

"Only to give you a word of advice."

"And what would that be?" She wrapped her hand around the hoe handle, holding it out in front of her.

Mr. Archibald hadn't taken a single step inside. That didn't make her feel any safer. "You keep to your side of the river. It's safer there."

"I've a job to do and the perfect right to come and go as need be." She tightened her grip.

"We don't take kindly to the vermin infesting our town, Paddy. Further, we know how to smoke out the rats, send them running from their own sinking ship."

"We're none of us running."

"Yet," he added without hesitation. "You and your kind stay on your side of the river or we'll see to it you don't have a choice."

"I have to cross the river to do my job."

Mr. Archibald shook his head, giving a humorless laugh. "You won't have a job come morning. A few of us will be talking sense into Jeremiah this afternoon. Maybe you ought to try doing the same with your fellow Paddies."

She kept her gaze on him, watching for even the slightest movement in her direction. "You had to follow me all the way into this barn simply to tell me that?"

"Think of me as the tomcat seeing that the mouse scurried back home."

She didn't care for that image. "I've never known a cat that *herded* mice." They generally *ate* them.

Mr. Archibald grinned, the oily, worrisome smile she hated so much.

A second figure appeared in the doorway. Was she to be set upon by more than one Red like Ian had been? If so, the hoe would do her very little good.

"Pardon me, Mr. Archibald." Finbarr turned slightly, enough for a burst of sunlight to glint off the axe he held over his shoulder. There was a lad who knew how to pick a last-minute weapon. No hoes or shovels for him. "I've been sent to chop wood and need to fetch my gloves from inside the barn."

She felt the tiniest bit of relief.

Mr. Archibald gave Finbarr a long look before letting his gaze return to Katie. "Don't bother coming to the mercantile tomorrow. You won't be welcome." He shot her a satisfied smile and slipped out of the doorway.

Katie let her shoulders drop. She set the hoe against the wall.

"Did he hurt you, Miss Macauley?" Finbarr asked, taking a single step inside the barn.

She shook her head. "He blew a great deal of smoke, but he didn't hurt me."

His eyes narrowed as he studied her. "Your face is bleeding."

She touched the tender spot on her cheek where she'd hit the stall wall. Her fingers came up wet. In her fear she hadn't noticed she'd cut herself. "I slipped," she said.

"Mr. Archer will want to see that," Finbarr said.

Katie shook her head. "It isn't bad. I'd much rather get back to Mrs. Claire's and forget this whole thing ever happened." Fine words, those, but empty. She'd not be forgetting the fear any time soon.

She stepped out of the barn and once more into the biting wind.

"Can I walk you to Mrs. Claire's house?" Finbarr asked.

"You needn't do that."

He walked at her side. "I know you don't need me to, but Mr. Archer would wring my neck if he knew I didn't after what you've been through."

Finbarr swung the axe into the chopping block as they passed it. He explained almost sheepishly, "I wasn't actually supposed to chop wood. I just thought Mr. Archibald might leave you alone if I stood there with an axe."

"Did Joseph send you to rescue me, then?"

Finbarr secured the top button of his coat. "He's out repairing a fence and sent me in for some wire. I saw Mr. Archibald follow you into the barn. I assumed he was up to no good."

"Apparently you know him well." Katie tucked her hands under her shawl. The day was growing colder instead of warmer.

"I know *the feud* well," Finbarr corrected. "It makes people vicious."

"'Tis a full-on shame the town can't put this hatred behind them."

Finbarr nodded. "Part of me is convinced someone will have to die before they do."

Katie opened her mouth to argue against such a drastic prediction, but the words wouldn't come. Suddenly part of her was equally certain, and the realization frightened her.

Chapter Twenty-Five

The sudden drop in temperature sent Tavish to Granny's house to split logs. The night would likely be a cold one, and he didn't want them to find themselves out of firewood. The pile of wood behind the house was alarmingly low. Everyone's firewood supply was dwindling. The annual pre-winter wood run would have to be scheduled soon. Very few trees grew in Hope Springs—they had to go out and cut as much wood as a few wagons would hold to see them through the cold months to come. Depending on how bitter the winter grew, they sometimes went out again with sleds. But the forest was far away, more than a day's drive. 'Twas a dangerous thing to be out in the winter, given the unpredictable nature of Wyoming weather.

He carried an armload of wood inside, speaking to Granny as he made his way through the kitchen. "Let Katie know that I can cut more in the morning if you've run out."

"Tell her your own self, Tavish."

Sure enough, Katie stood near Granny, tucking a quilt about the dear old woman's legs. She must have arrived home while he was out chopping.

"You're back early," he said.

"I told Mr. Johnson that Granny was ailing, and he gave me the rest of the day to look after her."

Tavish could hardly have been more surprised if Katie had said Mr. Johnson had offered to lower the Irish prices to match the Red Road's.

"That is unexpectedly human of him, all things considered." He laid his armful of wood in the basket near the fireplace and set himself to the task of lighting a fire.

"I'll say this for Mr. Johnson," Katie said, "he has proven himself less of a monster than I at first feared him to be."

Tavish had seen and heard for himself the unkindness Mr. Johnson heaped on Katie, yet she had kind words for the man?

"I'm not saying he's a saint, so you can both quit looking at me like I've lost my mind." Katie offered a tiny, fleeting smile.

"Leave it to our Katie to work a miracle with one of the meanest men in town." Granny smiled, patting Katie's cheek. "Before long you'll have him walking up and down this road just friendly as can be with all of us."

Katie shook her head. "No one could manage that. I think we'd all agree the Reds staying on their side of the river would be best."

She had never been one to truly advocate for the separation in town. What had brought that comment on?

"Can you get along without me for a bit?" she asked Granny. "I'd like to change into some warm stockings and take a moment for myself."

"Of course, child."

Tavish took her hand as she passed. She stopped and looked back at him. He hadn't noticed until just then, but Katie was pale, her features drawn and tense. And, more concerning yet, she had a cut just below one eye.

"What happened? You've a cut on your face."

"I slipped on my walk home. It hardly hurts anymore," she insisted. "I need a moment to myself is all. I'll be grand in a bit."

He studied her expression and the stiff set of her shoulders. Something was worrying Katie, there was no denying it. He'd give her a moment, but once he had the fire set, he meant to do what he could to coax a smile or a laugh from her.

She slipped down the small corridor. An instant later, he heard the sound of her door closing.

"Our Katie keeps things tucked inside," Granny observed in her usual sage way.

"Aye, that she does."

He had the kindling laid and the beginnings of a flame started when the first strains of an air played expertly on a fiddle floated out of Katie's room. He stopped a moment and simply listened. No one could pull music from a fiddle quite like she could.

"She plays every day," Granny said. "Sometimes more than once. Always when she first returns from the mercantile, and often at night before we go to bed."

"That is a fine treat for the both of you." Tavish thought about his own quiet and lonely evenings and felt more than a twinge of envy.

"And for the Archers," Granny added.

"The Archers?" He hadn't expected that.

"Aye. Joseph comes by regularly with his wee ones to visit. Katie always plays for them so the girls can dance and sing."

"How often are they here?"

"Three or four times a week."

Three or four times a week? That was more often than *he* was there. Where in the world did Joseph find the time? "I suppose if I had a hired hand and a housekeeper, I could spend my evenings visiting as well."

"Oh, pish." Granny looked on the verge of rolling her eyes at him. "If you wanted to come more often, you'd find a moment here or there."

"I am not neglecting her, Granny." He set a log on the fire, watching to make certain the flames took. "I have been running Ian's farm as well as my own. I was off making my deliveries. Every free minute I have goes to building a room onto my house. A room *for her.*"

"And is that what she wants most from you, lad? A room?"

He added another log. "She's spoken of wishing for a room to herself all these years."

"But is it what she wants *most?* That's the question you ought to be asking yourself."

The fire was burning small and steady. Tavish stood and took a step back. "What does Katie want most?" he asked quietly. "She is not an easy one to understand."

"And I'd wager you are entirely unaccustomed to difficulty in courting."

"Difficulty?" He shot Granny an amused grin. Surely she was teasing him. "We're moving slowly, I suppose, but things aren't falling to ruin between the two of us."

Granny rocked back and forth, her gaze narrowed on him. "I remember your courtship with Bridget. At this point in your acquaintance, the two of you were driving the lot of us out of our minds with all the sweetness and loving between you."

Granny was near about the only person he could ever bear to discuss Bridget with. So much regret and sadness still clung to his memories of his young sweetheart. He'd put that behind him, he often reminded himself, but that didn't mean he wished to talk about her.

The plaintive air echoing from Katie's room gave way to another. She was choosing slow, sad tunes. Did that mean she was upset, or was it simply what came to mind?

"Perhaps I ought to go talk to Katie." He spoke the thought out loud, but before he'd taken one step in the direction of Katie's room, a knock sounded on the front door.

Granny leaned around to look out the window. Whoever stood there was motioned inside. A moment later, Joseph Archer stepped across the threshold.

"Is Katie here?" The question wasn't casual at all. Joseph actually looked concerned.

"She most certainly is," Granny answered. "Has something happened?"

Joseph looked between the two of them. "She didn't tell you?"

His tone had Tavish on edge. Something had happened, just as he'd suspected. He moved quickly down the corridor. Katie was keeping something from them, something Joseph was aware of and concerned about. "Katie?"

She opened her bedroom door. Her look was questioning, but she didn't speak.

"Joseph Archer is here," he said. "He seems to think there is reason to be concerned about you."

Tavish watched her closely. Her color dropped off further. Her gaze shifted up the corridor.

"Finbarr must have told him," she mumbled.

"Told him what?"

Katie walked uncertainly into the room where the others waited, Tavish close on her heels.

"Hello there, Joseph." Her tone was hesitant.

Did she expect to be scolded? What in heaven's name had happened? And why hadn't she told *him* about it?

Joseph crossed the room, stopping directly in front of her. He slipped his hand under her chin, tipping her face so the small cut under her eye was more visible. He'd known about the cut.

"Does it hurt much?" Joseph asked.

She gave the tiniest shake of her head. "It looks worse than it is."

Joseph kept her chin in his hand. "And he didn't hurt you? You swear to me he didn't lay a hand on you?"

"What?" Tavish blinked in surprise. Someone had hurt Katie? "Who?"

They both ignored him.

"He only followed me," Katie said. "He near frightened the very life out of me, but he didn't hurt me."

"Katie Macauley, what is going on?" Someone had followed her around, scaring her? Why was he only just hearing about this, and from Joseph instead of from her?

Her attempt to remain unconcerned fell far short of believable. "Bob Archibald only wanted to be a troublemaker—"

"Bob Archibald?" Tavish's stomach fell to his feet. His fists pulled tight.

Joseph lowered his hand from Katie's face but didn't step away. "Archibald followed her on the walk home. Finbarr saw him chase her into my barn and went in after him."

Tavish would have to thank his brother the next time he saw him.

"Finbarr came in with an axe," Katie added. "Very effective."

"Why didn't you come inside the house instead of the barn?"

"Because your gem of a housekeeper wouldn't let me in." Katie's tone had lost some of its distress.

Joseph frowned. "Did you explain that you were being followed?"

"I wasn't given the opportunity."

Tavish jumped into the conversation he was quite thoroughly being left out of. "If you're being followed, Katie, something has to—"

Another knock interrupted him.

Granny looked through the window. Her eyes grew wide. "Saints preserve us," she muttered, and crossed herself.

"Who is it?" Tavish hadn't seen her react that way to a visitor before.

"Jeremiah Johnson," she whispered.

Johnson? On the Irish Road? What in heaven's name was happening?

Katie took an audible breath. She looked almost ashen.

"I'll talk to him," Tavish said.

"No." She stopped him with a hand on his arm, her eyes firmly fixed on the closed door. "He's come to talk to me, I'm certain of it."

"You have had a difficult day already," he insisted.

"I've strength enough for this." Katie stepped past him, nervous but determined.

"Katie—"

Joseph cut across his words. "I think she knows her own capabilities, Tavish."

"This is none of your concern," Tavish said.

"Oh, I think it is."

"Hush, both of you," Katie shot back over her shoulder.

She opened the door. Mr. Johnson stood on the other side, his hat in his hands. The man actually looked the slightest bit humble, something Tavish had never seen from Jeremiah Johnson in all the years he'd known him.

"Good morning to you, Mr. Johnson," Katie said. "Have I neglected something at the mercantile?"

He shook his head. "I needed to talk to you." Mr. Johnson's gaze took in the others in the room. "In private, if that is permissible."

Katie nodded silently and stepped out onto the porch.

"I don't like this," Tavish said. "She shouldn't have to face him alone."

"Katie is resilient," Joseph insisted. "And Johnson won't do anything when she's on her own porch with several people within earshot."

"Spoken like someone who hasn't been on the receiving end of Johnson's ire."

Joseph looked unimpressed. "Johnson has been angry with me plenty of times. He can be nasty, but he's not a fool."

"I'd beg to differ."

"Perhaps you didn't notice, Tavish, but he came here not blowing steam out of his ears, but *asking* to speak to Katie, talking to her with more than a hint of civility." Joseph's calmness was maddening. "I've spoken with Katie many times of late about her interactions with her employer, and things between them have improved dramatically. There really is no reason for worry."

"I don't trust him."

"But marching out there with fists flying will only make things worse," Joseph said.

Tavish stepped directly up to the man, nearly nose to nose. "Who put you in charge of Katie's welfare?"

Granny shushed them loudly. "I declare, the two of you are worse than a couple of tomcats fighting over a molly. If you'd stop your screeching for one minute I could open the window and listen in."

Tavish didn't look away from Joseph. The man didn't look away from him, either. They'd never spoken their rivalry out loud, but Tavish knew it was well and truly there.

Cold air seeped inside in the next moment, as did Katie's voice. Tavish glanced toward the window, now open the slightest bit.

"I've done good work for you, sir. You cannot deny that."

"I'm not denying it," Mr. Johnson said. "I have no complaint with your work; I simply don't need you any longer. As I said, my son will soon be done with his deliveries for the season, and he can do the work that—"

"I'm not a simpleton, sir. Please don't treat me like one." She didn't speak with anger. Her voice was calm.

Tavish stepped closer to the window, listening.

"Mr. Archibald told me in clear language that he meant to see to it you fired me. Seems he was successful."

Archibald had managed to get her fired on top of everything else. Tavish reached for the doorknob. He'd give Johnson a piece of his mind.

Joseph Archer moved to lean against the door, preventing it from being opened.

"Joseph." He kept his voice quiet so he'd not be heard through the open window. "Katie needs—"

"She is holding her own, Tavish. Let her keep at it."

"You're tossing her to the wolves?"

Joseph eyed him challengingly. "She is not out of her depth. Let her handle her own difficulty."

Katie's voice floated inside. "Mr. Archibald will spread his anger about—that's his way—but I thought you a better man than that, Mr. Johnson."

"I am letting you go because of what Bob said, but not because he said I should."

"I don't understand."

How was Katie keeping her head in the face of all this? She'd summoned the courage to ask for a job in the first place from a man who'd declared he'd never hire Irish. Now she'd lost that position because of the Reds' hatred. Still, her voice was calm and collected.

"I saw something in Bob Archibald's eyes that worries me," Mr. Johnson said. "It was more than anger toward y'all. There was pure hate there."

"Hate you've decided to bow to," Katie pointed out.

"No. Believe me, Miss Katie, it's not that."

Miss Katie? The man was actually speaking respectfully to an Irishwoman. What kind of miracle had Katie wrought?

"If you keep working at my place, he'll only grow angrier," Mr. Johnson said. "I can't vouch for what he might do. I'm honestly worried for you should you continue in my employ."

An anxiety Tavish hadn't known in some time settled over him.

"Let me out, Joseph," he whispered pointedly.

Joseph shook his head. "She's getting through to him. Don't interrupt now."

He had a point, as much as Tavish didn't want to admit it.

"If you disapprove of the things he does, Mr. Johnson, why don't you tell him so?" Katie asked. "Why is it no one will stand up to him?"

"For likely the same reason none of y'all can talk sense into Seamus Kelly. The two of them can talk their way in and around and over near about anything."

Mr. Johnson had the right of it. Tavish had no intention of telling him as much, though.

"It seems to me, sir, that someone is going to have to stand up to one or the both of them or someone is going to get hurt, or worse."

There was silence on the porch after that. Silence inside the house as well.

"Thank you, Mr. Johnson, for coming and explaining in person. It takes a bit of the sting out. And please thank Mrs. Johnson and Marianne for their kindnesses to me these past weeks."

Kindnesses? Had the Johnsons truly been kind to Katie? Tavish would never have believed it even thirty minutes earlier. But after hearing this conversation, he began to wonder.

A moment later, Joseph stepped back as the door swung open. Katie's eyes darted from Joseph to Tavish to Granny, then back through all of them.

"How are you bearing up, Katie?" Tavish asked.

She sighed, long and deep. "Sometimes I hate this place." On that declaration, she walked past them and disappeared down the corridor.

She hated Hope Springs. Katie had given up her dream of returning to Ireland to stay there, and she hated it.

Tavish followed her path all the way to the open door of her bedroom. "Katie?"

She sat on her low bed, shoulders slumped. "I've had a hard day."

"Would you like to go for a walk?" he asked. "I could tell you a few of those stories that always make you laugh."

She didn't move to join him, didn't even look up. "I'm not wishing to laugh just now, Tavish."

"In my experience, that is often the time when you most need to."

She didn't respond, but simply sat still, her eyes unfocused.

He sat gingerly on the edge of the bed. For the first time in a long time, he was unsure of his welcome.

"Perhaps a walk without the stories," he suggested. "That might at least lighten your heart a little."

"I thank you for that, but I just need to sit here and think for now." She looked over at him. The sadness in her eyes stabbed at him.

"I can't bear to see you hurting like this, Sweet Katie." He took her hand in his. "What can I do to take it away?"

Her gaze returned to the small window high on her wall. Her brows pulled tight again, a tenseness in her stooped posture. Clearly he hadn't helped.

"Katie?"

"I need to let my heart hurt and my mind fret. If I don't, the pain and the worry will only grow."

He rubbed his thumb along the back of her hand, wishing she would look at him again. "You don't want me to cheer you up?" The remark was half teasing, half worry.

"Not right now."

The reply settled like a weight on his chest. Cheering people up was who he was, what he did. 'Twas his role in life, the thing he was best at. If she didn't want that, what did he have to offer her?

"Do you want me to go?" He hoped the answer was no.

Her look was apologetic. "I think I would like some time alone."

"Ah." If that was what she wanted, he could give it to her. He rose, but his heart seemed to drop. She didn't want him there. He didn't think that had ever happened before. "I'll see if I can do anything for Granny before I go."

She nodded.

"And I'm right up the road if you need anything."

He hesitated at the door. Would she call him back? Would she say she needed his teasing and his smiles after all?

But she didn't.

Joseph stood at the end of the short corridor.

"Katie says she wishes to be left alone just now," Tavish said.

Joseph ignored him and stepped into Katie's room. Tavish remained just outside the doorway, sorely tempted to step back in and send Joseph packing.

"Can I do anything for you, Katie?" Joseph asked.

I offered to help, Joseph, Tavish silently told his rival. *She only wants to be left alone.*

"Do you know, Joseph, before coming here, I'd never once been fired from any job." Her tone was equal parts frustration and sadness. Tavish ached to hear it.

"I hope, even with how thickheaded we all are around here, that you are still happy you chose to stay," Joseph said.

"Oh, I am. I'm only discouraged, is all."

Tavish leaned back enough to look through the doorway. Joseph stood by Katie's window, while she still sat on her bed. They weren't touching. Katie wasn't even looking up at him. Joseph didn't appear to be making any more progress than Tavish had.

"Is there anything I can do for you before I go?" Joseph asked again.

Katie shook her head. "I mean to sit here and wrap my mind around this latest frustration. I'll be right as rain soon enough, I'm sure of it."

"If it helps at all," Joseph said, "you have done more good here than I think you realize."

She gave Joseph a fleeting and somewhat forced smile. His reassurance didn't appear to be entirely believed. But then Tavish's attempts to lift her spirits hadn't been successful, either.

Joseph left shortly thereafter, with a parting word for Granny and a quick nod for Tavish. Hoping for another chance to speak with Katie, Tavish stayed and helped Granny for the next half hour. Katie never came out of her room. Easing burdens had always been a talent of his, the best thing he had to offer others. But Katie was growing more and more weighed down, more and more burdened, and he didn't know how to help her.

Chapter Twenty-Six

Two days had passed since Mr. Johnson's visit. Katie had found a bit of calm and a sense of purpose. She'd taken the position at the mercantile in order to help her Irish neighbors through the winter. Though she wanted to think Mr. Johnson had softened a bit during her time there and wouldn't raise the Irish prices now that she was gone, she couldn't be completely certain of that. She had little else to offer beyond her bread. If she could use the bit of her savings that wasn't already going toward the food and fuel she and Granny used from day to day, she could see that her Irish neighbors had bread they needn't pay for. With the money they saved, they might be able to endure a rise in prices.

She'd made her first free bread delivery that day. And though convincing her neighbors to accept her offering had been difficult, Katie had held firm. Hope Springs was home, and the people there were family. She would do everything she could to help them.

Biddy walked at her side, having made the deliveries with her. "Ian is slowly returning to himself. Though his head still pains him, he has much of his strength back. I find myself hopeful I will have my dear Ian back again."

Katie smiled. Her heart lightened to see Biddy looking less burdened.

"I seem to remember a certain woman telling me once upon a time that 'hope springs eternal.'"

"And I was right about that, you know. I only wish this town of ours lived up to its name more often than it does."

Katie gave her friend a quick hug. "I haven't lost faith in Hope Springs. We'll find our way out of the darkness of this feud, you'll see."

"Katie! Katie!"

She knew Emma's voice on the instant and turned to greet the sweet girl.

"Good day to you, Em—"

Emma looked worried.

Katie reached out and took her hands, studying her face for any clue as to what had upset the child. "What's happened, dearest?"

"Ivy won't come out of the barn."

"What is she doing in the barn?" Katie knew the tiny girl didn't have chores to be done there.

"She's hiding."

"A game, then?" Biddy guessed.

Emma shook her head.

"Why did you not tell Mrs. Smith that Ivy's hiding in the barn?" Katie asked. "Or your papa? Or Finbarr?" To have come all this way seemed a touch extreme.

"Papa is gone, and Finbarr is with him." Emma's frantic look remained. "And I can't tell Mrs. Smith because Ivy's hiding from *her.*"

Katie did not at all like the sound of that. She exchanged a quick look with Biddy. "I'd best go check on my girl."

Biddy nodded. "Are you still planning on us for supper?"

"Aye." Katie stood. "I will see you tonight, Biddy." She took Emma's hand. "Come on, then. We'll coax Ivy out."

They walked quickly down the road toward the bridge. Ivy hiding in the barn did not, in itself, seem worrisome. But Emma was so clearly upset about it, Katie couldn't help feeling anxious.

"What exactly sent Ivy into hiding?" she asked.

Emma's brown eyes were too heavy and worried for Katie's peace of mind. "She knocked over the flour jar and it broke."

"She's embarrassed, then?"

Emma only shook her head, not explaining. Katie didn't press her.

They reached Joseph's barn. From the doorway, she heard a voice.

"This is entirely unnecessary and is taking up far too much time." The words held more than a hint of scolding. "Stop this tantrum and come down from there."

"Is that Mrs. Smith?" Katie asked.

Emma nodded.

"Shall we go have a wee little talk with her?"

The suggestion did not give Emma the bit of confidence Katie had hoped it would. Did Mrs. Smith worry her so much that even having an empathetic adult at her side not make Emma feel any better about confronting the woman?

"Come down here this instant." Mrs. Smith's impatience sharpened the words.

Emma paled. "May I wait out here, Katie?"

"If you'd rather remain here, or go up to the house, you most certainly may, darling," Katie told Emma. "But if you'd like to come in with me, I'll keep you right at my side where you know you'll always be safe."

Emma took a deep and fortifying breath. A look of determination crossed her face.

"There's my brave girl." Katie squeezed the hand still held firmly in her own. "Let's go rescue your sister."

Mrs. Smith stood at the bottom of the ladder leading up to the loft, her hands fisted on either hip. "If you don't come down here this instant, Ivy—"

Katie spoke over the cross words. "In my experience, Mrs. Smith, she responds much better to her name spoken in a kind voice."

Mrs. Smith spun about to face her. "This is none of your concern, miss."

"On the contrary." Katie stepped up next to her. "These girls are rather dear to me. Their welfare will always be my concern."

The woman only grew more outwardly exasperated. "Their welfare is not in question. Neither of them is in any danger. The littlest one simply refuses to come down, and I cannot leave her up there alone."

"Scolding her is unlikely to encourage her to come to you," Katie pointed out.

"If you can do a better job of it, please do." Mrs. Smith motioned toward the loft, stepping back with a look of haughtiness that grated. Clearly she thought Ivy would respond no better to Katie.

"Why don't you return to your work?" Katie suggested. "I will attend to the sweet angel in the loft."

"She is not being very angelic today," Mrs. Smith said. "I told her she would not be punished for what was clearly an accident, but it's as if she cannot understand simple—"

"Let me stop you right there." Katie kept her calm only with great effort. "'Tis never a wise thing to speak ill of any Irishwoman's children within her hearing."

"*Your* children?" Clearly the sentiment surprised Mrs. Smith.

"Indeed."

Emma clutched Katie's hand in both of hers. Katie slipped the girl just a touch behind her.

"And, if you would be so good as to give Mr. Archer a message for me, please tell him I've taken the girls to spend the day with me, and he can fetch them whenever it is convenient."

Mrs. Smith seemed to debate a moment before relenting with a shrug and a look of acceptance. She moved with quick strides out of the barn.

Katie looked down at Emma and received a tentative smile.

"Shall we go up after Ivy?" Katie asked.

Emma nodded.

Katie climbed the ladder, stopping when her head cleared the floor above. Ivy sat across the loft but within sight, her arms wrapped around her bent knees. Hay stuck out of her braids and clung to her stockings. Sad tears sat on her cheeks.

"Hello, Ivy, angel. Won't you come over and talk to me?"

Ivy stood and dragged her feet as she walked to where the ladder leaned against the loft. She plopped back down, sitting cross-legged on the floor.

"Why are you up here alone?" Katie asked.

Ivy's lip quivered. "Mrs. Smith is mad at me."

"I hear you broke the flour jar."

Ivy nodded. A tear dripped off her chin.

"Were you afraid she would be angry?" Katie thought of Mrs. Smith's sharp words. "Did she yell at you, or scold you harshly?"

Ivy dropped her head down, her forehead on her knees.

"Darling?" Katie pressed.

"She looks at me like she's angry. I don't like it."

"Does she hit you?"

Ivy shook her head, and Katie felt some of her anxiety lessen.

"Does she yell or shout?" Katie looked down at Emma, standing at the foot of the ladder.

"No," Emma said. "Not really. But she talks so . . . so hard at us."

Poor things. They needed love and kind words; they needed a mother. She understood that need, having spent most of her childhood alone and longing for someone to care about her.

She turned her attention back to Ivy. "How would you like to come have a wee céilí down at my house, sweetheart?" She reached out and stroked Ivy's hair. "I might even make biscuits. I know how much you love my sweet biscuits."

She heard the tiniest murmur of "Cookies."

"Yes. *Cookies.*"

Ivy peeked out at her. "With sugar on top?"

Katie nodded.

Ivy scooted along the floor of the loft until her feet dangled over the edge. Katie kissed her wet cheek.

"Can you come back, Katie?" Ivy asked. "Can you come back and make Mrs. Smith go away?"

Ivy always reminded Katie of her poor sister. In that moment 'twas as if little Eimear were there again, telling Katie how very cold she was, begging her to do something to make her warm again.

"I made Mrs. Smith go away for now." Katie knew it was only temporary comfort, but she had nothing else to offer. "And I mean to take you home with me for the rest of the day. Will that do?"

Ivy looked the smallest bit relieved.

"Why is it you hide up here, sweetie?"

Ivy shrugged a single shoulder. "It's quiet."

Katie could appreciate that. She'd often volunteered to sweep the larder at her first place of employment for just that reason. 'Twas a quiet place with no one about to yell at her or hurt her. She could cry there and not be punished for it.

She looked about the dim loft with its piles of hay. "There are many places to hide," she said.

Ivy nodded, another tear trickling down her face. Katie's heart cracked deeply at the sight. Joseph couldn't possibly be so inattentive as to not see his girls' unhappiness.

"Let's go up to my house, Ivy. We'll forget all about Mrs. Smith for the evening. There'll be no haylofts or hiding or mean voices. Only sugar-topped cookies for my two very good girls."

She climbed down the ladder, keeping a close eye on Ivy as she did. With both girls once again on solid ground, Katie held a hand out to each of them.

These girls would have a pleasant night, one filled with all the laughter and smiles and music she could give them.

Joseph's patience was quickly running thin. A man did not like returning home to find his entire family missing. "Katie took the girls?" he repeated Mrs. Smith's words, trying to make sense of them.

"Yes. Ivy threw something of a tantrum over a broken flour jar and refused to come down from the hayloft." Mrs. Smith spoke as she scrubbed the sink basin. "Miss Macauley arrived in the midst of it and, declaring she could do a far better job of addressing the situation than I could, sent me off with instructions to tell you she had taken the girls to her house for the remainder of the day."

He didn't fully understand what had passed between the women, but he felt some relief in knowing Katie was with the girls. They, at least, would have passed a pleasant afternoon, which was far more than he could say for himself.

Three hours of trying to talk sense into the thick heads of the Red Road had taken a toll. He was tired, frustrated, and drained.

"You are certain she took the girls to Mrs. Claire's house?"

"Yes. And that is where she said you could fetch them whenever it was convenient for you." She looked up from her scrubbing. "I realize I didn't ask your permission before allowing them to be taken, but seeing as you spend so much time there with Miss Macauley and generally take the girls with you when you go, I didn't think you would object."

He didn't object; he was simply tired. "Make yourself some dinner. I don't know when I'll be back."

By the time he reached Mrs. Claire's house, he was exhausted beyond reason. He was sick to death of the feud, tired of fixing everyone's problems. He needed sleep. He needed peace. Neither seemed likely anytime soon.

He rapped quick and hard on the door. Mrs. Claire waved at him through the window, motioning him inside.

Joseph stepped through the door, hung his hat on an obliging peg, and unbuttoned his jacket. He told himself not to let his weariness make him impatient. Katie was standing in the middle of the room playing a lively tune on her violin. The girls were dancing about her, giggling and grinning wider than he'd seen in a while—well, at least since the last time he'd come to fetch them at Mrs. Claire's house.

And why is it I still think of this as Mrs. Claire's house *and never Katie's?* Katie somehow didn't fit there, even after all the weeks she'd lived with the older woman.

Ian sat next to Biddy, his arm about her shoulder. It relieved Joseph's mind a great deal to see his friend continuing to recover. Ian's Michael sat in the corner, reading a book even as he tapped his foot to the music. Little Mary sat on the floor, leaning against her father's legs, grinning as she watched Katie play.

Joseph's gaze returned to Katie. He felt as though he could breathe again. More even than her music, her presence brought him a feeling of peace he had desperately needed of late.

The tune came to an end. Both girls dropped to the ground, laughing and exhausted.

Katie looked down at them. "Have you worn yourselves out yet? I don't know that my fingers can keep up with the two of you much longer."

"Mrs. Smith doesn't play the fiddle for us," Ivy said from her spot on the floor. "Or laugh with us, or sing songs. She just frowns and grumbles."

Mrs. Claire spoke up. "Look who's come knocking on our door, girls."

They all looked in his direction.

"Joseph," Ian greeted. "It's good to see you again."

"And you. How are you feeling?"

Ian nodded firmly. "Better every day."

Joseph watched for Katie's usual smile of welcome and for the girls to run straight to him as they always did. He needed both in that moment. The girls huddled close to Katie, who watched him sidelong and a bit uncertainly.

"Don't either of you have a hug for your papa?" He wasn't above begging.

Ivy pulled away first and rushed to him. He dropped to his knees and pulled her close.

"We've been dancing all day, Pompah. It's been ever so much fun."

Joseph caught Emma's eye. The hesitation there broke his heart. Though he had tried to explain to her why he had needed to speak sharply to their neighbors at the church, he still saw lingering hints of uncertainty in his little girl. He wished he knew how to make things right between them again.

"I've missed you, Emma." He had, indeed, more than simply being physically separated from her during the day.

A smile tugged at her mouth. She crossed to him, as well, and stepped into his embrace.

"Have you enjoyed spending your day with Katie?" he asked.

"We always love being with Katie," she answered without hesitation. "She said maybe someday Marianne could come dance with us too. That would be a fine thing."

Despite the small changes Joseph had seen in Jeremiah Johnson, he didn't for a moment believe he would allow his daughter to spend an afternoon down the Irish Road. But Emma and Marianne were such close friends, the only friend Emma really had, and he couldn't bear to disappoint her.

"Perhaps someday we can have Marianne come to our house and Katie can join us there. Then you and your friend can dance all you want."

Emma's smile grew more natural. Joseph kissed her cheek, then Ivy's.

"We need to be on our way," Biddy said. She crossed to where Katie stood in the middle of the room, and embraced her. "Thank you again for the supper and for your music. Heavens, Katie, what your music does for us."

"It is a balm, isn't it?" Katie answered. "I grow more grateful for the music every day."

Ian stepped past his wife. Joseph kept his girls at his side, but stood as Ian approached. He shook the hand Ian offered and gave him a firm slap on the shoulder.

"It *is* good to see you doing well, Ian."

"'Tis good to be doing well," Ian said. "And"—he glanced quickly at his wife, then back again to Joseph, and lowered his voice—"I thank you for the hay you sent over."

"I only wish I could do more," Joseph said.

He knew Ian was tiptoeing close to financial disaster. They hadn't been able to make more than a pittance toward their land payment. He'd lost crops. And he'd soon have another mouth to feed. Joseph did what he could, but the man's pride had been pricked a lot lately. And anything Joseph could do had to be done as much in secret as possible. Only his insistence that he wouldn't show the town any mercy had kept things relatively peaceful.

"We're ready to be off, dearest," Biddy said from the doorway.

The O'Connors stepped outside. Emma and Ivy moved to the door and waved.

"Could I have a moment of your time, Katie?" Joseph asked.

She looked a little surprised, but nodded and motioned him toward the hallway. He followed her into her small bedroom.

He spoke while she put her violin away. "Mrs. Smith told me something of what transpired this afternoon, though I confess her explanation confused me a great deal. She said something about a flour jar and Ivy hiding in the loft."

"Aye." Katie loosened the hairs on her bow, but didn't look up at him.

"Did something else happen? I haven't been able to think of a reason why you'd find it necessary to take them home with you over something so small."

Katie closed the violin case. "Mrs. Smith has a sternness to her manner that makes the girls uncomfortable—not quite frightened, but not at all contented, either." She kept her hands on the case, her body turned so she very nearly had her back to him. "They were both clearly unhappy, Joseph. Miserable, almost."

Joseph's heart stilled. Were his girls truly so miserable?

"I have managed to talk this over with them in bits and pieces throughout the day," Katie went on, "and I am convinced Mrs. Smith doesn't hit them or even shout at them. She simply doesn't love them the way they need. She's not as kind as she ought to be."

Katie turned to look at him, a plea in her eyes. "So, yes, I took the girls from home today and kept them here with me. I am sorry I didn't seek your permission first, but I couldn't bear to see Ivy's tears even a moment longer, nor Emma's worries. Those girls are too dear to me to ever allow them to feel that way if I can do something to relieve their unhappiness."

Her sharp defense of his girls warmed his heart. When was the last time someone had loved them anywhere near as much as he did? They needed this. They needed her. *He* needed her.

"I didn't realize Mrs. Smith was mistreating them."

Katie shook her head. "I don't know that she is being *un*kind to them. They simply don't like her or her manner."

Joseph paced away, thinking. "Mrs. Smith's references were impeccable. She has worked with children before. She came highly recommended." He stopped at her tiny, curtainless window. Uncertainty warred with anger in his mind. The girls would have told him if they were so unhappy with Mrs. Smith. His girls always turned to him when they were in need.

"Perhaps her previous charges weren't so easily wounded," Katie suggested.

Wounded. The idea pierced him. He rested his forehead against the window frame. Mrs. Smith hadn't ever given any indication that she was the kind to ignore a child's needs. And yet, he valued Katie's opinion and trusted her word too much to discount what she'd said. "I have failed my girls, haven't I?"

He heard the sound of her skirts swishing as she walked. She stopped directly beside him and laid her hand on his arm. "I think you're being far too hard on yourself, Joseph. They are loved and they know that they are loved, and that makes all the difference in the world."

The love that Katie had for Emma and Ivy was undeniable. She'd been so unsure of herself, so uncomfortable with the girls at first, but she'd worked at coming to know them. She'd dedicated herself to making them happy. She'd learned to love them.

"Thank you," he said.

"'Tis a pleasure to have them here with me. They really were no trouble at all."

He reached out for her, wrapping his arm around her waist. He, apparently, had a knack for torturing himself—he was all but embracing her, and his pounding heart was well aware of it. "I wasn't thanking you simply for watching them today, Katie. I am thanking you for caring about them and for loving them."

She smiled fondly. "They're easy to love, Joseph."

He intended to say something that would express how easy *she* was to love, but the words disappeared. Something overtook his judgment. He slipped his arm more fully around her waist and pulled her up to him.

He kissed her. Months of longing for this woman grabbed hold of him. He whispered her name against her lips, a deep, desperate need pounding in his heart. If she'd pushed, fought him at all, he would have let go. Instead, she seemed to melt against him. Her small hand clutched the front of his shirt. Her mouth answered his. She kissed him in return.

The air filled with the scent of her. His Katie, the first woman in years to touch his heart in any way. His Katie. Here was the moment he'd dreamed of and thought about for weeks but had doubted would ever happen.

Then he felt her stiffen, as if suddenly realizing who she was kissing, who she was leaning on and clinging to.

She pulled back. The look of surprise and anxiety on her face struck him like a fist. Her face went pale.

"Katie. I'm sorry. I didn't—"

She didn't wait for his explanation. She spun about and rushed from the room.

That was badly done. He'd thought of kissing her many times, but none of his imaginings had ended this way.

He pushed his hair back from his face, letting the air out of his lungs slowly. It didn't help. He still felt ready to explode.

You have to go say something. You cannot leave it like this.

He likely would be unwelcome, but he owed her the courtesy of a good-bye and, if she would allow it, an apology. Joseph was no coward to hide from a difficult thing that needed doing.

He moved with purpose down the hall. Mrs. Claire and the girls looked at him wide-eyed.

"Katie?" he asked Mrs. Claire.

"She flew by and straight out the back door."

Joseph followed that path and stepped outside. Katie stood not ten paces off, her back to the house, arms pulled tight around herself. She looked so alone, so small against the vast fields sprawled out beyond her. The wind pulled mercilessly at her hair, yanking strands of it loose and swirling it about her head. Even in his jacket, Joseph was cold. Were the jacket buttoned up, he'd likely still feel the bite of the wind.

He could think of no words that would help the situation. An apology for kissing her died unspoken. He was sorry she was upset, but he couldn't regret the kiss. Given some encouragement on her part, he'd have kissed her again on the spot.

Joseph walked up behind her, keeping his steps slow so she would have ample time to move away or tell him to leave her be if she wished. He knew she could hear his approach.

She didn't so much as glance back at him.

He slipped his jacket off when he reached her and set it on her shoulders. Katie let it sit there, not shrugging it off or tossing it at his head. After an awkward and silent moment, she pulled it more firmly around herself, holding it in place with a single hand.

He couldn't bring himself to mention their kiss. "I was wrong about Mrs. Smith being a good match for our family," he said. "But even if I found a replacement before winter comes and makes trips to the telegraph office impossible, no one could be here before spring."

Katie hadn't walked away but neither had she acknowledged him.

He pressed on—he couldn't think of anything else to do. "Can the girls come here during the day? Mrs. Smith won't speak sharply to them while I am there, but I have work that has to be done in the fields during the day. It wouldn't be permanent—I'm sure you have enough to keep you busy without them here as well. But I need to know they're happy, and there's no one in the world I trust more than you."

She kept her back to him. The air around him filled with the flowery scent he would forever associate with her. Joseph stuffed his hands in his pockets—the urge to reach out for her was too great.

Her silence wasn't at all encouraging. The tiny ember of hope he felt was growing dimmer by the moment.

"Katie?"

"The girls can come here," she said quietly. "For as long as you need them to."

"Thank you." He spoke as low as she did. There seemed nothing more to say. She didn't look at him, didn't lean even the tiniest bit in his direction. Clearly she wanted him to go. "I'll bring Ivy by in the morning after Emma is at school."

She silently nodded.

Joseph left her there. He would allow her and Mrs. Claire to have their home to themselves.

When he reentered the house, he saw the girls sitting with Mrs. Claire, listening to her tell a story. "We should be getting home," he said.

Neither looked the least bit happy at the prospect. He would need to have a good, long talk with them both as they walked, reassure them they would be spending their days with Katie.

He nodded the girls toward the door. He paused long enough to bid Mrs. Claire a good night.

"Might I give you a piece of advice, Joseph Archer?" the old woman asked.

"Of course."

"Kiss her again."

"Kiss her—? How did you know I—?"

"It wasn't yesterday I was born, Joseph." Mrs. Claire pierced him with a look. "Kiss her again sometime, but do the thing properly the next time."

While the idea was appealing, Joseph wasn't entirely convinced. A woman who flees in tears after a man kisses her generally isn't eager to be kissed by him again.

Chapter Twenty-Seven

Katie had had a long week. The girls were coming to her house each day: just Ivy while Emma was at school, and then both girls for the rest of the day until their father was done with his work. She and Joseph had somehow made the arrangements without looking each other in the eye, without hardly speaking, in fact.

Still, the two times she saw him each day, briefly in the morning and even more briefly in the evening, all she could think of was that kiss. Heavens, that kiss. She'd fallen clear to pieces at the first touch of his lips to hers. Tavish had kissed her some weeks earlier near the bridge, had kissed her quite thoroughly in fact, but she'd not reacted in quite the same way. She'd enjoyed it, to be sure. But she hadn't cried. Even a week later, thinking back on Joseph's kiss, she couldn't explain the tears. She hadn't been upset by it, certainly hadn't been disappointed. Just thinking back on it made her heart pound so hard she half expected to see it come flying out of her chest. With that pounding, though, always came a fresh threat of tears.

Katie hadn't the first idea what to make of it. Was this the sign she'd been waiting for, her heart's efforts to declare its preference? If so, why did she still enjoy Tavish's company? He'd come by a couple of times, and she'd been quite happy to see him. When Joseph came by in the evening to claim the girls, the simple sound of his knock set her heart skipping about and a whisper of uncertainty tiptoeing over her skin.

I'm so very confused, Eimear. I haven't enough experience with love to know what all this means.

She did her best to turn her thoughts to less uncertain topics. She stood at the window, looking out at the snow-covered landscape. Winter had come suddenly.

Employing both stubbornness and smiles, she'd managed to convince the Irish to continue accepting her bread for free. 'Twas a small thing, but she hoped it would help them at least a little. She would use up her savings quickly over the winter keeping her neighbors fed, but perhaps her efforts would mean they would all still be there come spring.

"This book has silly pictures."

She looked back at Ivy. Heavens, the child had her music-pictures book out. "Please be very careful with that, darling."

Ivy's big brown eyes turned up at her. "Is it your favoritest book?"

"It is my *only* book." She slid it out from under Ivy's ominously dripping nose, saving it from certain ruin. "Your papa gave it to me."

"Pompah likes books." 'Twas a relief to see Ivy smiling again. The sight of her tearstained face peering down at her from the loft still haunted Katie. "He has so, so many books." She held her arms out wide as she spoke. "He likes them a whole lot."

Katie slipped the book back on the table near the chair where she sat each night. "What else does your 'Pompah' like?"

"Cookies!" She giggled.

Katie tipped her head and allowed a half-smile. "*Your papa* likes cookies?"

Ivy hooked a finger over her lip, grinning. She nodded, laughter sparkling in her eyes. "We should make him some today."

"Cookies for *him?* Are you certain you don't want the cookies for *you?*"

Ivy bounced, her smile fully blooming.

Katie scooped her up into her arms. "You are too adorable for words, dearest."

Ivy wrapped her legs around Katie, settling into her embrace. She fiddled with the loose hair hanging about Katie's ears. They'd rather perfected the position.

"We need to go fetch your sister from school," Katie reminded her. "And when we get back I need to make my bread for the day. Suppose we make cookies tomorrow, will that do?"

Ivy looked a little disappointed but took the news in stride. Katie set her on her feet once more and set about the task of preparing her to brave the increasingly cold weather. Ivy pulled faces while Katie buttoned up the girl's coat. How could Katie help but laugh?

"You and Emma are the funniest little girls in all the world."

Ivy looked positively proud of the assessment. "Were you funny?"

"When I was little?" She wrapped Ivy's scarf about her neck. "I was a very serious little girl, actually."

"Did you have a mama?"

Katie nodded as she put Ivy's knit hat in place. "And a papa and older brothers. And I had a little sister."

Ivy's eyes opened wide. "Like me?"

"She was very much like you." Katie took Joseph's coat off its hook—he'd left it on her shoulders the night of their kiss and had absolutely refused to take it back. Though he'd not said as much, he likely knew she didn't yet have a coat of her own. He hadn't forgotten her story of being painfully cold as a child and, with the coat and the woolen stockings, meant to keep her as warm as possible. She'd never known a man quite as thoughtful as he was.

"Is your sister in Ireland?" Ivy put her hand in Katie's.

'Twas not the time to speak of death and loss. "She is. She's in a little, tiny town near a river."

"Does she like rivers?"

They spoke that way as they walked toward town, the cold wind battering them. Ivy had so many questions. Katie did her best to answer without speaking of things that were too difficult and too raw. As they came within sight of the school, Ivy asked the question Katie had most worried she would bring up.

"Where are your mama and papa?"

"They are in a town called Belfast."

They stopped in front of the blacksmith shop where the Irish always waited for their children. The area had been shoveled, the snow piled out of the way. Winter had only just begun; those piles would grow taller and taller.

"Will your mama and papa come see you ever?" Ivy asked, huddling close against Katie.

"No, dearest. They won't."

Ivy's brow puckered. "Don't they miss you?"

They didn't, actually. No letter she'd received had ever spoken of missing her or wishing she was nearby. Even the letter Katie had sent after hearing of her father's illness had gone unanswered, though ample time had passed for her to receive a reply.

"My papa is very ill," she said. "He cannot travel this far."

Ivy's expression turned sad. "Do you want to see him so, so much?"

Katie nodded. She did want to see him before he died. That wish hovered in her mind, though she kept it clear to the back.

"Oh, oh, oh!" Ivy took a quick breath, a look of pure excitement on her face. "Maybe my pompah could be your papa. Then you won't be so sad."

She only just kept back a laugh. Joseph standing in for her *father?* That was ridiculous in the extreme.

"Oh, sweetie." She bent down and kissed the top of Ivy's head. "You are a darling."

The schoolchildren poured out of the building. Many of the children ran through the drifts of snow, sending the powder flying in all directions. Dismissals had grown more chaotic, and not simply because of the weather. Children wove around each other, trying to find their parents. Parents did their utmost to keep an eye on the little ones while eyeing their enemies across the street.

Emma found Katie easily—they always met at the nearest corner of the blacksmith shop, directly under the first post.

"How was your school day?"

"Fine." Emma's answers were usually short. Katie had come to understand that, to know she wasn't being pushed aside.

"Pompah is going to be Katie's papa now," Ivy declared.

Emma looked surprised. "Can he do that?"

"Ivy doesn't want me to be lonely," Katie explained. "My father is very far away."

"Oh." That seemed to satisfy Emma. She scrunched her nose up, taking in a loud sniff. She did it again.

Katie took a noseful of air herself and knew immediately what Emma was smelling. Smoke.

Panic filled her chest. Smoke meant fire. She looked back over her shoulder. Dark smoke billowed from the top of the blacksmith shop. The entire crowd seemed to become aware of the danger behind them at the same time. Shouts filled the air. People ran in all directions, grabbing their children. So many people tried to fill the small space.

Katie clutched the girls to her side. She couldn't seem to get away from the smithy. Every step she took only put her in the path of someone else fleeing the flames that had begun to leap from the roof of the shop.

Ivy and Emma were pleading with her to get them away from the hot air and the smell of cinders. Katie struggled to keep calm. Her feet and legs and back burned with remembered pain.

"This way, girls." But she was thwarted by the panicked crowd.

Tears stung her eyes. Her only thought was escape, to get as far from the fire as she could.

As the air grew dark with smoke, a figure wove through the crowd to her side. *Joseph?* She couldn't tell.

"Pick up Ivy," the deep voice instructed, even as he swung Emma into his own arms.

It was Tavish. She was grateful to have him there. Panic was quickly overwhelming her. Tavish wouldn't abandon her in her time of need.

"There's fire," she said. "We can't get away from it."

Tavish didn't waste a single moment with words. Emma latched onto him, just as Ivy wrapped her arms around Katie's neck. Tavish took hold of Katie's arm with his free hand and guided them all around the swirling mass of fleeing townsfolk.

"Please get us away from here, Tavish. Please. Please." Katie tried hard not to cry, but fear gripped her heart so tightly it hurt. She could feel Ivy weeping against her shoulder.

The roar of flames grew more ominous. Even the air was hotter. She couldn't bring herself to look back. She knew what she would see. The blacksmith shop was likely engulfed in flames. Even over the sound of so many shouting people, Katie could hear the girls whimpering. The smell and feel and sound of the fire and the frantic townspeople left her frozen in place.

"Katie?" Tavish spoke as calm as could be. "We need to get the girls home. Their father will want to know they're safe. Can you keep going?"

She took a deep and shaky breath. Could she? Katie didn't even know. In that moment she didn't feel capable of movement, of whole thoughts, let alone the strength to calmly walk down the road. They'd been standing so close to the building. The fire must have been burning the entire time they'd stood there. She hadn't even realized it.

Each breath came quicker and shorter than the last. Her lungs simply couldn't take in more air. Had Seamus Kelly escaped his shop before it burned? Merciful heavens, any number of children had been gathered around. They might have been caught, burned, trapped.

"Seamus?" She mouthed the name to Tavish, unable to find her voice.

"He is at home today," Tavish answered.

Katie held Ivy tightly, so afraid for the girls, for herself, for everyone nearby. Though nearly twenty years had passed since she'd run for her life through a cascade of falling thatch, she remembered it as clearly as though it were happening again in that very moment. She could feel the heat on her face, the searing pain in her feet.

Hot tears ran down her face as she struggled for composure.

Tavish set Emma on her feet and took Ivy from Katie's arms. He extended a hand to her. "I'm taking you away from here, Katie. All you need to do is put one foot in front of the other. I'll do the rest."

Katie nodded. "And the girls?" she managed to ask.

He tipped her a whisper of a smile. "I don't intend to leave them behind."

She couldn't think clearly, otherwise she'd not have even wondered if he meant to look after Emma and Ivy. *He shouldn't be left to care for them in the first place. That's your responsibility, Katie.*

"I'm falling clear to pieces, Tavish."

Tavish pulled her close. "I'll hold you together, Sweet Katie. All the way back up the road."

He took the situation firmly in hand. Ivy was instructed to hold Katie's hand. Emma took Tavish's. They were on their way up the road, trailing most of the rest of town.

Katie's breaths poured out of her. She walked, but hardly recognized the road or the landmarks she passed. Tavish's arm remained firm around her, guiding her so she need not even think of what they'd left behind or the memories it had conjured. She concentrated on breathing in and out, on calming herself, but found the task beyond her abilities.

The girls shivered in the cold. Katie held Ivy as close as she could, but her mind couldn't seem to think of what else she might do to help them. Tavish's eyes darted about as if searching for something.

The rumbling of feet and voices echoed all around them. From both sides of the Archer home came a full mob of people. They glared from across the way, eyeing each other with accusations and anger and fear.

"Have they come to put out the fire?" Emma asked.

Tavish didn't answer. Katie couldn't. They'd likely come fully intending to brawl.

Was this it, then? The feud would end in a fire, both sides jumping into the fray and destroying themselves?

Fire always destroyed. It broke and it burnt and it killed. Always.

"Girls! Katie!"

At the sound of Joseph's voice, both girls broke free and ran to their father. Katie felt an almost overwhelming urge to do precisely the same. The exact feeling of relief she'd tried to describe to Biddy and Granny swept over her at his approach. Even knowing he hadn't been in town, emotion swelled inside at the simple reassurance that he was safe.

He reached her in the next moment, an arm around each of his girls.

"Katie?" He looked at her with growing concern. "Are you hurt?"

"She is afraid, Joseph," Tavish whispered.

Joseph looked her over. "Pull yourself together, Katie. There is no time for this."

Tavish took half a step between them. "Be a little understanding. With her history—"

"I know her history perfectly well. I know she is terrified." His piercing gaze returned to her. "But in this moment, right now, you need to keep going. We will have a war on our hands unless cool heads can prevail, and if Tavish and I don't return to town, there won't be enough voices of reason."

His words brought tears to the surface again. She needed a hug or a kind word. She needed a place to hide away from it all. Until Joseph spoke of her continuing on alone, she hadn't realized how much she'd hoped for a comforting embrace.

Tavish jumped into the conversation. "Leave her be, Joseph. She is—"

"What she is, is stronger than you are giving her credit for." Joseph's eyes darted between her and Tavish before settling on her face. He seemed unconcerned by her tears, if he noticed them at all. "I won't leave the girls with Mrs. Smith, not when they are already this upset, and I cannot leave them on their own. Can I trust you, Katie, to keep them safe and hold them together until I return? Can I trust you with that?"

"I don't know."

He stepped closer. Tavish did as well, facing Joseph as though they were foes locked in combat.

"All I am asking is that you stay strong long enough to look after them. When I come by to claim them, you can fall to pieces all you want. You only have to stay standing until then."

"I don't know if I can."

"There is no time for indecision," Joseph said. "The people in this town will kill each other if we don't stop them. Tell me yes or no, so I can do what needs to be done."

There would be no sympathy from that quarter.

"You could take them to Biddy's," Tavish suggested.

She looked to Joseph. The disappointment that flashed over his features cut her deeply. *There is no one in the world I trust more than you.* He'd told her that behind Granny's house. He trusted her, and she was letting him down.

Katie bit back a new wave of tears. 'Twas little wonder he was disappointed in her—she was disappointed in herself. "Come fetch them at Mrs. Claire's when you're ready." Her voice didn't remain entirely steady, but she'd summoned the strength to make the declaration, and that was something.

He gave a quick nod, instructed his girls to stay with her, and he and Tavish walked quickly toward town.

Though in her heart she was still weeping, outwardly she found a place of calm. She would see to the girls, look after them until their father returned. Then, and only then, would she let the weight of fear and memories break her down.

Chapter Twenty-Eight

Even on his way to stop a brawl, Tavish was a breath away from throwing a punch at the man walking by his side. He'd not have thought Joseph Archer the kind of person to toss harsh words at a woman so clearly suffering as Katie was. Joseph had brought fresh tears to her eyes, something Tavish wasn't sure he could forgive.

"You might have been a little easier on her," he said.

"Not if I wanted her to stay standing through this."

"She was doing fine before you came." Tavish had, after all, led her from town. He had supported her through the entire ordeal. She had been holding up—struggling, yes, but holding up.

"I, for one," Joseph said, "couldn't ever be satisfied knowing Katie was doing merely 'fine.'"

"That is not at all what I meant, and you know it."

They were quickly approaching the edge of town. Raised voices could already be heard.

"Katie needed a push," Joseph said.

"What she needed was compassion."

They'd nearly reached the town and the line of people on either side of the snow-dusted road, staring each other down. It was one fight after another in Hope Springs.

Joseph didn't look at him when he spoke, but there was an inarguable challenge in his tone. "It seems Katie will have to decide what she needs."

They were no longer speaking of her response to the fire. "Katie's already made that decision."

"Has she?" Joseph spoke with infuriating calm.

Tavish loved Katie and was certain she loved him in return. He could make her laugh when tears hovered in her eyes and bring a smile to her face when she was burdened. He'd never seen Joseph do that. And yet, Joseph seemed so certain of his own claim on Katie's heart.

"The troops have already assumed the formation." Only when Joseph motioned toward the gathered townspeople did Tavish realize he *wasn't* referring to their rivalry over Katie.

Tavish knew exactly what was going on ahead of them. The Irish had gathered around the smithy—what was left of it, at least—to show the Reds that they placed the blame for its destruction on the Reds' shoulders. The Reds had gathered around the mercantile because they fully expected the Irish to retaliate. 'Twas likely only a matter of time before they did just that.

"So what happens now? Do you start evicting the town?" Tavish and his parents were the only members of his family who would be safe. The rest of his siblings had come up short on their payment.

"Not if they disperse," Joseph said.

Tavish made his way to Seamus's side. "How bad is it?"

"I've lost it all." Seamus stood with his fingers shoved into the pockets of his vest, eyeing the charred remains of his business. Each exhaled breath formed clouds in front of him, adding to the desolation of the scene. "'Tis nothing but a pile of ashes and a few salvageable tools. I'll not have the money to replace this. Not for years, maybe. Longer, more likely. I can't recover from this."

Smoke rose off the charred wood.

"Everyone will help you rebuild, Seamus. Every one of us."

He shook his head. "They can't pay for their own homes, Tavish.

How're they going to rebuild my business? They haven't the money to replace my tools or my supplies." His tone tightened with each word. "This has ruined me. *Ruined* me." Seamus spun about and pointed directly at the Reds across the way. "And they know it!"

The Red Roaders stood with arms folded across their chests, unmoved by Seamus's anger. He took a step into the road. Tavish held him back with a firm hand on his shoulder. A single thrown fist or shove would set off the entire crowd.

"Keep calm, Seamus."

"Don't tell me to keep calm." Seamus's pulse pounded through the veins in his reddened neck. "There were children about, Tavish. *Children,*" he shouted at the Reds. "And these would-be murderers started a fire. Someone might've been killed."

Bob Archibald emerged from the gathering outside the mercantile. "Be careful where you throw your accusations, Paddy. Who are you to say any of us did this? Maybe you were too careless."

"You know full well I wasn't even here."

The men had come too close to each other for Tavish's peace of mind. They'd lunge for each other's throats any minute.

Joseph stepped between the men, though he addressed Tavish. "Talk the Irish back."

Tavish looked over his shoulder. Sure enough, his countrymen were inching closer to their neighbors.

"We've lost a business, Joseph," Seamus growled. "Our only remaining one, since they forced Katie to turn her bread business into a charity."

"If there's blood in the streets, Seamus," Joseph answered, "they'll lose more than a business." He turned his glare on Archibald. "The same goes for the Red Road, Bob."

"We've been accused of trying to murder children. You can't expect us to stand back and be insulted."

"That is exactly what I expect you to do." Joseph remained calm despite the antagonism crackling in the air. He addressed the Reds. "If you are not here to help clean up the ashes and soot, then I suggest you go home."

"Why? So these foreigners"—Bob motioned at the Irish with his stubbly chin—"can burn down the rest of the town while we're not looking?"

"Don't fret over that. I don't mean to steal your favorite trick." Seamus leaned in, spitting his words.

"Are you accusing me of something, Irishman?"

"Are you feeling guilty?"

"Not in the least."

"Tavish!" He turned about at the sound of Da calling out his name. He, Thomas, Keefe, and Ian were doing their utmost to keep the Irish from rushing at their Red Road neighbors. O'Donaghue could be counted on to be carrying a shillelagh, perhaps MacCormack as well.

He joined the voices calling for calm. But who was keeping the Reds reasonable? *They* weren't used to taking one on the chin in the name of peace.

He looked back, just as the Reds inched forward as a whole. There'd be a full-on battle any moment. Irish voices shouted right along with American voices, anger filling the air. Tavish tried to make himself heard, at least by those nearest him.

"We can't—"

No one was listening.

"Da!" But he couldn't hear him.

Someone rushed forward, nearly knocking Tavish over. He kept his place, trying to hold the crowd back. His boots slid beneath him on the slippery snow.

A piercing whistle silenced the mob. Then a voice spoke into the quiet.

Joseph. Again.

"You were all in church two weeks ago. You know the consequences of a brawl. A single drop of blood today and everyone here who is behind in their payments by so much as a halfpenny—and there are only two or three of you here who don't fall under that category—will find eviction notices nailed to your door by day's end."

Faces paled. Movement stopped. Relief mingled with anger in Tavish's chest. Joseph had stopped a fight that had been a second from exploding, but he'd done it by threatening people Tavish cared about.

He looked to Da, who seemed as unnerved as he felt. Ian stood not far off. He looked exhausted. He and Biddy hadn't made their full payment, so he stood in danger of losing his farm. He was in no condition to be thrown from his home. If the worst happened, would they be willing to stay with him? Would their pride get in the way?

It won't come to that. We'll keep the peace somehow.

"Go home. All of you," Joseph demanded.

Bob Archibald didn't budge. Neither did anyone else.

"How do we know they won't set fire to the mercantile the moment we're gone?" Archibald demanded.

Tavish quickly eyed all those nearest him, silently warning them to keep quiet.

"Because the supplies in this mercantile are all we have to see us through this winter," Joseph said. "The snows have come. Johnson's boy will be here any day, and his will be the last deliveries coming into town until spring."

"And without a smithy, we can't risk breaking a wheel or an axle trying to go for more supplies," Tavish pointed out. "If any horse needs a new shoe, there won't be any way of getting one. If anyone's tools or equipment needs repairing, we no longer have a forge where that can be done. Losing the mercantile on top of that will ruin us all. Every one of us, Red and Irish alike."

A new worry settled over the group. They'd known lean years, when winter arrived early—as it had that year—and lasted longer than usual. Until the trail to the train depot was clear, nothing would go in or out of town once the Johnson boy was back. Even if they pooled every penny they had, no new smithing supplies could be obtained until the spring thaw. The mercantile was the town's only lifeline now.

"Seamus, keep a few men here, only as many as you need to help you clean this up." Joseph looked out over the Reds. "Johnson?"

"Here, Joseph." Mr. Johnson stepped to the front.

"If you feel you need a few men to stay around, just in case, pick them out."

Johnson nodded.

Joseph addressed them all again. "The rest of you, go home. See to your families and your land and leave your neighbors to do the same."

Bob Archibald's scruffy face turned smug. The whole thing had clearly gone in his favor. No one, not even his fellow Red Roaders, could possibly think he *hadn't* been involved in burning down the blacksmith shop. He'd destroyed a man's business, stolen his very livelihood, and he'd gotten away with it.

Tavish understood the need for peace, but he hated that it always seemed to come on the backs of the Irish.

"See to our own." Bob nodded as he spoke. "That is a good idea." His gaze narrowed on Seamus. "We'll see to our road. You had best see to yours."

"Is that a threat?" Seamus growled.

"Only a friendly suggestion."

Joseph laid a warning hand on both men's arms. Tavish reached out, taking hold of Seamus's other arm. "Let's see to cleaning up," he said. "That needs to come first."

Joseph gave him a nod of acknowledgment. Tavish didn't feel much like being Joseph's ally. But what choice was there?

Joseph had the money and the power and the influence. Tavish had very little in comparison.

But you have Katie. And that is more important than anything else.

Snow had fallen heavy and thick by the time Joseph reached Mrs. Claire's door that night. The sun had long since set. He was tired and worn and worried. The town hadn't made peace; they'd simply declared a temporary cease-fire. He'd seen guards posted where the road passed his property to begin its winding trek past the Reds' houses. The Irish had followed suit; men stood on the Irish side of the bridge, taking turns to watch for their enemies.

Did they mean to stand in the snow all night long? He could only hope they'd thought to rotate out, rather than leave any one person exposed to the elements for so long. For just a moment he'd thought about stopping and trying to talk sense into them all. But he'd beaten his head against that particular wall too often of late. It seemed wise to take on only one losing battle at a time.

Speaking of which, he had to face Katie. He knew he had wounded her feelings earlier with his sharp words and lack of empathy. Tavish had played the "loving beau" role to perfection, and Katie had fallen to pieces under the umbrella of his affection. Joseph hated having to appear indifferent to her suffering, but she'd needed someone to remind her how capable she was. She was stronger than she'd allowed herself to be.

Very little light spilled from the windows of Mrs. Claire's house. Joseph didn't see the sweet old woman sitting in her usual seat by the window. He pulled his pocket watch out, doing his best to see the face in the dimness.

Nine o'clock. It was little wonder he was hungry and exhausted.

The girls would be asleep. Katie and Mrs. Claire might be as well. If he knocked, he might wake them up. Still, he wouldn't stand out on the porch all night, and he wasn't returning home without Emma and Ivy.

He leaned his head against the closed door, trying to summon the energy to decide what to do next.

The town had lost its smithy. He doubted those who'd celebrated the destruction understood just how devastating that could be for a community as isolated as Hope Springs. The anger simmering on the Irish Road wouldn't remain under the surface long. It would boil over, matched only by the hatred of the Reds. It was really only a matter of time.

From inside Mrs. Claire's house, he heard the faint sounds of crying. One of the girls? Joseph opened the door, peeking inside. If Emma or Ivy was hurt or upset—

He saw no one but Katie. She sat in the far corner of the room with a blanket draped over her shoulders, her knees bent, arms wrapped around her legs. Her head was bowed too much for Joseph to see her face, but it didn't entirely muffle the sound of her sobs.

Words failed him. Katie didn't cry often. Seeing it killed him a little every time.

The room was empty except for her and the low-burning fire. She was nowhere near the fireplace. Of course she wasn't.

He crossed to where Katie sat. For a moment he searched for something to say. Nothing came to mind, so he simply kneeled beside her.

Her head jerked up. Tears streamed from her red, puffy eyes. Pain clenched Joseph's chest at the sight.

Something like panic crossed her face. She swiped at her wet cheeks. "I only just—I didn't—Only after the girls were asleep. I—" Her face crumbled as she took in a shuddering breath. "I know you told me not to fall apart until you came to get them, but—I tried, Joseph. I just . . . I hate fire. I hate it so much."

"I know." He rubbed her arm, unsure what else to do. His first inclination was to put his arms around her, but the last time he had done that, he'd ended up kissing her, and she'd run away.

"I didn't cry until the girls were asleep. Not until then." She sniffled. "No one else is awake. It was just me, so you can't yell at me for that."

"I wouldn't yell at—"

"I don't work for you, or anyone else. I'm no one's servant anymore, so I can cry anytime I want to." Her voice broke more with each word. "I am not a servant, and I am not a child. No one can yell at me for crying anymore."

"You were yelled at for crying?"

Katie dropped her head onto her knees again. "I've had a hard day, Joseph."

He shifted from his knees to a seated position next to her. Again, he had no idea what to say. She'd been scolded for crying, and not only during her childhood. He'd chided her for it just that afternoon.

"No wonder Tavish told me I was being heartless."

She turned her head but didn't lift it. "He said that?"

Joseph chuckled ruefully. "He didn't mention that when he came by?"

"He hasn't come by."

"He didn't come over at all?" Joseph frowned. Tavish had left town hours earlier.

Katie shrugged a little. "Mrs. Claire saw him pass by with Ian. She said Ian didn't look well at all."

Ian's pallor had noticeably increased after Joseph issued his ultimatum. Ian hadn't made his land payment. Had evictions proven necessary, he would have been forced to take Ian and Biddy's home away from them. Even understanding the necessity of it, Joseph had hated himself in that moment. What kind of man lays such an enormous burden on the shoulders of a suffering friend?

"He is putting on a brave face, but he isn't recovering very fast," Joseph said. "I am doing what I can to help him and his family, but I feel helpless in so many ways. I worry about him, but I can't seem to do anything substantial to help him."

"I feel the same way about Biddy," Katie said.

What would I do without Katie? She listened to his worries without dismissal or judgment. She understood his concerns and struggles. Until he'd met her, he hadn't realized just how lonely he really was.

"If you can think of anything I might do for Ian and Biddy, let me know," he said. Katie could be counted on to be aware of people's hidden needs.

She reached up and touched his face. He took in a quick breath. The woman had no idea what she put him through.

"You are a good man, Joseph Archer," Katie said quietly.

He didn't want to send her running from him again. If he didn't think about the warmth of her hand on his face or that tantalizing scent she wore, he might make it through their conversation without making a fool of himself.

She rested her head on her knees again. A wisp of hair settled across her temple. His eyes lingered on that bit of hair. He forced his gaze away—if he didn't concentrate on something else, he'd have to sit on his hands to keep himself from touching her.

"Did you have a difficult time with the town? You look troubled."

He was troubled by too many things to even count.

She smiled at him. "Would you like me to play my fiddle for you?"

Her fiddle. He loved hearing Katie play.

"Music soothes the soul," she said. "My fath—my father told me that," she finished on a whisper. Her smile vanished.

Her father was dying. Joseph had mailed her letter weeks earlier, then another of his own after that, but no answers had been waiting for him at the telegraph office when he took his grain to the depot. He had hoped to receive some word from her parents to help ease the pain in her heart. Here was yet another way he'd failed her.

"Mourning for a parent is a difficult thing," he said.

Katie shook her head swiftly and adamantly. "I'm not mourning."

He begged to differ. He knew the look in her eyes well enough. "You have to let yourself grieve, Katie. It will eat away at you otherwise."

She sat up, leaning against the wall behind her, her arms wrapped about her middle. "I can't. If I start crying about this, I'll never stop."

He knew, at some point, she would have to let herself weep for the loss of her father. She would have to grieve for all the pain she'd passed through as a child. But she had cried enough for one day.

Her stockinged feet peeking out from under her dress gave him the perfect change of subject.

"You're wearing my stockings."

"If I were wearing *your* stockings, they'd never fit." She managed a fleeting lift to her lips.

He leaned against the wall as well, matching her posture and position. "My coat doesn't fit you either, but you wear it."

Katie rested her head on his shoulder. Joseph did his best not to breathe too deeply. If he moved in the slightest, she might pull away.

"It is too big, but it's far warmer than my shawl."

Joseph adjusted the blanket barely staying on her shoulder. That put his arm conveniently where it needed to be, though he hesitated a moment before settling his arm around her. She held her blanket close, but leaned more heavily against him.

He settled in, seated against the wall with the most amazing woman he'd ever met in his arms. It was the closest thing to heaven he could imagine.

"Did I ever thank you for the stockings, Joseph?" She sounded a little sleepy. He hoped that meant she was relaxing, letting some of her tension slip away.

"You did thank me for them," Joseph assured her.

"They are so warm." She wiggled her feet, her missing toes giving an oddness to the movement. "My feet won't ever be cold again."

Her tale of losing her toes to frostbite and infection still haunted him. "I hope they won't be."

She shifted enough to look up at him. Her eyes were still red and swollen, but she looked at least a little less burdened. "Between your stockings and coat and my fiddle and those sweet little girls, I might just survive all this."

"That is exactly what I am counting on."

Her eyes opened and closed slowly.

"You should go to bed, Katie."

"I can't. The girls are sleeping there." Her head returned to his shoulder.

He leaned against the wall again, content to have her at his side. "Why didn't you send them up to the loft?"

She yawned. "I was playing my fiddle for them in my room and they fell asleep. I couldn't bear to wake them up."

She'd given his girls the gift of her music and the peace it brought. It was little wonder they loved her so much.

"Did you know, Katie—when you were still living at our house and would take your violin out by the grove of trees, I used to sit on the back porch and listen."

Hearing her play at night had quickly become a highlight of his evenings. He'd spent each day hoping she would play that night. Hearing her music never failed to astound him, but there were no words adequate to describe *seeing* her play. The music transformed her. He didn't think he ever saw her quite as at peace as when she played her violin.

"I have missed your music since you moved out." He ran a hand along her hair, relishing that rare moment of closeness.

"I play for you nearly every time you're here, Joseph." She snuggled in closer to him. The woman was determined to torture him. "Perhaps you need to come by earlier in the day so you can hear it longer. I think you need the music."

All I need is you.

Katie grew still, her head still leaning heavily against him. Her breathing slowed and deepened. Joseph memorized the feel of her so perfectly tucked against his side. What he wouldn't give to spend the rest of their lives like that. But was that what she wanted?

He breathed deep the flowery scent of her hair. She might very well choose Tavish in the end. But he had this one moment with her.

With the patter of little feet, the moment ended.

"Pompah?" Ivy stepped out of the hallway, rubbing her eyes.

"Over here, darling," he whispered.

She stumbled about, clearly half-asleep. Ivy curled up on his lap and promptly fell asleep again. He stayed that way, with Ivy and Katie asleep beside him. This was how he'd always imagined his family life would be. Happy children who knew they were loved. A capable and determined woman at his side, one he loved so much it hurt sometimes.

Life with Vivian hadn't been that way. She'd been unhappy most of the time. In the end, she'd abandoned them all. Happiness was there beside him now if only she would choose to stay.

He dozed off and on for a while before realizing they couldn't spend the entire night sitting on the floor. He slipped Ivy from his lap, settling her next to him. Careful not to wake Katie, he took the blanket from her shoulders and laid it over Ivy.

"I will be back in just a moment," he whispered to his little girl.

Shifting about with Katie leaning against him proved something of a trick, but he managed it. He slid one arm under her bent knees and the other behind her back. He moved slowly to his feet, not wanting to wake her or Ivy or anyone else in the house.

Katie didn't move. Even so deeply asleep, she looked exhausted. Was he asking too much of her, sending the girls over every day? She was baking bread for free for the entire Irish Road. And, though she insisted otherwise, Joseph knew she carried the full burden of keeping Mrs. Claire's home tidied and in good repair, as well as cooking every meal and seeing to all the laundry.

He didn't know where else to lay Katie down except back in her own bed. Ivy had left the door to Katie's room open when she'd wandered out. Fortunately, she'd also left the quilt tossed back on the bed. That would simplify things tremendously.

The bed, however, was not empty.

Emma lay with one arm and half a leg dangling over the side. He carefully set Katie down on the bedtick and pulled the quilt over her.

"Let us hope Emma keeps still tonight," he whispered to her, "or you will hardly sleep." He brushed his hand along her face. "I love you, Katie." He kept the whisper almost inaudible.

Her eyelids fluttered and she smiled a bit. Had she heard him?

"Katie?

But she didn't answer, didn't stir. Joseph stepped around to the other side of the low-lying bed and rolled Emma more fully onto it. He tucked the blankets around her as well. The movement was enough to wake her the tiniest bit.

"Papa?" Her voice was equal parts confused and sleepy.

"Go back to sleep, sweetheart."

Her eyes opened a sliver. Her forehead creased. "Where am I?"

Emma disliked being away from home. She worried when her usual routine was upset. "You're with Katie. She's right here."

The worry immediately melted from her expression. She silently nodded and closed her eyes. His little worrier was put at ease so quickly simply by knowing Katie was nearby.

"I know just how you feel," he whispered.

Ivy was still asleep in the main room under the blanket. Joseph picked her up and carried her to the chair by the fireplace. He settled in with her there. It would be a long night trying to sleep sitting up, but he couldn't justify waking his girls after the day they'd had and making them walk all the way home in the falling snow. And, though he struggled to admit it even to himself, he didn't want to leave. He spent so much of his days trying to think of an excuse to visit Katie or prolonging the time it took to pick up or drop off the girls each day. For that one night, he could stay in the house where she lived and pretend that he belonged there.

Chapter Twenty-Nine

Katie's bread deliveries were slow the next day, both on account of the snow lying thicker on the ground than before and her own weariness. But Tavish was walking with her as she made the deliveries, and his company made the outing more pleasant than it would have been otherwise. She held her now-empty bread basket against her hip with one hand and rubbed her neck with the other. Her whole body had ached all day.

"Have you a stiff neck, Sweet Katie?" Tavish asked. He held the basket that yet had a few loaves in it.

She twisted her head from side to side, though it hardly helped. "I had a little girl kicking me most of the night. I'm afraid I didn't sleep well."

"And you didn't push her right out of bed and onto the floor?" His smile added a laugh to the question.

Katie shoved him with her shoulder, shaking her head at his teasing. "A horrible thing to even suggest, you troublesome man. She was there first, although 'twas my own bed, and I'd be a selfish person indeed to toss a child out onto the cold ground. Of course, she fell asleep there first, so in that sense it was really *her* bed, at least for the one night." She thought back over that quickly. "I confused my own self with that explanation."

Tavish chuckled. "Perhaps if you'd had a decent night's sleep, you'd be making a bit more sense."

Who else could make her laugh even when she was utterly exhausted? She liked that about Tavish. How could any person *not* like that about him? 'Twas little wonder he had such an abundance of friends.

"You know," Katie said, "if you'd come by last night like a decent sort of person, you might've carried the girls up to the loft when they drifted off, and I could have had my bed all to myself."

"My fault, is it?" He grinned, not the least apologetic.

"Whether or not it was, I plan to blame you for it."

He took the empty basket from her and set his basket inside it, tossing her a smile as he did. "Troublesome woman."

Katie appreciated Tavish's lighthearted banter; it kept her from focusing so fully on her worries over her neighbors and distracted her from the painful memories of yesterday's fire. It didn't truly relieve her troubles, but did offer her a momentary escape.

She looked out over the landscape, the trees touched with snow, the rooftops white as well. Soon enough she would need a sleigh to make her deliveries.

"I would guess one of these is for me." Tavish held up a loaf of bread. "While the other one must be for Ciara."

He and his sister were the only two people left on their route. "Sorted that out on your own, did you?"

"You can't get anything past me," he said. "Smart as a whip, I am."

"How is your fancy new room coming along?" she asked. "It looked nearly finished when we walked past."

"The outside is finished off, which is a very good thing considering the snows have arrived." He shook his head in frustration. "But I have a great deal of work left inside. There are just so many things needing attention right now."

"I know." She felt overwhelmed thinking on all that had happened. "'Twas a hard day yesterday, as so many have been lately. A hard, hard day."

He looked immediately contrite. "I should have come by to see how you were doing," he said. "I should have. By the time I got Ian home and his animals seen to and then my own, it was late. I suspected you were likely asleep already."

His reasoning was sound, and he had been helping his brother, who had been through so much, yet she still felt a twinge of disappointment that he hadn't come by.

But Joseph had, despite a long day and the late hour.

Aye, but his girls were there. He hadn't a choice, really.

Good heavens, this is all so confusing.

If only she had some experience to draw on. Life hadn't precisely given her ample opportunities to see what it meant to be loved or in love. If only she'd had a mother to explain those things to her when she was young.

They'd reached Ciara's house, but neither turned up the path. Raised, angry voices pulled their attention toward the nearby bridge instead.

"What in heaven's name is that?" Katie didn't at all like the sound.

"Where's the guard?" Tavish asked.

"Guard?"

He nodded. "The Reds and the Irish both posted guards at the head of their roads last evening."

She hadn't heard that. "*Armed* guards?"

"Aye." He didn't even look surprised.

"This has been done before?" How could the town live this way, always landing themselves in conflict—*armed* conflict?

"Only once." He glanced at her, the laughter in his eyes gone. "It didn't end well."

Katie's heart dropped clear to her boots. "What do you mean, exactly?"

He noticeably hesitated. Did he think he needed to protect her from some past unpleasantness, that she wasn't equal to the weight of it? She was no wilting flower.

"Tavish."

"No one died" was the extent of his explanation. He moved with determination toward the bridge. "Don't dwell on it."

"Tavish, wait." She moved quickly to catch up with him. "'No one died' isn't very reassuring."

He gave her a quick smile. He nodded to the baskets in his hands. "I'll get Ciara her bread, Katie. Why don't you head back to Granny's?"

"I mean to see what the trouble is," she said, "same as you."

"Katie." There was his scolding face. He didn't pull it out often, but she knew it when she saw it. "If the guards have left their posts, and the confrontation is loud enough to hear it from here, this is likely to get ugly."

"I've seen 'ugly' before, Tavish."

"Not like this—"

"Aye, because 'no one died.' You forget, Tavish, in my past, people did die."

He shook his head. "I'm not marching you onto a battlefield, darling. You don't need more unpleasant memories."

"This town is ripping itself to pieces. The people here are my friends. If something isn't done, my life here, a life I love despite all the difficulties, will be a memory." She wasn't about to be left behind when there was a problem of such importance to be solved.

"Katie."

"I am stronger than you're giving me credit for." Hearing Joseph's words tumble from her own mouth was something of a surprise. She'd been trying not to think of him while walking about with Tavish.

He looked a bit surprised at her words as well. She fancied she could see the debate tumbling about in his eyes. 'Twould be a kindness to simply make the decision for him.

"Off we go, then." She marched directly past him, over the bridge and the river below with its chunks of ice and swirling darkness.

The gathered mob was easy to spot against the stark white snow covering every inch of the landscape. The scuffle—for it clearly was one—stretched out across the near end of town. Katie took a deep breath as she pressed forward.

Armed guard.

Likely to get ugly.

No one died.

But she was strong enough. She could face this.

Tavish kept shaking his head even as they walked toward the group gathered on the road. "You really should go back home. This—"

"This town is my home now. I'll not go hide in a corner while it falls apart." She meant the remark to be one of determination, but it sounded far more like pleading. Not the best way to convince Tavish she was a pillar of strength. "You've a choice, Tavish. Either walk at my side as I face down the dragon, or do your best to keep up."

He didn't answer right off, but looked at her as though trying to sort her out. Before he spoke even a word, Seamus—Katie had learned to recognize his thick brogue and sharp words—shouted an unflattering assessment of someone's parentage.

Tavish's gaze flew in that direction.

Katie pressed ahead. Voices of reason, Joseph had called it the day before. The town needed someone to speak up for sanity and peace and reasonableness.

The shouting only grew louder as she approached. Their voices melded together in a head-splitting blend of insults and profanities. Fists were flying amongst the men. A few women were gathered about as well, hurling angry words at one another. It was a brawl if ever Katie had seen one.

She tried catching the attention of those she knew, pleading with them to stay calm. Her words did no good. Either they couldn't hear her, or they refused to listen.

Katie took hold of Marykate Kelly's arm, trying to pull her from a shoving match quickly escalating between herself and a woman of the Red Road.

"This is madness," Katie insisted. "Brawling and fighting won't solve our difficulties."

Mrs. Kelly was too lost in her anger to even acknowledge Katie.

"Please, Mrs. Kelly."

Katie was shoved aside with the growled instruction to "Keep out of it."

She moved from person to person, pleading with them for calm. No one would listen. Their hatred made them deaf to reason.

This has to stop. But what could she do?

The sudden sound of shattering glass brought immediate and tense silence to the combatants. As one, they turned toward the mercantile.

One of Mr. Johnson's front windows lay in mangled shards on the porch. The wind blew in through the opening, knocking over displays and goods.

Katie abandoned the brawlers and rushed toward the mercantile. "Mr. Johnson?" she called out, hoping no one had been nearby when the glass broke. Behind her the shouting and sounds of fighting only intensified.

"Mr. Johnson? Marianne? Thomas? Mrs. Johnson?"

She stepped inside the mercantile, glass crunching beneath her feet. A rock easily larger than her fist sat amongst the broken glass in the middle of the room. Mr. Johnson emerged from the storeroom with a broom in hand. The poor man looked pale, shocked.

This ridiculous, terrible feud. How far would they take it?

"I'll fetch the other broom," Katie said.

"No, Miss Katie." Mr. Johnson stopped her with a raised hand. "The Reds will retaliate for this, no matter that I don't intend to ask them to. And your own people might turn on you if you're seen helping their enemy."

"But I cannot leave you to address this alone, not when I can help."

Katie had never seen Mr. Johnson look so utterly defeated. "You are too good for this town, Katie Macauley."

There were moments when Katie could hardly believe this was the same man who'd belittled her so mercilessly when she first arrived in Hope Springs. That he, of all people, had changed as much as he had gave her hope for the rest of them.

"Let me help," she offered again.

He shook his head. "I don't want anything to happen to you, and I will worry less if you aren't here in the thick of all this."

She opened her mouth to protest, but the sound of a tiny whimper caught her attention. A step toward the back corner revealed the source of the little voice.

"Sweet Marianne." Katie knelt in front of the child. "Are you hurt?"

Marianne shook her head, but such fear filled her face.

"Were you in here when the window broke?" Katie asked.

The girl nodded.

Katie hugged Marianne close to her, aching for the fear the girl felt. She remembered all too clearly how overwhelming and frightening a place the world could be for a child. Marianne's little arms clung to her.

"Let us get you back into the house, darling," Katie said. "Your mother is there. She'll keep you close and safe."

She felt Marianne nod, though the girl didn't move to stand.

"If I promise to walk between you and the windows, would that make you worry less?" Katie offered.

"Yes, please."

Poor thing.

They made the slow trek across the shop. Mr. Johnson watched his little girl with a look of loving concern that Katie had longed to receive from her own father. She'd seen the same look on Joseph's face when watching his daughters. If only the people in Hope Springs would take a moment to realize how alike they were, that their worries and concerns were truly the same, then perhaps they'd set aside some of their hatred.

Katie opened the door behind the shop counter, the one leading into the Johnson's home.

"Mrs. Johnson?" she called out.

The woman came round the corner as fast as her quickly approaching delivery would allow. "Marianne. Good heavens, were you out there for that?"

Marianne rushed from Katie's side into her mother's waiting arms.

Content that the girl was now safe and cared for, Katie moved back toward the door.

"Thank you, Miss Katie," Mrs. Johnson said.

Katie smiled and nodded her acknowledgment. She and the Johnsons were not precisely friends, but they were most certainly no longer enemies. She clung to that knowledge, telling herself the town might someday reach that place with one another.

She stepped past Mr. Johnson, eyeing the mess made by glass and wind, wishing he would have allowed her to help. Outside, the brawl had spread clear to the riverbank and all around the charred remains of the blacksmith shop. Tavish was trying to talk sense into the crowd, but his efforts were being met with fists and shoves.

She walked among the mob, feeling helpless and angry and exhausted. They would destroy each other if given half a chance. Nothing seemed capable of stopping them.

A scream rent the air and a shout of "gun!" Katie's heart leaped to her throat, even as she half ducked, half hid behind one of the porch poles at the mercantile.

Sure enough, one of the combatants held a handgun, eyeing those around him with an almost crazed look. How had things come to this?

"Enough!" Joseph stood just outside the ring of angry townspeople, a hard expression on his face.

Katie wanted to call out to him, to warn him of the gun, but fear and worry silenced her.

"Put it away, Gregory." Joseph addressed the man with the weapon as calmly as could be. "No one will be shot here today."

His gaze took them all in. Katie had never seen him so cold. So unnervingly still.

"I told you the consequences of violence and unrest in the streets. You knew that this would cost you your homes, whether Irish or Red." Another sweep of his steely gaze set the entire group back a step. "Either you didn't care or you find the consequences worth the opportunity to fight like savages in your own town."

"Joseph—" Damion MacCormack began a protest, but got no further than that one word.

"No mercy for the merciless, MacCormack," Joseph answered. "No mercy."

"You can't take my home, Archer," Mr. Archibald growled.

"I *own* your home, and you missed a payment." Joseph's eyes darted between them all. "You have all forfeited your claims on my sympathies. I will have full payments by day's end from each and every one of you," he snapped. "Failure to do so will result in evictions. Am I understood?"

Utter silence fell over the crowd.

Joseph turned his back and walked with quick and determined steps up the road.

Katie knew all too well the fear she saw in the faces around her. They had lost their homes. With snow thick on the ground. With no place of refuge within two days' drive.

This couldn't happen. The children would suffer for it. So many people would be in desperate straits.

Katie abandoned her place behind the mercantile post and hurried after Joseph. Tavish emerged from the chaos and caught up to her. She didn't acknowledge him. She had to stop this. People would freeze and starve and suffer.

"You can't do this, Joseph." She followed close on his heels, Tavish close on hers.

"They knew the consequences of this." He didn't look back at her.

Was this the same man whom she'd found just that morning sleeping with a five-year-old girl sprawled across his chest? The same man who'd listened so tenderly to her sob through her worries the night before?

He seemed so cold and uncaring. With bruised faces and bleeding noses, the townspeople, who had only moments before been beating each other without restraint, were making their way from town as well. Looks of accusation joined muttered words of contempt. Even facing the loss of their homes, they couldn't set aside their anger.

"Joseph."

"If they wanted to stay in Hope Springs," he said, still marching away with no hint of hesitation, "they should have left the guns at home. They should have stayed there themselves."

"They're frightened." She picked up her pace enough to step in front of him. "They know half the town hates them—that just across the way are people with guns. *Guns,* Joseph."

He stood with his hat in one hand, arms at his sides. He'd adopted that exact posture the first day she met him. 'Twas his "I won't be swayed" posture.

"I am sorry the Irish will be impacted by this—"

"I wasn't speaking only of the Irish. Every person here today was afraid. Every person here was hated by half the other people. All of them."

He looked at her for the first time since she'd stepped around him. "You weren't arguing for your countrymen alone?"

"I cannot believe you would think that of me." She was so angry, she wanted to scream.

"I'll take you home, Sweet Katie," Tavish said.

But she wasn't ready to go. "I have no desire to see anyone thrown off their land, Joseph Archer. I know how that feels. I know the fear and the pain and the devastation of that. And I have never—" She took a sharp breath through her nose, trying to keep herself calm and collected. "I have never taken sides against anyone in this town. I won't turn my back on any of them now."

"They didn't give me a choice."

She threw her hands up. "You *always* have a choice."

"I don't have any leverage but this." He spoke in the determined, confident tone she'd tried to emulate so many times but never seemed to manage. "They won't stop otherwise."

"Well, now they will because they will be gone." Just the thought brought tears to her heart.

Tavish slipped his hand in hers. "Let's head back up the road, Katie. There'll be difficulties enough to deal with there."

She'd had her say but felt like she'd not made any progress.

Tavish tugged a bit, but she didn't step away.

"You can't do this, Joseph."

Some of his confidence slipped. "I can't do anything else. They won't listen to reason." His tone took on a hint of pleading. "They won't stop if there are no consequences. As much as I hate forcing these families out, it is the only thing that will stop the violence."

"Not everyone who was part of this today are the usual troublemakers," Katie said. "Mr. Clark from the Red Road is usually peaceable, as is Mr. Murphy from the Irish. You have to know they were simply here at the wrong time and were caught up in what others started."

Tavish kept a hand on her arm as she stood there, pleading with Joseph. He didn't stop her, didn't interfere. And he was no longer insisting she return to Granny's.

"Joseph." She would convince him to show some compassion. She couldn't live with herself if she didn't at least try. "I know what it is to wander through the cold, with no place to go and no food to eat. You'll be tossing out children too, Joseph. How many will lose their toes or their fingers in this cold? How many will end up in the frozen ground?"

He turned his face away, but she moved back into his line of vision.

"Please don't do this," she whispered.

"I have to." His shoulders visibly dropped. The pain in his expression struck Katie with such force that she couldn't breathe. "Gregory Tyler had a gun today. If this doesn't stop, others will do the same next time, and in their hatred, they will fire on each other. This will become a town of murderers."

She knew he was right. "And if this doesn't stop, you will have to do this again, won't you? Evicting more and more until the town is either peaceful or empty."

A bone-deep tiredness entered Joseph's eyes. "The only way to save this town from itself is to be cold and cruel."

Cold and cruel. Two things Joseph was not. The necessity of it was clearly eating away at him.

Her heart broke for him.

"I wish I could do something, Joseph."

He pushed out a heavy sigh. "And I wish I could do something *different.*"

Katie felt utterly helpless. So many people were suffering.

"The girls may need to stay with you and Mrs. Claire a little later today than usual," Joseph said. "I have to deliver evictions." An ache filled his voice.

"They won't be able to make their full payments, then?"

Joseph shook his head. He walked past them up to his house without looking back. The sight of him so alone, his shoulders drooping in a way she'd never seen before, broke something inside her. Pain clutched at her heart.

Oh, Joseph.

"Let us hope this truly does end here today," Tavish said, still standing at her side though she'd nearly forgotten he was there.

Tavish walked with her toward the Irish Road. Eoin O'Donaghue kept guard at the icy bridge. Katie looked back over her shoulder in time to see Joseph step inside his house. Beyond that, Bob Archibald stood talking to someone standing guard with a shotgun in his hand at the turn-off to the Red Road.

Hope, Biddy had told her, springs eternal. Katie was struggling in that moment to believe that was still true.

Chapter Thirty

Tavish passed a difficult night. The eruption of violence had him worried. So did Katie. The events of the day before had shaken her. The look of resignation she'd worn as they walked up the Irish Road weighed heavily on his mind. He wanted to do something to help her, to reassure her, but had no idea what.

The sky was still dark along the eastern horizon when he decided he wasn't likely to get much sleep. He dragged himself to the corner of his house that served as a kitchen and set about making himself a pot of coffee. Though he couldn't put his thumb on when or how the change had occurred, things were different between him and Katie. She was more distant, and he didn't know how to get her back.

The sound of raised voices echoed from outside. Apparently there were others on the Irish Road too burdened to sleep. Joseph had made good on his threat. Five families on the Irish Road had received notices of eviction and were ordered to vacate their homes within ten days.

But why would they be out on the road at this hour? Heaven help them all if someone had decided to attack the Reds in the middle of the night.

Tavish crossed to his front window. A significant number of people were running down the road. But it was not an angry mob; his neighbors were panicked and afraid.

He snatched his coat and hat off their pegs and pulled on his boots. He rushed out onto the road. He didn't need to ask what had brought them all out on a bitter cold morning. He could smell smoke heavy in the air.

His gaze followed the rush of people. Down the road, precisely where the bridge sat, a column of flames reached toward the sky.

Tavish ran down the road. Frantic shouts echoed in chaotic patterns against the backdrop of crackling flames and the taste of ash in the air. The Irish huddled along the riverbank, chipping at ice in an attempt to reach the water beneath.

Tavish dropped down beside Keefe. He snatched a rock from the bank and pounded at the ice nearest him. It was too thin for standing on, but still thick enough to frustrate their efforts. Buckets sat empty, a stark symbol of the losing battle they were fighting.

Someone a pace off managed to break through to the river water. A brigade formed on the instant. They tossed bucketfuls of water at the flames, but Tavish could see in their faces that they knew as well as he did that they were too late.

Long minutes passed as they fought the flames. Bits of the bridge dropped into the water, steam and smoke rising up as it did. The bucket brigade slowed as the fire extinguished itself.

Tavish stood amongst his now silent friends and family. The sun peeked over the horizon, illuminating the smoldering skeleton of their bridge. Keefe was directly beside him, a look of horrified shock on his face.

"What . . . ?" Tavish couldn't find any other words.

"Damion and Eoin came to relieve Matthew Scott from guard duty. The bridge was burning." Keefe spoke with very little inflection, his eyes never leaving the charred pillar stubs sticking out of the icy river. "He woke us, but it was already . . ." He shook his head.

Tavish looked over the crowd. "Where is Matthew?"

"We don't know." Keefe rubbed at his face. "He wasn't here. No one's seen him. Ciara ran up the road to check at his place, see if he'd gone home. He's disappeared, Tavish."

Matthew wouldn't have abandoned his post. He would have fought whoever had come to set fire to the bridge. And now he was missing.

Saints above.

Tavish spotted Katie among the crowd and made his way to her. Her troubled gaze took in the river and the banks and the smoldering bits of wood jutting out of the water. She stood with her arms wrapped about her middle, the hem of her nightgown peeking out from beneath the bottom of the overly large man's coat she wore, the same coat she always wore. It was one of Joseph's—Tavish knew it was.

She glanced at him then back at the river. "How do we get across now?"

There was the rub. The bridge was the only way to cross the river from the Irish side. "We don't," Tavish answered. "Even if we head in the other direction, the river loops back and grows wider and flows faster. This is the only place to cross."

"We're trapped, then?"

"Like rats," Seamus growled from nearby. "And every one of those blasted, no-good Reds knows it." He paced away, muttering a string of words Tavish hoped Katie couldn't overhear. "Burned down my shop. Burned down the bridge. They'll be setting fire to our fields and houses next."

Tavish kicked at the blackened bits of wood on the riverbank. "They can't set fire to anything over here. We can't get over there, but neither can they get over to this side."

"'Tis little comfort," Seamus grumbled. "We also can't get any food over here. We can't make our drive out for firewood without crossing the river. What happens when our supplies run out? We all sit here, frozen and starved in our homes? Those of us who even have homes left, that is."

Katie's coloring fled entirely.

Tavish held back the very real worry he felt, focusing instead on thinking of a way to take this worry off her shoulders. "We'll think of something, Katie. Don't fret."

"Don't fret?" Frustration immediately took hold of her tone. "Few families have the supplies to see them through the winter. We can't wade across so wide and deep a river with ice floating all around in it. There's no means of getting food here or firewood. We've not even reached the worst of the winter yet. That seems like ample reason to fret."

"I only want you to not be burdened by it." This seemed to be the theme of their disagreements lately. He wanted to help, but she didn't want the help he offered.

Ian joined them at the riverbank. "The river freezes at some point every winter." He spoke as though reassuring himself. "Eventually we'll be able to walk over."

"How long is 'eventually'?" Katie asked.

"It always freezes by January," Ian said.

Katie stepped away a pace. "We've not even reached December yet. How many families can last until January?"

"I don't know." Ian slowly shook his head. "I don't know."

Katie rubbed her arms. Her brow creased, mouth twisted in thought.

Tavish looked to Ian, unsure what he ought to say to Katie or do. But his brother was looking out over the impassable river.

Katie rubbed her thumb over her lips, eyes unfocused. Was he permitted to make suggestions or offer encouragement, or was he supposed to keep quiet and let her think? He had no idea.

Her hand dropped away suddenly, her eyes opening wider. Katie stepped almost to the water's edge. She cupped her hands around her mouth.

"Joseph!"

Sure enough, Joseph Archer was rushing toward them, barely visible in the dim light of sunrise. "I found Matthew Scott in my barn," he called out. "He'd been hit on the head."

"Saints above," Katie whispered.

"Is he living yet, Joseph?" Anne Scott called back. "Is he well?"

"He'll be fine." Joseph stopped in his tracks as his eyes surveyed the remains of the bridge. His shocked expression gave way to obvious worry. His gaze immediately flew to Katie. "You're well? You're unhurt?" he called out.

She nodded. "How did Matthew end up on that side of the river?" she asked.

"He hasn't said." Joseph's eyes never left Katie. "He is still a bit rattled."

Tavish watched the two of them, an uneasy feeling growing inside.

"How are the girls?" she asked.

"They are still sleeping," Joseph answered. "Finbarr is as well."

"Finbarr?" Tavish jumped into the conversation.

"He stayed last night on account of the snow," Joseph said, barely acknowledging Tavish. "Do you need anything?"

She smiled and held her hands up. "Nothing that you can do from over there."

They were smiling at each other from across an icy river with a burned-out bridge. Tavish hadn't received even the most fleeting of smiles. Something was decidedly not right about that. He'd had her affection first. Why, then, was she smiling at Joseph?

Tavish came up even with her and put an arm around her shoulders. Joseph's gaze didn't linger on them; he didn't even hesitate with his next comment. Apparently Tavish hadn't made the statement he'd thought.

"Tavish, I don't see your parents. Will you tell them Finbarr is here and well?"

"I will," Tavish answered.

"Tell the girls I'm sorry they'll not be coming by for a while," Katie called out.

"Of course."

Tavish could feel Katie shivering. "It's awful cold out, sweetheart," he said. "Perhaps it'd be best"—he felt he had to tiptoe around even the most commonplace of suggestions—"if we headed back now."

She agreed and didn't seem offended. A good sign, that. He felt on firmer footing now. He plopped his hat on her head, smiling at how large it was on her.

"So your head'll stay warm," he explained.

She pulled the hat down around her ears and glanced up at him, her eyes barely peeking out from under the hat. She even smiled. At *him.* Not Joseph. That was how it should have been.

"Thank you, Tavish." But she turned back toward the river before she'd taken a single step back up the road with him and called back to Joseph, "Do you think the girls might meet me here this evening? I would like to wish them a good night."

"Certainly," Joseph called back. "Would six o'clock work for you?"

Katie nodded. She waved to him. Joseph waved back.

It's nothing to fret over. Simply a bit of friendliness. That's all it is. Nothing more.

Tavish took her hand. He made a mental list as they walked back up the Irish Road of things she'd let him do for her. He could offer Katie his hat. He could suggest a warm house on a cold morning. She wouldn't get angry at him over those things. Joseph hadn't been scolded for asking if she was well or if she needed anything. So that was, it seemed, permitted. He could build on that short list.

And he could set his mind to other troubles as well. Every Irish family would need to make an accounting of the supplies they had and make plans to help those most in need.

And they all needed to start praying for a very hard, very fast freeze.

By nightfall, a clear path had been worn in the snow on the Irish Road. Every family had made the journey to the burned-out bridge, many several times over. Shock had given way to anger and worry.

Those whose notes had been called in the day before clearly didn't know what to do. They had been given ten days to vacate the homes they'd lost, and yet there was very little chance of crossing the river by then. They nervously stayed in the houses they could no longer claim as theirs, knowing it was only a matter of time before they would be forced out for good.

Most of Tavish's family, along with Katie, gathered at Ian and Biddy's, attempting to find some way to sort out the mess.

"I can understand Seamus's anger," Da said after a full quarter-hour spent discussing the ways Seamus was whipping his neighbors into a frenzy, assembling a list of all the ways they would exact their revenge once the river was crossable. "But we've a crisis on our hands, and we can't waste our collective time and energy on planning mobs."

"So long as Seamus is bent on doing just that, we'll not get anything useful out of him," Tavish said.

"What if he could be convinced to set himself on the immediate problem?" Katie asked. "If we could get him to concentrate on something productive, he'd not be stirring up another hornet's nest."

"I've never known him to be turned from his purpose." Indeed, Tavish had known few people as mulish as Seamus Kelly.

"But I could at least try," she insisted.

Tavish came within a breath of warning her away from an errand that would most likely end in disappointment. But every time he'd offered any bit of advice to her lately, she'd simply grown frustrated with him. He didn't even know what to say to her anymore.

"What did Joseph have to say?" Da asked Ian.

Ian had accompanied Katie to the river for her good nights to the Archer girls.

"He's as baffled as we are," Ian said. "We can't last long on this side of the river with no way of getting goods across. There's too little ice for walking on, let alone driving over, and too much ice to allow any kind of boat to cross. We've a few ideas we mean to try, but . . ." He ended on a sigh.

Biddy took Ian's hand in hers and leaned against his arm. Tavish sat next to Katie, not touching, not even really looking at her. Somewhere along the way, things had gone wrong between them.

"Things might grow terribly bad while we wait for a means of crossing the river," Da addressed the family. "But we're a family, and we look out for one another."

They always had and always would.

Tavish's parents and siblings bid one another farewell. Da lingered over his good-byes to Katie.

"I hope you know, lass, that I include you in my family." He smiled fondly, but with a look of concern in his eyes. "If there's anything you find yourself in need of, anything at all, you come and tell me. And I hope you'll not find me a bother if I check in on you regularly."

She shook her head and gave him a hug. "You told me months ago that you meant to be a father to me. I mean to hold you to it."

Da chucked her under the chin, just as he had all of Tavish's sisters. "I'm not embarrassed to tell you, I've grown terribly fond of you, my girl. Like one of my own."

Katie bid farewell to Ma as well, before pulling on Joseph's coat. *Joseph's coat.* Seeing her wear it drove the knife a little deeper.

"Can I walk you home, Sweet Katie?"

She nodded and even smiled a bit.

Tavish lit the lantern he'd brought with him. They stepped out into the cold night, snow falling on them. Neither of them spoke for a drawn out moment.

Katie broke the silence. "I think I'll go talk with Seamus tomorrow. I can't say I will do any good, but I mean to try."

"I would be happy to talk to him for you, Katie."

"*For* me?" She clearly didn't like that phrase.

"Yes." The statement came out as a question.

"Why do you do that, Tavish?"

"I'm only trying to do something helpful for you." Surely she understood that.

"Why don't you try doing something helpful *with* me for a change?"

She picked up the pace. He matched his strides to hers.

"Is there something so wrong with wanting to take a few burdens from your shoulders? Heaven knows you have plenty of them."

She kept walking, not answering or looking at him. He could see, though, she was deep in thought.

"Would you rather I not be part of your life, Katie?" Even suggesting it made him uneasy. What would he do if she said she wanted him gone? His heart had been set on Katie almost from the first moment they met.

"Leaving me behind while you deal with the difficult things is hardly being part of your life. Grand gestures are all well and good, Tavish, but a person needs to be part of all the little moments, not just the big ones." Her voice had lost some of its fight. She sounded worn down, confused. "Sometimes, it's as if you think I'm a child, that I can't face my own worries so you have to solve them all for me because I'm not capable."

"I don't think that at all."

"I know." So why did she sound disappointed? "But that's how it feels."

They walked on without talking. Katie had never been truly angry at him before. The few times she'd been a touch put out with him, he'd always been able to make things right again with a bit of teasing and a few smiles.

She was upset with him for doing what he did, for being who he was. How did a person apologize for that?

He slid his hands into his coat pockets. The night was colder than before, and for reasons unrelated to the weather.

"Do you ever wonder, Tavish, if we're entirely right for each other?"

The question felt like a fist to the gut. They seemed to be having a rough patch, but Tavish would never have guessed she was questioning their connection so deeply.

"We took to each other from the very first, Katie. We get along famously."

Even in the dim light cast by his lantern, her drawn brows and downturned lips were apparent. This was no offhand conversation. Katie was deeply pondering things.

"But is that enough?" Was she posing the question to him or to her own self? "We are friends, for certain. Close friends, even. And I'm not unaware of how much you were willing to give up for me. When I think of that sacrifice—"

He didn't like the tone of indebtedness that entered her voice. "Like I said at the time, I made that decision with no strings attached, no promises or obligations on your part."

She looked at him for the first time since they'd begun this difficult conversation. "You said you wanted a chance to see if we could become more than dear friends. Have we?"

He didn't know quite how to answer. He'd planned to ask her to marry him, never doubting they could be happy together. But lately they'd been growing apart.

"Do you think of me during the day, Tavish?" Her eyes were devoid of accusation, but he felt it just the same. "Do you ever have a problem arise and think to yourself, 'I wish Katie were here so I could talk with her about it'?"

He couldn't say that happened too often. Not because he didn't think of her nor because he didn't value her thoughts and opinions, but because he didn't want to burden her. Life had been difficult enough for her without adding his troubles to hers. More than any person he'd ever known, Katie deserved to be treasured. He wanted her to not be so alone in the world, to know she didn't have to spend the rest of her life carrying her burdens on her own.

Was that so wrong of him? He didn't even know what to think of it, except to worry that he was losing her. They'd reached Granny's house. Katie didn't step inside.

Tavish knew he had to say something but struggled to find the words. "Are you ending things between us, Katie?"

"No." The word, though a little hesitant, calmed his growing sense of panic and eased the pain in his heart. "I'm only trying to make sense of too many things just now," she said.

He took her hand in his and looked directly into her eyes. "We will sort this out, my Sweet Katie. We'll find our answers."

She nodded. It wasn't a full reassurance, but it helped.

"Good night, then," he said.

She watched him a moment, then leaned in and kissed his cheek. She lingered a moment there.

Tavish closed his eyes and shut out everything but that moment. It didn't feel like a reconciliation. It felt like a good-bye.

She slipped into the house. He remained on the front step, trying to breathe.

Chapter Thirty-One

"The rope is too short, Joseph," Ian called out across the water. "If I tie the ends here, it'll still not reach the fence."

Joseph rubbed his gloved hands, trying to get the painful cold out of them. "Is there anything over there you can tie it to, just for now?"

Ian could always splice more rope to its length, if only they could keep the blasted thing attached to both banks. For nearly a week, he and Ian had been attempting to devise some means of getting supplies across to the stranded Irish. And for nearly a week, everything they'd tried had failed. They'd tried floating baskets across on those days when the ice didn't extend from bank to bank, but they couldn't control how the baskets traveled and most simply rushed off downstream to be lost. Even guided by the waterlogged ropes, most baskets had taken on water or been tipped over by the strong currents. And for the past two days, ice had been covering the entire width of the river, but it broke at the slightest weight.

"There aren't even any bushes around here." Ian stood looking about. "If we can't get the rope to Keefe's fence, we might as well be spitting against the wind."

"Is there enough there to tie to another length of rope?"

Ian cupped one hand around his mouth while clutching the rope with the other. "Seamus! We need more rope. I'm close, but I have to have more length."

Seamus set down the latching hook he was whittling and rushed up the road. All the Irish men who knew how were whittling devices to hook baskets to the rope. The women were weaving the baskets. If they could only manage to get the system of ropes and pulleys working, the baskets could be pulled across without needing to even touch the fragile ice.

"Papa?"

Joseph turned at the sound of Emma's voice. "You're supposed to be eating your dinner, sweetie."

She came up next to him, snuggling into his side. It was far too cold for such a little thing to be out. "Is Katie here yet?"

Of course Emma was watching for Katie. He should have known she would be. He'd been covertly looking for her himself.

"Not yet."

As if his words summoned her, Katie reached the riverbank directly across from where they stood. Tavish moved from his extended family group to stand next to her. Joseph envied him. He was there with Katie, while Joseph could only look on from across the water.

I could use your calming presence, Katie.

"Katie looks cold, Papa."

"She does, indeed." The coat she wore—the one he'd given her weeks earlier—was better than what she'd had but still insufficient for the brutal winters in Wyoming. He wished he'd left her his warmer coat. He'd been trying to think of a way to get her one of her own without offending her pride. He'd never have guessed something as drastic as this would get in the way.

"Katie doesn't like being cold," Emma said.

Joseph hoped she was wearing her thick woolen stockings. At least her feet would be warm. Though she'd sworn they didn't hurt, he'd seen their gnarled, scarred state and couldn't be certain she wasn't hiding her pain.

"I'm sorry, Mr. Archer." Finbarr rushed over to him, blankets draped over his arm. "Emma slipped out before I could stop her." He jerked his head toward the river. "She wants to hear Miss Katie play her fiddle."

Joseph could understand that. Katie had come to the river every evening since the bridge had burned and played for her neighbors as they worked. Though they claimed to simply wish to be on hand to help should something be rigged up, Joseph guessed Katie's music had as much to do with their nightly return as anything else. They worked faster after her arrival, even in the bitter cold.

Finbarr spread out a blanket for Emma and himself to sit on. Joseph, as always, would continue working and moving about. He would listen, but he wouldn't rest. He checked Emma's coat and scarf and tight knit cap before wrapping her as tightly as he could in one of the blankets Finbarr had brought out.

"If she starts to shiver," he told the boy, "even just a little, you take her inside no matter her protests."

"Yes, Mr. Archer."

Across the river, Katie sat on a blanket of her own. Tavish draped another blanket over her shoulders.

That won't do a fat lot of good. It'll fall off as soon as she raises her arms to play. If she'd been on his side of the river, he'd have found her a coat, no matter how big or mismatched. He would have found something that would stay on despite her movements. Katie shouldn't be cold. Not ever again.

She looked out across the river. Not at Finbarr. Not at Emma. Directly at him. He hoped she was smiling underneath the thick scarf that she had wrapped around the lower half of her face. He waved at her, not caring that his very real attachment to her was obvious in the gesture. He missed her so deeply after a week of nothing more than brief conversations shouted across the river. He missed her with every beat of his heart, with every breath he took.

Katie waved back, then pulled the mitten from her left hand.

His stomach had tied into knots every evening watching her play. Her bare hands must have hurt terribly by the time she finished each night.

The strains of her violin filled the air around them. Conversations hushed. Eyes turned in her direction. Relief filled the weary faces. Katie offered them all a gift with her music. She gave them peace and a balm to their troubled hearts.

He checked the ropes and the branches they were looped over. A couple circuits of the small stand of trees satisfied him. Things were secure. There was little else he could do on his side of the river.

He leaned against the tree nearest the banks and just listened to Katie's music. She had a gift. And the joy she took in the music filled her to the point that no one looking at her could possibly miss it. He could easily picture her sitting in any of the grand concert halls in New England, listening to a symphony. She could likely outplay any of the musicians that graced those stages. She had every bit as much talent as any of them; she simply played a different kind of music.

I would take you to those concert halls, Katie. I would take you there every night if I could.

He would give her the world if she wanted.

"Joseph!"

When had Katie stopped playing? And why was she shouting to him?

She pointed toward Emma. "Tell Emma to keep her hands under her blanket. She'll freeze her fingers clear off."

Emma complied even as Katie called out the instructions. Finbarr shot him an apologetic look.

Joseph called back across the river. "You should keep your hands covered as well."

Katie shook her head. "I can't play if my hands are tucked away."

"You can't play if your fingers 'freeze clear off,' either, Katie Macauley." The entire Irish gathering cringed in unison at his mispronunciation of her last name. He didn't butcher it as badly as he once had, though. "I'm doing better," he told them all.

The laughter and good-natured ribbing he received from the other side of the river went on and on. It was good to see them smiling. Seamus Kelly, who in previous disasters would have spent every moment calling for revenge and focusing his neighbors' minds on their anger, was joking along with them. No one could miss the anger that yet simmered in his expression; neither did Joseph doubt Seamus still intended to retaliate in time. But seeing the man set his anger aside, at least a little, was encouraging.

"There is nothing quite like Irish laughter, is there, Mr. Archer?" Finbarr grinned, looking across at his countrymen.

"You arc a happy group; that is indisputable."

He watched them interacting and enjoying each other. Biddy brought Ian a cup of coffee. Tavish laughed with his younger sister. Neighbors helped one another, working together. They were freezing and facing hunger, and still they smiled and joked and laughed.

"Joseph."

He didn't recognize the voice until he looked over. "Good evening, Reverend Ford. What brings you around?"

The preacher looked across the half-frozen river. "The feud that has torn apart this town has gone on too long," he said. "It is time, I think, that I made a stand for peace rather than fanning the flames as I too often have."

It said something about the state of Hope Springs that hearing a man of the cloth speak of choosing to side with peace and goodwill was so shocking.

"I'm pleased to hear that," Joseph managed.

"Jeremiah is sending supplies in the morning so the Irish can get what they need once you've worked out a system."

"Jeremiah Johnson?" Joseph stared. He'd seen a softening in Mr. Johnson's behavior toward Katie, but he hadn't expected such an overt show of support for all the Irish.

Across the river, the crowd stood perfectly still, watching Joseph and the preacher. They couldn't hear what was said, and they looked worried.

He turned back toward them, calling out, "The mercantile is sending supplies tomorrow. If we can get this working, you'll have what you need."

Cautious cheers accompanied their looks of hope.

"There has been too much hurt and harm here," Reverend Ford said. "I wouldn't listen when Miss Macauley scolded me for my part in it. She was the first to point out that I had an obligation to do more. She was right."

"I've discovered she usually is," Joseph whispered.

Across the river, a wave of activity rippled through the Irish camp. The promise of supplies gave them the extra push they needed to forge ahead with their efforts even as the temperature continued to fall.

Katie took up her instrument again, choosing a livelier tune than before. Her fingers had to be absolutely frozen. That sent his thoughts momentarily to Emma. He glanced over. Finbarr had pulled her up close to him, rubbing her arms. He was a good young man, the perfect protective older brother to Emma and Ivy. The adoration in Emma's eyes every time she looked at the boy spoke volumes. Her tender heart had latched on to him from the very beginning.

"The Johnson boy brought this back from the depot." Reverend Ford handed Joseph a sealed envelope—a telegram.

"Thank you." Joseph tucked it into the pocket of his coat. He would open it later.

"I have never heard Miss Macauley play the violin," Reverend Ford said. "She is very talented."

"That she is. I have heard her music many times, but it still amazes me."

"Does she often play for them?"

Joseph nodded. "Every week at their parties. She played while she lived here. She played nearly every night that my girls were going to her home during the day."

Reverend Ford stood watching and listening, his brow pulled tighter and more deeply furrowed than Joseph had ever seen it. The man was seeing Katie clearly for the first time. Had he chosen to disregard her because of her public scolding of him? Toward how many other Irishmen in town had he been just as blind?

"Ian O'Connor has spent hours every day trying to get this rope system worked out, despite still being plagued by pain from the beating he took. Seamus Kelly lost most of his blacksmithing equipment when his shop burned down—likely by the same people who burned the bridge—yet he's working himself to exhaustion whittling what he would otherwise have forged to help in this effort."

He watched the effect his words had on the preacher. Amazement, wonder, and something very much like discomfort.

"They take turns tending each other's children while groups of Irish come work. They endure the cold so there'll be enough people here in the very instant we find a way to get supplies to them. I'm glad to hear that the supplies will be coming soon, but the weather is turning—we can all feel it. Perhaps as early as tomorrow it will be too frigid to spend so much time exposed to the elements, but the river won't have frozen solid enough to safely walk on. They will be trapped."

Reverend Ford's gaze turned to him, clearly troubled. "The Irish haven't been entirely innocent in this feud, you know."

"I know. Both sides have done their share of provoking the other." He held the preacher's gaze, hoping Katie's example of selflessness and his own pointed words would finally get through. "It's gone too far this time. Families have lost their homes. People are stranded without supplies. Matthew Scott was beaten into unconsciousness and tossed into a barn, all for trying to stop this"—he motioned to the skeletal remains of the bridge—"from happening. Lives are in danger now, Reverend."

They stood for a drawn-out moment in silence. The sounds of work and low conversations floated over the water, Katie's continued playing adding depth to the scene.

"Do you think, Joseph, it would help if I spoke to the Red Road? Reminded them of their Christian duty? Of their *human* duty?"

Joseph nodded firmly. "I am certain it would."

"And surely they don't wish to see more families evicted."

How Joseph prayed it wouldn't come to that.

Though Matthew's injuries had left his memory too vague to know who had attacked him and set the bridge afire, Joseph was nearly certain it was Bob Archibald. The man had been served an eviction notice after the brawl in the streets and given ten days to be out just as all the others had. If Joseph could have proven Archibald was responsible for this act of arson, he would have revoked the grace period and seized the property immediately.

With Johnson no longer stirring up the Reds, and Seamus, at least for the moment, not on the warpath, Archibald was the biggest threat to the possibility of peace. If he could be taken out of the equation, they might have a chance.

The reverend stood with a look of deep uneasiness on his face. "I should have taken a stand against this sooner. I should have."

"But perhaps it isn't too late."

Reverend Ford seemed to square his shoulders. "Would you be willing to host a meeting, of sorts, if I called one? Your home has been a place of neutrality, more even than the church, I'm sorry to say." He did, in fact, look ashamed of that. "If even some of those on the Red Road were willing to come and listen, perhaps we could change things before the situation grows even more dire."

"Have them come tomorrow after supper," Joseph said. "There's no point putting this off, not when we could use help getting supplies over the river. And you are right: If we can convince even a few to let go of their hatred, we might change the course of this entire thing."

Reverend Ford agreed, though tension and worry clouded the small ray of optimism in his eyes. Joseph understood the feeling. They were facing an uphill battle.

The preacher walked slowly back toward the road, looking across the river more than once. Joseph hoped this was the beginning of a much-needed change in Hope Springs.

A chilling blast of wind penetrated his thick coat. The temperature would drop drastically once the sun fully set.

Joseph knelt down on the blanket, facing Emma. "You have to go back inside now, Emma. It is far too cold."

"But I want to hear Katie play. We can't go to her house so I never hear her anymore."

"Have you found the tune the two of you have been looking for all these months?"

Emma's gaze dropped in something very much like guilt.

"Emma?"

"I don't remember it anymore," she admitted in a whisper. "I didn't tell Katie, though, because I didn't want her to stop playing for us."

"My sweet Emma," Joseph said. "Katie knows you love the music. She knows we all do; that's why she plays for us. She won't stop giving you her music no matter that you're not searching for something in particular."

She looked up at him, her eyes both hopeful and pleading. "Do you really think so?"

"I am absolutely certain of it."

Emma's shoulders rose and fell with a deep breath. "I wish she wasn't so far away."

Joseph chucked her under the chin. "You miss Katie, do you?"

Emma nodded.

"So do I," he quietly admitted. "But eventually the river will freeze thick enough, and we'll go fetch her. Then we'll see if we can't convince her and Mrs. Claire to come spend the rest of the winter at our house."

"What if they won't come?" Emma looked worried.

"Then we will take them all the food they could possibly need and plenty of wood for burning."

Emma pondered that a minute. "I wish she would come live with us again, Papa. I liked it when she lived with us."

He glanced at Finbarr. The boy was trying hard to appear as though he couldn't hear them.

Joseph kept his response light. "I think you miss her cookies and cakes most of all."

Emma smiled. "No. I miss *her* most of all."

"Go along, sweetie," he said. "Go warm up in the house and get ready for bed."

"But, Papa—"

"Come along, sweet girl," Finbarr cut in. "I'll walk back up with you."

Emma agreed. Bless Finbarr for stepping in and helping out. Finbarr walked back with her, keeping her close to him and her blanket firmly wrapped around her shoulders. He was a fine young man, one Joseph was proud to watch growing up.

Katie had stopped playing. She was only just closing her violin case, the instrument stowed away inside. She and Tavish were having a conversation punctuated with smiles. Was she really as happy with Tavish as she seemed? Joseph knew she could be happy with him as well if he were only given the chance to show her as much.

Tavish walked off with Katie's violin. She pulled her coat more tightly around herself as she turned to look across at Joseph.

"Did Emma go inside?" she called out.

Joseph nodded. "It's too cold."

"Aye, and that's the truth with no twists about it."

Her Irish turns of phrase made him smile.

"My fiddle keeps losing its tune from the cold, and my fingers hurt so bad I can't hardly stand to move them about." She rubbed her arms. "I need to go check on Granny. It looks to be a bitter night, and she isn't always careful to gather enough blankets before going to bed."

"Good night, Katie." How he wished they had even a little privacy so he could tell her how much he admired the care she took of her neighbors. He might even have worked up the courage to tell her more of his feelings. But those things shouldn't be shouted.

She was gone quickly, the cold speeding her steps. As soon as the river was crossable, he told himself, he would find a moment to lay his heart out to her. She might reject it. She might have already given hers irretrievably to Tavish O'Connor. But he would try. Come what may, he would try.

Chapter Thirty-Two

Word spread quickly down the Irish Road the next day that there would be no meeting at the riverbank that night. The day had been too cold, with the air only growing more frigid. Everyone had agreed it would be for the best if they kept to the warmth of their houses.

Katie buttoned up Joseph's coat, more grateful for it the past nights than she could say. Katie was bound for the river. None of the Irish would be there. But if there was even a chance Emma or Ivy or Joseph—she wanted to see him most of all—meant to go out that night, Katie wanted to be there. She needed to see them again.

She made certain Mrs. Claire had a warm fire and an adequate supply of blankets before leaving. She left her fiddle behind. As much as she would have liked to play for them, her fingers couldn't bear another night in the cold. The fiddle itself likely couldn't either.

The biting air hit her like a slap. *Heavens, but it's cold tonight.* She secured her scarf over her face. She'd been warned not to breathe in through her nose without it. Only her feet were even the tiniest bit warm. *Thank you for that, Joseph.* She'd worried that night months ago when he saw her bare feet that he'd be disgusted by the sight of them, that he'd think less of her. But he'd understood. He'd understood enough to give her stockings to keep her feet warm and safe.

Katie had nearly reached the spot where the bridge had stood. The Irish were, of course, nowhere to be seen. But across the river, lights shone in the lower level of the Archer home. Silhouettes filled the windows.

Was Joseph having a party? She doubted it. More likely a gathering or meeting of some kind.

Wagons sat around the house. Horses stood about, draped with thick blankets, their breath clouding in front of them. This was no small affair.

A light flickered in the barn. Perhaps some of the guests were searching for a place in the barn for their horses.

Except why would they be searching in the loft?

Katie debated turning back. Joseph wouldn't be waiting for her down at the river with a house full of people. The girls wouldn't be out alone.

Unless Finbarr has brought them.

The least she could do was check. Her teeth chattered so hard her jaw hurt. Though she'd miss seeing the girls, Katie hoped they hadn't come out in this weather.

The rope Joseph and Ian had looped from one side of the river to the other was still in place. They'd managed to tie it to Ciara's fence but couldn't anchor it in quite the right way for getting supplies across the water.

Crunching snow pulled her gaze and her thoughts toward Joseph's barn. The shutter over the window facing her was closed, but she could see an outline of light, flickering like a single candle. Who would be in a barn loft in such cold weather?

She saw movement in the shadows at the base of the barn, then a sudden burst of flame. As always, the sight made her breath catch.

Someone had lit a torch. 'Twas a man, she could see that much. He was stocky, with broad shoulders. Katie watched as the man stepped from the shadows. He turned the tiniest bit, just enough for his face to be illuminated by the torchlight.

Bob Archibald.

A weight settled in her stomach. Katie had never seen the man without an evil glint in his eye. What trouble was he about this time?

Bob Archibald moved around the barn and out of sight. Katie inched to the edge of the river, watching for him to come back into sight. Minutes passed. She argued with herself, first insisting he wasn't doing anything untoward. After all, there was a gathering just across the way at Joseph's house, a gathering of the Red Road, she was certain. Mr. Archibald wasn't likely to be up to tricks when amongst *his* side of this feud. And yet, the sick feeling in her stomach only grew.

He suddenly reappeared, moving quickly toward the house. He was nothing more than a shadow again. What had he done in the barn?

A more worrisome question occurred to her: *Where's his torch?*

Bob disappeared into the house. He didn't look back.

She ran down the list in her mind of the many fires the town had seen in the past weeks. A small one at the smithy, followed by the larger one that destroyed it completely. The bridge burning to nothing but charred posts sticking out of the river.

She knew, even without smoke or flame, that he'd left the torch inside the barn, that he'd lit something on fire. She looked around frantically. There was someone in the loft. She'd seen the light up there. Someone was in the barn, and Bob Archibald more likely than not had set a fire inside.

"Help!" she called out. "Someone! Help!"

Nothing answered but the wind.

What could she possibly do? Someone was in danger. She couldn't simply walk away.

Perhaps whoever was there would think to get down. But who would be hiding in the loft anyway?

Hiding. In the loft.

"Merciful heavens." Ivy hid in the loft. Emma said she did it all the time. "Oh, sweet heavens."

Katie looked out frantically over the river at the rope hanging there. She had to cross it. She simply had to.

She hooked her arm over the rope, holding it with both hands and stepped out onto the ice.

Please let this hold. Please. My baby girl's in danger.

Her mind could think of nothing but Ivy.

She moved one step at a time along the slick ice, leaning heavily on the rope to keep her balance. How she hoped Joseph and Ian knew how to tie a good knot. If the ice broke underneath her, would the rope be enough to hold her? Would she fall through the ice? She held desperately to the rope, looking around while her mind spun. Was there any other way to do this? Was she panicking for no reason?

'Twas then she saw the first wisps of smoke rising from the barn. One of her girls was in danger. She would cross the river no matter what it took.

Afraid the force of a step would crack the fragile ice, Katie slid carefully but quickly. She held her breath as she reached the middle of the river.

One step at a time. Just one. Just one.

Without warning, the ice beneath her right foot gave way. The rope dug painfully into her armpit with the weight of her falling body. She desperately clung to the rope as her feet sought for something solid. Freezing water rushed into her boot, soaking through her stocking. She couldn't find the ice, couldn't find anywhere to put her foot.

Help me, please.

Smoke continued inching out of a lower window of the barn. No one was coming from the house. She'd seen no one leave the barn. With every bit of strength she could muster, she pulled herself forward on the rope, sliding the foot that still had contact with the ice and praying she wouldn't slip. Her arms burned with the effort of keeping herself out of the water. Finally, she had both feet on the ice. There was no time for relief or rest.

On she moved. The ice gave again. Fear clutched her heart. Not fear for herself, but the horrifying possibility that she wouldn't make it to Ivy in time. She reached her leg out as far she dared and set her toes on the ice. The rope tore at the sleeve of her coat as she dragged herself forward. Both her feet were soaked. She shook with cold and effort.

"I'm nearly there, Ivy," she said. "I'm nearly there."

The moment her feet reached the far bank, she ran.

"Help!" she shouted. "Someone!"

She threw open the barn doors. The air inside was far warmer than it was outside. She could smell smoke.

A flood of memories washed over her. Her mother's screams. Her sister sobbing in fear. A rain of fire as the thatch roof of her childhood home fell down around her. The searing pain of her feet and legs burning beneath her.

You cannot stop now, Katie Macauley.

"Iv—"

Someone rushed passed her into the barn. After a quick moment, she realized it was Finbarr.

"Help me put this out," he called back over his shoulder.

She moved to the back corner, where the smoke was thickest. The wall had begun smoldering, though there were no flames yet. The bits of hay on the floor were, thankfully, wet enough to be smoking more than burning.

Finbarr tossed a wool horse blanket to her. He beat at the heap of smoking hay with a blanket of his own. She understood without instruction. If they could beat down the fire before it got out of hand, they could save the barn—and Ivy.

Together they beat frantically at the cinders. The smoke grew ever thicker.

Just as she swung the blanket again, flames erupted on the wooden back wall. She stepped back.

I hate fire. I hate fire.

"I'll let the animals out." Finbarr rushed in that direction. "Get to the house."

She stood a moment, too afraid to even move. Fire continued to spread. The entire wall would be aflame in a matter of minutes. Everything in that barn would burn.

Sweet heavens. Ivy.

Katie rushed to the ladder and climbed toward the loft.

"Miss Macauley!" Finbarr called. "You have to get out!"

She reached the loft, eyes scanning the darkness. "Ivy? Are you up here? Ivy?"

No response. The candle she'd seen flickering before seemed to have been blown out. Perhaps Ivy had extinguished it when she heard Mr. Archibald come in.

"Ivy, I saw your candle, dear. Please, you have to get out. You have to come with me *now.*"

The air tasted of smoke. Katie swallowed down a sob.

"Ivy, please."

Over the sound of crackling wood and Finbarr shouting for the animals to leave, Katie heard a tiny voice. "Katie?"

"Sweetheart?"

Where had Ivy been the last time Katie had found her hiding in the loft? *The near corner.*

Katie moved quickly in that direction. It was too dark to see anything. She dropped onto her hands and knees, searching with her hands. "Ivy? Please don't hide from me."

The smoke grew thicker with each passing moment. Katie's lungs fought to pull in a breath of clean air. Her mind screamed for her to run away as far and as fast as she could. The barn was on fire. *Fire.*

"Katie, I'm scared." Ivy's voice shook.

"Where are you, sweet one? Keep talking so I can find you."

"The people were mad." Ivy coughed. "And it smells smoky."

Her eyes were adjusting. She could make out a tiny silhouette in the corner.

"Come along, Ivy." She moved quickly toward her. "Come with me. We need to go."

"I'm scared. I'm scared." Ivy coughed in the smoky air.

Katie took hold of Ivy's arm. "We have to go quickly." The taste of ash filled her mouth.

"I can't see you, Katie." That was Emma. She was up there as well? *Merciful heavens!*

Panic like she'd never known surged through every inch of her. She felt about frantically until she found Emma's arm. "We have to get out now, girls. We have to."

She kept a hand on both of their arms as she struggled to her feet. The girls were coughing harder. They fought her efforts to pull them toward the ladder, but she didn't let go. She would not leave them.

"It's smoky, Katie."

"There's a fire down below, girls. We have to get out."

"But, Katie—"

She tugged on their arms again. "We have to go, Emma. We have to."

"But we can't leave Marianne."

She froze. *Marianne? Marianne Johnson?* "Marianne's here as well?"

"Everyone was shouting."

"Marianne!" She coughed. The air had grown thick and hot. "Was she sitting with you? Have you any other friends up here?"

"It's just us, Katie."

"Marianne! Answer me, child. We have to get out. Marianne!"

The back wall was full on fire, flames leaping toward the ceiling. The hay in the loft would catch any second. She had to get Emma and Ivy out, but she couldn't leave Marianne behind.

What do I do? What do I do? 'Twas little Eimear again, a poor child's life in danger, and she was the only one there to help.

"Marianne!"

Ivy and Emma were coughing near constantly. But Katie heard another cough. If she could just follow it—

She heard Finbarr's voice instead. "Miss Katie, you have to get out. The whole place'll come down on your head."

"Help me, Finbarr. Emma and Ivy are up here."

"Saints above." He scrambled up the ladder.

"Marianne Johnson is over here as well, but I can't find her."

"Marianne!" Finbarr ran across the loft. He coughed hard. "Marianne!"

Suddenly the crackling grew to an almighty roar. The hay had caught. Her pulse pounded hard in her head. They likely had mere minutes.

"Katie." Ivy whimpered at her side.

Emma had grown silent.

"Take the girls, Finbarr. Get them as far from here as you can. I will find Marianne—"

"No, you go. I'll look."

"Finbarr—"

"Go, quickly."

Steam rose off the hem of Katie's dress, the heat of the fire pulling the last of the river water from her clothes.

"Don't leave me here," a frightened little voice pleaded in the darkness.

"Marianne?"

"Don't leave me. Please."

"We won't leave you," Katie called out. "I promise."

Finbarr was a step ahead of her, moving toward Marianne's voice.

"Come with me, Marianne," he said. "We have to run."

"Finbarr." Katie's eyes stung painfully. Each breath burned. "There's no time."

He grabbed Marianne, holding her fast as they all rushed toward the ladder.

Katie swatted at the girls' dresses as cinders set the hems smoldering.

"The ladder's on fire, Katie." Ivy clung close to her.

"No, dear." *Not yet.* "Down. Quickly."

Both girls pulled away, afraid. Katie looked down at the flames and smoke below. She couldn't let herself be paralyzed by it. *Hold yourself together until the girls are safe.* She'd done it before. She could do it again.

"Come down with me," she said. "We'll go together."

She took the first step over the edge, her foot finding the rung, then the next. "Come on."

Ivy stepped over. They took one rung at a time. Emma hesitated, looking back over the loft.

"Finbarr!" Katie called out.

He appeared in the next moment, Marianne still clutched tight to him.

It was enough for Emma. She climbed down the ladder too. Katie stepped onto the ground below and reached for Ivy.

"Katie." She was crying, shaking.

"Run, Ivy. Run straight from the barn and don't stop until you reach the house."

She could hear voices shouting outside. The people in the house had discovered the fire.

"Your father'll be out there, dearest. You run to him, now. Run!"

Ivy took off like a bolt. Emma hadn't come all the way down the ladder yet. She'd stopped halfway. Finbarr stopped above her, Marianne clinging to his neck.

"Come on, Emma," Katie encouraged.

"I'm scared, Katie. It's all on fire. Everywhere."

"I'm scared too, sweet girl. But we cannot stop now." She held her hands up, but Emma wasn't near enough to reach. "Hurry, please, darling."

Her legs were suddenly hot. She glanced back. *Heavens, I'm on fire!* She swatted at her skirts, slapping out the flames.

"Emma! Now!" That startled her into action. A moment later, she was within reach. Katie grabbed her and set her on the ground.

A loud, ominous creak sounded above the rushing flames. They had to run. The whole place was coming down.

"Run, Emma!"

Through dropping hay and ashes and cinders, they ran. The barn groaned. Katie looked up. The entire roof was engulfed in flame. 'Twas that night all over again. The roof above her coming down. Running for her very life.

The entire barn seemed to shift around her. Emma was very near the doors, but not quite out yet. Katie ran faster than she ever had. The walls gave way. Emma looked up and screamed. The terror cut at Katie's heart.

She lunged forward, pushing Emma through the barn doors and out into the night. Katie spun back around, frantically reaching for Finbarr and Marianne. They were just out of reach. Something heavy and hot knocked her down. An almighty crash filled her ears, then silence.

She couldn't get up. She couldn't breathe. Somewhere in the background she heard voices shouting. Pain pulsed through her in waves. She tried to pull in air, but there didn't seem to be any.

She closed her eyes and tried to endure the pain. She hurt so much. So deeply. Her thoughts began to muddle.

The sound of Father playing his fiddle came to her from across the years. "Ar Éirinn" filled her mind. 'Twas the tune he'd played the night of the fire, and the one that always made him feel close again.

"I'm scared, Father," she silently told him. "I'm here, dying, alone." Just as he was. He was dying, and she wasn't there with him. She was dying, she knew she was, and he wasn't there with her.

Each breath grew harder, more painful. No thoughts came after that. Only pain. So much pain.

Chapter Thirty-Three

Joseph sat on a chair beside his bed, listening to the clock tick and the sound of Katie struggling to breathe. His precious girls slept on the floor, wrapped in blankets. They'd refused to leave despite his insistence. He'd not said anything about it, but they seemed to sense that Katie's life was hanging in the balance.

He held her broken hand between both of his, the pain in his heart only growing. She needed a doctor, but the closest one was a two-day drive away and the roads leading to the depot wouldn't be passable until winter was over.

He gently kissed the tips of her fingers, the only part of her hand he hadn't wrapped in bandages. So many bones were broken, but he didn't know how to set them or how to piece the rest of her back together.

The sound of her struggling for air had been his constant companion for hours. She likely had broken ribs and lungs full of smoke and ash. The girls coughed a lot as well, though they'd not been crushed by the falling barn as Katie had. They were already sounding better. Katie only looked worse.

"I don't know how to make her well again." He didn't know if it was a prayer or if he was simply so out of his mind with fear that he was talking to himself. "I can't breathe for her. I can't give her my hand."

Her hand. If she lived through this, her hand would still be as broken and disfigured as her feet. More so, in many ways. How much tragedy would life require her to endure?

"How is she, Joseph?" Reverend Ford asked from the doorway.

"She needs a doctor," Joseph said.

"I'm afraid I don't have one of those." His footsteps drew closer.

"Then she'll need a miracle—or are you fresh out of those as well?"

Reverend Ford stood at the foot of the bed, watching Katie with a somber expression. Did the preacher see death hovering in her features as clearly as Joseph did?

Mrs. Smith came inside, carrying a steaming teapot. They had established a familiar pattern over the night's watch: Mrs. Smith would make a concoction of herbs and water, then bring the teapot up to fill the air with soothing steam. It did seem to help, if only a little. His opinion of his housekeeper was not generally high, but he was grateful for her that night.

"The young lady's coloring seems a little better, Mr. Archer." He knew enough of Mrs. Smith's bluntness to know she meant what she said.

He didn't see any change, but took some comfort in the possibility that Katie's condition had improved at all.

"Now you men step outside the room. I've a poultice to replace."

Joseph kissed Katie's fingers one more time before laying her bandaged hand on the bed beside her. He didn't know exactly what Mrs. Smith's poultice contained, but if there was any chance it would help, he would happily be thrown from his room again and again for days on end.

He waited for Reverend Ford to step out before closing the door behind them both. He leaned against the wall, letting it hold his weight. The strength to stand on his own had disappeared in the dark of early morning, many hours ago.

Joseph rubbed his face, fighting angry, exhausted, desperate tears. He had to hold himself together. His girls would be awake soon. They would need him. And Katie had no one to care for her but him. The Irish were still trapped across the river.

"I would be happy to sit up with Miss Macauley. You need to sleep."

"I can't."

"Your housekeeper and I can tend to—"

"It isn't that. I *can't* sleep. I have tried, and I can't." He tipped his head back, taking in a deep breath. "It is there in my mind. Every time I close my eyes, I see it again. I hear it. The sound of the barn giving way. The sight of Emma not quite outside and me knowing I couldn't possibly get to her in time."

That moment would likely haunt him for the rest of his life.

"Then, suddenly, Katie was there, pushing Emma clear."

"Miss Macauley was your miracle tonight, Joseph. No one even knows how she got across the river."

Or how she knew the girls were in the barn.

"For just that moment, I was so relieved." His heart dropped at the memory. "Then I watched as the walls fell and she was trapped. And I thought, as we were digging her out, that if we could just get her clear, everything would be fine. But when we found her, she was so broken. She was hardly breathing. I thought—for a few terrible seconds, I was certain she was dead."

His entire world had ended in that moment.

He could only just push the smallest of breaths past the lump in his throat. He paced away. His mind had struggled all night to comprehend the enormity of what had happened.

"You said people would die if this feud was left unchecked." Reverend Ford's voice was soft and heavy. "I confess I dismissed your words as irrational and angry. I should have done more."

If the preacher was looking for words of comfort or assurance that he had done enough, he wouldn't be hearing them from him. Joseph had spent years trying to warn the town against the path they were treading. He'd given up friendships and companionships trying to save them from themselves.

Now this.

"Has anyone confessed to setting the fire?" he asked.

The preacher looked uncomfortable. "No."

"How very typical." He paced away, unable to keep still. "An innocent child is dead. A sixteen-year-old boy is hovering near that precipice as well. A warmhearted and loving woman lies in that room fighting for her very life. All because *someone* set a fire in the name of a senseless feud. A child is dead, Reverend. Dead, and still they cling to their loyalties."

Reverend Ford paled, his eyes growing more red-rimmed.

"One of their own killed one of their children, and it's not enough to change a single thing." He spun about. "How many of this town's children will they bury before they've finally had enough?"

He left Reverend Ford standing alone in the hallway. His emotions were in such turmoil, he didn't trust himself not to lash out with more than words. The man didn't deserve it, not entirely. He had been there the night before trying to talk sense into them. The preacher had taken a stand, late though it was. Perhaps nothing could have prevented that night's tragedy.

Joseph rapped lightly on the guest room door and heard a muffled invitation to enter. The room was as dim and cheerless as his own, the poor soul on the bed as still as Katie.

"How is Finbarr?"

Matthew Scott, his own head still bandaged from the blow he'd taken only a week earlier, sat near the bed. "He's breathing, but that's about all I can say for him."

Joseph stood at the head of the bed, looking down at the boy. He was almost unrecognizable, his face swollen and bruised and burned. They'd treated his injuries as best they could, but they could only do so much.

"How is our Katie?" Matthew asked.

"Not any better."

"I should've gone with him," Matthew said. "While the Reds were here chewing your ear off about this feud, Finbarr told me he saw Bob Archibald sneaking in through the back of the house, looking guilty as sin, but he didn't know what about. He said he meant to go have a look around." Matthew shook his head, mouth pulled tight. "I should've gone looking with him. It's too much to ask of a lad."

Bob Archibald. Joseph had suspected him all along. Fire was the man's weapon of choice. Everyone knew that.

"You couldn't have known about the fire," he said.

"They were nearly out," Matthew said. "Katie was but a step from safety. Finbarr was right on her heels with the poor little Johnson girl. They were so close."

Joseph leaned his forehead against the tall post of the headboard as images flooded over him again, unbidden and unwelcome. They'd found Finbarr practically touching Katie, he was so near her. He had Marianne in his arms, shielding her tiny body. He'd clearly tried to save her from the weight of the falling walls and vicious flames, but they'd tumbled to the ground wrong. Marianne's neck was broken. She was dead, likely in the very instant the barn fell on them.

They were so close.

Marianne was Emma's dearest and closest friend. They were little peas in a pod, oftentimes giggling outside school or church. Only by chance had Emma escaped with her life when her friend had not. That chance would eat away at him; he knew it would. And it would plague his sensitive little Emma. Would she blame herself the way Katie did for her sister's death? The thought weighed on him.

"I wish Finbarr's parents could be here," Matthew said.

Joseph knew the details of the night's tragedy had been shouted across the river to the Irish families who had come when they saw flames licking the sky. The O'Connors would know the graveness of Finbarr's injuries. He couldn't imagine being separated from either of his daughters in the aftermath of all that had happened.

Joseph set himself to the task of changing the bandages on the side of Finbarr's face. He knew little about treating burns beyond the absolute necessity of keeping them clean. The boy didn't even wince as the bandages tugged at his wounds.

Matthew followed his lead and checked the bandaging on Finbarr's chest and arm. They worked in heavy silence. There seemed no sufficient words for that night's suffering.

"Papa?"

He spun on the instant, determined to shield Emma from the sight of Finbarr's injuries. She was too sensitive, too attached to the boy. "Go back to sleep, sweetheart. In your own bed or back in the room with Katie, either one, but you need to go to sleep."

She walked directly to the opposite side of the bed, not giving him a chance to reach her first. Her sweet angel face paled as she looked at Finbarr. She reached out her hand to touch the boy's face.

"Very gently, Emma," he instructed. "You must be very, very gentle."

She brushed her fingers ever so softly along his right cheek. His left side had taken the brunt of the falling building and the fire.

She coughed but never looked away from Finbarr. "Is he going to die, Papa?"

Joseph took a sharp breath in through his nose, trying to maintain his composure. "I don't know, Emma."

She kept her fingers on Finbarr's cheek. The boy was such an odd combination of friend and brother to her, the first boy to touch her heart. She must hurt to see him so injured.

"Katie sounds like she is dying," Emma whispered. "Like her body won't let her breathe."

"I know." He blinked back a tear. If he broke down, Emma would be even more frightened than she already was. "We're doing everything we can for her, I promise you."

She looked up at him for the first time since seeing Finbarr. "Where is Marianne, Papa?"

He hadn't expected to have this conversation with her yet. He hadn't decided what to say. She watched him with those hurting and painfully hopeful eyes as he moved to her side. He knelt on the floor, looking directly at her and searching for the right words.

"Finbarr tried very hard to get Marianne from the barn." He swallowed against the painful thickness in his throat. "The fire spread very fast, and the walls couldn't keep standing after being burned so much. They—"

Emma put her hand over his mouth. "I don't want to talk about it anymore." Her voice broke and, with it, his heart. She had lost too many people in her short life.

"Tell me when you do want to talk, sweetheart."

She nodded, then turned away from him, facing the bed again. "I want to help Finbarr."

Joseph took her hand. "Emma, darling, there is nothing you can do."

Her expression only grew more determined. "I want to help him."

The stubbornness of her declaration only made the hopelessness of the situation all the more poignant. If only there was a task he could give her, anything to make her feel less helpless.

"Can I hug him?" She turned her eyes to Joseph, clearly expecting to be denied.

"His body is very broken, dear. A hug might hurt."

She shook her head. "I can be careful. I won't hurt him, I promise. I wouldn't ever hurt him." A tear escaped the corner of her eye. "I love him, Papa."

Joseph wiped the moisture from her cheek with his thumb. "I know, Emma."

"I'll be very soft," she promised.

He couldn't deny her this small thing. It couldn't possibly make Finbarr's condition worse. Joseph lifted her up so she could sit on the edge of the bed. With utmost care, Emma scooted across. She slowly lowered herself to Finbarr's side. She tucked herself in the cradle of his arm, resting next to him with one of her arms across his chest.

"Let her stay with the lad a moment," Matthew whispered, having come around the bed to Joseph's side. "It might give him a bit of comfort, and her as well."

Joseph's heart broke for his poor girl.

"I'll keep a watch over them both," Matthew added. "You go sit with your Katie again."

"*My* Katie?"

Matthew didn't explain. He just motioned Joseph toward the door and retook his seat beside the bed.

He'd only just reached the doorway when Emma started to hum, the effort marred now and then with the need to clear more ash from her lungs. Joseph stood, listening. It was Katie's tune, the one her father had always played for her, the one Katie so often played for the girls to help them sleep. In her pain, Emma had once again turned to Katie for comfort.

She needs Katie. I *need Katie. If I can't help her, how will I live without her?*

Reverend Ford had left. The hallway was empty. Joseph stood at his bedroom door, watching Katie lying still on his bed. If only something would change, anything to give him a reason to hope.

Mrs. Smith noticed him after a moment. "Did Emma find you?"

He nodded. In the short silence that followed, he listened to Katie breathe. Hers was not the occasional cough that plagued Emma and Ivy. Every breath Katie took was a struggle. "She doesn't sound any better."

"Nor any worse," Mrs. Smith said. "She's as tough as nails."

"In some ways, yes." But Katie was also fragile at times. She'd been hurt too often and too deeply not to carry scars inside and outside.

Mrs. Smith vacated her seat, allowing him to resume his post. He scooted the chair close enough so he could hold Katie's hand again. Ivy still slept in a ball on the floor nearby, wrapped tightly in a quilt.

"I'll confess, Mr. Archer, I didn't much care for Miss Macauley when I first arrived. It seemed everywhere I turned I was met with reminders of how she'd done things here and how perfect she'd been." Mrs. Smith's tone had lost much of its usual sternness, taking any insult from her words. "I resented her for that and, though it shames to me admit it, I took that frustration out on the girls, speaking to them more sharply than I ought to have spoken. But I've come to realize something. She really was perfect for your family in ways I never could be. The family I'd worked for the past years was not a loving one, and I was ill-prepared to fit into a household like yours. She stood as a constant reminder that I wasn't fitting in here, and I disliked her for it."

Joseph looked down at Katie. "She scolded the preacher on her very first week in Hope Springs. And Seamus Kelly. And Bob Archibald. And Jeremiah Johnson. I have been informed of the error of my ways as well." He managed the tiniest of smiles at the memories. "She sets us straight when we need it. She has something of an iron will at times."

"But with a heart soft as warm butter, it would seem." Mrs. Smith left on those very insightful words, leaving Joseph alone with his thoughts.

He moved to the bed, sitting on the very edge. He brushed a hand over her hair. "You do know, Katie, that you aren't allowed to give up, don't you? Even if you choose Tavish, even if you decide to go back to Ireland after all, you have to pull through this."

Her next breath seemed to catch a moment. Her expression hadn't changed in all the hours she'd been lying on the bed, but it did in that instant. Her brow creased and her eyes scrunched tight. The color drained even more from her lips. The look was one of sheer, unrelieved pain.

"I'm here, Katie." He brushed his thumb over the lines of agony etched in her face. A tear escaped her eyes. Joseph kissed it away. "I'm here, Katie. I won't leave you."

Chapter Thirty-Four

Pain woke Katie with a jolt. It burned through her. Unrelenting. Unforgiving.

Someone spoke. She couldn't make sense of the words nor identify the voice. Something about it, though, told her this was her shelter from the storm.

For hours, days perhaps, she'd hovered between light and dark, struggling against pain and heaviness. But there was always a distant voice soothing her in her worst moments.

She tried to ask her unknown guardian angel to help her, to do something to ease the agony, but she couldn't form the words. Katie shifted. The movement sent burning pain shooting through her arm and side. She sucked in a sharp breath, causing herself even more agony. She whimpered into the quiet around her.

A gentle hand brushed lightly over her face, and the same whispered voice she'd heard a moment earlier spoke again, this time in words she could understand. "I'm here, Katie."

'Twas a man's voice, deep and soothing and reassuring. She knew it, recognized it, but the fog of pain and exhaustion kept her from piecing together exactly whose voice it was.

More voices chimed in, swirling and swishing about. Katie tried to open her eyes, but could only manage the tiniest sliver. She could make out shadows moving around her, but nothing more.

The bed shifted as though someone had been sitting beside her and stood up. Departing footsteps sounded. She *was* being abandoned. Her light in the darkness was leaving her. With tremendous effort she moved her lips, but she couldn't get the words to sound.

"Rest, Katie. We're here with you." That wasn't him. Her mind refused to identify anyone; she wasn't even sure where she was or how she'd come to be there, but she was utterly certain this new voice was not the person she needed.

He'd left her. Just like everyone always did. Flashes of memory attacked her in quick succession. Smoke. Fire. Shouts of panic. Moments from her childhood melted with more recent horrors.

Hot tears gathered in her eyes. She couldn't make sense of her memories. Her mind filled with fire and fear.

Pain as intense as though a hot iron was pressed to her very bones seared through her left arm. She couldn't move it; she didn't dare try. Each breath hurt more than the last. She hadn't the strength to even open her eyes again.

Please. She didn't know if she was silently begging for relief from her agony or to simply be allowed to lose herself once more in sleep. Only one thing was certain in her mind: she could not endure much longer.

Someone took hold of her right hand. She found an unexpected comfort in the gentle but firm connection. The pain remained, but that touch, more so than any of the voices around her, reassured her she wasn't alone. She clung to it, holding fast with what little strength she had.

"We have some medicine for you," a voice whispered close to her ear, the voice she'd been listening for. He'd come back to her. "It will help you sleep."

She couldn't seem to make her voice work. How could she beg him not to leave her again if she couldn't speak?

A foul concoction was tipped down her throat. She managed to swallow some. She sputtered, which led to coughing. Her lungs wouldn't settle. No air seemed to get through. Each breath burned as if she'd filled her mouth with ash.

"Breathe slowly," she was instructed. "Your lungs will calm."

She held his hand and took breath after breath, trying to keep calm. Slowly her body stopped fighting her. Air came in and out. The coughing stopped. Though the pain in her side and her back, the pounding in her head, and the agony in her left arm did not disappear, they seemed to lessen.

"Rest, Katie. I won't leave you."

A feeling of peace settled over her. It was more than his promise to stay at her side, more than the relaxing effect of whatever medicines she'd been given. Even in her suffering and fear and confusion, one vital thing had become clear.

She knew the voice. She knew who it was her heart had cried out for in the dark pain she'd been unable to escape. She knew him, and he was there with her.

Joseph.

Chapter Thirty-Five

Through the combined efforts of the Irish and a good number from the Red Road, a rope bridge spanned the nearly frozen river the day after the fire in the barn. Tavish was the third person across, his parents having been granted the right to go first by virtue of Finbarr's condition.

What he found at the Archer home left him speechless. If not for the tufts of singed ginger hair and Matthew Scott identifying the swollen and bandaged young man in the guest bedroom, Tavish wouldn't have known it was his brother. Even his eyes were hidden behind bandages.

"Is he blind?" Da asked Joseph when he came in to check on the family.

"We don't know. He hasn't been awake, so there has been no opportunity to ask him."

Tavish looked down at his brother, an ache growing in his chest. "His eyes *were* damaged, then?"

Joseph nodded. "We looked at them before applying the bandages. I'm no doctor, but it didn't look good."

Ma had sent Matthew off to rest, taking over Finbarr's care. She nodded as Joseph spoke, but didn't look away from her son.

Joseph leaned against the wall near the door. Heavy bags hung under his eyes. He clearly hadn't shaved. If he hadn't taken time to wash up or sleep, the situation was even worse than it seemed.

Dread settled uncomfortably in Tavish's heart. "How is Katie?"

Joseph didn't answer, but he instantly looked more tired.

Tavish's stomach dropped to his toes. He moved quickly out of the room and across the corridor to where he'd been told Katie was. Joseph's housekeeper and Reverend Ford were packing Katie's bandaged left arm and hand in ice.

Even from the door he could hear her labored breathing. She wasn't as still as Finbarr, but neither was she thrashing about. Her expression held such pain, it hurt to look at her. Beneath the deep bruises and dark cuts, her face was pale as snow.

Saints above.

Tavish caught the preacher's eye. "What can I do to help?"

"Not much, unfortunately. Other than bringing in ice from the river, we really don't know what to do."

A tiny, agonizing moan escaped Katie's throat. Tavish sat in the chair next to the side of the bed. Her expression pulled tighter. She shifted the tiniest bit, then again. Tavish took her uninjured hand in his.

"You're going to be fine, Katie." He could think of nothing else to say. He didn't even know if she could hear him.

Another sound of anguish followed.

"Go fetch Mr. Archer," Mrs. Smith told the preacher.

Reverend Ford was already halfway out the door, apparently not needing the instructions. It seemed they'd done this before.

Katie began coughing, gasping. Panic swirled through Tavish's mind. Was she choking? What ought he to do?

"Does Joseph have medicine for her?"

Mrs. Smith shook her head as she calmly checked Katie's forehead with the back of her hand. "She rests better when he's here. That is about all we can do for her."

Tavish kept hold of Katie's hand. "We're here, Katie. Try to keep calm."

She didn't seem to hear him. His efforts at comforting her did nothing.

Joseph strode into the room in the very next instant. "Did she awaken?"

"No." Mrs. Smith stepped back, making room for her employer to come closer. "But she's fussing again. I would guess it's the swelling in her hand. The skin is pulled so tight it has to be very painful."

Katie continued coughing. Tavish watched helplessly. Each breath she took ended in a deep wheeze.

Joseph leaned over and whispered something in her ear. With one hand he stroked her cheek, then her hair.

Tavish watched for the miracle Mrs. Smith had practically promised Joseph could perform. To his surprise, he saw one—a small one, but something of a miracle just the same. Katie still struggled with each intake of air—her expression remained pained—but she breathed more slowly and the lines of pain around her mouth eased.

"There you are." Joseph stood a little straighter, his whispered words reaching the rest of them, though he clearly still spoke to Katie. His gaze flitted directly past Tavish and settled on Mrs. Smith. "Can we give her more powders?"

The housekeeper shook her head. "The bottle says not for two more hours. I dare not risk it without a doctor assuring us it won't harm her."

Joseph looked haggard, worn to the bone. "What about lavender tea? That helped her sleep before."

Mrs. Smith nodded. "And I'll replace the poultice on her chest. That should help her lungs clear."

On cue, Katie coughed again, the sound dry and raw. Mrs. Smith hurried out to fetch her supplies.

"Help her sit up a little," Joseph instructed Tavish. "We have to get her to drink some water."

Tavish slid an arm under Katie's back and helped lift her. She winced, and he paused.

"This is hurting her." Tavish could see that it was. Joseph hadn't raised Katie from his side. "Maybe if we lifted both sides so she wasn't tilted so much."

Joseph shook his head. "This arm has to stay in the ice."

Tavish held Katie up that small bit, fighting the urge to lay her back down. She whimpered in this new position. Joseph took a cup from the bedside table and slowly trickled water into her mouth.

She swallowed, her eyes scrunching tight with the effort. A few more coughs, then a few more sips, and they laid her back down.

Joseph reached for her blanket and pulled it back up to her shoulders. He dabbed at a bit of water hovering at the corner of her mouth, brushed her hair out of her face, then adjusted the tub of ice her arm sat in. It was all very automatic, almost habitual.

"You've done this a few times."

Joseph nodded wearily.

The depth of her suffering pierced Tavish. "Her hand seems particularly bad." Only the very tips of her fingers peeked out from the heavy bandaging, and he could see how terribly swollen and discolored they were.

"It was crushed when the barn fell. There are bones in a few fingers that feel like little more than powder."

Merciful heavens.

"Papa?" Emma Archer stood in the doorway.

"You are supposed to be sleeping," Joseph said.

"I want to see Finbarr."

Joseph shook his head. "Finbarr is sleeping."

"I know." Her tone turned pleading. "I won't wake him up; I only want to see him."

Katie started coughing again. Joseph's eyes darted between her and his little girl. Mrs. Smith's words hit Tavish with renewed understanding.

She rests better when he is here. Joseph didn't want to leave while Katie was struggling, but his daughter was in need as well.

"I can take her," Tavish offered, grateful to have found something he could do to help. "I'll ask Ma if Emma can peek in on Finbarr."

"Thank you." There was no doubting Joseph's sincerity, nor his complete exhaustion.

Tavish felt entirely expendable. He wasn't ready to truly think on the reasons why Katie would find comfort in Joseph's presence and not his. He could do nothing but accept it for the time being and do what he could to help.

Finbarr woke the morning after the Irish crossed the river. The entire family breathed a collective sigh of relief. He had no memory of the fire, no understanding of what had happened. Da and Ma decided that, until he was stronger, it would be for the best if they kept explanations to a minimum. He was told only that he and Katie had both been caught in a fire in Joseph Archer's barn. Eventually he would be told how close the Archer girls had come to being trapped there as well. Someday they would tell him Marianne Johnson had died in his arms.

Tavish did his best to lift his family's spirits. The effort felt nearly futile in the hours after Finbarr told them he couldn't see. One eye provided little more than shapes, the very beginnings of faces, but through the other eye, Finbarr confessed in raspy, quiet tones, he could see nothing at all.

Mr. and Mrs. Johnson and their two boys came by again and again to look in on Finbarr and Katie. They begged for something to do that might help. Mrs. Johnson ended up sitting in Finbarr's room, with Ma's arm around her shoulders, as they both wept. Though the words hadn't been spoken, everyone seemed to understand. The grief was a piercing ache they all shared, one nobody quite knew how to relieve.

A dark cloud of discouragement hung over the house. Everyone tiptoed around. An almost eerie quiet had settled there. Biddy had come across the river and stayed to help with Katie. Ian helped with Joseph, who looked like he hadn't slept at all.

"I have to stay here with Katie," he muttered every time anyone suggested he rest.

"I'm worried for him," Ian said late the second afternoon as he and Tavish stood in the doorway of Katie's room. "He can't push himself like this much longer."

"Aye, but he won't listen to reason."

"Of course not." Ian's words were heavy. "He loves her, but he can't do anything to relieve her suffering. He's watching her die."

If only Ian was exaggerating. Katie's condition was grave. Seeing her in such pain was eating away at Tavish.

His gaze settled on Joseph, where he sat at the bedside, arms tented and hands locked together as if in prayer. "She's different with him."

"His presence does calm her quite a bit," Ian said.

Tavish shook his head. "I don't just mean now. Even before all of this, the two of them—" He couldn't find the right words to explain what he'd been seeing and feeling. Perhaps he didn't want to find the words. He stepped a few paces away from the door. "I've been frantic for weeks, afraid I would lose her to him. But—" Saying the words hurt more than he'd expected, but he had to get it out. He knew Ian would understand. "If she needs him, Ian, if he is what will pull her through this, if *he* is the one who will make her happy, I . . . I can't . . ."

Ian didn't say anything. He moved to Tavish's side and set an empathetic hand on his shoulder.

"She deserves to be happy," Tavish said. "She deserves it more than any person I've ever known."

"What about you, brother? Don't you deserve to be happy?"

"I've seen her with him, Ian." He pushed out a heavy breath. "I've seen the way they change each other for the better. I couldn't be happy if I took that away from her."

"But you and she—"

"—haven't been the same lately." Tavish finished the sentence with the hard truth of the matter. "I simply haven't been willing to admit it to myself."

"I'm sorry," Ian said. "I truly am."

"So am I. But this is right. I know it is." The admission hurt more deeply than he could even express, but he could no longer deny it.

Ian watched him a moment, not with pity but with compassion. "You're a good man, Tavish O'Connor."

Tavish shook his head, overwhelmed by all that had happened. He took hold of the doorknob to Finbarr's room. "I mean to look in on our brother."

He slipped inside the quiet room where Finbarr was sleeping. Ma kept vigil at his bedside. Mr. Johnson stood at the bureau, setting out bottles of powders and ointment. They looked up as Tavish entered.

He offered the most sincere smile he could manage, hoping his grief didn't show. There was enough suffering without him adding to it.

"I need to be with my wife," Mr. Johnson told Ma. "Please send word if there is anything the boy needs. He or Miss Katie. Anything at all."

"I will," Ma said.

Mr. Johnson's eyes met Tavish's as he passed. The tears that hovered there tore into him. There was too much pain in too many hearts. Including his.

Chapter Thirty-Six

Joseph felt sick inside. He'd dreaded this moment all day. Mrs. Smith carefully unwrapped the bandages on Katie's left hand.

No one had spoken the obvious truth out loud, least of all Joseph.

Katie's fingers were dying. The ice had helped slow the swelling. They had tried every salve, every folk remedy anyone down either road could think of, but Katie's fingertips had still turned black.

Katie winced and groaned with each movement of her arm. She hadn't slept in hours but seemed to hover half-conscious and visibly racked with pain. Her eyes had opened a few times but didn't focus on anything. Her lips moved with silent pleas. Tears welled in her tightly closed eyes. She was in utter agony, and nothing Joseph had done had helped in the least.

He held his breath as Mrs. Smith exposed Katie's fingers. His heart stopped. The blackness had spread nearly the entire length of her fingers. He saw resignation and mournful acceptance on the faces of Biddy and Ian and Mrs. Smith.

"What haven't we tried yet?" he asked, shaking his head furiously. "Did you ask Mrs. Claire? She might remember something she learned as a girl. Or down at the ranches? They see injuries like this all the time. They might know something we don't."

"Joseph—" Ian began.

He spoke directly over him. "The ice didn't help, but we haven't tried heat. What if we alternate between the two?"

Biddy was already shaking her head. "This cannot be reversed. You and I both know that."

"I *don't* know that," he said sternly. "We haven't tried everything. Heat might get the blood flowing better. That could help. It could."

"Joseph." Ian took over for his wife. "There's nothing—"

"No." He barked out the word. "We have to keep trying."

"Until when?" Ian asked. "Right now it's only her fingers. But left unchecked, her entire hand will die, then her arm. What happens when the blackness passes her shoulder, Joseph? What if the dying spreads to her heart or lungs?"

He couldn't listen anymore. He couldn't. "We have to think of something else. There's a way to fix this. There has to be."

Biddy set a hand on his arm. "We can cut off the fingers, Joseph. She'd be left with the rest of her hand intact. But if we wait—"

"We cannot take her fingers, Biddy. I can't let that happen." Pinpricks of pain stabbed at the corners of his eyes. A thick lump grew in his throat. "I won't."

"It's only fingers," Ian said. "She can live without her fingers."

"No." Joseph paced away. Panic roared inside. He would explode soon, he knew he would. "We have to leave her fingers. We have to. You . . . you don't understand."

He pushed both hands through his hair, fighting the urge to simply shout with the frustration of it all. Katie was suffering. He wanted to take that away, but what they were talking about was unthinkable.

"I *don't* understand." Biddy watched him from the bedside, worry lining her face. "I know you don't want to cause her pain, but we cannot leave her like this."

"No one takes her fingers." He growled it out, driven by desperation. "We'll think of something else. But we won't take her fingers. We won't."

They all watched him, brows pulled down, confusion in their eyes and faces. How could they not see what they were doing to her?

"It is one hand, Joseph," Ian insisted. "Only a hand."

"It's more than that. It's her music." The echo of his words stabbed his heart. "She plays her fiddle with her left hand. She can't play without her fingers. If we amputate them, she'll never play her fiddle again."

He could see by their faces they hadn't pieced that together, and the realization gave them pause.

"Music is like breathing to her," he said. "If I take that away from her, it'll kill her." He swallowed on the last words, fighting to control his emotions. "I can't do that to her. I can't."

Katie had sacrificed her feet for the sake of her hands all those years ago in the cold Irish winter. She'd run back into her burning house to save the very violin she'd played for him and his girls these past months. Music was everything to Katie. It held her happiest memories. It was her strongest connection to her home. It was her one abiding source of peace. He could not—*would* not—take that from her.

"She isn't able to make this decision herself." Ian's calm was both admirable and grating. "Someone has to decide."

He shook his head again and again, the movement only growing more frantic. "I say no. Absolutely not."

Another voice entered the argument. "Katie and I have an agreement between us." Mr. O'Connor stood in the doorway of the room. His expression was somber. Apparently he'd been listening for a while. "She hasn't a father here to look out for her, so I offered to stand in for him. She did me the honor of accepting that offer, and I've taken the responsibility very seriously."

He looked around the room. When his eyes met Joseph's, something like empathy, understanding, and a plea for trust passed between them.

"I love her like my own daughter, Joseph. I'd not let anything hurt her if I could help it. And I'd never take her well-being lightly."

Mr. O'Connor meant to take the weight of this choice on his own shoulders? Joseph hated that he was even considering handing such a crucial decision over to anyone else.

Mr. O'Connor was not a tall man, but he could command a room. He stepped up next to Joseph. "I understand about Katie's music. I saw the love she has for it and her need for it in her eyes the first time I ever saw her play. Let me promise you now, I don't take that lightly. Not in the least."

Joseph could feel the man's sincerity. The tension squeezing his heart lessened the slightest bit.

"Katie trusted me enough to think of me as family." Mr. O'Connor spoke only to him. "Can you trust me to care for her as I would my own child? Can you put that trust in me, Joseph Archer?"

Could he?

"I swear to you—I'll bring in the preacher and give my word on his Bible if that'll help you believe me—that I won't make any choices without thoroughly weighing the consequences. I swear it on the souls of the sons I lost—may they rest in peace. I swear it to you."

There could be no stronger assurance than that. Joseph nodded, even as he fought down a fresh surge of desperate emotion.

Mr. O'Connor set his shoulders. With mingled compassion and determination, he spoke again. "The first order I'm giving is for you to leave."

"I . . . *what?*"

Mr. O'Connor didn't waver. "You are not equal to what the next hours may hold, son. You'll not do our sweet lass here any good if you fall apart. You'll crumble clear to pieces if you stay. You have to leave her in our care and trust us to look after her."

That hadn't been part of the original bargain. He couldn't agree to it. "I promised her not to leave. I've promised her again and again that I would stay with her. I won't break my word."

"Then make her a new promise, Joseph. Tell her you'll be nearby. Tell her you're leaving her in the care of trusted people."

"I can't—"

"She will understand." Mr. O'Connor pulled him across the room to Katie's bedside. "We can give you a few moments alone." The others in the room nodded. "Then you need to go. Go love your daughters—they need you too. Go rest your mind and body. Your Katie needs you to be strong enough to leave."

Even as the room emptied, Joseph doubted he had the strength to simply leave Katie there, knowing the enormity of what she faced. But he knew for a fact if her fingers or hand or arm had to be amputated he couldn't sit there beside her while the deed was done. Even understanding the necessity, he would likely fight them every step of the way.

Mr. O'Connor was right. He had to find the strength to walk away and let them take care of her.

He sat on the edge of the bed, looking into her pale face. The agony he saw there broke his heart. He knew, though he struggled to admit it, that much of her suffering came from her hand. His mind understood what had to be done, but he couldn't force his heart to accept it.

"I wish I could make it go away," he whispered to her. "If I could give you my hands, I would. I would do anything for you, Katie."

He gently took her blackened fingers in his hand. He could do nothing to save her from this. Nothing at all.

"I am so sorry." He placed a featherlight kiss on the back of her hand. "So very sorry."

Her whimper of pain nearly broke him.

"I know I promised not to leave you." He struggled to push air through his tight lungs. "But I'm not strong enough to watch them do what they need to do."

He ran his fingers along her hair, letting his eyes linger on her face. She was the most beautiful thing in the world to him. He could only hope she would forgive him for what was about to be done to her.

She grimaced, shifting about as if searching for a position that would relieve her pain. A tear trickled over her temple.

"I love you, Katie Macauley." He swallowed with effort. "I have almost from the very beginning. The longer I know you, the more I—" The pain of regret and worry forestalled any further admissions. "I need to go sit with the girls," he said. "The O'Connors are going to look after you. I promise I'll be back. I promise."

A moment later, Mr. O'Connor peeked inside. He didn't say a word; he didn't have to. They both knew what came next.

Joseph forced himself to stand and walk away from Katie's side. This had to be done.

Mr. O'Connor set a reassuring hand on Joseph's shoulder as he passed. Joseph nodded his understanding. Reverend Ford, Karl Kester, Ian, and Seamus Kelly waited in the corridor. The reverend had likely come to pray over their efforts and Katie's well-being. Ian and Karl, no doubt, meant to help hold her down through the agony of an amputation—there was nothing for the pain but ineffectual powders and all the liquor they could gather up.

Not until the men had stepped inside the room and closed the door behind them did Joseph piece together Seamus's role in the coming operation. As a blacksmith he had tools—those that hadn't been destroyed by fire—and was skilled with his hands, and he was by far the strongest man among them. Seamus was the one who would be cutting off her dead fingers.

Joseph slumped against the wall. He blinked hard against the tears that gathered hot and furious in his eyes. A blacksmith had removed Katie's toes. Now the same thing was happening all over again. For all his money and influence, he couldn't even give her a real doctor.

He had failed her. Utterly.

Chapter Thirty-Seven

Marianne Johnson was buried on a clear Sunday morning. The frozen earth seemed as unable to accept the child's death as the townspeople were. Every able-bodied man, Irish and Red Road alike, took it in turns to pound into the icy ground. Hands bled with the effort. Hearts broke. Tears were shed in abundance. In that moment of such acute sadness, an odd sort of healing began.

The fire had not cared about nationality. Everyone in town felt the tragedy.

Finbarr sat by the graveside throughout the service, his eyes heavily bandaged. Tavish didn't know what would become of his brother. The lad had always spoken of working his own land someday. Could a blind man live on his own in such an unforgiving land? And what of the boy's heart? Finbarr had spoken very little since awakening after the fire, even less after he'd finally been told of Marianne's fate. What he did say lacked the joy and lightness that was so much a part of him. He didn't smile. He didn't wish to talk to anyone.

The only person who seemed able to get through to Finbarr was Emma Archer. She sat next to him at her dearest friend's graveside service, holding his hand as if he were the only one of the two of them needing comfort, though her fragile heart must have also been breaking.

Tavish's eyes turned toward the road. He could just make out the distant shape of Joseph Archer's home. Katie was still there, just as she'd been the past two days, lying in the dark in Joseph's bedroom. The last he'd seen her, she was resting more peacefully than she had before the operation. Her breathing was less strained.

She pricked at his heart. She likely always would.

He was letting her go. He would still do all he could to help with her recovery, but he was stepping back, giving Joseph the room he needed to fill the role that was rightly his.

Jeremiah Johnson stood beside his daughter's grave, the very picture of a broken and grieving father. "I asked Reverend Ford if I might say a word or two." He took a moment, clearly attempting to get himself under control. "I need to thank Finbarr O'Connor for—for risking his own life for my daughter."

Tavish watched his youngest brother sit in stoic silence. With the top half of his face bandaged, his emotions weren't readable. But his mouth was pulled tight, as still as stone.

"There is some small comfort in knowing Marianne was not alone when she died." Mr. Johnson blinked a few times, his Adam's apple making several trips up and down as he swallowed his emotions. "And I need to say that I have been moved by the outpouring of support and kindness we've received, from both the Red Road and the Irish Road. I've not always treated my Irish neighbors with fairness or kindness, and I am . . . humbled to be receiving their comfort now." Mr. Johnson's voice broke. "I wish I could say, had the situation been reversed, had it been an Irish barn burning with Irish inside, that the Reds in this town would have rushed in as quickly and selflessly as this Irish man and woman did."

Such a speech would have been unimaginable only a few short weeks ago, even a few days ago. If only Katie were there to hear it.

"Miss Macauley was always kind to Marianne in the time she spent working in my shop, even though I was often cruel. Marianne, herself, scolded me for my uncharitable heart." His pained whispers brought fresh tears to every eye. He wiped at his eyes with a white handkerchief. "I've paid a terrible price for my pride and my hatred. Though I can't promise to be perfect, I mean to be better." His shoulders squared. His eyes met Da's. "I'd like the chance to start again and make things right."

Da gave Mr. Johnson a nod of acceptance.

Mrs. Johnson wept openly. Tavish's heart broke to see it. No mother should have to bury a child.

Reverend Ford read the remainder of the graveside rite, declaring ashes to ashes and dust to dust. Each person tossed a handful of dirt into the painfully small hole.

Tavish waited until everyone had left except the Johnsons and Reverend Ford and Finbarr. Emma had only abandoned her post at her father's insistence.

The Johnsons' oldest son, Joshua, a young man not many years older than Finbarr, approached. The sight of his red-rimmed eyes cut Tavish deeply. He was grieving a sister, something Tavish could comprehend, if not fully understand. He had sisters. The loss of any one of them would hurt terribly. He'd lost two brothers and a fiancée and that pain had never fully left him.

"My pa says to tell you that he'll see to it Finbarr reaches the Archer place so you don't need to wait for him."

Tavish looked uncertainly at his brother. Would Finbarr resent being left to these people who, only a few days earlier, were considered enemies?

"He's in a difficult place just now," Tavish said. "He blames himself, hates himself for what happened. I don't know that I can leave him."

"Pa understands that," Joshua said. "He blames himself as well, and his heart is torn to pieces. What your brother did for my sister—" He took a quick breath, blinking fiercely. "He is safe with our family, I promise you that."

The sincerity of his declaration couldn't be doubted. "Thank you," Tavish said.

The walk back to the Archers' house, where the rest of his family would be waiting, was a contemplative one. Finbarr was facing a future nearly as uncertain as the one their family had faced during The Famine, and Tavish could do little to help. He'd lost Katie—not to death, thank the heavens, but to a man he might one day be willing to admit was better suited to her. He knew letting her go was right, but it didn't stop the loneliness.

Finbarr will need me, whether he likes the idea or not. Helping him get through the coming days and months, maybe years, will help me do the same. He'd have a purpose, a distraction.

Katie would be happy; that was critically important.

He would learn to be happy, too.

Chapter Thirty-Eight

"Katie?"

A small voice was whispering her name.

"Katie?"

There was no urgency to it, no fear or worry. 'Twas as if someone simply wanted to get her attention.

She tried to open her eyes, but they fought her. A general ache filled her as though she'd worked herself too hard the day before and her body was protesting the effort.

"Katie?" Little hands touched her face; she could make out the feel of each tiny finger. In a flash of understanding she knew who was speaking to her: Ivy.

She worked to move her arm enough to feel about for the girl. Her fingers brushed what felt like a leg next to her.

"Are you awake, Katie?"

Not particularly.

"Ivy, come down from there. Katie needs to rest. And it is your bed-time as well." *Joseph.*

A sudden, almost desperate, need grabbed her. She wanted to see him. She wanted him to come sit by her. Though she couldn't explain the near panic she felt, she couldn't bear the thought of him leaving her there.

Her voice refused to cooperate. She pried one eye open, struggling with the other. Ivy's sweet, angel face hovered just above her.

"She's looking at me, Pompah!"

"Truly?"

Immediate relief filled Katie's mind. She could hear Joseph's footsteps approaching. He wasn't leaving her. She had both eyes open and nearly focused by the time he came within sight.

"How are you, Katie?" he asked. "Do you need anything?"

With effort, she shook her head. All she needed was him, and he was there.

"I've been practicing my loop and loops," Ivy said eagerly. *Loop and loops.* That was the phrase Ivy used to mean the crocheting Granny had taught her. "Do you want to see?"

Katie smiled and nodded. Ivy all but jumped off the bed and ran from the room. Joseph took Katie's hand, pulling her gaze back to him. Dark circles shadowed his eyes. Weary lines weighed down his face.

"You look tired." Her voice was scratchy, her throat sore.

Joseph only smiled. "It is so good to hear your voice again." He spoke little louder than a whisper.

She was awakening more by the minute, her surroundings growing clearer. Why was she in Joseph's room? She hurt too much for it to be anything but a lingering illness or rather extensive injuries.

"I am very confused."

Joseph ran his hand along her cheek. He looked at her as though she were some great treasure. Katie couldn't recall anyone looking at her in just that way. She wanted to enjoy it, but flashes of something—memories or lingering nightmares, she couldn't say which—kept pulling her from the moment. Smoke. Fire. Hay.

"There was smoke," she muttered.

"Don't think on it now. There'll be time—"

Her mind filled with the roaring sound of fire consuming everything in its path. She could see the flames. Taste the smoke in her mouth once more. The girls were there. Afraid. In danger.

"Fire." She heard the fear in her voice.

"No, Katie. The fire's out. You're safe."

She shook her head, but it wouldn't clear. She didn't feel safe. "The girls." Ivy had been there a moment before, safe. But not Emma. "Joseph!" Panic swept over her. "Where's Emma?" She tried to sit up, but the effort sent scorching pain up her left arm. Even as she dropped back down in agony, her heart raced with fear. "Emma?"

"Emma is fine," Joseph said. "She's with Finbarr."

"Was she hurt? Is she—?" Her voice quivered. She didn't finish the thought.

Joseph seemed to grasp what she couldn't quite say. "Emma and Ivy are both whole and unharmed. You saved them both, Katie. They are fine."

Katie could remember the fire, but not where it had been or when or how it had started. She had clearly not escaped injury, but that was unimportant. The girls were safe. The thought brought immediate relief.

Finbarr had been in the fire too. She remembered him there, but no details beyond that. "Finbarr is well? He wasn't hurt?"

Joseph hesitated. A knot formed in Katie's stomach.

"He was injured," Joseph said after a moment. "But he is recovering."

There was more he wasn't saying, she could sense it. She felt at a disadvantage, lying there like an invalid. The same terrible pain shot through her arm when she tried to sit up again.

"My arm hurts." She groaned out the words.

He nodded. "Let me help you."

Slowly and carefully, they managed to get her sitting more upright, pillows stacked behind her. The searing pain in her arm continued. She glanced down, but her arm was wrapped so thickly in bandages she could make out nothing but a lump of fabric in the basic shape and length of her arm. The anguish of her injuries was so great she couldn't tell where the pain ended and where it began.

Joseph gently turned her face toward him with the lightest touch of his fingers. "Can I get you anything? A drink of water? Something to eat? We have medicinal powders to help with the pain."

"I hope you didn't pay the Irish price for the powders, Joseph. It's too dear."

He smiled a tiny bit. "You have missed quite a lot while you've been sleeping. Jeremiah Johnson has renounced the practice of charging an Irish price."

She was too shocked to even speak, almost unable to think.

"Furthermore, he brought the medicine here free of charge with instructions that his store is entirely at your disposal should you need anything else."

"I don't understand."

Joseph sat on the bed, facing her. "Your efforts at teaching them to be better have paid off."

If tensions in town were improving, something Joseph had wanted since long before she'd met him, why wasn't he happy? Her left arm hurt too much to move, so she raised her right hand, brushing her thumb along the dark smudge beneath his eye. "You look so tired."

He took her hand in both of his and kissed her fingers. She didn't know what had inspired this affectionate side of him but found she liked it very much.

"This has been a terrible week," he said. "I don't think there is a person in all of Hope Springs who isn't exhausted."

Again she saw something in his face that told her more had happened than he'd let on, that the past week had held greater difficulties than her injuries and Finbarr's.

"Look, Katie! Look!" Ivy rushed back inside, a knotted mess of yarn held high in her fist.

She climbed up onto the bed, pushing against her father as she did. Joseph moved to make room for her. He sat with his back against the headboard, directly beside Katie. He only released her hand for a fraction of a moment. Even in her pain and confusion, Katie smiled.

"Mrs. Claire says I'm getting better and better," Ivy declared, holding up her crocheting for Katie to inspect. "We stayed at her house while you were sleeping. She told me to do my loop and loops so I would stop bothering Emma while she was crying."

"Emma was crying?"

Ivy paused only long enough for a quick nod. "And I saw Finbarr crying, and Pompah, and Marianne's mama and papa. Everyone. Mrs. Claire and I did loop and loops, and—"

Ivy rambled on, but Katie didn't really hear her. Marianne's name sparked a memory, one as clear as a cloudless morning. She could hear Marianne's voice. *Don't leave me here.* She could hear each word and with it the sound of crackling fire. *Don't leave me here. Don't leave me.*

Where was Marianne? Joseph hadn't said anything about her.

Emotion blurred Katie's eyes, pricking at her heart. She'd never been one to really believe in premonitions, but in that moment she knew. Without asking. She simply knew.

"Katie?" Joseph whispered as Ivy chattered on.

Katie slowly lifted her eyes. She silently mouthed Marianne's name.

In a movement so miniscule she almost missed it, he shook his head.

The tears came without warning. *Sweet little Marianne.*

She'd pleaded not to be left behind. Katie could still hear her frightened voice. *Don't leave me here.*

The memory of Marianne's words mixed with the echo of poor Eimear's voice from so many years earlier.

Katie, I'm cold.

Don't leave me.

I'm cold.

Two little girls she was supposed to protect. Two sweet children who had depended on her. Trusted her. Both were dead. Both of them. It was her fault. Again. It was all her fault.

Her breath shuddered through her. She ignored the pain, simply allowing the grief to crash over her like a punishing wave. Joseph put his arm around her. She leaned her head against his shoulder. Tears rolled over her cheeks and down her chin.

"Ivy," Joseph interrupted her chattering, "would you go ask Mrs. Smith to bring Katie something to eat?"

Katie buried her face further into Joseph's sleeve, hoping Ivy wouldn't see her tears. The child had clearly witnessed too much crying over the past days. She heard Ivy climb off the bed, her footsteps fading.

She and Joseph sat a moment, neither speaking. Katie had no words. Joseph, she imagined, was searching for the right ones.

"I don't know that it helps at all, but it happened very quickly." He lightly rubbed her upper arm as he spoke, the gesture gentle and caring. "She was gone in an instant, we are absolutely certain of it. There was no suffering, no pain."

But there was still the inescapable fact that another small child she might have saved was dead, was likely already lying in the frozen ground. How vividly she remembered helping her father dig her sister's tiny grave.

I should have been faster. I shouldn't have wasted time with words. I should have . . . I should have . . .

She sobbed, sending shards of pain through her ribs.

Joseph kept her at his side, silently smoothing her hair with his fingers. He didn't speak, didn't offer empty words of comfort. He simply held her as she cried.

She opened her mouth to ask him to stay with her. But the words died even as they echoed in her mind in Marianne's frightened voice. *Don't leave me.*

Katie could do nothing but weep as her heart broke irreparably in two.

Chapter Thirty-Nine

Joseph stepped away from Katie for only the briefest of moments to look in on his daughters, checking to see if they were sleeping. No one in the house had rested well since the fire. They had passed a long and grueling week. Ivy was plagued by nightmares; Emma wouldn't eat.

He'd spent the hour since Katie had awoken holding her while she cried. She hadn't spoken, hadn't looked up at him. She simply cried against his shoulder. Deep breaths had ended in whimpers of pain. He'd sat there, silently, with an arm around her. She had been deeply suffering, and he, like a useless idiot, hadn't been able to think of a single thing to do or say.

"Is something wrong, Papa?" Emma's sleepy voice floated through the dim room.

"No, sweetie. I'm only checking to see that you're sleeping."

He saw her shift beneath her quilt. She didn't get up, didn't seem truly awake. He slowly closed the door, careful not to make noise. The girls were finally sleeping. He stood in the hallway, searching for the strength to make it through the rest of the evening.

"Joseph."

He turned at the sound of Biddy's strained voice. She stood in the doorway to his room, her arms full of bandages. The bleeding at the stubs of Katie's fingers had slowed, but not stopped entirely. Mrs. Smith had lectured them all on the importance of changing out the linens used to bind Katie's wounds. Women on the Irish and Red Roads had volunteered to wash the strips of fabric Katie and Finbarr had used up over the past days.

The tight pull around Biddy's mouth instantly worried him.

"She's unbound her hand," she whispered, the words quick and concerned.

Not yet. She isn't ready for this yet.

He moved swiftly inside the room. Katie sat with her feet hanging off the edge of his bed. Her arm, bandaged and splinted from wrist to elbow, was unwrapped from the wrist down. She kept completely still, her gaze never leaving her fingerless hand. The only sound in the room was her too-quick breathing.

What do I say? I can't fix this.

She didn't look up as he reached her. He knelt on the ground in front of her. Katie's eyes remained riveted to the red, tender remains of her left hand resting on her lap. The look of horror on her face cut him deeper than any knife could.

Maybe he should have said something when she first woke. He should have broken it to her gently rather than leaving her to discover it this way. But when could he have possibly told her? There'd not been a chance before she'd realized Marianne's fate. She had been in no condition for further difficulties afterward. He wondered if she'd already realized she couldn't feel her fingers and had pieced together what had happened.

Coward. You only told yourself that to avoid this moment.

"What happened?" Katie spoke not in the broken whisper he'd expected but in a voice so flat it worried him more than her silence had.

"Your arm broke when the barn collapsed, and your hand was crushed." He watched for her reaction, needing to know if he was causing her more pain. He saw nothing. He couldn't even say for certain that she heard him. "We did everything we could, but it was so badly broken. It couldn't be saved."

"I need my hands, Joseph." Her tone was direct, all but empty of emotion.

"Katie, I—"

"I don't know how to do anything without both hands." Her words picked up speed, the first hints of worry entering her voice. "How will I do any of my work? How will I bake my bread?"

"This town won't let you go hungry or be in need while you're adapting," Joseph insisted. "You can relearn."

"What good will I be?" she muttered. "If I can't work, I'm worthless."

Joseph took her face in his hands, turning it so she was looking at him. "You have never been worthless, Katie Macauley. Not ever."

He'd never seen such bleakness in any person's eyes.

"I can't play my fiddle." The words trembled, yet she sat stoically still.

The loss of her music hurt the deepest. He'd known it would.

"I am so sorry." He had said those four words to her more than any others over the past few days. They were woefully insufficient but the only ones he had.

He let his hands slide down her arms, careful of her left arm, which was still splinted and bandaged, and took her hands in his. It broke his heart to feel the difference between the two.

She lowered her gaze again. "I stole my father's fiddle. I took away his music." Her quiet words grew more steady, a terrible hopelessness entering her tone. "Now *I've* lost the music as well. That's fitting, I suppose. The cruelest of punishments. I rather deserve it, actually."

He had fully expected her heartache, but he hadn't anticipated the guilt she had so quickly tied to it.

Her shoulders rose and fell with an unsteady breath. "Life just takes and takes. I can't bear it anymore. I can't."

She pulled away from him, moving her legs back up onto the bed. This was one of the moments Joseph had worried about. She needed the peace and reassurance playing her music brought her, but where would she find that now?

Katie slipped under the blanket, her back turned to him. She blamed him as much as he blamed himself it seemed. He should have done more to stop this. He should have thought of something else to try before letting this happen. Joseph dropped his head against the bed.

Life just takes and takes. She was suffering, and he couldn't help. He couldn't do anything for her.

Biddy came in the room and knelt on the floor beside him. She held out the bundle of bandages. "Her hand still needs wrapping," she whispered.

He shook his head. Katie wanted nothing to do with him.

"During the darkest times in Katie's life," Biddy lowered her voice even further, "everyone abandoned her. She has faced every hardship alone because no one would stand by her. Don't you do that to her as well, Joseph Archer."

"Nothing soothes her like playing her violin, and she doesn't have that now." Joseph kept his voice as quiet as Biddy's. Katie didn't need to overhear them discussing her.

"And there is no way to change that now, so you need to help her through this."

He sat back on his heels, a weight settling in his chest. "You should be talking to Tavish; he is the one who knows how to make her laugh and smile."

"When a person is dying inside, she doesn't need a jester." Biddy set the bandages in his hands. "She needs a champion."

Joseph thought about that for several long moments after Biddy left the room. Katie needed so much. He despaired of being equal to helping her through the struggles that lay ahead of her. She had lost something vitally important to her, something he couldn't give back. Even if those failures made her hate him in the end, he knew he could never abandon her.

He came around to the other side of the bed. Katie's eyes were closed, tears trickling over the bridge of her nose. She'd shed too many tears.

Joseph pulled the chair close then sat, trying to decide the best way to ease her worries. He slipped his hand beneath her wounded one.

"I'll be very careful," he told her.

Each wince struck him like a blow, but he kept working. Katie didn't speak, didn't even open her eyes. The gravity of the situation sat heavy on his shoulders. He'd never known anyone with her fortitude and determination, but her inner reserve of strength seemed to be failing her.

Tavish would have teased and joked with her until she smiled. He would have banished her tears with laughter. Joseph didn't have that talent. What did he have to offer her? He could talk her ear off about budgets and profit projections and sound like a sentimental fool speaking endlessly of his daughters and his land. That wouldn't help at all.

He tied off the bandaging, then slipped her arm back under the quilt. He sat silently beside the bed.

She needed her music, but he couldn't give that back to her. She still hurt over her father's rejection, but he couldn't change that either. Her family was in Ireland, too far to send for or bring by.

He did, though, have the telegram Joshua Johnson had brought back after his last trip to the train depot. It wasn't exactly a declaration that she was loved and cherished. But it was something.

"A few days ago I received an answer to a telegram I'd sent to Belfast."

He thought he saw the smallest of reactions in her face, though she kept her eyes shut.

"I have a business associate there, and I asked him if he could look in on your family." That sounded so presumptuous. Had he crossed a line? "I only wanted to know if there was anything that could be done to help."

Katie's breathing had slowed. She sounded calmer, or at least like she was listening.

"Mr. Butler wrote that he visited with your parents."

Katie's eyes opened, but she didn't look at anything in particular.

"He said your father's illness is a weakness of the heart. He's easily tired but isn't in pain." Would that help her worry less? "Someone named

Brennan is staying with them, helping." Joseph thought that was one of Katie's brothers. "Mr. Butler said they have very kind neighbors looking out for them and a competent apothecary giving him powders for palpitations. He said they seem to be doing well."

"Did they ask about me?" Katie spoke quietly, a quivering undertone of hope in her words. "Or have a greeting for me or anything?"

The very question he'd been afraid she would ask. He'd procrastinated telling her about the telegram for just that reason.

"The telegram wasn't long. I am confident they sent a letter, and it simply hasn't arrived yet."

He had wanted her to hear something personal from her parents, even the most basic words of caring and concern. He'd asked Mr. Butler specifically to ask Mr. and Mrs. Macauley for any greetings they might have for their daughter, assuring him he would cover the cost of a longer telegram if necessary.

After reporting on the general state of the Macauley household, Mr. Butler had added "No messages for Miss M." That was the entirety of her parents' greeting to their only living daughter.

"They didn't say 'hello' or ask how I was," Katie muttered. "My mother usually tells me to work hard. She didn't even say *that,* did she?"

Like an idiot, he'd made her feel worse. He thought she would want to hear that her father wasn't suffering. His well-being seemed to mean a lot to her, whether or not he'd earned her devotion.

"Life takes and takes, Joseph." She closed her eyes again. "It just takes and takes."

I not only can't make things better, I make them worse.

Chapter Forty

Tears were threatening once more. Katie had kept them at bay for days, but only by refusing to even think about all that had happened. She had tried to hide from her breaking heart, but it lingered there, aching and pricking at her.

Joseph hadn't looked in on her all day. She'd missed him, and he hadn't come by. The day was growing harder, and she felt herself drowning in her own sorrows.

"Good afternoon, Katie." Biddy stepped inside the room. "How are you?"

If Katie had had any doubts about her feelings for Joseph, the fact that she was disappointed that *he* wasn't standing in the doorway spoke volumes of her love for him. "I'm struggling, Biddy."

Biddy came over to her chair. "Aye. You've a difficult road to walk just now."

She felt entirely unequal to that trying path. "I don't like to think of myself as a weak person."

"Weak? I can honestly tell you, my friend, that I have known few people in my life with the strength you show every day."

Katie let her head hang. She didn't feel strong. Not in the least. "I cannot do this alone. I know I can't. I . . ." Emotions bubbled, obscuring her words. "I need Joseph. I haven't needed anyone since I was a child. Needing people meant being hurt; it meant being weak. But I need him here."

She brushed at the tears trickling down her cheeks.

"You love him, Katie." Biddy squeezed her shoulder. "That is not a weakness. Love gives us strength when our own fails us."

"My strength seems to have left me entirely." Indeed, the tears wouldn't stop. "So, it seems, has Joseph."

Biddy sat in the chair near Katie and took her one good hand between both of hers. "That is your worry and exhaustion speaking. You know as well as any of us that your Joseph would never abandon you. He is down the Irish Road, fetching his girls. He'll be back before long."

My Joseph. The words acted as a balm to her aching soul.

"I would advise you, though, to pull yourself at least a tiny bit together before Joseph returns." Biddy appeared perfectly serious. "He's worrying fiercely about you. The poor man's a mess."

"I'm a bit of a mess myself."

Biddy patted her fingers. "Are you hurting, Katie? Mr. Johnson sent plenty of powders."

"My arm and hand hurt terribly," she confessed. "And I'm absolutely certain I have burns on my back."

"That you do." Empathy shone in Biddy's eyes. "And broken ribs and more bruises than Joseph could bear to see. You'll be pained for some time, I'm afraid."

"Pained by a great many things."

Biddy pulled her hands free and stood. "Mrs. Smith is suggesting boiled potatoes for your lunch, but I thought colcannon would be far better. Which would you like?"

"What kind of Irishwoman would I be if I didn't choose colcannon?" Katie even managed a bit of a lighter expression.

Biddy nodded firmly. "No kind of Irishwoman at all." She stopped at the doorway and looked back. "I know it's tired you are, and worried and burdened. But all will be well in time, I promise you that."

She wanted to believe it. She wanted to be done with the pain and regret. Time heals wounds, she'd heard said, but too many of her scars had been painful and bleeding for far too long. She no longer had her music to turn to. She had but one remaining source of comfort.

"Do you know how much longer Joseph will be?" she asked.

Biddy smiled softly. "Not long, I'd imagine. He seldom leaves, and never stays away long."

Love gives us strength. Katie had little experience with such things, but told herself to trust that promise.

"And if you're feeling up to it, there's someone else wishing to see you just now," Biddy said.

Tavish stood in the corridor just beyond the doorway. *Dear, kind Tavish.*

"Come in. Please," she said.

He crossed to the chair next to the bed. "You're looking better, Katie."

She gave him a look of utter disbelief. "Seems to me, Tavish, you ought to be fitted for a pair of spectacles."

He grinned and chuckled lightly. "No matter your protests, you *are* looking better. And this entire town will be glad of it. Joseph especially."

Tavish knew, it seemed. And though he smiled, Katie could see his disappointment.

"Tavish, I—"

He reached out and took her hand. "I understand, Katie. I truly do."

She wanted to believe him. But she hated the thought of causing him pain. "You were willing to give up everything for me."

"Oh, Katie." He shook his head. "You love him, I can see that. *Everyone* can see that. And you're happier with him than you are with anyone else. Are you going to sit there and tell me that's not true?" He gave her a look heavy with doubt.

Simply thinking of Joseph and the strength and love she felt whenever he was near, brought a fresh tear to her eye, and an immediate feeling of peace settled on her heart.

Tavish smiled knowingly. "That right there, Katie, is proof to me that he'll make you happy. And that is what I want most for you."

"You are a good man, Tavish O'Connor."

He released her hand and leaned back in his chair, a laughing smile on his lips. "Ian told me the same thing not many days past. Either my brother is growing daft in his old age, or I am turning out to be a rather exceptional human being."

"I would wager 'tis a bit of both." She appreciated the light moment, though it slipped away quickly. "I want you to be happy, too."

"I will be, Katie. I will be."

He stayed a few minutes longer, talking on various topics. Conversation was easier between them than it had been in some time but nothing like it had once been. They were finding their new place in each other's lives, this time as friends. And though she worried for him and ached for the pain she'd caused him, she found some hope that he would, indeed, find his own happiness.

Chapter Forty-One

Though the Irish and Reds had done a fine job of stabilizing and improving the rope bridge they'd constructed, Joseph still worried about his girls crossing it. The river was frozen over, just not solidly enough to trust the ice. He didn't breathe easy until all three of them were back on his land, safe.

Ivy hadn't stopped talking since they left the Dempseys' house. His little chatterbox seemed almost back to normal. If only the nightmares would leave her be.

Emma had spent the day stuck to Finbarr's side like bark on a tree. Joseph had worried she would drive the poor boy mad. He wasn't the carefree, sunny young man he'd been before the fire, though he let Emma sit at his side. Neither of them talked, not even to each other, but there was a contentment there that Joseph hoped would one day see them both return to the happy children they once were.

He held the kitchen door open for the girls. Their faces were red from the cold. "Run upstairs and change into your flannel nightgowns," he instructed. "I will come up and read to you before you go to bed."

Ivy skipped off.

"Papa?" Emma lingered in the kitchen. She had been so quiet, so pulled into herself. It killed him by inches to see her that way. "Could we say good night to Katie before we go to bed?"

"Katie is still hurting. And she is very tired. We don't want to wear her out."

Emma's mouth turned down. "And she's sad, like Finbarr."

Nothing slipped past Emma.

"Yes, they both feel very sad."

"They'll be happy again, Papa. You'll see." Her declaration bore the imprint of a question, as though she needed him to confirm her hopes.

"Of course, sweetheart. They only need time."

She looked immediately relieved, though the worry in her eyes didn't entirely disappear.

"I'll be up soon, dear."

Emma nodded and followed the path Ivy had already taken.

I pray you're right, Emma. I can't bear to see Katie in so much pain.

Mrs. Smith was in the parlor, working on a dress she'd been sewing over the past few weeks.

"Did Biddy leave already?" he asked.

"About an hour ago. She was feeling tired and intended to go home and rest."

He would have to think of a way to thank Biddy for all she'd done. He knew the trip down the Irish Road and across the river was not an easy one for her with the added difficulties of pregnancy, and yet she returned again and again. He could never have seen Katie through this recovery without her. "How has Katie been today?"

"Better." Mrs. Smith gave him an understanding smile. Did everyone in the town know of his feelings for Katie? "She has been asking for you for hours."

"She has?" *I should have come back sooner. I should have been here.* "Is she still awake?"

"When I was last up there she was." She motioned with her head toward the stairs. "And she asked if you were home. Again. It seems she would very much like to see you." Something like a laugh twinkled in her eyes.

He and Mrs. Smith had settled their differences over the last few days. While the girls weren't entirely comfortable in her presence, he had come to appreciate her ability to run the house and her willingness to help in Katie's recovery.

He gave her a quick smile of gratitude and hurried up the stairs. Katie had been watching for him all day. He didn't mean to keep her waiting even another minute.

Please let her be improving. Talking. Smiling. At least a little better.

His heart pounded against his ribs as nervousness clawed at him. He wasn't sure he could endure seeing her in pain much longer. He stepped through the doorway to his room, telling himself not to get his hopes up.

She sat on the bed, leaning toward her feet, her hair spilling down in front of her face. He couldn't tell what she was doing. She didn't sound like she was crying. He heard no moans of pain. She certainly didn't seem to be sleeping.

He stepped closer. With her only hand she was valiantly attempting to get a stocking on her bare foot. She couldn't quite manage it though: each time she tugged it toward one side of her foot, it popped off the other.

A smile tipped his mouth. *This* was his Katie, facing problems head-on. She was no longer curled in a ball under the blankets, looking off into nothingness.

He moved quietly to the bedside as she tried the stocking once more. Without a word, he reached over and hooked one finger around the edge of her stocking, holding it in place so she could finally get it on. From that point, she managed the task with relative ease.

She glanced up at him through the fall of her hair. "I didn't expect this to take so long."

Joseph sat on the edge of the bed, facing her. Katie pushed her hair out of her face. Her eyes, thank heavens, weren't as bleak as they'd been the last time he saw her. She looked better, stronger.

"I had this wonderful plan to come downstairs before you returned," Katie said. "You were going to be very impressed." She let out a puff of breath, sending a few loose wisps of hair wafting upward. "The stockings were harder than I expected."

She never did give herself enough credit. "You managed to get both of them on. That's something."

"I'd meant to put my boots on as well, but I couldn't find them. And, thinking on it now, I likely couldn't have tied the laces anyway."

Joseph laid a hand on her ankle, rubbing his thumb along her thick stocking. "One thing at a time, darling."

She blushed so deeply and so immediately he couldn't help chuckling to himself. She lowered her eyes. "You've never called me darling before."

"Haven't I?" He'd thought of her that way for a long time.

Katie gave him a tiny smile. "I do like 'darling' far better than 'Miss May-kuh-lee.'"

She was smiling again. For the first time in more than a week he felt an easing of the pressure squeezing his heart. "What if I agree to call you darling from now on, and you agree to call me Joseph?"

Her expression was equal parts disbelief and amusement. "I always call you Joseph."

"I know. I just really like the way you say it."

She gave him a sidelong look. "Are you talking sweet to me, Joseph?"

He leaned in close to her. He'd never known anyone whose eyes were as purely brown as hers. Not even a flake of any other color touched their depths. Beautiful. Simply beautiful.

He touched his fingertips to her bottom lip, tracing its upward turn. "I have missed that smile, Katie." He cupped her face with his hand, memorizing the look and feel of her there, less burdened, less pained than she'd been since the fire. "I worried so many times during the last ten days that I'd never see you smile again."

Her face fell. What had he said wrong?

"I know I've been difficult. I'm sorry about that."

"No, no. That is not at all what I was saying." He lifted her good hand to his lips. A single kiss on the back of her hand proved insufficient. He pressed another to the base of her fingers, then another to the tips. "I thought I lost you, Katie." He held their clasped hands to his face. "I thought it far too many times."

He would never entirely free his mind of the terror he'd felt while digging through the rubble of his barn, trying to convince himself she was still alive beneath it.

Katie leaned toward him, close enough to talk in whispers. "I think you rather like me, Joseph Archer."

"I rather do." He bent closer, the tiny gap of air between them all but disappearing.

"Katie! Katie!"

Why was it children had such a terrible sense of timing? He'd been not even a half-second away from kissing Katie. He couldn't do so now with Ivy already climbing up the side of the bed.

"Katie, you're awake. I've been waiting for days and days and days for you to be awake again. Can I sit with you?"

"Of course, dear," Katie said.

Joseph helped Ivy up. "Be very careful. Katie is still hurt."

Katie pulled her hand free of his to guide Ivy to the head of the bed and help her sit comfortably.

"Pompah didn't come in to read to us, so I said to Emma, 'I'll find him and just you watch me.' And Emma said, 'I can't watch you if you've left the room.' Then I stuck my tongue out at her, and she stomped her foot." Ivy grinned up at Katie, admiration filling every inch of her face. "I haven't seen you in forever and ever, Katie. Are you still sad?"

Katie chucked her under the chin. "Less sad all the time, sweetheart."

Ivy's brow pulled in almost theatrically. "Mary said her grandfather told her papa that you don't have any fingers left." She glanced at Katie's unbandaged hand. "But you have fingers; I can see them."

Joseph set his hand on Katie's shoulder. He would turn Ivy's line of questioning if Katie needed him to.

But she proved resilient. "I have fingers on *this* hand, but not on the other. The fingers on that hand were too broken."

"Ah." Ivy nodded as though the entire thing made sense. "Did you know Finbarr's eye is broken, too? He can't see anything out of it. Not at all."

"I had heard that."

"Ooh, ooh." Ivy popped up onto her knees, facing Katie, her eyes wide with excitement. "He could have an eye patch, and you could have a hook on your broken-up hand. Then you could be pirates. You would be the very best pirates. Oh, Katie, you could be just like Grace O'Malley, *Irish Pirate Queen*."

"Where in heaven's name did you learn about Grace O'Malley?" Katie's eyes darted between Joseph and Ivy.

Emma answered instead. "Papa read us this book."

All eyes turned to the doorway. Emma stood there, clutching a volume of *Irish Legends and Histories* against her chest, her arms wrapped around it.

The look Katie gave Emma nearly took Joseph's breath away. She loved his daughter like her own, that was clear. His sweet, hurting Emma had found the caring, loving mother she'd needed the past years.

"My sweet Emma." Katie held her hand out, an invitation Emma didn't hesitate to accept. She too climbed up on the bed, snuggling next to Katie, just as Ivy was. Katie held her in a tight and loving embrace, saying again and again, "My Emma."

His girls were happy and loved and safe. Joseph's family was complete and together. He placed a kiss on the top of each of his girl's heads.

"Do I get a kiss, as well, Joseph Archer?" If Katie's flushed cheeks were any indication, she didn't mean a quick peck on the top of her head.

Of course, with both of the girls as an audience, he couldn't possibly kiss her as deeply or as thoroughly as he wanted to. Still, he had no intention of turning her down.

Joseph slipped a hand under her chin, tilting her face toward him. He lightly kissed the very corner of her mouth, then the other. Two tiny giggles stopped him before he could kiss her again.

He pulled back enough to see Katie's smile. Though she'd winced more than once as the girls had settled in and though worry and pain still sat heavy in her eyes, she was returning bit by bit to the strong and hopeful woman he loved.

"Perhaps I should read the girls their story." He made quite a show of rolling his eyes at their interruption.

Katie took his hand. He held it fast, cherishing the feel of her reaching out for him. "Read to all of us," she said.

He didn't have to be asked twice. Joseph adjusted Emma enough so he could sit next to Katie, with Emma nestled more or less between them. He held the book in one hand and Katie's hand in the other.

Ivy put her arms around Katie, being noticeably careful of her injuries. "I love you, Katie," she said earnestly. "Please don't ever, ever, ever leave us."

That brought Emma's eyes to Katie's face again. Joseph could all but hear Emma making the same plea.

Katie's expression gentled. "Not ever again, my sweet girls." She squeezed Joseph's hand, her eyes moving to look at him. She smiled slightly. "Not ever again."

Chapter Forty-Two

Katie had fallen asleep to the sound of Joseph's voice, her two angels pulled up close beside her. Though the pain remained, both in her body and in her heart, she felt a growing sense of peace.

Morning brought setbacks. She tried to use her left arm and the remnants of her hand to change her stockings and, rather than finding success, she discovered her wounds were too raw and new. She'd been reduced to tears of agony and frustration. Walking from the bed to the chair at Joseph's fireside hadn't been easy since waking from her injuries, but she was particularly achy and stiff that day, making such a simple thing nearly impossible.

You need to be cheerful, Katie Macauley. This is no time for selfish wallowing.

But she hadn't the strength in her for cheerfulness.

In the quiet of her solitary room she could hear voices below—quite a few if she didn't miss her mark. Did Joseph have company?

She tucked the blanket more firmly around herself. Today was not a day for visitors. Not even the mouthwatering mixture of smells floating up from below tempted her to leave the quiet protection of her hideaway. She wouldn't add to Joseph's burdens by forcing her weariness on him, but she wasn't equal to the task of hiding her pain that day.

Joseph came in the room about lunchtime. "How are you today?" Something in his tone told her he already knew.

She tried to force a smile, tried to think of some light and airy response. But the words died. "I'm having a hard day."

He came and knelt in front of her chair, resting his arms on her knees. "What can I do, Katie?"

"I'm frustrated is all."

"Well"—Joseph took her good hand in his, smiling gently—"I do have something I think will help lift your spirits a little."

His encouragement touched her, but her doubts remained. Joseph kissed her knuckles. He'd done that again and again the night before. The simple, loving gesture both calmed her and set her heart fluttering in her chest. She needed this man more than any person she'd ever known.

"I have come to invite you downstairs."

"Downstairs?" She shook her head. "I want to stay up here. I'm not ready to see people, Joseph."

He pressed her hand to his heart and looked deep in her eyes. "I know this is hard, darling, but being with people who care about you and love you will help."

"I can't." Her words shook. Though she knew herself ill-prepared to face the world, she hadn't anticipated the immediate emotional toll of the mere suggestion.

"You have strength enough for this." He squeezed her fingers and set her hand on her lap. He stood. "I see you've pulled your stockings on already."

"'Twas a pathetic struggle, that," she confessed with a sigh.

He pulled a box off the bureau and brought it over to her. Indicating the box, he said, "You've needed these for a long time. Yours were destroyed in the fire."

He lifted the lid and tipped it enough for her to see a pair of fine, new boots inside. She recognized them immediately. They were the very boots she had admired nearly every day she'd worked for Mr. Johnson.

Joseph didn't wait for a comment or reply. He pulled one out and loosened the laces. "I realize you can't tie them yet," he said as he slipped the boot on her right foot. "We'll think on that, though, and find a way for you to manage it. Something will occur to us, I'm certain of it."

He tied the laces in a loopy bow, then repeated his efforts with the other boot.

Katie could do little but stare. She had never in all her life owned such a fine pair of shoes. They were new and lovely. Her grotesque and misshapen feet looked almost elegant housed in such fine, deep-brown leather.

"I haven't the money for these," she whispered. "And I cannot ask you to—"

"Katie." 'Twas a scold if she'd ever heard one. "Let me first say, they aren't from me. The Johnsons sent them with very strict instructions that I was not to let you refuse."

"The Johnsons?" Why would they send her such a gift? She'd failed to save their daughter's life. They ought to despise her.

She wagered Joseph knew precisely why the offering confused her, but he didn't explain. He returned to the bureau and pulled open one of the smaller drawers at the very top. He took something out, though Katie couldn't make it out.

"This"—he set a neatly folded bundle of flowered fabric on her lap—"is from me."

She unfolded it. "Oh, heavens." Katie had never seen such a beautiful shawl in all her life. Deep blue flowers sat on a background of cream, with a blue crocheted edging so intricate and delicate she couldn't keep herself from touching it.

She looked up at him, utterly speechless.

"Put it about your shoulders, darling. You have a few people downstairs who are anxious to see you."

"Is this a bribe, then?" She had to confess that, if it was one, it was working brilliantly.

He smiled at her. "No. I have actually had it for three months, trying to find the right moment to give it to you."

"And this was that moment?" She slid the shawl around her shoulders.

Joseph helped her adjust it. "I know going down there will be hard. I only hoped this would buoy you up a bit."

She took a fortifying breath. "Promise to stay with me, Joseph, and I can face anything."

Joseph closed the distance between them, pressing a sweet and tender kiss directly on her lips. The warmth of him so close, the feel of his breath on her face, brought the familiar combination of contentment and heart flutters.

She'd first learned to recognize the smell of his shaving soap while working in his house. The scent had long since become one of her favorites. She took a deep breath of it while he was so close, fully expecting him to pull back after their very brief kiss.

He didn't.

His fingers wove through her hair, holding her close while his lips explored hers. Katie let her hand travel the length of his neck and settle on his chest. His heart pounded beneath her fingers. She pushed away all thoughts of injuries and regrets and uncertainty, and simply lost herself in that moment. All her life she'd been alone. Now here was this man, so kind and loving, who had stayed with her through the most terrible moments she'd passed. And he loved her as much as she loved him.

He broke the seal of their lips, leaning his forehead lightly against hers. They sat that way for what felt like minutes on end, though likely not more than a few seconds.

"I really do need to take you downstairs." He clearly regretted the necessity.

Katie could sincerely smile at the sentiment. She'd have liked to remain there just as they were, as well.

"Shall we?" She kept her tone encouraging, despite a lingering wish to avoid the crowd below. Joseph had done so much. She wouldn't make trouble for him over something so simple.

He nodded and, with obvious reluctance, pulled back once more.

"I should warn you I'm still not very sure on my feet."

He gave her a look of amused scolding. "I hadn't meant to make you walk, darling."

That was all the warning she received before he slipped his arm under her legs and the other behind her back. The thoughtful man had even chosen the side that allowed her to link her good arm around his neck.

He lifted her with little trouble and carried her from the room. The voices grew louder as they reached the staircase.

"How many people are down there?" She felt increasingly nervous now that she was facing this gathering.

"We are packed to the rafters. Nearly the entire town has come to see you."

Katie leaned into him, watching with discomfort as the bottom of the stairs loomed near. Her heart jumped into her throat as they rounded the corner. *Merciful heavens.* The room was bursting at the seams.

Katie bent her arm more closely around his neck, feeling entirely unequal to the immediate attention she received from the room. The crowd grew instantly quiet, all eyes following her arrival.

Biddy stood near the stairs, with Ian directly beside her. She reached out and quickly touched Katie's arm. "You're looking better, Katie."

She *felt* better having her dear friend nearby. Her eyes fell next on Tavish and his mother, not much farther into the room. Tavish smiled at her in his usual friendly way. Facing a crowd when she was yet pained and ill proved easier with so many familiar faces.

Mr. O'Connor stepped up beside Joseph. He chucked her under the chin, his traditional way of greeting her. "We've missed having you among us, Katie, *mo 'níon.*"

Mo 'níon. My daughter.

"And I have missed you," she said.

He smiled fondly before turning his gaze to Joseph. "I'll let you set her down. I just needed to see for myself how she was."

Joseph nodded and carried her further into the crowded room.

"Some of these are Red Road," she whispered to Joseph.

He pressed a quick kiss to her temple. "That is a distinction that means less and less with each passing day."

He set her down on a chair in the middle of the room and took his place in the one beside it. She'd seldom felt so out of her element. Her hair wasn't done up. Though her shoes and shawl would pass even the most rigorous inspection, she doubted the rest of her looked fit for company.

Ivy and little Mary O'Connor sat not far off, playing with matching carved horses. It was good to see Ivy happy and lighthearted. Emma sat with Finbarr on the sofa. Emma smiled at Katie.

Her eyes fell on Mr. Murphy amongst the gathering. "I thought you'd been forced to evict the Murphys," she said, her voice lowered. There were others among their number whom she knew had lost their claim on their homes the day before the bridge was burned.

"This town means to make a new start," Joseph answered quietly. "I have torn up the eviction notices and everyone, except the Archibalds, is back in their own homes. This feud will be laid to rest once and for all."

"Truly?" She could hardly believe it.

"Truly."

Seamus Kelly stepped out from among the crowd, his gaze kind as he looked at her. "Joseph Archer's asked us for a favor," he said. "Something that started out small, but grew, likely beyond what he'd expected."

Katie glanced at Joseph, but saw no clues in his face.

"Joseph explained to us that you'd lost more than merely a bit of your hand to our fighting. Though we can't give it back, we want to give you something we hope will help." Seamus nodded to the group of people gathered nearest him. "We started with a handful of Irish, listening to Joseph humming a tune to us."

A tune?

"But word spread among the Reds, and they wanted to give you something as well." Seamus slipped his hands in his trouser pockets. "We only hope we do it well enough for you."

Seamus stepped back into the group, and Thomas Dempsey lifted his tin whistle to his lips.

Katie knew the tune within three notes. "Ar Éirinn." Her father's song. *Her* song. A lump of emotion threatened to choke her even as tears gathered fast and thick in her eyes. That song was her connection to home. No one played it quite the way her father did. She had reproduced it from her memories of him, but no one had ever come close to the pure melody he'd managed.

She felt Joseph's hand slide into hers, but she didn't look at him. A flute, two or three violins, a guitar, another few whistles all joined Thomas. Someone from the Red Road even had a harp. She hadn't heard a harp in years.

Katie watched them, her lips pressed together, so consumed by emotion she could hardly breathe.

"I know it isn't the same as playing it yourself," Joseph whispered into her ear. "But I wanted—we all wanted you to have *something*. They've been practicing for days. Red and Irish. Together."

A sense of amazement joined her grief as she looked over those gathered around. There was no division along national lines, no repeat of the glares she'd seen between sides the first Sunday she'd been in Hope Springs. They were gathered together without threats, without angry words.

And they were playing the song that had, for her, always been the one unfailing source of peace in her life.

She looked up into Joseph's dark eyes. "You taught them the tune?"

He gave a small nod. "I've heard you play it so many times I have it memorized. It fills my mind whenever my thoughts turn to you."

Katie blinked back tears even as more fell down her cheeks. She leaned her head on his shoulder and turned her gaze to the musicians again. Their song washed over her like a calming wave. She found she could even smile as she listened.

Pain and heartache and death had ripped at the very fabric of this town. Healing was slow and difficult, but they were managing it. And so was she.

The tune came to a beautiful end. The gathering applauded. Katie offered a grateful smile to the musicians.

The music continued, with the Irish playing their traditional tunes and the Reds sharing songs they knew. The gathered townspeople mingled and mixed, crossing boundaries that had once been unscalable walls. Food appeared in abundance, both traditional Irish fare and dishes Katie had learned to make since arriving in America.

"Perhaps your Irish parties will become more general affairs now," Joseph suggested. He looked uncertain, almost nervous. He lowered his voice and leaned close. "I hope hearing that song wasn't painful for you. I—"

Katie set a single finger on his lips to stop his words. "I loved it. That you knew exactly the song, and took the time to arrange this . . ." She couldn't find the words. "I loved it." Katie locked her gaze with his, needing him to feel and see the depth of her feelings. "I love *you,* Joseph Archer."

He kissed her quickly, once, then again, brushing a finger along the line of her jaw. "And I love you, Katie Macauley."

He mangled her name in a way he hadn't in many weeks, mispronouncing it even worse than he had when they first met. She gave him an exaggerated shudder.

"We need to do something about your unpronounceable name." 'Twas a pointed remark, one accompanied by a look of such earnestness she knew on the instant he meant it as more than a jest.

"Perhaps I need a new one," she suggested.

He whispered, his breath tickling the hair that hung loose over her ear. "There is no 'perhaps' about it, Katie. I mean to see to it you have a new last name, and I know exactly which one it ought to be."

Her pulse leaped, pounding with excitement. She knew he loved her as much as she loved him, but, though they'd spoken the night before of always being together, he'd not specifically brought up the subject of marriage until now. Even having known that was his intention, hearing the words filled her heart to overflowing.

"You do realize," she said, unable to hold back a smile, "if you change my name, you have to keep me."

He pressed a kiss to her temple. "My darling, darling Katie." He wrapped his arms around her and held her.

His embrace felt like home in a way nothing had in years. To love and be truly loved in return was a gift she'd only ever dreamed of. But she knew, sitting with Joseph, in the sanctuary of his home and his affection, that she had found the place where she belonged.

Katie sat in the comfort of his arms the rest of the day while the town worked at healing their wounds. There would be harder moments as the weeks and years rolled on. They had deeper conflicts that needed addressing. But there in Joseph Archer's home, the very beginnings of a new day dawned.

Chapter Forty-Three

People, Katie had been told, kept lists of their favorite moments and brightest days. Her life had contained so few bright moments, the idea of tracking them had never occurred to her. But standing in the guest bedroom at the Johnsons' home the morning of her wedding day, she felt certain that day would live forever as the best of her life.

Mrs. Johnson had delivered a healthy son less than a month after the fire. They'd named the boy Connor Gabriel. Connor in honor of Finbarr O'Connor, for his efforts to save Marianne, and Gabriel in honor of Mr. Johnson's late brother. The family still carried the weight of mourning, but there was a bond there that gave Katie hope they would eventually emerge, if not whole, closer to one another.

They had offered their home for her to make her wedding preparations, as it sat closer to the church than any other building in town. She wore the boots they'd given her as a gift in the aftermath of the tragedy. The women on the Irish Road had made the sky-blue dress she wore. Joseph's shawl hung about her arms, adding an elegance she was grateful for and the feeling that he was there even in the last moments of her life without him.

She had mostly recovered in the two months since being trapped beneath the remains of his barn. Her broken arm and hand no longer hurt when she moved them. She'd even relearned how to do quite a few things. She could breathe without pain. The burns she'd sustained were little more than still-pink scars.

Through it all, Joseph had been at her side, doing anything and everything she asked, more even. Though she'd moved back to Granny's home three weeks after the fire, he had visited her every day without fail.

There would be no more visiting. They would be together.

Katie smiled at herself in the tall mirror. Life had often been cruel, but it had brought her to this moment, to a measure of happiness she had never known before. For that she was grateful.

A knock sounded at the bedroom door, a knock she knew without having to even think on it. 'Twas the exact rhythm Joseph tapped out on a door.

Katie crossed the room and pulled the door open enough to peek out. She gave him a teasing look of reprimand. "You were supposed to go to the church, Joseph Archer. I do believe you're lost."

He quirked an eyebrow, even as one corner of his mouth pulled up. "I know exactly where the church is, Katie, and I fully intend to be there today. But one of the ranch hands from up the road just returned from the train depot."

"He traveled there in the winter?" After more than two months of cold and snow, Katie had gained a deep respect for the severity of a Wyoming winter.

"I know. They're a little crazy out on the ranches." He smiled. "Nonetheless, he brought back something you need to see."

"On my wedding day? It must be particularly important." Her teasing tone dropped off as his expression grew inarguably serious. "What is it?"

"May I come in?"

She nodded and pulled the door open.

He stepped inside, dressed in his Sunday suit. "The ranch hand left this at the house. It—" Joseph's eyes widened, his words trailing off. "You look beautiful."

Heat crept up her neck at the intensity of his gaze. "Did you push your way in here to tell me that?" If she could tease him, she might not blush quite so hard.

He shook off his distraction and pulled a folded bit of paper from his jacket pocket. "There was a letter at the post office for me, with one inside it for you."

"A letter for me?" Only one person ever wrote to her. *Mother.* Katie's heart fell to her feet. Father had not been expected to live out the year. Was this the news she had dreaded hearing?

She looked to Joseph, pleading silently with him. She couldn't bear to hear such a thing on today of all days.

Joseph came to her side and wrapped an arm around her. "I received a letter that explained this one. I would not have brought it today if it was a painful thing."

Katie nodded, breathing through the tension in her lungs. "Will you read it to me?"

"Of course, darling."

She sat on the oak chest at the foot of the bed, preparing herself for whatever the letter might contain. "It is from my mother, isn't it?"

Joseph's gaze was steady and reassuring. "No, Katie. It is from your father."

Her breath caught. A fierce uncertainty clasped her heart. *Father.* He had never written to her nor sent a single word of greeting in the nineteen years since she'd seen him last. Not once. Not ever.

Joseph unfolded it.

"My dear Katie,

"I hope this letter finds you well. Though I know you to be a woman grown, when I close my eyes to sleep at night I see you as the wee girl you once were. I worry for you and think of you every day. It's twenty years since I lost you, the last child I had in my keeping. I regretted the boys' leaving. I mourned your poor sister's passing. But you, my brave little bird—losing you hurt like nothing before or since.

"The priest and the doctor both say I haven't long for this world, and I find my mind reflecting on the years of my life. I think back on the letters your mother sent to you and the words you sent us in return. I think of all the times you asked after me, and I, coward that I am, could not bring myself to answer. I tried, Katie. Heaven forgive me, I tried but couldn't bear it. I'd failed you, left you to the keeping of strangers and the unkindness of a cruel world. My heart smote me for doing that to my dear girl and, in my guilt, I couldn't bear to send so much as a greeting.

"This man, Mr. Butler, says you are cared for in your new home in America. He tells me a Mr. Joseph Archer has developed a fancy for you, the same Mr. Archer who has offered to see your mother and me through these final weeks and months. He strikes me as a fine man, and my heart finds peace knowing you're with good people who can do for you what I was never able to.

"I've not given you much in your life, my girl, and that weighs on me greatly. I know you to be one who doesn't scare at the necessity of work and that, I pray, has seen you through the hard times you've faced. And I hope you've continued with your music. The tunes of home have ever been a comfort to me. I left our fiddle with you so you'd have a bit of me in your life no matter how far away from each other the years pulled us."

Katie wiped at her streaming eyes with the hand towel she found on the washing table. *Our fiddle.* He didn't consider it *his,* but theirs. And he'd left it behind on purpose? All these years she'd hated herself for stealing it, when he'd meant it as a gift, an offering of himself.

Joseph's voice trailed off. She lifted her eyes and found him watching her, his eyes searching her face. "Do you need me to stop?"

She shook her head. Hearing from her father after so many years of longing for him was difficult, but she couldn't bear to leave the rest of his letter unread.

Joseph's eyes returned to the pages in his hand.

"Your Mr. Archer has purchased a headstone for our Eimear's grave, a proper and fine one. Knowing our little girl will not be forgotten by the world has given your mother a measure of peace she's not known in many years. He has also offered to return to us the land we lost in The Famine, as ours to keep—not as tenants, but as owners. And he's asked only that, in return, we send you woolen stockings regularly. Brennan means to accept the offer, and it does my heart good."

Katie looked up into Joseph's face, hardly believing all he'd done. These arrangements must have been made many months earlier, before anything between them had been settled. "Oh, Joseph," she whispered.

He sat beside her on the wooden chest. He kept the letter in one hand and put his other arm about her, pulling her close. He continued reading.

"I realize my words are likely too few and a great many years too late, but I've little else to offer you. I've asked Mr. Archer to do a few things for me, and I hope they will help you think on your father with more kindness than I deserve.

"Remember me in your prayers, my dear girl. If heaven is merciful, I will be with our Eimear again soon, the both of us smiling down on you. Be happy, sweet bird.

"Your loving father,

"Sean Macauley."

Her heart ached, even as a warmth that had eluded her for nearly twenty years spread through her. These were words she'd never thought to hear from her father. She'd needed them, longed for them, and given up all hope of ever having them. To hear him say he loved her, that he thought of her and missed her, meant the world to Katie.

Joseph gave her a handkerchief to replace the cloth she'd soaked through with her tears. Katie leaned her head against his shoulder as she wiped at her wet cheeks and eyes. He held her close to him.

She didn't know how long they sat there as her heart slowly, silently poured out of her. So many regrets settled in her even as weights were lifted by her father's words.

After a time, she found the strength to ask one of her many questions. "He said he asked you to do something. What was it?"

Joseph rubbed at her upper arm. "He asked me to see to it you learned to read if you hadn't been taught already. He said your brothers have all learned and, in his words, you are 'a far sight brighter than they ever were' and if they could master it, you certainly could."

Somehow her father had known how much she'd longed to learn to read and write. Even separated by years and oceans, he'd known that.

"I was also asked to do what I could to make certain you were never cold." His other arm wrapped around her, pulling her into a full embrace. "He has been haunted for twenty years by the memory of you nearly freezing to death, without a home to shield you or a proper coat or shoes to wear. Even after all these years, he worries about you being cold again."

Katie put her arms around Joseph as well, needing his strength as she faced the demons of her past. "I have thought for most of my life that he didn't love me, that he didn't even like me."

Joseph kissed her forehead, lingering there as he held her close. "He does, Katie. So deeply. So much. He spent as much time pleading with me to look after his 'sweet bird' as he did threatening me in proper fatherly fashion if I ever mistreat you at all. He told me his ghost will haunt me mercilessly if I make you the least bit unhappy."

Katie half smiled, half sobbed at that. "Never take lightly an Irish threat of haunting, Joseph Archer. Our afterlife activities are a serious matter."

"I assure you, my darling, as a father I know that is a warning to be taken very seriously."

A feeling of peace settled over her. Worries she had carried all her life were lifting from her heart.

"You gave Eimear a headstone and Father his land back."

"It mattered too much to you for me to leave it undone." He spoke so matter-of-factly, as though there had never been a question of doing this amazing thing for her. "I want to take you back there, Katie. I want to take you to visit Ireland, to see your home. And I'd like to introduce the girls to your mother."

Though she had come to terms with her decision not to return home and the knowledge that she would never see her family or homeland again, that loss had been a painful one. To return again was an unspeakably beautiful gift.

"My dear, sweet Joseph. I didn't think I could be any happier, and then you give me this."

He set her a little away from him, watching her with concern. "Are you happy, Katie? Truly happy? With all you have been through, I worry that you aren't, that you have resigned yourself to some degree of contentedness. But, my darling, I want more than that for you. I want you to be happy."

"I am," she assured him. "I absolutely and completely am."

"You've lost your music. That worries me a great deal."

She reached up and touched his face. "If I promise you that even that doesn't cloud my joy, will you let your heart quit aching over it?"

He smiled. "I will try."

"I love you, Joseph."

"Perhaps you should marry me then?"

Good heavens. "We aren't late, are we?"

He shook his head. "But I do need to get over to the church. Ian will never let me live it down if I'm late to my own wedding." He got to his feet.

"Will you kiss me before you go?" she asked.

He shook his head. "No, because then we *will* be late."

She laughed at that. "Then will you do something else for me?"

"Anything at all, darling."

She moved to stand in front of him. "Will you read my father's letter to me again sometime?"

"Whenever you need to hear it, Katie. Until you can read it yourself."

To read her father's words her own self? "That would be wonderful."

"And then"—he lifted her hand to his lips, kissing her knuckles like he always did—"then *I* will write you letters and leave them around the house for you to find."

He meant to write her love letters. "And I will write *you* letters as well."

He tipped his head, his gaze locking with hers. "Do you promise?"

Katie nodded.

He kissed her forehead, but stepped away quickly. At the doorway, he looked back. "Don't be late."

A quarter of an hour later, she walked with Biddy to the church. Biddy moved slowly, the weight of her pregnancy taking its toll. Her new little one was due to arrive any day.

"I'm so happy for you, Katie." Biddy squeezed her hand. "And for Joseph."

Katie sighed contentedly. "Yes, it seems this is to be a day filled with happiness."

The girls, bundled in their heavy winter coats, met Katie at the church's back door.

Biddy gave her a quick hug. She stepped into the church, leaving Katie there with her sweet girls.

Ivy slipped her hand into Katie's right. Emma took hold of her left. In the weeks since Katie's fingers were removed, Emma had become entirely comfortable holding her oddly shaped hand. The girl seemed less unnerved by it than Katie herself was.

Ivy grinned from ear to ear. Emma wore a look of focused determination. She glanced up at Katie. "I am glad you're marrying my papa."

Her heart felt ready to simply leap out of her chest. She, who'd spent so many years entirely alone, was surrounded by people she loved and who loved her in return. "I am very glad too."

Mr. O'Connor stepped out of the chapel. "Are you ready, then, *mo 'níon?* You'll turn to ice out here in the cold."

"He's right, girls," she said. "Inside with you where it's warm."

She followed them in and helped them off with their coats, hanging them amongst so many others. She slipped out of her own coat, a beautiful green one Joseph had given her.

"We've saved two seats for you right in the front, lasses," Mr. O'Connor told the girls. "Hurry up, then."

Katie straightened her shawl and smoothed out her hair. Mr. O'Connor offered her his arm. She slipped hers through it.

"Are you ready, my girl?"

"Absolutely."

They walked around the back wall of the chapel. Every bench was full. The town didn't divide itself by nationality any longer. Friendships had been formed across the old chasm. The change, slow as it was, still amazed her even after the passage of two months. Her thoughts, however, didn't stay on her neighbors.

Joseph stood at the front of the chapel, smiling at her as she walked up the center aisle. The look in his eyes warmed her from head to toe. She was loved. Deeply and truly. And she loved him with all her heart. From that day on, they would have the rest of their lives to spend together.

Mr. O'Connor walked her to where Joseph stood. "You take care of her, Joseph Archer."

"I intend to."

Mr. O'Connor kissed her cheek and gave her a smile of joy. "We love you, Katie-girl."

He stepped back, and Joseph took Katie's hand. His fingers wove through hers.

"I missed you," he whispered as they turned to face Reverend Ford.

"It has only been twenty minutes, Joseph." But she smiled at the sentiment. She had missed him as well.

The ceremony was simple and touching. The words weren't fancy, but Katie cherished every moment. Joseph slid her ring on her right hand, a necessary break from tradition.

Reverend Ford pronounced them husband and wife. Joseph kissed her before the preacher had a chance to instruct him to do so.

He kissed her slowly, taking his time. Katie put her arms around his neck and kissed him in return. He held her tight, and the world around them disappeared.

Life, with all its past ugliness and pain, had brought her to a perfect, glorious moment. She had a home and a family. She had Joseph, her wonderful, loving Joseph.

He broke the kiss, but kept her in his embrace.

"I love you," she said.

He kissed the tip of her nose, then her top lip.

"Enough of that, you two," Mr. O'Connor called out with a laugh. "We've a bit more to do here and a party to start up."

Katie turned to Ivy, sitting beside Finbarr, and gave her a knowing nod. The girl recognized her cue. Ivy hopped off the bench and hurried to where Katie stood, handing her a fingerless glove.

"Katie?" Joseph asked.

"We've a fine surprise for you, Joseph."

He looked curious, just as she'd hoped he would.

Seamus came and stood next to her, helping her slip an odd contraption they'd created onto her mangled left hand. She buckled it good and tight and thanked Seamus.

Emma came up next, carefully carrying Katie's fiddle and bow. Katie slipped the bow inside the strip of leather across her left palm. She and Seamus, with the entire O'Connor clan offering suggestions, had designed a way to keep her bow in a hand with no fingers.

She took her fiddle in her right hand, something she imagined would always feel a little odd, and slipped it under her chin. She took a deep breath, feeling unexpectedly nervous.

Her playing was still very unsure, nothing like the music she had once played, but it was a beginning, a promise of beautiful things to come. The chapel filled with "Ar Éirinn," a tune she loved even more than before. The notes filled her heart with her father's kind and loving words, with the comfort of knowing her family was home again, with thoughts of this town that had at last become a place of hope and healing.

Joseph stepped up behind her and wrapped his arms around her waist, setting his head against the side of hers, managing to hold her in a way that allowed her to continue to play. "Oh, Katie," he whispered. "You have your music."

Playing her fiddle again, knowing her father had meant her to have it, with Joseph holding her, Katie's heart filled with utter peace.

Her song ended and, inexpert though her offering had been, the chapel erupted in cheers and applause. Hardly an eye was dry, including Joseph's.

"You have your music," he said again.

"'Twill be many years before I can play well, but there's still joy in scratching out a tune, however unrefined."

He took her face in his hands. "I don't think I have ever enjoyed your playing as much as I did just now. It was the most beautiful thing I've heard in some time."

They were soon surrounded by well-wishers, people offering congratulations and expressions of happiness.

Mr. O'Connor put Katie's fiddle away. Joseph helped her unbuckle her bow holder, shaking his head in clear amazement. Katie couldn't seem to stop smiling.

The wedding guests trickled out, making their way to Joseph's newly reconstructed barn where the entire town had been invited to join in the celebration. Biddy and Ian hugged Katie and Joseph once more for good measure. Finbarr and Tavish offered sincere and heartfelt congratulations. Though Finbarr hadn't recovered his sight, he seemed to be slowly adjusting to his new life, and Katie held out hope that he would return to the cheerful lad he'd been. And Tavish did seem to be happy, just as he'd told her he would be. Mr. O'Connor gave her a fierce hug and told her again how much he loved her.

Katie had told Biddy this was to be a day filled with happiness. How true that was.

Only Katie and Joseph and the girls remained. Joseph pulled all three of them into his embrace. Katie kissed the top of each girl's head, then Joseph's cheek. Her family. This was her family.

"This is the best day ever," Ivy declared, her smile the widest Katie had seen.

"I agree." Joseph's gaze held Katie's. "The best day ever." He kissed her. "So far."

She loved the thought of that. They would make each day better than the last. And they would be together. Always.

Acknowledgments

With gratitude to the following:

The Wyoming State Historical Preservation Office; the library at Cornell University; The Farmers' Museum in Cooperstown, New York; and the Bunratty Castle & Folk Park in County Clare, Ireland, for invaluable information and insights.

Krista Lynn Jensen and Ranee S. Clark for answering endless questions about Wyoming and helping me make the setting of these books as accurate as I could.

My amazing critique group: Annette Lyon, Heather B. Moore, J. Scott Savage, LuAnn Staheli, Michele Paige Holmes, and Robison Wells, for support, guidance, and friendship. And a deep and sincere thank you to Jennifer Savage for countless acts of service and friendship, and for making me, red hair and all, feel like one of the family.

Pam van Hylckama Vlieg for being the greatest support, advocate, and agent I could hope for. Your guidance and encouragement are a gift for which I am daily grateful.

Lisa Mangum for amazing, detailed, and thorough edits. Without question, this book is stronger and better than it could possibly have been without her eye for detail, her unparalleled sense of story, and her always-reliable advice.

And most importantly of all, to my family members and friends who have, over the past year, walked at my side as I have begun my battle with an unexpected and unforeseen disease. Life has not taken the path any of us anticipated, but the courage I have seen in my children, the love and support I receive daily from my husband, and the help, prayers, and kindnesses of my parents and siblings and extended family have given me strength in the midst of a very difficult struggle, and have helped me find the courage to face an uncertain future.

Thank you to the many friends and readers who have reached out with words of support and encouragement, something I have appreciated and needed more than you likely realize.

Discussion Questions

The Feud

1. Much of the hatred and violence of the town feud is fueled by only a few individuals. Why do a few loud voices of dissent so often overpower voices of reason? In what ways have you struggled to take a stand against something only to be drowned out by other voices?

2. Mr. Johnson had a brother who died at the battle of Gettysburg, fighting against an Irish regiment. How has this experience likely influenced his hatred toward the Irish? What things in Seamus Kelly's past might also have left him quick to fight and slow to choose peace?

3. After assisting Mr. Johnson with his injuries, Katie laments that the Red Road and the Irish seem unable to see how alike they are. What similarities are there between the groups that might have helped them relate to one another? In what ways do we sometimes dehumanize others with whom we have disagreements?

4. When Ian is laid low, and later, when many relatively peaceful families are forced from their homes, Katie struggles with seeing the innocent paying the price for the hatred of others. In the end, this pattern holds true in terrible ways, and yet it is that price which finally brings healing

to Hope Springs. Why do you think the town was unwilling to set aside their hatred before being devastated by it?

Joseph and Tavish

1. What are each man's strengths? Weaknesses? What do they have to offer Katie that she needs? What does she offer to each of them?

2. Joseph feels that, not having had the opportunity to court Katie while she lived in his home, he needs to at least try now that he is free to do so, whether or not it makes a difference. Tavish, recognizing that Katie's past makes her wary and slow to open up, knows his courtship will take time and feels that Joseph is infringing on *his* chance to court Katie. In what ways are they both right? Why was this conflict between them unavoidable?

3. Katie didn't grow up with a mother or sisters or with any examples of romantic, loving relationships to learn from. How did this upbringing make it harder for her to sort out her feelings for Joseph and Tavish? Katie worries that she seems foolish to those looking on from the outside. Consider times in your own life when you have been unfairly judged by those seeing, but perhaps not fully understanding, your struggles.

4. Biddy points out that Katie's dilemma is made more difficult because Joseph and Tavish are both good men and could make her happy. Often choosing between two good options is the hardest choice of all. What clues led you to know she would make the choice she did? What do you think finally convinced her of what her heart wanted most? Would you have made the same choice she did? How might her life have been different if she'd chosen the other path instead? What ultimately made her choice the right one for her?

Katie

1. More than almost anything, Katie wants to be loved and to be an important part of the lives of those she cares about. With which people in Hope Springs does she find this connection, and in what ways?

2. How do her efforts to help her neighbors, as well as her enemies, bring healing and peace to Katie's heart?

3. After the fire, it seems Katie has lost everything: she will not see her family again, they have not written to her, she doesn't have her music to soothe her, and she is haunted by the suffering she could not prevent. In what ways does she recover those things and more? What losses might she likely continue to struggle to accept?

4. After all she has been through in her life, especially in the months since arriving in Hope Springs, do you think Katie will be happy? Will Joseph? Tavish? The rest of the town? Why or why not?

About the Author

© Annalisa Photography. Used by permission.

SARAH M. EDEN is the author of several well-received historical romances, including Whitney Award finalists *Seeking Persephone* (2008) and *Courting Miss Lancaster* (2010). Combining her obsession with history and an affinity for tender love stories, Sarah loves crafting witty characters and heartfelt romances. She happily spends hours perusing the reference shelves of her local library and dreams of one day traveling to all the places she reads about. Sarah is represented by Pam van Hylckama Vlieg at Foreword Literary Agency.

Visit Sarah at www.sarahmeden.com.